ASSASSIN

ASSASSIN

DAVID
HAGBERG

A TOM DOHERTY ASSOCIATES BOOK / NEW YORK

ASSASSIN

Copyright © 1997 by David Hagberg

This book is printed on acid-free paper.

A Forge Book
Published by Tom Doherty Associates, Inc.
175 Fifth Avenue
New York, NY 10010

Forge® is a registered trademark of Tom Doherty Associates, Inc.

Library of Congress Cataloging-in-Publication Data

Hagberg, David.
    Assassin / David Hagberg. — 1st ed.
       p.   cm.
    "A Forge book"—T.p. verso.
    ISBN 0-312-85028-X
    I. Title.
PS3558.A3227A9   1997
813'.54—DC21   96-54159
                                      CIP

First Edition: June 1997

Printed in the United States of America

0 9 8 7 6 5 4 3 2 1

For Lorrel

**Special thanks to Tania Doherty
for her kind help.
The mistakes are entirely mine.**

The Russian constitution is ". . . absolutism tempered by assassination."

—Ernst Friedrich Herbert von Münster

Assassination is the extreme form of censorship.

—George Bernard Shaw,
The Rejected Statement

If it were done when 'tis done, then 'twere well
If were done quickly; if the assassination
Could trammel up the consequence, and catch
With his surcease success; that but this blow
Might be the be-all and the end-all here,
But here, upon this bank and shoal of time,
We'd jump the life to come.

—Shakespeare,
Macbeth

ONE
MARCH

ONE

Kirov, Russia

Yevgenni Anatolevich Tarankov was called the Tarantula because of the gargantuan web he'd spun over all of Russia in the past five years. From friends in the Kremlin and inside the old KGB, through the peoples of the central Russian plains and wheat fields still dotted with intercontinental ballistic missile silos, and beyond, to the independent-minded residents of the wild far eastern regions of Siberia, he was feared and loved. He was a force to be reckoned with. A Russian force, campaigning for the leadership of his country the Russian way, with bullets and bread.

He was a man in his early fifties, whose most prominent features were his eyes, which were large, black and expressive. When he smiled his eyes lit up with a pleasant warmth like a crackling fire on a cold Siberian night. But when he was angry, the fire was replaced by a sharply bitter man-killing wind that, as a poet from St. Petersburg wrote, "... chilled a man's soul so completely that he forgot there ever could be such a season as summer."

He was unremarkable in appearance, typically Russian of moderate height with a thick waist, a bull neck and a massive head that looked common beneath a fur hat. But if his eyes were windows into the soul of Russia, his intellect was the engine that drove his successes and earned a grudging respect from his enemies, and an adoration bordering on religious faith from his followers. With Tarankov you either felt safe, or you felt as if your life were teetering on the slippery edge of an ice-coated cliff that dropped five thousand meters into a black hole from which escape was impossible.

It was his vision for the future of Russia. The nation would either regain its greatness or it would fall into a bottomless pit of despair.

It was morning and sharply cold as he stood on the swaying platform on the last car of his twenty-car armored train headed west from Yekaterinburg. They'd passed through the industrial city of Perm a few hours ago, and soon they'd enter Kirov, their next target city, where the killing would continue.

He leaned against the rail, smoking a German cigarette, enjoying the calm before the storm. The sky was overcast, which seemed to be appropriate this morning, the air bitter with sulphur oxides from what few factories were still in operation. The people here, he mused, were like the air and countryside—gray, dull, used up, without hope.

His East German wife, Liesel, came out with his morning brandy. Like him she was dressed in combat fatigues, without insignia. "Radar is clear so far," she said. Her Russian was still heavily accented though she'd lived in Russia since she was a seventeen-year-old student at Moscow State University.

"Not a day for flying in any event."

"They'll wish they had," she replied. She hunched up her coat collar and shivered, then sniffed the air and smiled slyly. "It's come, Zhennia, can you smell it?"

He returned her smile. "I can smell air pollution. Is that what you mean?"

"Hope, Zhennia. That's what you're smelling, and nothing is sweeter than hope."

"You sound like a recruiting poster now."

"Maybe." She pursed her full lips. "Already a lot of young boys believe it. Believe in you."

"Better the factory workers and the farmers want to follow me."

"Them too," Liesel said. "But it's the young men who'll make it happen." Her eyes flashed. "There'll be a bronze statue in Dzerzhinsky Square of a young soldier, his rifle raised over his head, his face pointed up to the sky in hope." She smiled again, this time coyly. "Just like the Minuteman in Concord."

"With a pool of blood at his feet," Tarankov said. The brandy had made his stomach sour.

Liesel shot him a sharp look, her violet eyes flashing with passion, her angular face screwed up in a grimace. She was a direct woman who never took sarcasms well. She expected short, succinct answers. In school her double majors had been mathematical logic and analytical psychology. She understood what motivated people, though she most often didn't like it.

"It's better to lose a river of blood now, than the entire country later," she said.

"Russian blood."

"*Da*, Russian blood, but from traitors, Zhennia." She swept her hand outward. "Look what they've done. Look what they're doing. It's time for a clean sweep, even in the darkest corners. The filth has to be cleaned away before we all choke on the dust. And you're the only man in Russia capable of doing it."

Tarankov looked at his wife with warmth and affection. For a brief moment he could see them alone, away from the struggle, in a dacha by a lake somewhere in the far east. A part of him desperately wanted the peace and quiet away from the struggle, back to a past, easier life.

In the early days after the war, his father had been on the team of rocket scientists who'd built the Russian launch center at Baikonur. Tarankov had fond memories of evenings spent listening to his father and fellow Russians and captured German scientists passionately talk about a science that would not only take them to the moon and beyond, but would also be capable of launching nuclear weapons intercontinentally. The Soviet Union would become the dominant force on the planet, and these men, his father included, would be the means to achieving that goal.

By day, his mother who was a gifted mathematician in her own right, and his aunts and grandfather, who were poets and historians, educated him. Philosophy and psychology were equally important as mathematics and physics. Literature and poetry were on par with chemistry and astronomy. Those days were simple, and he missed them now.

He attended Moscow State University, joined the Young Pioneers, the Komsomol and the Communist Party, and when he graduated with masters degrees in mathematics, physics, philosophy and psychology, he enlisted in the newly formed Strategic Rocket Force as a captain.

But then disaster struck. His father and mother had become too moderate and too vocal in their views. They were friends with Andrei Sakharov, but they did not have the physicist's importance so they were sentenced to a Siberian gulag for crimes against the State, where five years later they both died.

It was the beginning of Tarankov's real education, he once admitted to a friend. At that moment he became a realist. He embraced the Soviet Union and the Communist Party as he never had before, working equally as earnestly with Gorbachev's moderates as with Vladimir Zhirinovsky's ultranationalists. But when the Wall fell he shed no tears. Nor did he openly mourn the loss of the Baltic states and the disintegration of the Soviet Union. Instead, he began to consolidate his power base in the military, the Militia, the old KGB, the Kremlin and the Communists.

They passed a shack in the morning mist, a curl of smoke rising from the chimney. Then another shack, and two more, as they entered the outer suburbs of Kirov which was an industrial city on the Vyatka River.

"Just eight hundred kilometers to Moscow," Liesel said, straightening up. "Not so far. Maybe eight hours or less."

"More like eight light-years," Tarankov replied. He finished his brandy and handed the glass to his wife. "Have Leonid join me."

"Here," a dark figure said from within the shadows of the doorway behind them.

Liesel was startled, but Tarankov didn't bother to turn. Leonid Chernov was like an extension of his own personality, a brother, a kindred spirit. They understood each other.

"I'll see that Colonel Drankov is ready," Liesel said, and she left.

"There could be resistance in Kirov," Chernov said joining Tarankov. "It might be better if you remained aboard until we have Government Square secured."

"Do you think that's for the best, Leonid Ivanovich?"

"For your personal safety, yes." Chernov shrugged. "For the cause . . . no."

Tarankov turned to look at his second in command who was ten years younger than him and stood a full head taller. Like everyone else aboard the train, including Colonel Drankov and his two hundred highly-trained commandoes, Chernov wore Russian battle fatigues with no insignia. They were a well-oiled team. Everyone knew everyone else, and all of their duties were clearly defined and perfectly understood. Everyone from the lowliest APC driver to Tarankov himself was equal, only their jobs and responsibilities differed.

"That's the whole point."

Chernov smiled humorlessly, but said nothing.

"Maybe I'll make you director of my KGB."

"Maybe I won't want it."

"There aren't many causes left worth your special talents," Tarankov said.

"Now it's you who are the idealist."

They passed the railroad siding for the Kirov Lumber Works complex, which looked all but deserted this morning. Where the yards should have been teeming with workmen, only a half-dozen men stood atop piles of lumber as the train roared by. A few of them waved, but most of them merely watched.

"They know we're coming," Tarankov said.

"It would seem that not everyone is thrilled by the prospect."

Tarankov studied his number two's eyes, but this morning he could discern nothing other than an amused indifference. They'd been together for more than five years, and in that time there'd been a few moments like these in which Chernov was unreadable. Stalin had once said the same thing about his secret service chief Lavrenti Beria, a killer whose cause and loyalty wasn't always so easy to determine. "What are you thinking?" Stalin asked. "You don't want to know," Beria replied. "Except that I'm yours."

So long as it suits me, Tarankov finished the thought as he was sure Stalin had.

They passed other factory complexes that like the lumber works were mostly deserted of workmen. The word had spread that Tarankov was coming. They would be gathering downtown to witness what a western journalist described as ". . . a revolution so typically Russian that no one in the West has a chance of understanding it. The distance from apathy to passion is nowhere shorter than it is at this time and place in history."

They roared into the city at more than a hundred kilometers per hour, not slowing down until they'd passed through the central switching yards and entered the downtown section where the tracks made a huge loop to the north, passing over the river still choked with dirty ice floes. The main railway station was two blocks off the city square, and as they approached it Chernov ducked inside for a moment returning with Tarankov's Makarov pistol and his fatigue cap with a red star on the crown.

Tarankov put on his hat, strapped on his pistol and checked the gun's action. Carrying a sidearm was his only concession to his personal safety. But everyone from Liesel to his military commander insisted on it, and at the rallies the crowds seemed to expect it. This was war.

Thousands of people lined the tracks, many of them waving the hammer and sickle flag of the Soviet Union. Others raised banners with Tarankov's name, and still others held posters with his picture. Most of them chanted his name, many of them held up their right fists in the sign of solidarity. There were no police or military in sight.

"It could be a trap," Chernov said.

"Then we die here," Tarankov replied, not taking his eyes off the crowds. His chest was swelling and blood pounded in his ears. He was more alive now than he'd ever been. Russia was his.

The train rumbled to an abrupt stop a hundred meters east of the big, iron latticework central depot, its iron wheels screeching on the tracks, throwing up sparks. Loading doors on twelve of the cars crashed open, and a dozen troop-carrying armored vehicles roared into life, their half-tracks clattered down steel ramps, and they quickly formed into a unit of a hundred commandoes, and four smaller squadrons of twenty-five men each.

Liesel, also wearing a sidearm, joined Chernov and her husband on the rear platform. They climbed down and boarded the lead APC in the main group from which Colonel Vasili Drankov would direct his forces. This was their tenth campaign in the past eighteen months, but Kirov, which was a city of 300,000, would be by far their largest conquest. Any number of things could go wrong, and they all knew it. By sheer weight of numbers the citizens could stop them dead, just as Yeltsin's supporters had protected the White House during the Kremlin coup.

Drankov saluted. "Radar is still clear. Air traffic has even been diverted from the civilian airport. And all the military channels are dead between Moscow and the air base as well as the army post."

Thousands of people raced down to the train, but mindful that something was about to happen, kept clear of Gruzinskaya Boulevard that led from the station to the city square. The noise was deafening, a roar that began to coalesce into the single chant: "Tarankov! Tarankov! Tarankov!"

"The military would be stupid to interfere," Tarankov shouted.

Liesel at his side was beaming. Chernov stood in the gunner's turret surveying the crowds and watching the taller buildings for snipers.

"This won't be another Chechnya," Drankov said with assurance. "Not with all this support. These people don't like the apparatchiks any better than anyone else we've seen. But the Party is still timid of Moscow."

"Not for long," Tarankov said harshly. "This time we'll give them a message they won't soon forget."

"As you wish, Comrade," Drankov said tightly, and he began issuing orders by radio. The main body of their forces would head directly into the city square which was at the heart of the government and financial district. Units One and Two were to head directly to the television and radio stations and the biggest newspaper, and summarily execute not only the government censors, but the left-wing intellectuals and democratic reformers who'd been identified by Tarankov's people months ago.

Unit Three was to proceed to the Arbat Bank, which was a branch of the powerful government-directed Bank of Moscow, execute its president and chief officers and rob the vault. The money and gold, if any, was to be brought back to the square and distributed to the people after Tarankov's speech. The confusion it would cause would help cover their retreat should the local militia decide in the end to retaliate. Anything was possible.

Unit Four was to round up the mayor, the entire city council, the chief prosecutor and his staff, the directors of public works, housing, transportation and all six of the regional court judges, and bring them to the central square.

The four smaller units roared off in a cloud of diesel fumes, and as Drankov's main unit headed up Gruzinskaya Boulevard, Tarankov spoke into a lapel microphone that relayed his voice by radio to loudspeakers atop all their assault vehicles.

"COMRADES, MY NAME IS YEVGENNI TARANKOV, AND I HAVE COME TODAY TO OFFER MY HAND IN FRIENDSHIP AND HELP."

The crowds lining the boulevard fell silent as Tarankov's voice rolled over them like waves on a vast shoreline. As the column passed, the people pressed in behind and followed the armored vehicles up to the square.

"OUR COUNTRY IS FALLING INTO A BOTTOMLESS PIT OF DESPAIR. OUR FORESTS ARE DYING. OUR GREAT RIVERS AND LAKES HAVE BECOME CESS-

POOLS OF WASTE. THE AIR IS UNFIT TO BREATHE. THE ONLY FOOD WORTH
EATING FILLS THE BELLIES OF THE APPARATCHIKS AND FOREIGNERS. OUR
CHILDREN ARE DYING AND OUR WOMEN ARE CRYING, BUT NO ONE IN MOS-
COW CAN HEAR THEM. NO ONE IN MOSCOW WANTS TO HEAR THEM."

The column moved at a steady four kilometers per hour, which made it
easy for the crowds on foot to keep up with it, and which would give the
four outriding assault units a chance to complete their assignments by the
time the main force reached the square. The plans had been orchestrated
by Chernov, and no one questioned his brilliance. Every town they'd entered
had become theirs within thirty minutes, without exception. Kirov, though
larger, more sophisticated and much closer to Moscow, was proving to be
no different than the much smaller, rural towns.

"OUR HEALTH CARE SYSTEM IS BANKRUPT. OUR MILITARY HAS BECOME
LEADERLESS AND USELESS. HOOLIGANS AND PROFITEERS ERODE OUR LIVELI-
HOODS LIKE CANCER. THE MAFIA EATS BEEFSTEAKS AND CAVIAR, DRINKS
SWEET CHAMPAGNE AND DRIVES CADILLAC AND MERCEDES CARS WHILE RAP-
ING OUR DAUGHTERS, WHO HAVE NO HOPE FOR A FUTURE."

Bankrupt, cancer, rape, were what Chernov called "buzzwords." He'd
spent three years working out of the Russian embassy in Washington.

"AIDS AND DRUGS AND MINDLESS MUSIC ARE ROTTING THE BRAINS OF
OUR CHILDREN. THE WEST HAS IMPOSED ITS FILTH UPON US BECAUSE WE
ARE THEIR ENEMY AND THEY WANT TO BURY US."

Tarankov could look out the slit windows and see the people walking
beside his lead APC. Many of them were crying, tears streaming down their
weathered faces. Some of them smiled, while others walked with hands
touching the side of his armored truck. Many of them were military men in
shabby uniforms.

They were his people. They were the soul of Russia, and by their tears
and their smiles, by their touching his truck, they were crying out to him
for salvation.

Still talking, Tarankov pushed open the side door, scrambled out of his
seat and jumped down onto the street with the people before Drankov or
anyone else could stop him. He was still connected by radio link to the
loudspeakers on his units all across the city by now.

"MOSCOW . . . HOW MANY STRAINS ARE FUSING IN THAT ONE SOUND FOR
RUSSIAN HEARTS!" he quoted Pushkin.

The crowd roared its approval.

"WHAT STORE OF RICHES IT IMPARTS!"

Women and men and old babushkas crowded around in an effort to
touch him. His voice seemed to be everywhere, it seemed to be coming from
heaven itself.

"I WILL RETURN YOUR PRIDE, YOUR HOPE, YOUR DIGNITY. I WILL RETURN
THE UNION!"

Chernov climbed down from the APC, and he and Liesel joined Tarankov
for the last half-block into the square. Unit Four had pulled up and was

herding its prisoners from the city and federal buildings into a clear area in front of the frozen fountain. The square was jammed with people, tens of thousands of them, possibly more than one hundred thousand, one third of the entire population.

A broad path opened automatically for Tarankov and his column as if he were Moses parting the Red Sea.

"IT IS BETTER TO LOSE A RIVER OF BLOOD NOW, THAN THE ENTIRE COUNTRY LATER, EVEN IF IT IS RUSSIAN BLOOD. BECAUSE WE WILL ONLY SPILL THE BLOOD OF TRAITORS."

A lot of the people in Kirov knew what had happened in other cities that Tarankov had visited, and now that the prisoners were in plain view an odd, ugly mood began to sweep over the crowd. Liesel called it the "blood lust," when a crowd suddenly began to act as a single entity. A wild animal that wanted to kill.

"LOOK AROUND AND YOU WILL SEE WHAT THEY HAVE DONE," Tarankov's voice boomed across the square, now ringed with his mobile units.

"Units One and Two are completing their mission," Chernov said at his ear. "Radar is still clear."

Without breaking his stride Tarankov led his column into the square down the long path to where the two dozen city and district officials were lined up. They hadn't been allowed to get their hats and coats, and they stood shivering in the bitter northwest wind that gusted across the square. It would probably snow later today, but most of them understood that they wouldn't be alive to see it.

"IT IS TIME FOR A CLEAN SWEEP. THE FILTH MUST BE RUTHLESSLY CLEANED AWAY BEFORE WE ALL CHOKE ON THE DUST."

A low, guttural murmur spread across the square.

"WHEN OUR STRUGGLE IS COMPLETED, I WILL RAISE A BRONZE STATUE IN MOSCOW'S DZERZHINSKY SQUARE WITH MY OWN TWO HANDS. IT WILL BE OF A YOUNG SOLDIER, HIS RIFLE RAISED OVER HIS HEAD, AND HIS FACE POINTED UP TO HEAVEN IN HOPE."

"Unit Three has completed its mission," Chernov said. "All units are on the way back. ETA under five minutes."

Tarankov held a hand over his lapel mike. "Was Unit Three successful?"

Chernov spoke briefly into his lapel mike. He nodded. "No gold this time but they got millions in roubles, and a very large amount of hard currencies. Mostly Swiss francs."

"Distribute the roubles, we'll keep the francs for our expenses," Liesel said.

Chernov waited for Tarankov to respond.

"It's expensive running a revolution, Zhennia," Liesel prompted.

Tarankov looked at his wife, then nodded after a moment, and Chernov relayed the order. Reality was sometimes a bitter pill, something his countrymen for all their tribulations under Stalin had never learned. He would have to teach them.

The armored column stopped fifty meters from the fountain. Drankov's commandoes piled out of the transports to take up defensive positions in case they had to retreat under the press of the crowds, or under fire by an organized force.

Tarankov continued up the broad path, his stride long and purposeful. Ten meters from the prisoners he unbuttoned the flap on his holster.

Kirov's Mayor Eduard Bakursky, a democratic reformer who'd been trying unsuccessfully to jumpstart the city's flagging economy, stepped to one side and pulled out a pistol that one of the commandoes had slipped him.

The prisoners nearest him reared back.

"You bastard!" Bakursky shouted. He raised the pistol and started shooting, the bullets apparently going wild. They were blanks. He'd been set up.

Tarankov stood his ground and calmly drew his pistol, switched off the safety and fired two shots, one hitting Bakursky in his chest, and the other catching the portly man in his thick neck just below his chin. He was driven backward into the frozen fountain, his blood splashing across the ice and snow.

"TRAITOR," Tarankov shouted, his voice thundering across the square. "TRAITORS TO THE PEOPLE, ALL OF YOU."

He shot the man who'd been standing next to the mayor, and as the prisoners tried desperately to get away, Tarankov followed them, emptying his pistol into the group.

The Unit Four commandoes opened fire with their Kalashnikovs on full automatic, killing the remaining prisoners within seconds.

As the sounds of the final shots echoed off the buildings and faded, the huge crowd suddenly erupted in a frenzy of cheering and clapping and whistling. They began to sing the old Communist Party anthem, *The Internationale*, though probably not one in a thousand knew that the song originated in France in the last century. But it didn't matter. The people were happy. Blood had been shed, but it was a just killing. The revolution had finally come to Kirov and the crowd was drunk with the thrill of it.

And Tarankov too was drunk on their passion, as he turned to address his people.

The Kremlin

Russian President Boris Yeltsin, red faced and sweating, stumbled on the stairs into the old Soviet Presidium building, and one of his bodyguards had to reach out to stop him from falling. Lunch with Prime Minister Yuri Kabatov and his staff of old women had been nothing short of grueling. Only with vodka could he keep his sanity, although on days like this he wondered why he bothered.

His chief of staff, Alexi Zhigalin, and his military liaison, Colonel Igor Lykov, were waiting for him upstairs in his outer office, and their faces fell when they saw what condition he was in.

Zhigalin handed him a glass of tea. "Generals Yuryn and Mazayev are on their way over, Mr. President. Are you up to seeing them?"

Yeltsin flung the glass across the room, and brushed the impertinent pissant aside. "Unless NATO's tanks are knocking at our back door, the generals will have to wait. Two hours," he thundered as he entered his office.

Zhigalin and Lykov exchanged a glance. "It's the Tarantula. He's struck again, this time in Kirov," Zhigalin said, his long, narrow face even more pale than usual.

Yeltsin pulled up short and turned back, shooting the two men an ugly glance. "The madman's name is Yevgenni Tarankov. You will not utter that other name in my presence again."

"There was a massacre in the city square," Lykov said, the heels of his highly polished boots firmly together.

Yeltsin thought he looked like a drugstore cowboy. A fairy. But what he was saying was finally beginning to penetrate the fog. "In Kirov?"

"Yes, Mr. President," Lykov said. "The mayor and his staff along with all the district judges, and some others were gunned down. Tarankov himself apparently shot Mayor Bakursky and a couple of others to death."

"Where was the Militia, the army?"

"General Kirpichko was apparently on joint army–air force maneuvers a hundred kilometers north of the city. By the time he could return, Tarankov was gone."

"But they didn't chase after his train?"

Zhigalin shook his head. "It wouldn't have done much good, Mr. President. The people of Kirov support him. Now that our officials are dead it would take a full military intervention to bring order—"

"Do it," Yeltsin said.

"Sir?" Lykov asked.

"Find out where he's going, get there before him, and either arrest him or kill him."

"It wouldn't be so easy as that, Mr. President," Lykov said. "He has many supporters in the military and the Militia. Even in the Security Service. And his commandoes are better than the best of our troops."

Yeltsin walked back to Lykov and looked him up and down as if he were a raw recruit at parade inspection. "He has two hundred men with him. The best troops in all of Russia. Each one better than any ten of ours."

"Yes, sir."

"Then send ten thousand soldiers to arrest him. Send tanks, rocket launchers. Send helicopter gun ships. If he's near water, send ballistic missile submarines. But arrest him!"

"The people are with him," Zhigalin said.

Yeltsin turned his now steady gaze to his chief of staff.

"Then arrest them as well—"

"Quite impossible, Mr. President," FSK Director General Nikolai Yuryn said coming in. "We would have the healthy beginnings of a full scale armed insurrection. It's exactly what he wants." The FSK, or Federal Service for Counterintelligence, with its headquarters at the Lubyanka, was the internal security arm of the old KGB.

Militia Director Captain-General Mikhail Mazayev came in behind him. Both men were in uniform.

"Nikolai is correct, of course, Mr. President," Mazayev said. "By playing into his hand we'd be making matters worse."

"What do you suggest?" Yeltsin asked. He was at a slow boil and his generals knew it. The tension in the room was electric.

"I suggest that we bide our time," Yuryn answered. "He will make a mistake sooner or later. He will go to excess—all men of his ilk do at some point. It's inevitable. When that happens the people he claims to champion will desert him. Probably his own people will kill him."

"Are all of you agreed on this course of action?" Yeltsin asked reasonably.

"*Da*," Yuryn said. He was a large man, even bigger than Yeltsin, and he towered over everyone else in the room, especially the diminutive Zhigalin.

The others nodded.

Yeltsin let his shoulders sag as if he were defeated, started to turn back to his office, but then stopped, his face even redder than before. "Find out where Tarankov is going. Get there before him with as many troops and as much equipment and ordinance as you think you'll need . . . no, twice that much . . . and either arrest him or kill him. Have I made myself clear, Comrades?"

"Perfectly," General Yuryn said indifferently. "I'll have the order drawn up and on your desk for signature by morning."

"Do you feel you need such a document?"

"Yes, Mr. President, respectfully I do."

"Then have it here within the hour," Yeltsin said, and he went into his office and slammed the door.

TWO

Tarankov's Train

Yevgenni Tarankov replaced the telephone on its cradle, sat alone staring at a map for a full five minutes, then left the train. They were stopped on an unused siding about three hundred kilometers east of Moscow. Camouflage netting was draped over the entire train even though it was the middle of the night, they were still under a thick overcast and the sideboards had been lowered, making them appear to be a freight train with markings for Volgograd.

The nearer they got to their prime objective the more Chernov and Colonel Drankov insisted on such stringent security measures.

In four days they would hit Nizhny Novgorod, which would be their most ambitious, and therefore most difficult and dangerous target. After this morning's success at Kirov he'd felt that they were gaining a momentum that soon would be unstoppable. But all that was changed. He lit a cigarette, then stepped away from the tracks out from under the netting suddenly feeling confined, claustrophobic.

Two of his commandoes appeared out of the darkness. "Comrade, may we be of assistance?" one of them asked in a respectful but firm voice. They were armed with Kalashnikovs.

"I'm going for a walk."

"Yes, sir. Would you please extinguish your cigarette?"

Tarankov looked sharply at the trooper. He wasn't over thirty, none of Drankov's commandoes were. But he looked like he ate barbed wire for breakfast, and wrestled black bears for sport. In the dim light reflected from the snowcover the man's face seemed as if it were carved from granite. He towered nearly two meters and easily weighed one hundred kilos, but standing nearly motionless it seemed as if he had the moves of a ballet dancer. He didn't flinch under Tarankov's hard gaze.

Tarankov dropped the cigarette into the snow, and when he looked up the second commando had disappeared without a sound.

"What is your name, soldier?"

"Lieutenant Ablakov, sir."

"Gennadi?"

The man cracked a smile, pleased. "Yes, sir."

"Are you married?"

"Yes, sir. My wife is living with her mother in Yakutsk."

"It's a hard life there, but she is out of harm's way. Do you have any worries?"

"No, sir. But I miss her."

"As you should, Gennadi," Tarankov said gently. "Do you understand what we're doing?"

Lieutenant Ablakov straightened slightly. "I wouldn't be here if I didn't."

It was a good answer, Tarankov thought. Ablakov and the others were respectful of him, but not fearful. That, of course, would have to change in time. But for now it was a useful attitude. Stalin understood that the people around him in the beginning would develop a familiarity that in time would become unacceptable. Diminishing his absolute authority. It was the reason for many of his early pogroms. Penicillin cured the infection, but too much penicillin killed the patient so it had to be flushed out.

Chernov came out and together they walked to the last car beneath the netting where Tarankov lit another cigarette.

"They don't like you wandering off alone," Chernov said.

Tarankov looked into his chief of staff's eyes. The man had been the best Department Viktor killer the KGB had ever fielded. Even better than the legendary Arkady Kurshin who'd worked under the old Baranov regime. Those had been hard times, which demanded hard men. But, Tarankov mused, these were even harder times.

"Without you there would be no movement. Drankov and his men would be gone within the hour."

"What about you?"

Chernov shrugged. "There's always work to be done. I might return to Moscow. I have friends."

"You need an organization."

"Such institutions exist."

Tarankov chuckled. "In Iran, perhaps?"

Chernov cocked his head. "They could use a steady hand," he replied. "What's troubling you tonight?"

Tarankov looked away. They were in a forest here, the shadows dark, and mysterious. Russian shadows, he thought. Hiding something. "No one in Russia would raise a hand to kill me."

Chernov said nothing.

Tarankov turned back to his chief of staff. "Yeltsin has ordered my arrest because of Kirov."

"That's not unexpected."

"They'll be waiting for us in Nizhny Novgorod. Army, Militia, FSK helicopter gunships. A real coordinated effort."

"It'll take more than that."

"Five thousand troops under arms."

"Nizhny Novgorod is a city of over a million people. If they rise up, the entire Russian Army could do nothing but watch," Chernov said. He studied Tarankov's eyes. "Do you want to call it off?"

"This time they mean business, and they have four days to impose a curfew and make it stick. It takes a Russian a lot longer than that to rebel."

"Then we'll go first thing in the morning, before they're fully prepared," Chernov said. "If you avoid Nizhny Novgorod because of the army, they won't have to arrest you. Yeltsin will have won his point. Even a Russian will be able to see that."

"*If* the army shows up," Tarankov said.

Chernov was suddenly bemused. "You've already thought this out," he said. "You know exactly what we're going to do."

"*Da.*"

"Do you have a timetable?"

Tarankov nodded, content for the moment to let Chernov work it out for himself.

"Am I to be told, or do you intend keeping all of us in the dark?" Chernov asked with some irritation in his voice. He was afraid of no one. It was his greatest strength as well as his greatest weakness.

"We'll go to Nizhny Novgorod next week. But first we'll hit Dzerzhinskiy in the morning, and then I'll send you to remove our biggest obstacle."

Chernov's eyes narrowed. "If you mean to do what I think you mean to do, there could be dangerous repercussions. Not only in Moscow, but in the West as well. At the moment Washington sees you as an internal problem, vexing only to the Kremlin. If I do this thing, that perception will change."

"True, but it takes Americans even longer than Russians to react. Look how long it took before they moved against Castro or Noriega or Saddam Hussein. By then it will be a *fait accompli*, because Russia will be mine."

"This is different."

"Yes, because we will once again become a definite threat to their security. But by the time Washington realizes the fact, our missiles will be fully reprogrammed and operational."

"What missiles are left."

"You only need to kill a man once to ensure his death, not ten times."

"Very well," Chernov said after a moment. "I'll brief Drankov and his unit commanders. What are we targeting in Dzerzhinskiy?"

"The Riga electric generating facility."

A slow smile curled Chernov's lips. "The nuclear power station."

"*Da.*"

Dzerzhinskiy
A Moscow Suburb

The train slowed to a crawl in the chilly predawn darkness. Two commandoes leaped from the lead car and raced thirty meters ahead to the mechanical switch, shot the lock off, and moved the lever to the right which shunted them off the main line and onto the spur which served the power station.

They placed a small shaped charge on the switch, backed off ten or fifteen meters, and turned the firing plunger. The small explosion destroyed the switch making it impossible now for the tracks to be easily moved back, which could trap them on the spur.

As soon as the men were back aboard the train, it gathered speed past an abandoned brick works and a tumbled down foundry, slowing again to a crawl five hundred meters farther just before a tall chain-link gate guarding entry to the station.

The same two commandoes leaped off the train and placed charges on both sides of the gate. Moments later the much larger explosion ripped the gate off its hinges, sending metal parts and chain link fifty meters into the air, and just as effectively shattering the morning stillness.

Riga Nuclear Power Station Number One, which had opened eight months ago despite massive protests, was an engineering marvel by any standard. Constructed as only Russians know how, the huge containment dome and twin cooling towers rose above the shabby suburb of factories, houses and apartment complexes that were little more than hovels. The enormous amounts of water needed to cool the two reactors was drawn from the Moscow River and piped underground in concrete races ten meters in diameter; large enough so that during construction the largest earth movers were dwarfed.

By building the power station in Dzerzhinskiy the Kremlin sent three clear messages to the people and to the rest of the world. Russian engineering could solve any problem, even making it possible to build a nuclear power plant so far away from a water source. The Russian government was in charge of the nation and knew what was best for its people. And, since the facility was less than six kilometers as the crow flies from the Kremlin, the people were assured that Yeltsin believed the Riga station would not become another Chernobyl. Riga was safe.

So far unpublicized, but generally known in the suburb, was that in the first eight months of operation the complex had suffered four major accidents including one that SCRAMed the system less than ninety seconds before a total meltdown occurred.

The reactor was like a sword of Damocles hanging over the neighborhood. No one who lived in Dzerzhinskiy worked in the complex, but everyone in the suburb had to live with the threat.

Because of the sensitive nature of the power station, and the demonstrations against it, the complex was heavily guarded by crack FSK troops, some of whom had served in Afghanistan, and others in the battle for Chechnya. It amused Tarankov, as the train again gathered speed for the last kilometer to the loading docks and Central Control, that although Chernov and the others did not want him wandering around alone in the dark countryside for fear of a sniper, they were willing to let him go with his troops into a hornet's nest.

He watched from his operations center on the observation deck in the rear car with Liesel, Chernov, a communications specialist and a weapons officer. His personal quarters on the lower deck were polished wood and brass, but up here the deck was equipped with state of the art communications and radar equipment, as well as firecontrol for 22mm automatic cannons fore and aft, and a smaller version of the navy's close-in weapons system, capable of radar-tracking incoming targets, including incoming aircraft and missiles, and firing 12.5mm depleted-uranium slugs at a rate of six thousand rounds per minute. This one car presented a formidable force by itself.

"They know we're here," comms specialist Junior Lieutenant Yuri Ignatov, said. He entered the information he was picking up by radio into his battle planning computer, which was similar to the BSY-1 used on nuclear submarines. In this case the computer would spit out weapons and tactical options based on real time information it was being fed, and relay it to Colonel Drankov and his unit commanders.

Even as the information came up on the display screen, they could see the troops spilling out of the bunkers to the southeast of Central Control. A pair of rocket launchers came up from a tunnel and started to turn toward the train.

"Take them out," Chernov ordered.

Their weapons officer, Lieutenant Nikolai Zabotin, entered the new targeting data into his console, and as they got within two hundred meters of the rocket launchers, cannons on the lead car ripped both trucks apart, shredding metal, rubber, plastic and human flesh indiscriminately. Both launchers went up in huge balls of flame, scattering burning debris and ordnance over the FSK ground troops pouring out of the bunkers.

"We're a hundred fifty meters out, prepare to dismount," Chernov radioed Drankov. He reached up and braced himself against the overhead.

The others did the same, as the train's coordinated braking system, which operated much like anti-lock brakes on a luxury car, slowed them almost as quickly as a truck could be slowed in an emergency, and ten times faster than any ordinary train could slow down.

As soon as their speed dropped below twenty kilometers per hour, the battle doors on each car slid open, hinged ramps dropped down, and Drankov's commandoes aboard their armored assault vehicles shot from the train like wild dogs suddenly released from confinement, firing as they made sharp turns into what remained of the FSK's first response force.

Tarankov keyed his microphone. "This is Tarankov. Send Units Three and Four to blow the main gates."

"The alert has been called to the main Militia barracks," Ignatov said.

"The people will fill the streets before they can get here."

"The Militia might run them over," Ignatov said.

"Three and Four enroute," Drankov cut in.

They could see the two units peel off toward the west, while One and Two headed toward the main electrical distribution yard on the opposite side of the complex.

By the time the train came to a complete halt across from the Central Control building, Drankov's main force had taken out the last of the FSK troops, and his men were racing through the building, blasting their way through doors leading into each level, then leapfrogging ahead.

Within eight minutes from the start of the assault the main gates were down, and the first of thousands of people from the suburb were pouring into the compound, the main electrical distribution yards which covered more than fifty hectares were destroyed, the two reactors were shut down, the four water races were collapsed with heavy explosives, the control room with its complex control panel and its computer equipment was completely demolished, and every on duty guard, engineer or staff member was dead or dying.

"Five minutes and we've got to be out of here," Chernov said. He'd donned a headset and was listening to the military radio traffic between the Dzerzhinskiy Militia and the main barracks downtown.

"Sound the recall," Tarankov said.

Liesel was beside herself with excitement. "This'll teach the bastards a lesson," she said.

"One they won't soon forget," Chernov shot back.

Tarankov opened the hatch and climbed out onto the catwalk as the crowds swarmed across the vast parking lot toward the train.

"Five minutes," Chernov shouted.

"COMRADES, MY NAME IS YEVGENNI TARANKOV, AND I HAVE COME TODAY TO OFFER YOU MY HAND IN FRIENDSHIP AND HELP."

THREE

Tarankov's Train

Have you had any sleep?" Tarankov asked.

Chernov shook his head as he placed the last of three cases of Marlboros into the trunk of the Mercedes 520S parked beside the tracks. The top two layers of cartons actually contained cigarettes. He closed the trunk, leaned back against the car and accepted a cigarette from Tarankov, though he hated the things.

"It went well this morning," Tarankov said. "Moscow is going to have to deal with power outages for a long time. It'll make things worse for them."

"Yeltsin and his cronies have access to emergency generators. And if things get too bad they can always escape to the dachas."

"You don't approve," Tarankov said crossly. He was tired too.

"On the contrary, Comrade. I neither approve nor disapprove. But I'm a realist enough to understand that it's the ordinary people on the street who make revolutions possible. Once the leader is in power, he can do anything he wants, because he'll control the guns, and the butter. But if he loses the people in the beginning he will have lost the revolution."

"A good speech, Leonid. But you failed to take into account the fact I was cheered."

"By the people of Dzerzhinskiy who were afraid of the power station. By next winter when the snow flies again, and still there is not enough power in Moscow, the rest of the city will remember who to blame."

Tarankov smiled faintly. "By then the power will be restored." An event, he thought, that Chernov would not be alive to witness.

"That's as optimistic as it is naive, I think," Chernov said.

They were parked in a birch woods two hundred fifty kilometers north of Moscow. Tarankov gazed across a big lake, still frozen, his eyes narrowing against the glare from the setting sun, as he tried to keep his temper in check.

"Throughout the summer I will divert military construction battalions from as many division as it will take to get the job done in ninety days," he said.

"You *do* have a timetable," Chernov said, flipping the cigarette away. "If you're right, Dzerzhinskiy can be turned into an advantage. And Nizhny Novgorod can be important if the situation doesn't become untenable after tomorrow. But you still need Moscow and St. Petersburg. We can't kill them all."

"Only those necessary."

"They're not stupid. They'll figure out your plans, and try to block you somehow."

"It's already too late for them," Tarankov said. "You're close to me, have you figured it out?"

Chernov smiled. "It's not my job. I'm nothing more than a means to your end."

"What about when we come into power?"

"I'll leave, Comrade Tarantula, because I will no longer be needed. And we know what happens to people in Russia who are not needed."

"Maybe I'll kill you now," Tarankov said with a dangerous edge in his voice.

Chernov's gaze didn't waver. "I don't think that would be quite as easy as you might think," he said in a reasonable tone. He pushed away from the car, and Tarankov backed up a half-pace despite himself. "I have work to do, unless you have second thoughts."

"You're confident you can do it?"

Chernov nodded seriously. "Yeltsin could have been eliminated anytime over the past couple of years, but nobody wanted to take responsibility for it. He's not been worth killing until now."

"Am I worth killing, Leonid?" Tarankov asked.

"Oh, yes. Especially after tomorrow," Chernov replied. "And believe me they will try. Someone will almost certainly try."

"You will see that they fail."

"That, Comrade Tarankov, *is* my job." Chernov pointed to the cigarette in Tarankov's meaty paw. "But they won't have to send an assassin if you keep that up."

Tarankov grunted. "You sound like Liesel." He smiled. "One nag is enough."

"She's right."

"Good of you to say so," Tarankov said. "We'll wait for you at Kostroma. But if you get into trouble you will have to rely on the usual contacts in Moscow, we won't be able to come for you. Not until after Nizhny Novgorod."

"I'll be there," Chernov said. "Now, if you will excuse me, I need to get a few things before I leave. I want to be in Moscow before midnight." He abruptly went back to the train and boarded the second car from the rear, not seeing the intense look of anger and hatred that flashed across Tarankov's heavy features.

Chernov's car contained the officers' wardroom and kitchen, as well as quarters for him, Colonel Drankov and the four unit commanders. The colonel and two of his officers were smoking and drinking tea in the wardroom when Chernov passed. They did not look up, nor did he acknowledge them. Their relationship was exactly as he wished it to be: one of business, not friendship.

In his compartment, which consisted of a wide bunk, a built-in desk and two chairs, a closet and a well-equipped bathroom, Chernov laid out the uniform of a lieutenant colonel in the Kremlin Presidential Security Service, then pulled off his boots and combat fatigues.

Someone knocked at his door. He quickly looked around to make sure nothing of importance was lying in plain view, then flipped a blanket over the uniform. "Come," he said.

Liesel Tarankov, wearing a UCLA Sailing Squadron warmup suit, came in. She looked Chernov up and down, then glanced at the turned down blanket. "I thought you were getting ready to leave us, not go to bed."

"I was changing clothes. Is there something I can do for you, Madam?"

"I want to discuss your assignment."

"Very well. If you'll allow me to finish dressing, I'll join you and your husband in the Operations Center and we can go over the detail."

"No. I want to talk about it here and now." A little color had come to Liesel's cheeks, and a strand of blonde hair was loose over her left temple. She was fifteen years younger than Tarankov and not unattractive.

"Then I'll call him, he can join us here." Chernov stepped over to the desk and reached for the telephone, but Liesel intercepted him, pushing him away.

"Just you and me."

Chernov smiled. "Did you come here expecting me to make love to you, madam?" he asked in a reasonable tone. "Is that how you meant to control me?"

"I'm not ugly. I have a nice body, and I know things."

"What if I told you that I'm a homosexual."

She laughed. "I wouldn't believe it."

"I think you'd rather believe that than the truth," he said.

It took a moment for the meaning of what she'd just heard to penetrate, and when it did a flush came to her face. *"Schweinhund!"* She lunged at him, her long fingernails up like claws.

Chernov easily sidestepped her. He grabbed her arms, pinned them behind her back, and shoved her up against the bulkhead, his body against hers.

She struggled for a moment, but then looked up into his eyes and parted her lips.

He stepped back, opened the door, and spun her out into the passageway. "Go away before I tell your husband that you tried to seduce me."

"He wouldn't believe you," she shot back, a catch in her voice.

"I think he would," Chernov said disparagingly, and he closed and locked the door.

For a few moments he thought the woman was going to make a scene, but when nothing happened he got dressed. Before it was all over, he thought, he would fuck her, and then kill her. It would be the best thing he'd ever done for Tarankov.

The Kremlin

Chernov arrived at the Borovitsky Tower Gate, on the opposite side of the Kremlin from Red Square, at 11:45 P.M. One guard examined his papers, which identified him as Lieutenant Colonel Boris Sazanov, while the other shined a light in the back seat, and then requested that the trunk be opened.

He popped the lid then stuck his head out the window as the guard spotted the cases of cigarettes. "Take a couple of cartons. They won't be missed." His hat was pulled low, most of his features in shadow.

"Who are they for?" the guard asked.

"Korzhakov," Chernov said. Lieutenant-General Alexander Korzhakov was chief of presidential security, a drinking buddy of Yeltsin's and the number two most powerful man in the Kremlin.

"I don't think so," the guard said respectfully. "I think I'll call operations."

"This car was left unlocked for an hour on Arbat Street. The cigarettes will not be missed if you're not greedy, and you keep your mouth shut."

The first guard handed Chernov's papers back. "What are you doing here this evening, Colonel?"

"Delivering cigarettes."

The second guard pulled two cartons of cigarettes out of one of the boxes and stuffed them inside his greatcoat. He slammed the trunk lid, and went back into the guardhouse.

"I don't smoke," the first guard said.

"Neither do I, but they're sometimes better than gold, if you know what I mean."

The guard stepped back, saluted and waved Chernov through.

Chernov returned the salute and drove up the hill past the Poteshny Palace and around the corner to the modernistic glass and aluminum Palace of Congresses. It was a Wednesday night, the Duma was not in session, nor was any state function or dinner being held, so the Kremlin was all but deserted.

The guard at the entrance to the underground parking garage checked his papers, and waved him through.

Chernov took the ramp four levels to the most secured floor where Yeltsin's limousines were kept and serviced. He parked in the shadows at the end of a long row of Mercedes, Cadillacs and Zil limousines. The entrance to Yeltsin's parking area and private elevators fifty meters away was guarded by a lone man seated in a glass enclosure. Chernov checked his watch. He was exactly on time.

Two minutes later, the guard got up, stretched his back, left the guard box and took the service elevator up one level.

Chernov took a block of eight cigarette cartons from the bottom of one of the cases, and walked to the end of the parking row, ducked under the steel barrier and went back to the Zil limousine with the SSP 7 license plate. It was the car that would be used to pick up Yeltsin in the morning and bring him here to his office.

It was a piece of information that Tarankov got. Chernov trusted its reliability.

The freight elevator was still on sub level three, and would remain there for three minutes. No more.

Chernov climbed into the back compartment of the limo and popped the two orange tabs that released the seat bottom. Next he peeled the back from a corner of the bottom of the brick of cigarettes and stuck a radio-controlled detonator into the soft gray mass of Semtex plastic explosive. This he stuffed under the seat, molding it against a box beam member. The bottom of the car was armored to protect from explosions from outside. The steel plates would focus most of the force of the blast upward through the leather upholstered seat. No one in the rear compartment could possibly survive, nor was it likely that anyone in the car would escape critical burns and injuries The amount of Semtex was five times more than necessary for the job.

Chernov relatched the seat bottom in position, softly closed the door, and as the freight elevator began to descend, ducked under the barrier, hurried back to his car and drove away.

"That was quick," the guard at the ground level said.

"I just had to deliver something," Chernov said.

"Well, have a good evening, sir," the guard said. He raised the barrier.

Chernov headed past the Presidium to the Spassky Tower where the guard languidly raised the gate and waved him through. Threats came from outside, and besides no one of any importance was inside the Kremlin tonight. Anyway, all colonels were damned fools.

After clearing Red Square, Chernov drove out to Krasnaya Presnya past the dumpy American Embassy on Tchaikovsky Street to a block of old, but well-maintained apartments near the zoo and planetarium.

Traffic downtown was heavy, but out here the shops were all closed and the neighborhood streets were quiet, though lights shone in many windows. Russians loved to stay up late talking. In the old days they fitted blackout curtains on their windows. These days they weren't worried.

All that would change, Chernov thought as he drove around back and parked the Mercedes in a garage. Tarankov truly believed he had the answers for Russia. Likely as not, his revolution would bring them to war. But by then, Chernov intended on being long gone.

He waited for a couple of minutes in the darkness to make sure that he hadn't been followed, then climbed the stairs to the third floor, his tread noiseless. He produced a key and opened the door of the front apartment, and let himself in.

The apartment was dark, only a dim light came from outside. It smelled faintly of expensive western perfumes and soap. Feminine smells. Music came softly from the bedroom.

Chernov took off his uniform blouse, loosened his tie and went into the kitchen where he poured a glass of white wine. Removing his shoes, he walked back to the bedroom, and pushed open the door.

"Can you stay long this time, Ivan," Raya Dubanova asked softly in the darkness. She'd been a ballet dancer with the Bolshoi. Now she was an assistant choreographer of the corps de ballet. Her body was still compact and well muscled. She knew him only as Ivan.

"No," Chernov said sitting beside her on the bed. He put the wine glass aside and took her in his arms. She was naked.

"Can you stay at least until morning?" she whispered in his ear.

"I can stay with you tonight if you promise to wake me at six sharp," he teased. "But if you snore I'll have to go to a hotel."

"I don't know if you'll be capable of getting out of bed when I'm finished with you," she said wickedly. "Now take off your clothes, and come to me."

She'd been forced to be the escort of a Strategic Rocket Force general who Chernov was contracted to kill three years ago. He'd shot the man in his bed while Raya hid in the bathroom. When it was over she came out, looked at the general's body, took the gun from Chernov and pumped three bullets into it, then spit in the general's face.

She wouldn't stay in the apartment so Chernov brought her to this one. He came to her as often as possible, sometimes able to stay for only an hour or two, other times staying an entire evening.

She knew what he was, but she never asked who he worked for, or if he'd killed again. She was simply grateful that he'd saved her from the old man. And each time he came to her bed she showed her appreciation.

Tarankov didn't know about their relationship. No one did.

He undressed and joined her in bed. "I need a couple of hours of sleep," he said.

"We'll see," she said, straddling him. She raked her fingernails across his chest almost, but not quite with enough force to draw blood, and he immediately responded.

Maybe he wouldn't need so much sleep as all that, he thought, a soft groan escaping from his lips as Raya began to bite the tender skin on the insides of his thighs.

Red Square

At 8:00 A.M. the line in front of Lenin's Mausoleum was already long even though visitors were not allowed inside until 10:00. Chernov, wearing a worn overcoat, black fur hat and shabby boots, stood near the end of the line, his hands stuffed deeply in his pockets. The morning was bitterly cold, made worse by a sharp wind blowing from the Moscow River. Most of the people in line were old women, but there were a few foreign tourists and several men not ashamed to show remorse for the father of Russian socialism. Rain or snow it was a rare day that there wasn't a line in front of the mausoleum. It was the most anonymous spot in Red Square.

Two police cars, their blue lights flashing, came around the corner past the History Museum at a high rate of speed. They were immediately followed by four Zil limousines, and two final police cars.

Chernov waited for them to pass then slow down as they turned toward the Spassky gate. The first two police cars entered the Kremlin, and he pressed the button on the tiny transmitter in his pocket.

The third limousine erupted in a huge geyser of flame and debris. A second later the sound of the blast hammered off the Kremlin walls and boomed across Red Square.

Everybody in line instinctively fell back, raising their arms to shield themselves from falling debris. Even before the first siren began to sound, everyone scattered as fast as their legs could carry them.

Chernov allowed himself to be swept away, until he ducked around the corner on October 25th Street where he entered the metro station. He did not look back. He didn't have to, because he knew for certain that if Boris Yeltsin had been in that limousine, he was now dead.

FOUR

**The Russian White House
Moscow**

Russian Prime Minister Yuri Kabatov entered the Crisis Management Center deep beneath the White House. The chamber and its communications center had been hacked out of the bedrock shortly after the Kremlin Coup in which Gorbachev had been ousted, but nobody this afternoon felt comforted knowing sixty meters of granite separated them from the real world above because all the security in Russia hadn't been able to save the life of Boris Yeltsin.

"I don't think there can be any doubt who was behind this latest act of violence or why," Kabatov said, taking his seat at the head of the long conference table. He was satisfied to see that nobody disagreed with him.

In addition to his own staff those around the table who had responded to his summons included Moscow Mayor Vadim Cheremukhin and St. Petersburg Mayor Dmitri Didyatev, both democratic reform moderates like himself. The meeting had been delayed so that both men, whom Kabatov considered crucial to Russia's future, could be notified and make their way into the city; Cheremukhin from his dacha on the Istra River, and Didyatev from St. Petersburg.

Farther down the table were Militia Director General Mazayev and FSK Director General Yuryn. Yuryn sat erect, his thick hands folded in front of him on the table, a scowl on his gross features.

Some of Yeltsin's shaken staff had also arrived, among them the President's Chief of Staff Zhigalin, and his Chief Military Liaison Colonel Lykov.

Seventeen men in all, most of them moderates, had gathered to make what, Kabatov felt, would be the most important decision that had been made since the breakup of the Soviet Union.

"Without proof, Mr. Prime Minister, there's very little we can do if we are to continue as you wish under rule of law," General Mazayev said thickly. He had dark circles under his red eyes. He looked like he'd just sobered up.

"We're not going to have to worry about proof because the bastard won't deny it," Kabatov shot back. He was a terrier of a man, with a sharp, abrasive personality that matched his looks. "He'll say that his actions are for the best of the nation. He destroyed Riga Power Station so effectively that my engineers tell me it will be at least a year before it's back on line, maybe longer if there's other damage beyond what we already know. And the stupid kulaks up there cheered him. They actually cheered him. But this winter when they begin to freeze their asses off they won't blame him, they'll blame us.

"I'm also told that Yeltsin ordered his arrest in Nizhny Novgorod, and that Tarankov was tipped off. So he retaliated by having the president assassinated. This time if there are any leaks they will have to come from this room."

Kabatov was ranting, he could hear himself but he couldn't stop because he was deeply frightened. Yeltsin had been a drunken buffoon, but his security detail was simply the best in the entire world. They figured the explosive device had been placed beneath the back seat of the limousine. Supposedly no one outside the security detail, not even Yeltsin himself, knew which car that would be. And there were no early reports of any suspicious activity in or around the secured parking level beneath the Kremlin. Yet they were still cleaning his blood off the streets outside Spassky Tower with toothbrushes.

"The monster has to be arrested and brought to trial. It's as simple and as necessary as that if we're going to survive as a democracy. Now, I want your ideas on how to do it."

Alexi Zhigalin looked up defiantly. "Just kill him. We can find his train and send the Air Force in to blow it off the tracks, destroying him, that East German whore he's married to, and all of his fanatical followers. They're traitors."

"It could be done," Yeltsin's military liaison, Colonel Lykov, said. "I've already spoken with General Ablakin. If the FSK could help us with intelligence gathering, it could be pulled off within twenty-four hours. It would send a clear message—"

"To whom?" Kabatov interrupted. "If this were the United States and its president were assassinated, the government wouldn't kill the assassin."

"Jack Ruby probably worked for the CIA," Yuryn said.

"That's not been proven."

"We're not the United States," the FSK director said.

"No, nor are we England, or France or Germany or any other *civilized* nation if we kill Tarankov. Such an action would play directly into the hands of his supporters. Don't you think with a cause like that to follow, that popular support for whatever other lunatic decided to stand up to us would grow?"

"President Yeltsin maintained much the same view," General Mazayev said. "Look what happened to him."

"Are you saying that one man and a handful of thugs can hold an entire country for ransom?" Kabatov shouted.

"In Tarankov's view he is campaigning," Yuryn said.

"Campaigning for what? Yeltsin's vacant seat?"

"*Da.* And yours, Mr. Prime Minister, and that of the General Secretary of the Communist Party. And that as supreme leader of a new Soviet Union, the Baltics included. As you know, he has a lot of popular support."

"Gained by robbing people of their own money out of our banks and giving it back to them," Kabatov said with disgust. "Apparently he handed out something less than he robbed in Kirov. Something considerably less." He shot Yuryn a bleak look. "Campaign funds?"

"Probably," Yuryn replied indifferently. He worked for the federal government, not for the Prime Minister, though it was unclear at the moment who, other than Kabatov, was nominally in charge of the government.

"Your suggestion then, General Yuryn, is to kill him? Do you agree with Alexi Ivanovich?"

"On the contrary, I strongly recommend that we wait. As you say, when winter comes around and there is not enough power for Moscow the mood in the city will definitely change for the worse. But the blame can be shifted away from you, and back to Tarankov."

"How considerate of you," Kabatov said sarcastically.

"It is the same advice I gave President Yeltsin," Yuryn said. "General Mazayev and I happen to agree on this point. But the President insisted that Tarankov be arrested at whatever costs. I believe that order cost him his life."

"There was a security leak somewhere," Kabatov said.

"Presumably. Nor should you believe that there won't be a leak from this gathering. Such things happen despite our best precautions."

"Then it will have to come from one of you men," Kabatov said coldly, his eyes shifting from man to man. "This room was electronically sealed once I entered. Nothing of a mechanical or an electronic nature can get out of here. The only thing that will leave here this afternoon is what's in your heads."

Again Yuryn shrugged indifferently. "If you mean to actually arrest Tarankov and not simply eliminate him and his followers, then our staffs will have to become involved. The leak will come from there." The bulky intelligence service chief leaned forward in his chair and tapped the table top with a blunt finger. "If you go after him he will find out, and he will come after you." Yuryn looked at the others around the table. "He'll come after all of us."

"Are we to be held hostage?" Kabatov shouted, thumping his fist on the table. "Should we shut out the lights, crawl under our beds and hand the madman the keys to the Kremlin? Stalin assassinated Lenin in order to gain power. Has that happened again? Are we going to allow our nation to sink to those levels of barbarism? Pogroms. Gulags. Wars?

"What do you think the West's reaction will be when we pack up our tents and abandon the field? Without trade how long will Tarankov or any of us survive? Russian winters have killed more than foreigners. Russian winters have claimed plenty of Russian lives too. He must be taken alive and placed on public trial for all the world to see."

"It will tear the nation apart," Yuryn warned.

"We will lose the nation if we don't do it," Kabatov said wearily. "I didn't call you here today to argue the point. I called because I wanted you to tell me how to proceed." He glanced down the long table at Zhigalin. "Where is General Korzhakov?"

"He sends his apologies, Mr. Prime Minister, but he is busy with the investigation."

Kabatov shook his head in disgust. "Has any progress been made since this morning?"

"Some," Zhigalin said. He opened a report he'd brought with him. "I was given this just before I left the Kremlin. Apparently a man who identified himself as Lieutenant Colonel Boris Sazanov assigned to the presidential security detail, entered the Kremlin last night a few minutes before midnight. He said he was delivering gifts. One of the guards checked the trunk of the man's car and found several cases of American cigarettes. He got inside the parking garage beneath the Palace of Congresses where he remained for around five minutes. He then left by a different gate."

"Now we're getting somewhere," Kabatov said. "Has this Lieutenant Colonel Sazanov been found?"

"No such officer exists. Nor do we have much of a description. It was evening, the lighting was imperfect, and the guards said the man parked in such a way that the front seat of the car was mostly in shadow. Their impression was that he was large, under fifty, possibly under forty years old, and he spoke in a cultured, well-educated voice. He was probably a professional."

"A professional what?"

"Assassin, Mr. Prime Minister," Zhigalin said. "He drove a new Mercedes sedan, so it's possible he worked for the mafia."

"Maybe it wasn't Tarankov's people," Mazayev said sharply.

"Tarankov has friends among the mafia," Zhigalin shot back. "The bastard has friends everywhere."

"What else?" Kabatov asked.

"The guard at the Palace of Congresses got a partial license plate number, and the city is being searched for the car, as of noon without success."

"Why wasn't I told of this?" Militia General Mazayev demanded. The Militia were the police.

"The alert was issued routinely for a stolen vehicle," Zhigalin replied. "General Korzhakov felt that the initial stages of the investigation should be as low key as possible so as to lull the assassin into a false sense of security."

"Spare me," the Militia director said. He turned to Kabatov. "I'll put my people on it. *All* my people. We'll find this car and this colonel."

"How was the bomb detonated?" Kabatov asked. "If it was set on a timer, it would mean that the assassin knew President Yeltsin's schedule. That in itself might give us a clue."

"The bomb was probably fired from a radio-controlled detonator," Zhigalin said. "At least that's the preliminary finding. It means that the assassin stationed himself someplace so that he could see the presidential motorcade show up at the Kremlin. He pushed the button, the President's automobile exploded, and he calmly walked off."

"Someone in Red Square?"

"There was the usual line in front of Lenin's Tomb, some early tourists at St. Basil's and a few people just exiting the Rossyia Hotel, plus normal pedestrian traffic. Witnesses are being rounded up and questioned." Zhigalin glanced at Mazayev. "Again simply a routine investigation for the moment."

"If the man was a professional, as you suggest, then he is long gone by now," Mazayev said bitterly. "The city should have been shut up tight immediately after the bombing. We would have found the assassin."

"He's back aboard Tarankov's train," Zhigalin said. "If you want to find him you needn't look anywhere else."

"Whoever this assassin is, there is little doubt that his action was directed by Tarankov," Kabatov said. "On that there can be no argument. Which brings us back to arresting the sonofabitch. Are there any more suggestions as to how we should proceed?"

"President Yeltsin wanted him arrested when he showed up in Nizhny Novgorod," Zhigalin said. "We can go ahead with that plan."

"He won't show up there," Yuryn said.

"Why not?" Kabatov asked.

"Tarankov found out that preparations were being made in Nizhny Novgorod for his arrest, so he retaliated by staging the raid on the Riga facility, and then assassinating President Yeltsin."

"Do you know this for a fact?" Zhigalin demanded.

Yuryn shook his head. "If, as the Prime Minister suggests, Tarankov did order President Yeltsin's assassination, that would be the reason. He knew about Nizhny Novgorod."

"Assuming this is in fact true, how do we proceed?" Kabatov asked.

"Besides plugging the leaks so that Tarankov does not learn of our plans, we have to deal with two problems," the FSK director said. "The first is the western media. They want to know what happened this morning on Red Square."

"That's already being taken care of," Viktor Yemlin interjected from the end of the conference table. He was chief of the North American Division of the SVR, which was the foreign intelligence branch of the old KGB. Previously he'd worked as *rezident* for the KGB's operations in Washington and New York.

Kabatov had no love for the old KGB or its successors the FSK and SVR. He'd come under investigation by the intelligence service when he served as ambassador to the United Nations eight years ago. Despite his position, and the fact that the charges against him were proven to be groundless, he'd been treated roughly. But Yemlin was an important moderate, despite his position and background.

"Well?" he said, his dislike obvious.

"Explosive ordinance used for the protection of President Yeltsin that is normally carried in one of the escort limousines was defective and detonated by accident, killing three presidential security service officers and the driver. President Yeltsin's limousine was not touched."

"Why hasn't the President made a statement?"

"He died of a stress-induced heart attack this morning at 11:38 A.M. A body will be produced to lie in state, and his funeral will be scheduled for one week from today."

Kabatov grudgingly admired the tremendous lie. "Can the SVR pull it off?"

"I'm told we can, Mr. Prime Minister," Yemlin said. He was a distinguished looking man who reminded everybody of Eduard Shevardnadze with his kindly eyes and thick white hair. "But it will require the cooperation of everyone in this room."

"How long can such a lie be sustained?" Zhigalin asked.

Yemlin shrugged. "Historians opening records a hundred years from now might find out. It was only recently that the truth behind the executions of Tsar Nicholas and his family came out."

Kabatov nodded. "Very well, do it."

Yemlin smiled faintly. "It's already being done."

Kabatov held back a sharp retort. Instead he turned to Yuryn, who was staring thoughtfully at Yemlin. "What is the second problem we have to deal with?"

"Tarankov's next moves. If indeed he did order President Yeltsin's assassination it may have signaled the start of his end game. Though how he'll react to the SVR's coverup is anyone's guess, we need hard intelligence on his intentions. Without such knowledge trying to arrest the man will, in the very least, result in a bloodbath. If we'd known ahead of time about his raid on the Riga facility and had tried to stop him, the people up there would have gotten in the way. There would have been a lot of deaths. Killing him would be easier than arresting him. But if you mean to go ahead, give me time to put a man on the train."

"Do you have someone in mind?" Kabatov asked.

"I have any number of capable officers."

"The reason I ask is because by your own admission Tarankov has his support in every government agency, at every level."

"I have people who will do it," Yuryn said.

"When can you start?"

"If it's what you want, immediately," Yuryn said.

"It is," Kabatov said. "Arresting Yevgenni Tarankov is Russia's only hope, and our most urgent priority."

FIVE

Moscow

Viktor Pavlovich Yemlin returned home to his spacious apartment on Kalinin Prospekt shortly after 7:00 P.M., and poured a stiff measure of Polish vodka. He sat in his favorite chair, put his feet up and stared out the window at the lights of the city and the gently falling snow.

He was a deeply troubled man. In the old days, before his wife died of cancer, he would have enjoyed company at times like these.

Someone with whom to discuss his misgivings, his feelings of doom and gloom. But he had been a widower for so long that he had come to make peace with his solitude. In fact he rather enjoyed being alone, though he bitterly missed his only son, who'd been killed in Afghanistan.

He turned on the stereo with the remote control, and set the volume for the disc of Tchaikovsky's Violin Concerto in D Minor, his favorite piece of music, and laid his head back.

In his late sixties, Yemlin was not the man he should have been. Born in 1930 in Kiev, his parents had moved to Moscow at the start of the Great Patriotic War, and at twelve he ran away with his brothers to help defend Stalingrad against Hitler's army. After the war his parents died of heartbreak, because of seven boys Viktor was the only one to survive, and he'd survived flawed because his youth had been so dramatically cut short.

He was arrested and sent to count the birches in Siberia because he'd lied on his officer's candidate school and Moscow State University applications. He claimed he was older than he was so that he could count his military service for bonus points.

Four years later the NKVD, which was the forerunner of the KGB, discovered his name and his heroism in military records, and immediately recruited him. He was sent first to Moscow State University where he was educated in political science and international law and politics, to the prestigious Moscow State Institute of Foreign Relations, then to Officers Candidate School and the War College, and finally to the NKVD's School One.

He worked on a number of projects for the NKVD and then the KGB in eastern Europe, until General Valentin Baranov recruited him for the real work of a spy: That of the grand schemes of the seventies and eighties in which the Soviet Union would take over the world with the strong right arm of its KGB.

In a series of brilliant missions from Mexico City (the Soviet Union's largest and most active embassy and KGB station), to the United Nations in New York, and finally as *rezident* of KGB operations for all of North America out of the Soviet embassy in Washington, Yemlin proved himself to be one of the most capable and effective intelligence officers the Komityet had ever fielded.

He'd never been considered for promotion to head the agency, because he didn't have the right background or the correct political patronage for such advancement. But he was well respected by every KGB director he'd ever served under.

Now that the Soviet Union was no longer intact he should have been one of the bitter old guard for whom Tarankov's message was a siren's call to the old ways. Many of the men in the FSK and SVR were admirers of the Tarantula, hoping that a new Soviet Union would somehow rise out of the ashes of the old.

Instead, he had become a moderate. Years of living in the West's openness with its cornucopia of ideas and consumer goods had changed him. So subtly at first that even he wasn't aware of the differences in his outlook. But finally he understood to the depth of his soul that the great communist experiment of a world socialist movement had failed not because of corrupt, cruel leadership, but had disintegrated of its own ponderous, unrealistic weight. Tarankov was trying to bring it all back again, and a lot of people were listening to him. Russians were tired of being second class citizens, they wanted super power status returned to them. They were tired of being hungry, they wanted to be fed. And they were tired of an aimless existence that seemed to be going nowhere, they wanted to be led. Socialism didn't work, and Russians hadn't learned yet how to make a go of democracy. They were tired of trying.

After the meeting in the White House, Yemlin had returned to his office at SVR headquarters on the Ring Road and written his report. He was careful to draw no conclusions or make any substantive recommendations. But in his heart of hearts he agreed with General Yuryn: Trying to arrest Tarankov would likely end in a bloodbath in which dozens, perhaps hundreds of innocent people would get killed. And placing Tarankov on public trial would tear Russia apart. It would be just like the Red Army versus the White Army after the October Revolution. The nation would sink into a civil war that this time would drag on forever, and that no one could possibly win.

But if Tarankov were allowed to continue on his course he would probably win the next election in June three months from now. Either that or he would take the Kremlin by force.

Yemlin thought about that possibility. The raid on the power station in Dzerzhinskiy was within a half-dozen kilometers of the Kremlin. The bold attack had shaken the government to its core. Yeltsin's assassination twenty-four hours later had come as a worse shock. Perhaps they were witnessing the start of Tarankov's end game, as Yuryn suggested. If that were the case his next move would be even bolder, more daring, and certainly more destructive. Yemlin could think of a number of plausible scenarios in which Tarankov could simply swoop into Red Square, arrest or assassinate the moderates who opposed him in the Kremlin, and de facto take over the government. A Red Square filled with a million Tarankov supporters—Yemlin believed he had that many in Moscow alone—would block a military retaliation.

Yemlin also suspected that Prime Minister Kabatov's worst fears were true; that Tarankov's base of support went far beyond a bunch of starving kulaks who wanted to go back to the old ways. It involved more than just a handful of old hardliners in the government and the military and the old KGB, it cut across the board into every segment of the nation's population. He'd even heard noises from the Baltics, and from Ukraine and some of the other breakaway republics, that after all what Tarankov was trying to do was give the nation back its dignity.

He went to the sideboard, poured another vodka and took his drink back to the window where he lit a cigarette.

Yeltsin's chief of staff Zhigalin's suggestion that the Army and Air Force hunt down Tarankov's train and destroy it would not work either. The people would certainly rise up against the government, and what little remained of Russia's shaky democracy would disintegrate into anarchy. That's if the military would undertake such an operation without tearing itself apart first. There certainly would be desertions, and possibly an outright revolution amongst the troops, and much of the officer's corps. It might even happen that the army would move against the Kremlin, and when the government was secured invite Tarankov to take over.

Which once again brought him back to the conclusions he'd drawn several months ago. Tarankov had to be assassinated, but no one in Russia could be trusted to do it. The job would have to be done by an outsider. By someone who in the end could be blamed for the killing, because even if a Russian could be found to kill Tarankov, the people would believe the government had ordered it, and the revolution would explode.

If an outsider did it the killing could be laid on the doorstep of a foreign country, or at the very least it could be portrayed as the act of a lone gunman. A nut. Another Lee Harvey Oswald, who the Warren Commission determined had worked alone, not as a conspirator hired by the Soviet Union.

He'd shied away from that concept as well as he could through the summer and fall. But each time news of Tarankov's exploits came to him, he was drawn back to the inevitability of the idea.

In October he'd cautiously broached the subject with his old friend Konstantin Sukhoruchkin, the director of the Russian Human Rights Commission that Gorbachev had founded after the Kremlin Coup. Sukhoruchkin had agreed wholeheartedly without a trace of hesitation. Like Yemlin, though, his only reservation was that the assassin would only get one chance so he would have to be very good. He'd also suggested that between them they attempt to build a power base of support for the idea among the people who had the most to lose by a Tarankov dictatorship.

By the first of the year it became painfully clear to both men that task they'd set themselves to was not only dangerous—they had no idea who to trust or learn who they were—but it was foolish. No one in Russia could be trusted with such a secret. So Yemlin did the next best thing by contacting his old mentor Eduard Shevardnadze, president of Georgia, who would have as much to lose under Tarankov as they would.

Shevardnadze had agreed only to discuss the issue, and only when Yemlin felt that there were no other options left to them, and that time was running out.

Yemlin put out his cigarette, finished his drink and rinsed the glass in the kitchen sink. He pulled on his greatcoat and went down to a pay phone in the metro station a block away. He never used his home telephone for important calls, nor did he bother having it swept. All the old checks and balances were in place in the SVR, which meant all but the most senior officers were spot checked from time to time. The easiest and most cost effective way to do that was by monitoring telephone calls and opening mail. But Yemlin had been around for a long time, and he had a few tricks up his own sleeve.

Sukhoruchkin answered the telephone at his home on the second ring. "*Da?*"

"Meet me at the airport."

"Now?"

"Yes," Yemlin said. "It's time."

Yemlin called his contact at Vnukovo domestic airport. "We would like to go flying this evening, Valeri."

"It's a lovely night for it," his pilot replied. "The tops are low, so once we get above all this shit you'll be able to see the full moon."

"We'll be returning in the morning."

"As you wish."

Yemlin's final call was to a special number in the SVR's communications complex. After one ring he got a dial tone for an international line that could not, by design, be monitored. In two minutes he was connected with the residential quarters of the president of Georgia.

"This is Viktor Pavlovich."

"I expected you would call this evening," Eduard Shevardnadze said.

"Konstantin and I would like to see you tonight. Will you be free?"

"Are you calling from Moscow?"

"*Da*. But we can get down there by midnight unofficially if you will have a car and driver to meet us."

"What's the tail number of your airplane?"

Yemlin told him.

"Take care, my old friend. Once a word is out of your mouth you can't swallow it again."

It was an old Russian proverb which Yemlin understood well. He hung up and headed for a cab stand.

Tbilisi, Georgia

The aging Learjet, which Yemlin occasionally leased from a private enterprise he'd set up ten years ago for a KGB-sponsored project, touched down at Tbilisi's international airport a few minutes before midnight. As promised the 1500-kilometer flight above the clouds had been smooth, the full moon dramatically illuminating the thick clouds below them until they broke out in the clear at the rising wall of the Caucasus Mountains.

They were directed along a taxiway to the opposite side of the airport from the main terminal, where they were met by a Zil limousine and driver, who took them directly into the bustling city of more than a million people.

Although Tbilisi was on a high plain in the mountains it was much warmer than Moscow. And it seemed more prosperous than the Russian capital, with cleaner, brighter streets and shops, though closed at this hour, displaying a wide variety of consumer goods. Georgia was not without its problems, but they were being addressed and slowly solved under Shevardnadze's capable leadership. All that would change for the worse, Yemlin thought, if Tarankov was successful.

They were brought to the rear courtyard of the presidential palace off

Rustavelli Boulevard and were immediately escorted inside to a small private study on the second floor. Heavy drapes covered the windows, and a fire burned on the grate. The book-lined room seemed like a pleasant refuge.

Shevardnadze joined them a few moments later. He wore a warmup suit, and carried a book, his glasses perched on the end of his nose. He looked serious.

"Gentlemen, this is a meeting I'd hoped would never come about," he said, and they shook hands.

"I agree, Mr. President. This is not our finest hour," Sukhoruchkin replied. Unlike Yemlin and Shevardnadze, he was tall and very thin, with large round eyes under thick black eyebrows. Although he was of the same age his long hair, always in disarray, was startlingly black. He looked like the brilliant academic he was. Before he'd become director of the Human Rights Commission he'd been one of Russia's finest writers and philosophers. He and Yemlin had known each other since boyhood, and had married sisters. Sukhoruchkin's wife had died last year.

"You're in accord with Viktor Pavlovich?"

"I'm a man of peace, a philosophy I've espoused and taught all of my life. I believe to the depth of my soul in nonviolence. But now I regret to have to say that I believe just as deeply that there may be no other solution to the problem at hand."

"A problem we all share," Yemlin said.

Shevardnadze nodded. He put his book down, took off his glasses and motioned for them to have a seat in armchairs in front of the fire. He sat on the leather couch.

"I'm assuming that Yeltsin didn't die of a heart attack, though my intelligence service cannot tell me anything different."

"He was assassinated by one of Tarankov's men who posed as a presidential security service lieutenant colonel," Yemlin said. "He planted a radio-controlled bomb last night, and waited in Red Square this morning until Yeltsin showed up for work, and pushed the button.

"You wouldn't be here now if he were in custody."

Yemlin shrugged. "It's a moot point, Mr. President. Whether we had him or not—and you're correct, we don't—the attack on our Riga power station, and Yeltsin's assassination are Tarankov's doing, and we would have to go after him anyway. But now I believe he may have a plan to grab the presidency before the June elections."

"Which Yeltsin would have lost," Shevardnadze said. "Why is Tarankov taking such a risk?"

"Because Yeltsin ordered his arrest by whatever means of force necessary. He meant to put him on trial."

Shevardnadze shook his head. "Tarankov would probably have been acquitted, and it would have destroyed Yeltsin's government."

"The Prime Minister has ordered the same thing," Sukhoruchkin said.

"He means to arrest Tarankov and place the man on public trial, which in itself should be the correct action to take."

"If Moscow were London or Washington," Shevardnadze said.

"It will tear the country apart," Yemlin said.

"If he were killed by the army it would tear Russia apart as well," Shevardnadze said. "But if he's allowed to continue unchecked on his present course he will succeed. Is this what you believe?"

Both men nodded.

Shevardnadze looked into the fire for several long seconds as he gathered his thoughts. A weight seemed to settle on his shoulders, and he sighed as if to rid himself of an impossible burden. When he turned back his face was sad.

"I too am a man of peace, Konstantin Nikolaevich, as I know you are. I've long admired your writing."

Sukhoruchkin nodded in acknowledgement.

"If Tarankov comes to power he means to restore the old Soviet Union by whatever means are necessary," Yemlin said.

"We would give him trouble, but if he had the backing of the generals we couldn't win," Shevardnadze admitted. "The Baltics would cause him more problems."

"As would regaining Eastern Europe, but the bastard will do it, and no one will dare to stand up to him."

"Does he have the military behind him?"

"He will," Yemlin said. "There's no doubt of it."

"What about the SVR?"

"By whatever name it's called, it's still the KGB."

Again a silence fell over them as they each pondered what they were on the verge of agreeing to. It was an impossibly large step, a quantum leap, from the rule of democratic law in which they all believed, to an act of terrorism.

"Tarankov must be assassinated," Yemlin voiced their thought.

"I agree," Sukhoruchkin said with surprising firmness.

"As do I," Shevardnadze said. "But I know of no one in Georgia who is capable of such a thing. Nor do I suspect you'll find anyone in Russia whom you could trust."

Yemlin nodded.

"You have such a man in mind? A foreigner?"

"*Da.*"

"Who is he?"

"An American, Mr. President. His name is Kirk McGarvey. And if he agrees to take on the job, he'll do so for the same reasons that we want to hire him."

SIX

Paris

Spring had come early to France. Although it wasn't the end of March, the last two weeks had been glorious. The sky was pale blue, and each morning dawned crystal clear, as if the air above the great city had been washed and hung out to dry under a warm sun. Along the river the plane trees were budding. In sunny corners of the Tuileries some flowers had already began to bloom. And parks and boulevards and sidewalk cafes were filled with Parisians who'd been cooped up all winter, and with tourists who could scarcely believe their good luck.

Kirk Collough McGarvey sat with Jacqueline Belleau at a window table in the Restaurant Jules Verne on the third floor of the Eiffel Tower sharing an expensive bottle of Chardonnay while they waited for their lunches to be served. Jacqueline had insisted they come here today because this was where they'd met three months ago, and she was "romantic and French." He'd indulged her because it amused him, and he wanted to see what her next move would be. The French secret service, which was called the *Service de Documentation Extérieure et de Contre-Espionage*, or SDECE for short, was usually sophisticated in its business. But sometimes, like now, they were blatantly obvious. Jacqueline had been sent by the SDECE to seduce McGarvey to find out why he was back in Paris. The French were paranoid about former CIA agents taking up residence in their country, though not so paranoid that they would deny such men a visa. *"Hein, l'argent est l'argent, n'est-ce pas?"*

"That's a lascivious grin, if ever I've seen one," she said, catching him in his thoughts. "How do you say it, a penny for your thoughts?"

"I was thinking that Paris isn't like any other city. It keeps getting better."

She smiled, her oval, pretty features lighting up as if she were a kid at Christmas. "And that from a crusty old bastard like you."

He nodded. "That from a crusty old bastard like me." He admired her, not only for her stunning good looks—she could easily have been a runway mannequin, though not as thin as most of them were—but for her sharp intelligence and even sharper wit. She was unlike either of his ex-wives, or any other woman he'd ever been involved with. The number wasn't a legion, but they'd all been memorable because they'd all ended in failed relationships.

McGarvey, nearing fifty, was tall and muscularly built but with the co-ordination of a ballet dancer. He had thick brown hair that was turning gray at the temples, a wide, honest face, and penetrating eyes, sometimes green, at other times gray. He ran ten miles every day, rain or shine, from his apartment off the Rue La Fayette in the tenth arrondissement out the Avenue Jean Jaurès along the Canal de l'Ourcq. He swam five miles every afternoon at the Club American downtown, and as often as possible worked out at the Ecole Militaire Annexe with the French national fencing team.

Although he'd known plenty of women, he'd been a loner most of his life, partly out of choice, but mostly out of circumstance. In the parlance of the secret service, he'd been a shooter. A killer. An assassin. And every night he saw the faces of every person he'd ever killed. He saw the light fading from their eyes, the animation draining from their faces as they realized that they were dying. Each of them, even the very bad ones, had died the same way: surprised. That sort of a profession tended to be hard on a relationship, any relationship.

After graduating from Kansas State University with masters degrees in literature (his specialty had been Voltaire) and languages, he joined the Central Intelligence Agency as a translator and analyst. But the Cold War was in high gear and the Company needed talent because a lot of its agents were getting burned. They saw something in McGarvey that even he didn't know existed. His instinct for survival and self-preservation was a hundred times stronger than in the very best field agents. Combined with his physique, his facility for languages, his intelligence, and the results of a battery of psychological tests which showed him to be extremely pragmatic and under the correct circumstances even cold, he'd been offered the job as a field agent. But a very special agent. His training and purpose so black that only a handful of men in the agency and on the Hill knew anything about him.

Bad times, he thought now, studying Jacqueline's pretty face. She was forty, and from Nice, and was aging as only the Mediterraneans did. Like Sophia Loren she would become even more beautiful as she got older.

"Such deep, dramatic thoughts for such a lovely Saturday," she said, reaching across the table for his hand.

He raised hers and kissed it, tenderly and with a little sadness, because when this one was gone he knew he would miss her. "It's my day to feel a little lugubrious. Sometimes spring in this city does that."

"Hemingway," Jacqueline said. "I thought you were a fan of Voltaire."

He managed a slight smile. He'd never told her that, which meant her SDECE briefing had been very complete. It was one of the little inconsistencies he'd spotted from the beginning.

In the end the Company had sent him to Santiago to kill a general who'd massacred hundreds of people in and around the capital. But the orders had been changed in mid-stream without his knowledge, and after the kill McGarvey was out.

He'd run to Switzerland where for a few years he'd made a life for himself, operating a rare-book store in Lausanne. There, like here, the secret service worried about his presence and had sent a woman to his bed to keep tabs on him, though how they'd found out he once worked for the CIA was a mystery. When the CIA called him out of retirement for a particularly bad assignment they couldn't handle, he'd left her. The call to arms had been stronger than his love for her.

Greece, Paris, even back to the States for awhile, the CIA kept coming for him, and he kept losing the women in his life, and kept running from his demons. And now he was getting the odd, twitchy feeling between his shoulder blades that it was about to happen again. Lately he'd been thinking about returning to New York to see the only woman he'd ever loved unreservedly, and the only one who'd loved him back the same way. His daughter Elizabeth, now twenty-three and working as a translator and analyst for the United Nations. He smiled, thinking about her.

"That's better," Jacqueline said.

"I'll try to smile more often if it has that effect on you," McGarvey said.

"That too," she said. "But I meant here comes our lunch and I'm starved."

"You're not a cheap date."

She laughed. "You can afford it. Besides, there's something I haven't told you about myself."

He waited, an indulgent smile on his lips.

The waiter served their filet of sole and tournedos of beef plat du jour expertly, then refilled their wine glasses.

"What's that?" McGarvey asked.

"Whenever I have a good meal like this I get horney as hell. I'll show you when we get home."

The waiter nearly dropped the wine bottle. "*Excusez-moi,*" he muttered, and he left.

"That wasn't very fair," McGarvey said.

"Paris waiters are all shits. Nobody dislikes them worse than a Parisian. Maybe next time he won't eavesdrop."

"I think *you're* becoming a crusty bastard from being around me so much."

"Anatomically impossible," she said airily as she broke off a piece of bread and buttered it. "Crusty bitch, not bastard."

McGarvey raised his wine glass to her. "*Salut,*" he said.

She raised her glass. "*Salut, mon cher.*"

After lunch they took the elevator to the observation deck a thousand feet above the Seine, and looked out across the city. From here they could see people strolling through the park, and along the river. It was the most famous view of Paris from the city's most famous monument, and McGarvey felt at home here as he always had.

"When are you going to let me read your book?" she asked.

McGarvey was a hundred pages into a personal look into the life of the writer, philosopher Francois Marie Arouet, whose pen name was Voltaire. His working title was *The Voltaire I Knew,* but the SDECE almost certainly believed that he was writing his memoirs, a book that no one wanted written. He wrote longhand, and kept the manuscript and most of his notes under lock and key. So far his failsafes had not been tampered with.

"When I'm finished with it," he said. "How about an after lunch drink at Lipps?"

"You *are* a Hemingway fan," she laughed. "Let's walk along the river first. Then afterward we're going home."

"Sounds good," McGarvey said, and she turned to go, but he stopped her. "Are you happy, Jacqueline?"

A startled look crossed her face. "That's an odd question."

"Are you?" McGarvey studied her eyes.

It took her a moment to answer, but she nodded. "Yes, I am."

She was telling the truth, he decided.

They took the elevator back to street level, and headed past the sidewalk vendors and jugglers to the busy Quai Branly where they could cross to the river. Out of habit he scanned the quay; the pedestrians, the traffic, the taxis lines up at the cab ranks and the cars parked at the curb. His gaze slipped past a dark blue Citröen parked behind a yellow Renault, a man seated behind the wheel, and then came back. His stomach tightened, but he did not vary his pace, nor change his expression in the slightest. Jacqueline, holding his arm, detected nothing.

He turned left toward the taxis, and Jacqueline looked up at him.

"Aren't we crossing here?" she asked.

"I want you to take a cab back to my apartment. There's an errand I have to run."

"I'm not going anywhere without you," she said.

"Don't be so snoopy, or you'll spoil my surprise."

"What are you talking about?"

"I want you to wait for me at home. I won't be long, and when I get back you'll know what I meant."

"Why can't I wait here?"

"Because I don't want you to."

"Are you a macho pig?"

He laughed. "Not so long ago someone else called me that same thing. But right now you can either wait for me at my apartment, or go back to your own place and stay there. I have something to do."

She was torn by indecision, he could see it in her eyes. But finally she nodded. "Don't be long."

"Come on, I'll get you a cab."

"I can manage," she said, pulling away from him. She searched his face for a clue, then walked over to a cab, climbed in the back, and the taxi headed away. As it passed she looked straight ahead.

McGarvey waited until the cab was out of sight, then went back to the tower, where he bought another ticket for the fourth floor.

Upstairs, he leaned against the rail in front of the windows and lit a cigarette. The observation deck was busy. A few minutes later the man from the Citröen joined him.

"She is a very pretty woman," he said.

McGarvey focused on the man's reflection in the glass. "Hello, Viktor Pavlovich. Yes, she is."

"French secret service?" Yemlin asked.

"Probably."

"I figured that was why you sent her away when you spotted me. She'll wonder why."

"Will it matter if the French know that we've met?"

Yemlin thought for a moment. "Yes, it will matter very much. It will be a question of your safety."

"Are the French after you for some reason?"

"No, but they wouldn't be so happy if they knew why I'd come to see you," Yemlin said. He stared down at the street and the river.

"I'm retired," McGarvey said. "Anyway you'd be the last person I'd help. We go back too long on opposite sides of the fence for me to so easily forget."

"Eighteen months ago you came to me to ask a favor. And I did it for you, Kirk. Gladly. And as it turns out you did very well because of the information I provided you. All I'm asking now is that you hear me out."

McGarvey turned to look at the Russian. In eighteen months he'd aged ten years. He no longer seemed to be the dangerous adversary he'd once been when he'd headed the Illegals Directorate of the KGB, and later when he'd headed Department Viktor, the Russian assassination and terrorist division.

He'd been fighting capitalism, he'd told McGarvey. Fighting to save the *Rodina*—the Motherland—as they'd all been in those days. But there had been hundreds, even thousands of deaths. Tens of millions of deaths counting the ones Stalin massacred.

But who was innocent, McGarvey asked himself now as he had then. He had his share of blood on his hands. More than his share. Was fighting to save democracy any less noble for an American, than fighting to save socialism was for a Russian? He didn't have the answer.

"All right, Viktor, I'll listen to you. But that's all. I promise you that I'm out of the business."

"What about the woman?"

"I'll make my excuses. It'll be okay."

Yemlin glanced out the windows. "Let's walk in the park. Heights make me dizzy."

They took the elevator back down, then crossed Quai Branly and descended to the river walk where McGarvey and Jacqueline had been heading. An odd state of affairs, McGarvey thought. But then his entire life had been a series of odd affairs.

Traffic on the river, as on the streets, was heavy. The weather was bringing everybody outdoors. The river walk too was crowded, which was better for their purposes. It gave them anonymity.

"The situation is becoming very bad in Russia," Yemlin said.

"I know," McGarvey replied. "Have you caught Yeltsin's assassin yet, or did he get out of the city and return to Tarankov's protection?"

"President Yeltsin died of a heart attack—"

"That's not true. Nor do your security people carry any type of ordinance in their chase cars that would explode like that. The public may have bought it, but there isn't a professional in the business in the West who believes the story. The question is, why did you people make it up? Are you that concerned about Tarankov?"

"I don't agree with you, Kirk," Yemlin said. "The signals we're getting back from the CIA and SIS indicate they believe what we're telling them."

"What else can they do? Nobody wants to hammer you guys into the ground anymore. Fact is most of the world feels sorry for you. Your people are going hungry, you've polluted the entire country, your factories are falling apart, and nobody in their right mind wants to travel around Moscow or St. Petersburg without bodyguards. So Langley is saying, okay we'll go along with whatever they want to tell us for the moment. Let's see what shakes out. Let's see how they handle it. Armed revolution, anarchy, or a Warren Commission that nobody will believe, but that everybody will respect."

"You have no proof of that."

"Come on, Viktor, don't shit the troops," McGarvey said sharply. "You want to talk to me, go ahead and talk. But don't lie. Tell it like it is, or go back to Moscow. Who knows, it might get better."

Yemlin's shoulders sagged. He shook his head. "It won't get better. It can only get worse."

"Is Kabatov really in charge like the wire services are reporting?"

"Nobody else wants the job, and for the moment at least his is the most decisive voice in Moscow. But nobody thinks that the situation will remain stable until the June elections. At the very least what little order is left will totally break down, and the anarchy that the west has been predicting for us all these years will finally come to pass."

"What about the military? How are they handling Yeltsin's death?"

"Wait and see."

"No threat of a coup?"

"That depends on what happens between now and the elections. But it's certainly another very real possibility, Kirk. Our situation is desperate."

"Will the Duma elect an interim president?

"They're in session now. Kabatov has the majority support, again only because he's the lesser of any number of evils."

"Like Nikolai Yuryn?"

Yemlin looked at McGarvey with wry amusement. "You would make a good Russian politician."

They walked for awhile in silence, the traffic on the avenue above seemingly more distant than before. McGarvey knew why Yemlin had come to see him. The trouble was he didn't know what to do.

"What really happened, Viktor?"

"It was one of Tarankov's men, as you suspected, though we don't have much of a description yet, or a name. He got into the Kremlin by posing as a Presidential Security Service lieutenant colonel, planted a radio-controlled bomb in the limo scheduled to pick up Yeltsin in the morning, and pushed the button when the president's motorcade came across Red Square."

"He must have a good intelligence source. He probably was out of Moscow within an hour after the hit, long before the Militia could get its act together."

"He had a seven-hour head start."

McGarvey looked sharply at the Russian. "It's that bad?"

"You can't imagine."

McGarvey lit a cigarette. "There's a very good chance that Tarankov would have won the election. Why'd he take the risk?"

"Yeltsin ordered his arrest. It was going to be an ambush next week in Nizhny Novgorod. A few thousand troops and helicopters against his armored train and two hundred commandoes. There was a leak, the information got to Tarankov and he had Yeltsin killed."

"Now Kabatov is stuck in the same position. He has to go ahead with

Yeltsin's order to arrest Tarankov and then do what? Try to bring him to trial in Moscow?"

Yemlin nodded glumly. "It'd tear Russia apart."

"You'll lose the country if you don't. He's another Stalin."

"We came to the same conclusions. If we arrest him the people will revolt. If we leave him alone he'll win the election easily, or take over the Kremlin by force and kill everyone who opposes him."

"Who is the we?" McGarvey asked.

"Konstantin Sukhoruchkin, who's chairman of the Russian Human Rights Commission—"

"I know him."

"And Eduard Shevardnadze."

"Anyone else?"

"I've talked to no one else about it."

"Did you see Shevardnadze in person?"

"We flew down there the night before last. No one knows about the real reason for our trip. But we're all agreed on the correct course of action. The *only* course of action to save the Democratic movement in Russia. Yevgenni Tarankov must be assassinated by a foreigner. By someone not connected to Russia. By a professional, someone who is capable of doing the job and getting away. By you, Kirk."

"No."

The directness of McGarvey's answer knocked the wind out of Yemlin's sails, and he missed a step, almost stumbling. "Then all is lost," he mumbled.

McGarvey helped him to a park bench. Yemlin took a handkerchief out of his pocket and wiped his glistening forehead.

"I promised only to listen, Viktor Pavlovich. I'm retired, but even if I wasn't the job is all but impossible. Tarankov surrounds himself with a crack commando unit, his access to intelligence is very good, and he has the support of a large percentage of the population in addition to the military, the Militia, the FSK and even your own branch. Whereas the assassin would have no organization or backing because he would have to distance himself completely from you and the other two men. He would be operating in a country in which simply walking down the street could get him killed. And to top it all off, if Kabatov's government got wind that an assassin was coming they might try to stop him. After all, if Russia wants to model itself after a nation of laws then it must abide by those laws. They would have to come after the assassin, who even if he was successful would find it quite impossible to get out of the country alive."

Yemlin looked bleakly at him, but said nothing.

"Even if he did get away, then what?" McGarvey asked. "Nobody condones assassination. Even with a lot of money the places where the assassin could hide would be limited. Iran, Iraq, maybe a few countries in Africa, an island in the South Pacific. Not places I'd care to spend the rest of my days."

"That's assuming your true identity became known," Yemlin suggested weakly.

"That'd be the trick. But I'm not hungry."

"I don't understand what you mean."

"What would you offer me? Whatever, it wouldn't matter because I don't need it. I'm not rich, but I have enough for my needs. Or maybe you're offering me the thrill of the hunt." McGarvey smiled sadly. "I've had my share of thrills. The thought of another does little or nothing for me. Or maybe what you're really offering me is a chance to settle old scores. And there are a lot of those. But not so long ago I was told that I was an anachronism. I was no longer needed because the Soviet Union was no more. The bad guys had packed up and quit. It was time, I was told, for the professional administrators and negotiators to take over and straighten out the mess. At the time I thought was full of shit. But maybe he was right after all." McGarvey shook his head. "I have a lot of bitterness, Viktor Pavlovich, but no stirrings for revenge. You're just not worth the effort."

McGarvey walked over to the low stone barrier that was part of the levee that sloped down to the water. A bateau Mouche glided past and some of the tourists waved. McGarvey waved back.

Yemlin joined him, and took a cigarette. "Did you know that Marlboros cost less money in Moscow than they do in New York? You need hard currency, but that's progress."

"I've heard."

"The contrasts between Moscow and Washington are stark. But here the lines of division seem softer."

"I didn't know you'd spent time in Paris."

"A couple of years in the embassy," Yemlin said. "In a way I envy you. If I had the money I might retire here. Or perhaps somewhere around Lyon, perhaps on a small farm. Perhaps a few acres of grapes. I'm not a stupid man. I could learn how to make wine."

It was such an obvious appeal that McGarvey couldn't resist it. "You were a bad man in the old days, Viktor, for whatever reasons. But you've changed."

"We've all changed."

"I can't help you—"

"What if I offered you something more than money," Yemlin said. He spoke so softly that McGarvey barely heard him.

"What?"

"I have something that you've always wanted."

The afternoon was no longer as warm as it had been. "What's that?"

"It is something I only recently learned. In this you must believe me."

"Will you give it to me if I still refuse to kill Tarankov?"

"You must agree to consider the job. That much. Think about it, Kirk. If you give me your word that you will think about it, I'll give you what I brought."

McGarvey felt as if he were looking at himself through the wrong end of a telescope. He felt distant, detached, out of proportion. "I'll think about it, Viktor Pavlovich," he said. His voice sounded unreal, down the end of a tunnel.

Yemlin took an envelope out of his breast pocket and handed it to McGarvey. "This is your honor, Kirk. It's not much, but I think that in the end it is all that we have."

"What—"

"Your parents were not spies, Kirk. They did not work for us as you've believed all these years. They were set up."

SEVEN

Paris

Jacqueline Belleau arrived at the office of her control officer Alexandre Lévy on the top floor of the department store Printemps after lunch on Monday. She'd spent an oddly disconnected weekend with McGarvey after the strange scene between them on Saturday. He'd returned to his apartment a couple hours after he'd sent her away, with a beautiful Hermés scarf. A present, he said, he could not buy with her tagging along.

She was touched by the gift. It meant that their relationship was progressing faster than she'd hoped for. Yet she was disquieted by his behavior, which was more like something a spy would do than a lover. She supposedly worked for an attorney who maintained an office a block away, so he could have simply waited until today when she was gone to buy her the present. And for the remainder of the weekend he'd been quieter than normal, even a little moody, as if something were bothering him.

"Don't ever press him, Jacqueline," Lévy had cautioned her in the beginning. "He is a professional, and men like him can spot a plant a kilometer away. Just be yourself. Natural—"

"Without appearing that I'm *trying* to be natural, *c'est vrai, grand-père?*"

At sixty-three Lévy was by far the oldest case officer in the Service. With his thinning white hair, weathered face and kindly features, everyone called him *grandpère*, grandfather, but he didn't seem to mind. "And don't take your assignment lightly, it could get you killed."

"I understand," she'd replied.

Lévy took her hands. "Most importantly, *ma cherie*, don't fall in love with him. That too has happened before, and it will cloud your judgement."

Lévy and another man she recognized as Division Chief Colonel Guy de Galan, were hunched over some papers and photographs spread on the conference table.

"Ah, here she is now," Lévy said, looking up. "We've been waiting for you. Do you know Colonel Galan?"

"Of course," Jacqueline said. They shook hands.

"We had a tail on you this weekend, did you notice?" Galan asked. He was an administrator, but with his dark, dangerous air he looked more like a Corsican underworld thug than the head of the American and Western Hemisphere Division of the SDECE's Intelligence Service.

"No, but I make it a point not to look for my own people," she answered.

Galan nodded. "That's a safe thing to do." He handed her a 20×25 cm photograph of an older man, with thick white hair and a serious face, passing through passport control at what appeared to be Orly Airport. "Do you know this man?"

She shrugged. *"Non."*

"He is Viktor Yemlin, chief of the North American Division of Russia's SVR. In effect his job is much the same as mine. He arrived in France Saturday morning, where he went immediately to his embassy. An hour later he left behind the wheel of a Citröen with civilian plates, no driver."

He studied Jacqueline's reaction closely.

"Did he come here to see Kirk?" Jacqueline asked.

"He followed your cab to the Eiffel Tower, then waited in front until you'd finished lunch," Galan said. "Did you notice anything?"

"No."

"Well, McGarvey spotted him. After he sent you away, he and Yemlin met at the top of the tower briefly, then descended to the river. It took us a few minutes to get a team with a parabolic mike across the river, but by then it was too late."

"They're both professionals," Lévy said. "They make it a point not to have long conversations in public."

"Did you get any of it?" Jacqueline asked. She had a sick feeling at the pit of her stomach, but she didn't know why.

"Not much," Galan said. He handed her a single sheet of typewritten transcript.

". . . *must agree to consider the job. That much. Think about it Kirk. If you will give me your word that you will think about it, I'll give you what I brought.*" SPEAKER IDENTIFIED AS YEMLIN. (See attachment A101.)
    THERE WAS A PAUSE.
    "*I'll think about it Viktor Pavlovich.*" SPEAKER IDENTIFIED AS MCGARVEY (See attachment A102.)
    YEMLIN HANDS MCGARVEY A SMALL WHITE ENVELOPE, NO MARKINGS SEEN.
    "*This is your honor, Kirk. It is not much, but I think that in the end it is all that we have.*" (A101.)
    "*What . . .*" (A102. Sentence incomplete.)
    "*Your parents were not spies, Kirk. They did not work for us as you've believed all these years. They were set up.*" (A101.)
    "*Go home.*" (A102.)
    "*Just think about my request.*" (A101.)
    SUBJECTS LEAVE AREA. TRANSCRIPT ENDS.

Jacqueline looked up into Galan's eyes. He wasn't smiling.

"Considering who and what Monsieur McGarvey is, we think that the Russians have asked him to assassinate someone."

"He turned it down."

"He agreed to think about it, Mademoiselle. We'll query Washington on this business about his parents being spies, but if the information Yemlin handed over to him is valid—or if McGarvey believes it is—it may be the incentive he needs to take him from thinking about such an act, to doing it."

"There's no mention who the subject might be," Jacqueline said.

Galan shook his head. "No. Nor do we know if the subject is here in France, but we must consider that possibility."

Jacqueline's head was spinning. "Expel him. Kick him out of France, now, before he can change his mind."

"We won't do that, and I'll tell you why," Galan said. "If McGarvey decides to assassinate someone here in France, kicking him out of the country would do nothing but drive him underground. If we keep him here, we can watch him."

"That is your job, Jacqueline," Lévy put in. "You must find out for us."

"It may have something to do with this book he's writing," Galan said. "I want you to get it for us."

"He has safeguards. I've inspected them myself. If I open that cabinet he'll know."

"Photograph the safeguards and get the film to us. We'll take it from there. Believe me, as good as Monsieur McGarvey is, we're better."

Jacqueline nodded. She felt very small at that moment, her feelings confused, and contradictory. A part of her was excited by the new challenge. She'd been well-trained for exactly this sort of operation. Still another part of her felt somehow dirty. She was very mixed up.

"When he finally came home Saturday afternoon, did he tell you why he sent you ahead?" Lévy asked gently. He'd picked up something of her distress.

"He wanted to buy me a present in secret. A surprise."

Lévy and Galan exchanged a look.

"Did you believe him, Jacqueline?" Lévy asked. "Or did it seem odd to you?"

She lowered her eyes. "It seemed odd." She looked up defiantly. "But there have been any number of little oddities. Nothing significant, except that I think he may suspect what I really am."

"I would be surprised if he didn't suspect," Galan said. "Why didn't you contact your control officer if you had a suspicion that something wasn't completely correct?"

"Because I wanted to find out as much as I could. I wasn't sure."

"Are you sure now," Galan said. "I meant before you walked into this office and heard what we had to say, were you sure?"

"No."

"Then you should have called, *ma cherie*," Lévy said.

"Perhaps she should be pulled off the assignment—" Galan said.

"No," Jacqueline interrupted sharply. "There's no time to get somebody new. He'd know that we were on to him."

"Probably. But on the same token we don't want you to get hurt. Do you understand what I mean?"

She nodded, though she wasn't quite sure she completely understood. But she had a job to do. "I'll get you the photographs of his failsafes."

"It's very important that we know if he is taking this job for the Russians, and if the subject is in France. Could even be a Frenchman," Galan said. "Or a visiting dignitary. We must know."

"I'll do my best," Jacqueline said.

"*Bon.* I know you will," Lévy said. He opened a small medicine bottle and gave her a capsule. "Before you leave, take this with some water. You're going home for the remainder of the week with a light fever and a runny nose. This will induce the symptoms."

"Maybe he won't want me near him if I'm sick."

Galan chuckled. "I don't think Monsieur McGarvey is frightened of a few germs. Besides you won't really be ill."

She nodded and turned to go.

"Jacqueline, how do you feel about your American?" Galan asked, his tone surprisingly avuncular.

She looked at him, but could read nothing from his bland expression. "I like him," she admitted. "I think he is a good man who has worked too long in a very bad profession. He's retired now, and he wants to remain so."

Galan nodded his understanding. "I sincerely hope that you are correct."

SDECE Headquarters

Colonel Galan came to attention in front of the desk of the Director of the SDECE, General Jean Baillot, and saluted smartly. The general, a taciturn old veteran of the French-Algerian troubles, was working on some paperwork. He motioned Galan to have a seat.

Looking past the general out the leaded glass windows, Galan had a nice view of the Eiffel Tower. The office was palatial, furnished with genuine antiques, and was extremely comfortable. But he didn't think Baillot ever noticed. He was a man, his subordinates noted, of very little amusement. He would have been just as content working in a tent.

The general put down his pen and looked up. *"Oui?"*

Galan handed him the report he'd typed himself, summarizing everything they'd learned to date, as well as Jacqueline Belleau's orders to help them steal McGarvey's manuscript.

When he was finished, Baillot laid the report down, and once again looked up. "Why have you brought this to me, Colonel?"

"I need your authorization to ask the American Central Intelligence Agency for help."

"You wish to ask them about Kirk McGarvey's parents in order to see if the Russians are able to provide a motivation for McGarvey to do this job for them?"

"Oui, Monsieur le General. I would also like to have their latest information on McGarvey and Viktor Yemlin."

"Why?"

"The CIA's operation in Moscow is better than ours, and McGarvey was one of theirs. I want to know if they have any ideas who Yemlin wants McGarvey to assassinate."

General Baillot thought about the request for a moment, his penetrating eyes never leaving Galan's. "Is there any person presently in France whose death would benefit the Russians?"

"No one of any real importance, sir. Of course there may be upcoming state visits of a secret nature that my department knows nothing about."

"There are none," the general said flatly. "You have my authorization to ask the CIA for help. But you will do so through their Chief of Station Thomas Lynch here in Paris."

"Yes, sir," Galan said, and the general dismissed him.

At the door the general recalled him. "Kirk McGarvey is a dangerous man. But he is not an enemy of France. Do I make myself perfectly clear?"

"Perfectly, *mon General.*"

EIGHT

CIA Headquarters

Deputy Director of Operations Howard Ryan was a man who believed in isometrics. Walking into his third floor conference room at 7:30 A.M. sharp and taking his place at the head of the long table he knew that every man seated there hated him because he pushed. It was exactly as it should be, he thought with smug satisfaction. Hate generated energy. And energy was exactly what the Company had been lacking for many years.

Besides his assistant, Thomas Moore, the others he'd called to the briefing included the assistant to the Deputy Director of Intelligence, Chris Vizanko, whom Ryan considered to be little more than a street thug who didn't belong here, and the heavyset Director of Technical Services, Jared Kraus, who was a steady if sometimes ponderous presence.

Each man had brought his own "experts," something Ryan always insisted on. He told his people repeatedly that if they were not willing to bet their lives on the facts then they'd better surround themselves with experts. His staff called it "Ryan's insulation factor." If something went wrong, the more underlings around you to absorb the blame the better you'd come out.

But Ryan had pressures from above, as he was fond of reminding them. His came from the big leagues; the Director of Central Intelligence, the Senate Select Committee on Intelligence, the President's National Security Adviser and the President himself.

"Gentlemen, the Director is scheduled to brief the President at ten, and in turn he expects me to brief him at nine. It gives us less than a half-hour to come up with a consensus on the facts so that I'll have time to prepare my recommendations," Ryan began.

"If Boris Yeltsin died of a heart attack, he did so in mid-air," Vizanko said.

Ryan, who'd started out as an attorney for a prestigious New York law firm, did not like levity of any kind, and he shot the assistant DDI a sharp look of disapproval. "What do you have for me?"

"Jim Ravn's people managed to come up with blood and tissue samples from Red Square. The DNA in several of them was definitely Yeltsin's." Ravn was the Chief of Moscow Station.

"It's been more than forty-eight hours, what took so long?" Ryan demanded. He always wore three-piece suits. He took his ornate pocket watch out and looked at the time as if to make his point. It was a "Ryan" gesture, pretentious as hell.

"That's normally a two-week procedure, Mr. Ryan," Kraus said from his end of the table. "Ravn must have lit a fire under somebody to get it that fast."

"He got it from the Russians themselves. And those guys are definitely motivated right now," Vizanko said. "He also came up with a rumor that a body will be ready for display later today. The operative word is 'a' body, not Yeltsin's."

There was more deadwood yet to be cleared out of the Agency, Ryan thought. "Russian science and shaky rumors. This is what the world's best intelligence agency has managed to come up with?"

"With no reliable eyewitnesses who actually saw Yeltsin in the back seat of the limo that took the hit, I think it's the best we can do under the circumstances," Vizanko said. "It's Mr. Doyle's opinion that if Yeltsin had actually died of a heart attack, his body would have been placed on display within twenty-four hours. They just wouldn't have waited so long." Tom Doyle was Deputy Director of Intelligence.

"His bodyguards don't carry that kind of explosives in any event," Kraus said. "We think the device was Semtex. Ravn's people found evidence supporting that."

"What evidence?" Ryan shot back. He didn't like this at all. It was way too loose.

"Certain chemical compounds consistent with the plastic explosive were detected in the human tissue samples."

"Just what compounds? Specifically."

Kraus shrugged, and opened a file folder. He passed a report down the table to Ryan.

"As you can see, Mr. Ryan, page three and four outline the results of mass spectrograph tests on the material. The third and fifth sets of complex hydrocarbons, which you can see, do not match human blood or tissue, and in fact can be identified as—"

"I can read," Ryan said harshly. The graphs, columns and rows of numbers, and diagrams of what appeared to be a complex series of spikes and sawtooth patterns made no sense to him. He did not have a science background. But the material looked impressive as hell. It would make for a damn good presentation.

He ran his finger down several rows of figures, flipped to page four, and studied the graphs.

"I concur," he said, looking up. "Do we have any sense of how much Semtex was used?" He liked to toss in an unanswerable question now and then. It kept his people on their toes.

"That's on the bottom of page five, sir," Kraus said. "It was a radio-controlled package weighing in the neighborhood of six kilos. Probably placed inside the car, beneath the rear seat. The body armor would have effectively focused the blast upward."

Ryan looked at Kraus and the others to make sure they weren't having a laugh at his expense, then flipped to the next page. "I see it here," he said. "Good work."

"I don't think there's any question who pulled it off or why," Vizanko said. He passed down a thick folder. "Yevgenni Tarankov. They call him the Tarantula, and for good reason it looks like."

"Save me from wading through this, Chris. Do we have hard intelligence to support that speculation?"

Vizanko sat back, insolently. "Tarankov hit their Riga Nuclear Power Station in the Moscow suburb of Dzerzhinskiy the day before. You've already seen that report, and damage estimates. We think that Yeltsin finally got off his duff and ordered Tarankov's arrest." Vizanko spread his hands. "The Tarantula retaliated. Sure as hell sent the Kremlin a clear message."

"What's that?" Ryan asked coldly.

"Tarankov is going to take over in the June elections, if not sooner."

"By force?"

"It's a possibility that should be considered."

"I see," Ryan said. He turned to his assistant, Tom Moore. "Do you concur?"

Moore, "Sir Thomas" behind his back, even more staid and pedantic than his boss, took his pipe out of his mouth and studied the contents of the bowl. "I'd have to study the reports at length, Howard. But on the surface of it the possibility has enough merit to be kicked upstairs."

"Very well—"

"But of course I would advise caution. Meddling in Russia's internal affairs at this moment is fraught with danger, the least of which is our considerable dollar investment over there."

"My thoughts exactly," Ryan said.

"Won't matter much if Tarankov takes power," Vizanko said. "That bastard will nationalize everything, and there'll be very little that we could do to stop him. Half the Russian Strategic Rocket Force officers are on his side. We've already seen the analysis of those numbers. It'd take no leap of imagination to envision him scrapping SALT, and reprogramming his ICBMs."

"He doesn't have the money."

"I think he could get it, Mr. Ryan," Vizanko said. He shrugged again. "Anyway, it's a thought."

"Any other comments?" Ryan asked after a few moments. There were none. "Thank you for your help this morning," he said.

Ryan was in the DCI's office a minute before nine with two copies of his lengthy report, one of them in a leather folder for the President. He'd scanned the Directorate of Intelligence report and the Technical Services Division findings directly into his computer under the Directorate of Operations seal, heavily edited the material, added his own conclusions and included full color graphs, charts and maps, along with photographs of Yeltsin and his staff, Prime Minister Kabatov and his staff, Russia's key generals, and a selection of the few photographs they had of Tarankov. Ryan's second principle of insulation, was when a report was requested throw as much material into it as possible, then double that amount. The government, he was fond of saying, likes to see something impressive for the trillions it spends.

General Roland Murphy (retired) had been director of the Central Intelligence Agency for an unprecedented ten and a half years because he was very good, he had no party affiliation, and each president he'd served under found him to be indispensable, whatever his politics.

He and Ryan went back a number of years together. The general knew the family very well, and he'd hired Ryan away from the law firm to act as general counsel for the CIA, a job which Ryan had loved.

During his tenure, Ryan had developed an appreciation for, and a real expertise in, the hardball politics of liaison between the Agency and the Hill, an ability Murphy lacked. When the previous DDO had been killed eighteen months ago, and Ryan wounded in the same operation, Murphy had rewarded his friend with the directorate.

Murphy quickly scanned the report, which ran to nearly eighty pages, as Ryan poured a cup of coffee, and went to the big corner windows. The sky was gray, but all the snow was gone and spring was not far away. Ryan was indifferent.

"Very professional, as usual, Howard," Murphy said after a few minutes.

"Thank you, General," Ryan said, turning back.

"This'll impress the hell out of them, but the President likes straight answers. He doesn't want to be caught flat-footed like he was over the Japanese thing."

Ryan's jaw tightened, and he reflexively touched his face where he'd been shot by a former East German Stasi hit man. By all rights he should have been killed. But for the grace of God he would have been, and he carried the scar not only of his wound, but of the memory of the man who had put him in harm's way.

"I understand, Mr. Director," Ryan said. "I've included a summary on the last two pages which should make it clear."

"You can tell him that yourself. He pushed the briefing forward to nine-thirty, which doesn't give me time to wade through this."

"I'd be happy to brief the President," Ryan said, genuinely pleased. One of the keys to acquiring power, he'd always told himself, was to surround yourself with power. Another was knowing how to handle yourself when the time came.

The White House
Washington, D.C.

The President's appointments secretary, Dale Nichols, showed them into the Oval Office at precisely 9:30. Ryan had answered tough questions nonstop on the way over from Langley in the DCI's limousine; as a result he felt much better prepared than he had a half-hour ago. The general might not have been a politician, but he was as astute as he was expedient.

President Lindsay, a tall, Lincolnesque figure, was seated in his rocking chair across from his National Security Adviser, Harold Secor, Secretary of State Jonathan Carter and Secretary of Defense Paul Landry. Two extra chairs had been pulled up around the broad coffee table.

"Good morning, Roland," the President said. "I'd say from the cut of your jib that the news is less than good."

"Good morning, Mr. President. There've been better days," Murphy responded. "I think you know Howard Ryan, my Deputy Director of Operations."

"Good to see you, Ryan," the President said.

"It's good to be here, Mr. President," Ryan replied evenly.

No introductions were needed with Secor, Carter or Landry. They knew Ryan well from briefings before various committees and subcommittees on the Hill.

"Howard's more in touch with the nuts and bolts of the situation than I am, so I brought him along to conduct the briefing," Murphy said.

"Fine."

Ryan handed the President the leather folder. "The last two pages summarize what we know, but I can go over the high points with you, Mr. President."

The President motioned for him to take a seat, and he flipped through the bulky report. He didn't bother with the summary at the back. When he was finished he looked up. "I'll read this later." He handed the report to Secor. "In the meantime we have a problem for which I'm going to need some hard information. Prime Minister Kabatov telephoned me this morning, and asked for my help. He means to arrest Yevgenni Tarankov for murder and for destruction of one of their nuclear power plants. He's asked for my backing, and that of NATO to forestall what might develop into a military coup d'etat. I promised that I would get back to him this morning."

"He wants us to use our satellites to help track Tarankov's train," Secor said.

"Mr. President, may I ask what the Prime Minister said to you about President Yeltsin's death?" Ryan asked. He was on dangerous ground here. Ever since the debacle with the Japanese the President had become a tough bastard. He treated failure harshly.

"I assume you'll make a point," the President said.

"Yes, sir."

"The funeral has been postponed until next week. He hoped I'd understand, but they have their hands full over there at the moment."

"Mr. President, are you saying that Prime Minister Kabatov continues to maintain that President Yeltsin died of a heart attack induced by the car bomb in Red Square?"

"That's exactly what he's saying," the President said. "Do you know something different?"

"President Yeltsin was in the limousine that blew up. He was assassinated under Yevgenni Tarankov's orders because Yeltsin had ordered his arrest in response to the destruction of the Riga Nuclear Power plant."

"I wouldn't be a bit surprised," Secretary of Defense Landry said. "Does the bastard really think he can take over by force?"

"It's a possibility that we're monitoring very closely, Mr. Secretary," Ryan said.

President Lindsay ran a hand over his forehead. "What a mess. They're in over their heads, and they're finally beginning to realize the sad facts of life." He glanced at Murphy, then brought his attention back to Ryan. "How reliable is this information?"

"Unfortunately there were no eyewitnesses, Mr. President. But my people managed to come up with samples of blood and human tissue from the square, minutes after the explosion. A laboratory was set up, and they did in two days what would normally take three or four weeks to do. They came up with an accurate DNA analysis of the blood, and a mass spectrographic study of the tissues. The blood was Yeltsin's, there's no doubt about that. And imbedded in the human tissues we found conclusive evidence of Semtex, which is a powerful plastic explosive. The data are on pages seventeen through twenty-one. We're estimating that the bomb weighed around six kilos, and was placed inside the cabin of President Yeltsin's limousine—probably beneath the rear seat. The limo's external armor plating would have effectively contained the primary force of the explosion inside the cabin, tripling its effectiveness. It was radio controlled. Most likely the assassin was in Red Square within sight of the presidential motorcade. He pushed the button and escaped in the confusion."

Murphy gave Ryan an odd look, but Ryan shrugged it off. He was in his element now.

"Tarankov may try to take the government by force before the June elections, Mr. President," Ryan continued. "He has the support of much of the military, as well as at least half the officers in the Russian missile force. If he is successful it's likely he'll reprogram what missiles remain back to their old targets—cities in the United States. He'll almost certainly have no trouble finding the money to do so."

"That sounds a little far fetched, Howard," Secretary of State Carter said.

"I'd like to agree, Mr. Secretary, but the facts seem to indicate otherwise," Ryan replied heavily.

"What's the CIA recommending?" the President asked.

Murphy started to reply, but Ryan beat him to the punch.

"First, we need to proceed with caution, Mr. President. Meddling in Russia's internal affairs right now will be dangerous, considering our considerable dollar investment over there."

"Now, that I agree with," Carter said.

"We cannot ignore the situation," the President said.

"No, sir," Ryan responded. "What we need is a major intelligence investigation into Tarankov's chances for success, and exactly how deep his power base runs not only in the military and old KGB and Militia, but in the rank and file population as well. The people of Dzerzhinskiy cheered him when he destroyed the power station.

"I think we need to give Prime Minister Kabatov as much help as possible, but only in the form of assurances until we have more information. The Prime Minister is ordering the very same thing that resulted in President Yeltsin's death."

"What happens if we find out that Tarankov will be successful?" Secor asked evenly. "Do we step in with force?"

"In that case it would be a political decision. But if the man has popular backing he'll become president of Russia, and we'll end up having to deal with him. Perhaps it would be better to start hedging our bets now."

The President eyed Ryan coolly. "As you say, Mr. Ryan, the decision would be a political one. But I'm curious. What do you mean by hedging our bets?"

"We should send out feelers to him. Might kill two birds with one stone."

"How so?"

"Whoever we send as an unofficial envoy from this government would in reality be one of my people. He'd be instructed to explore possible future relations, while keeping his eyes and ears open to learn what he could."

"In effect we'd be stabbing Prime Minister Kabatov's democratic reform government in the back," the President said, his voice dangerously soft.

Ryan didn't miss the warning signals, but he was in too deeply now to back out. He chose his next words with care. "Not exactly, Mr. President. But we would be protecting our own interests, because short of sending direct military help to Prime Minister Kabatov there is very little of a substantive nature that we can do. If Kabatov's government falls, not because of anything we've done or not done, and Tarankov takes over, we should be prepared for him."

The President sat back in his rocking chair. "I want to disagree with you, Mr. Ryan. But the hell of it is, I can't." He looked at Secor for help, but his National Security Adviser shook his head.

"Do you have someone in mind for this . . . diplomatic mission?"

"Not at the moment, Mr. President."

"How soon could you work up a proposal?"

"Within twenty-four hours, sir."

"Very well, do it, Mr. Ryan," the President said. "In the meantime I'll telephone Prime Minister Kabatov and tell him that he has my complete support. If there's anything we can do for him *outside* of Russia's borders, we'll do it. If possible Tarankov should be arrested and placed on trial."

"Yes, sir," Ryan said.

On the way out of the White House Murphy chuckled wryly. "I hope you know that you were had back there."

"What?" Ryan asked.

"The President set you up, Howard. He has a habit of doing that. But you'll learn."

"I don't know what you mean."

"You've named your own poison, man. If the President goes for your proposal you'd better pack your long underwear, because you'll be the envoy."

Ryan's blood ran cold. "I'm a desk officer."

"You just graduated."

NINE

Paris

Traffic along the Boulevard Haussmann was intense as it was on every weekday except in summer.

McGarvey sat in the shade beneath an umbrella at a sidewalk café across the street from the huge department store Printemps, waiting for Jacqueline to come out. The law offices where she worked were in the next block. He'd expected her to return to work after lunch, but instead she'd come here. To do some shopping, he hoped, though he doubted it.

She'd been jumpy all weekend no doubt because of his own strange mood. Yemlin's information about his parents had deeply disturbed him, and he'd been unable to hide it from her. Each time she'd asked what was wrong he told her that he always got this way in the spring in Paris.

"Then let's leave the city," she said.

"What about your job?"

"I'll cut my summer vacation short. We could go to Cannes, or St. Tropez. It would be nice, I promise you."

"No."

"*Porquoi pas?*" she cried.

"I have something to take care of, that's why. I don't run away from my obligations."

She'd shaken her head. "You're a strange American."

He'd laughed. "We all are."

Jacqueline emerged from the department store, and McGarvey was about to get up and pay his bill, when something struck him as wrong. She turned in the opposite direction from her office, and headed off in a rush. McGarvey sat down. She'd been inside for nearly an hour but she'd bought nothing. She carried no shopping bags.

Ten minutes later he spotted another person he knew emerging with the crowds from the store, Colonel Guy de Galan, chief of the SDECE's Division R7, in charge of gathering intelligence from and about America and the Western Hemisphere. McGarvey had had a brief run in with the man a couple of years ago.

Galan stepped to the side, and pretended to look at the displays in one of the windows while he lit a cigarette.

It was a standard tradecraft procedure, but it would be impossible for him to spot McGarvey here. The point was, however, that he was taking precautions. He expected someone might be watching him.

After a few moments, Galan turned, scanned the traffic in the street and looked over in McGarvey's direction. But then he tossed his cigarette aside, and headed in the same direction Jacqueline had gone.

"How about that," McGarvey said, even more depressed than before. He'd been ninety-nine percent sure that Jacqueline worked for the SDECE. But there'd been that tiny one percent that he'd been able to delude himself with. Gone now, and it saddened him.

Time to get out, finally, like he'd been trying to do for any number of years. Each time he thought he had it made, though, someone came for him. Each time they came he jumped through the hoops.

"Maybe it's what you are, *Compar,*" an old friend had told him once. They'd been drinking, and saying anything that came into their heads. "Maybe the leopard doesn't like its spots, but tough shit. They're his and he's got to live with them."

"Gee, thanks, Phil, that helps a lot," McGarvey said. They'd just been bullshitting each other. But sometimes the truth came out like that. And sometimes it wasn't so pleasant to face.

McGarvey paid for his coffee and went in search of an imported food shop and then a car rental agency, not yet certain what he was going to do, but at least sure what his next move would be.

Bonnieres

The thirty-five-mile drive out of Paris on the N13, which for short stretches followed the banks of the Seine, was quite pleasant in the afternoon sun. He'd taken a direct route not bothering to watch for a tail until he was clear of the heaviest traffic. Twice he'd turned off the main highway, and once he stopped at a service station to check his oil, so by the time he reached the small town on the Seine he was sure that he was clean.

On the other side of the town he got off the main highway again, and followed a series of increasingly narrower roads that wound their way through the farmlands along the river, until he came to an old farm cottage in a valley at the edge of a woods overlooking the Seine. He parked in the protection of the trees five hundred yards from the house, and went to the edge of the field on foot.

The farm seemed to be deserted except that he could make out the faint sounds of machinery running, and the area immediately to the south of the house contained a compact array of solar electric panels that looked new.

McGarvey had been thinking about Otto Rencke a lot over the past few weeks, a sort of summing up, he supposed. It was something he'd been doing lately, dredging up old memories, old places and friends as well as enemies. Put them all in perspective. Writing the Voltaire book had got him started on that line of thinking, as history always did.

The last time McGarvey had used him, Rencke had been living in an ancient brick house that had been the caretaker's quarters for Holy Rood Cemetery in Georgetown. Rencke was working on a freelance basis as a computer systems consultant for the Pentagon and the National Security Agency. He had the almost superhuman ability to visualize entire complex networks of systems—supercomputers, satellite links, data encryption devices and all the peripheral equipment that tied them together.

Trained as a Jesuit priest, he'd been at twenty-one one of the youngest professors of mathematics ever to teach at Georgetown University. But he'd been defrocked and fired on the day they'd caught him in the computer lab having sex with the dean's secretary.

He'd enlisted in the army as a computer specialist but was kicked out nine months later for having sex with a young staff sergeant—a male. It didn't make any difference to Otto, he was satisfied with whatever came his way.

A year later he'd shown up on the CIA's payroll, his past record wiped completely clean.

McGarvey had first run into him when Rencke was revamping the Company's archival section, bringing it into the computer age. They'd worked together from time to time after that in Germany, South America and a few other places where Rencke had been sent to straighten out computer systems, sometimes for the Company, at other times for a friendly government.

McGarvey and he had formed a loose friendship, each admiring the other man for their intelligence, dedication and sometimes easy humor.

During his tenure at Langley Rencke had updated the CIA's entire communications system, standardized their spy satellite input and analysis systems so that Agency machines could crosstalk, thus share information with the National Security Agency and the National Reconnaissance Office on a realtime basis. He'd also devised a field officer's briefing system whereby up to date information could be funneled directly to the officer on assignment by satellite when and as he needed it.

But his past had finally caught up with him, and like McGarvey he'd been dumped. He'd moved to France a couple of years ago, and McGarvey came out from time to time to have lunch and a few drinks.

McGarvey went back to the car and drove the rest of the way down to the farmhouse, parking in the shade of a big tree in the front yard. He took the package from the imported food shop and went around back where Rencke was sitting cross-legged on a table in the courtyard.

"Hi ya, Mac," Rencke said brightly. He still looked like a twenty-year-old kid, with long out-of-control frizzy red hair, wild eyebrows and a gaunt frame, though at forty-one he'd finally begun to develop a pot-belly.

McGarvey tossed him the package. "I thought you might be getting hungry out here all by yourself."

"I'm always hungry, you know that," Rencke said. He tore open the bundle, which contained a half-dozen packets of Twinkies, which in the States were cheap, but in Paris cost six dollars each. Rencke was a self-admitted Twinkie freak, and McGarvey had never seen him eat anything else. "Oh boy, but you've got the look on you again," he said, opening one of the packets and stuffing his mouth. "Good. Bad for me, but good."

McGarvey pulled a chair over and sat down. "Are you staying out of trouble?"

Rencke shrugged and spread his hands out, scattering crumbs. He was dressed in filthy cutoffs and a tattered, gray T-shirt. "I try, honest I do. But this is a land of farmers' daughters. What can I say? But you're in trouble. It's a mile wide on your sour mug. Bad guys coming out of the woodwork again. That it? Thinking about tossing your hat back in the ring. Oiling your peashooter? Going hunting, Mac?"

"Those farmers' daughters have fathers." McGarvey smiled. "And one of these days you're going to get your ass shot off."

"The big question would be answered."

"What question is that, Otto?"

Rencke's face lit up. "The God thing, you know Jesu Cristo, Mohammed, and Harry Krishnakov. All that stuff. Aren't you just dying to know?" Rencke laughed out loud.

"You're nuts," McGarvey said laughing.

"Exactamundo, Mac. But I'm the best friggin' genius in town. Like a willing virgin, I'm ready and able."

"Troubles . . ."

"The Russian thing, isn't it," Rencke bubbled, and when McGarvey tried to speak, Rencke held him off. "Don't tell me yet. The Russians are up and at it. The Tarantula knocks out a nuke plant. Did them all a favor, if you ask me. Next thing you know old Boris gets himself popped off. His guys don't carry bombs in their cars. Maybe a shock grenade or two, but not the muscle to blow a car apart. So Tarankov did it because Boris wanted to take him down. Am I right, or what?"

McGarvey nodded.

"Oh, boy, I still have the magic!" Rencke opened another packet of Twinkies and stuffed them in his mouth. "So Tarankov means to take over, probably before the June elections. He's got the balls. From what I read, half the country is behind him. Sorta like a cross between Willie Sutton and Marie Antoinette. If they don't have bread let 'em cut cake they can buy with money heisted from the banks. But Kabatov's people think the way to go is arresting the bugger and putting him on trial. Right? Right?"

"That's what I was told."

Rencke jumped down from the table, and hopped from one foot to the other, his face lit up like a kid's at Christmas. "They do that . . . If they could pull it off, the whole country would go down the dumper. Be a two-flusher at least. But if they keep their mitts off he'll take over anyway, and maybe the whole world will take a crap." Rencke stopped, his face suddenly serious. "He's a bad man, Mac. The worse. If he gets into power he'll make Stalin and old Adolph look like pikers. Amateurs, know what I mean?"

"It's their problem, Otto. I'm not shedding any tears. They did everything in their power over the past seventy-five years to get to this point."

"Bzzz. Wrong answer recruit. He gets in and it becomes our problem," Rencke said. A sad, wistful expression came over his face, and he smiled. "The only solution is for someone to assassinate the bastard before it's too late. Someone has come to ask you to do it. Friend or foe?"

"Former foe."

"Yemlin. As in Viktor Pavlovich. He did you a favor with his Tokyo Abunai network, and now he's calling in the chips. He's a born again democratic reformer, is that it?"

"I'm out of the business," McGarvey said for his own benefit as well as Rencke's.

"How'd you manage to sidestep your little spook?"

"You're a bastard."

"You called me that once before, Mac. Just not true. My mother was a good woman. But I am a real shit, and I'm sorry if I hurt your feelings. But the question is valid."

"I managed."

"Does she suspect?"

"Probably."

"Not so good to have the French on your back," Rencke said, looking away momentarily. "What'd you tell him, Mac?" he asked dreamily.

"I told him no."

Rencke turned his wild eyes back to McGarvey. "Then what're you doing out here? Looking for a conscience, because if that's all it is, forget it. Tarankov is a bad, bad dog. I could show you things, Mac. Real things that'd curl even your gray hair."

"That's what I came out here for," McGarvey said.

"Research or justification?"

"Just research . . ."

Rencke wagged his finger at McGarvey. "As you're fond of saying, Mac, don't shit the troops. If you want my help you'll have to level with me. Because if you're going to do it I'll have to backstop you, which'll put my ass on the line. I've got a right to know."

"Just research for now, Otto. Because I honestly don't know what I'm going to do. I want to stay retired."

Rencke shook his head, the sad expression back on his face. "We both wish that were true, my friend. But the fact is you're getting bored again. I saw it the last time you came out here. And listen to me, without you there would have been a lot more bad guys killing a lot of really good people. You *have* made a difference, Mac. In a lot of people's lives. Don't ever doubt it."

"I do every day," McGarvey said.

"Comes with the territory," Rencke said. He turned abruptly and went into the house.

McGarvey waited outside for ten minutes, smoking a cigarette, enjoying the warmth of the afternoon. His ex-wife Kathleen had once called him the "last boy scout." Now Rencke had called him the same thing.

One thing was certain, he thought as he rose and went into the house, whoever agreed to kill Tarankov would have less than a one-in-a-thousand chance of pulling it off and escaping. It was an interesting problem.

The windows in the main room were boarded up and the fireplace blocked. Fluorescent lights had been installed in the ceiling, and air conditioning kept the house cool, almost cold. Computer equipment was scattered everywhere. A dozen monitors, one of them a forty-inch screen, were set up next to printers and CPUs around the room. In a corner what looked like a smaller version of a Cray supercomputer was processing something. The lights on its front panel flashed at a bewildering speed.

"I built that one myself," Rencke called from where he was seated at the big monitor, his fingers flying over the keyboard. "The lights are useless, but they impress the hell out of people."

"Who's seen it?" McGarvey asked, walking over.

"Nobody," Rencke said. "Take a look at this."

A map of Russia came up on the screen with all the major cities pinpointed in yellow. Starting with Yakutsk in Siberia and working its way west toward Moscow, the cities flashed red, and a number between ten and a hundred appeared beside each one.

"I won't bore you with details, but those are the cities Tarankov's commandoes have hit in the past couple of years. The figures are the number of people he's killed in each place."

Rencke erased the screen, and this time brought up a map of the entire old Soviet Union. "I designed a probability program from the basic premise that Tarankov succeeds in taking the Kremlin by force or by the ballot box. Either scenario made no difference." He looked up. "Ready for this, Mac?"

"Go ahead," McGarvey said.

Rencke hit a key. For a few moments nothing seemed to happen, until one after another, spreading outward from Moscow like some malignant growth, cities large and small began to glow red, numbers, some in the thousands, began to appear beside them. The figures next to Moscow and St. Petersburg showed the most growth, rising into the tens of thousands, but then Kiev and Nizhny Novgorod and Volgograd blossomed. The cancer spread next to Tallinn, Riga and Vilnius in the Baltics. Finally into Romania, and Bulgaria and Poland. The numbers were staggering, in the millions.

"The people will have jobs, they'll eat regularly, they'll have free medical care and free education all the way up to the doctorate level," Rencke said.

"How accurate is this?" McGarvey asked.

"Based on my primary premise, very," Rencke said. "How about nuclear accident projections, because they'll be reactivating their nuclear missile force, including their subs? Or, if you want to see something pitiful, how about projected NATO responses? Almost nil. How about the biggest one of all, Mac?" Rencke looked up, a maniacal glint in his eyes. "Thermonuclear war. Because if Tarankov takes power the nuclear countdown clock will start ticking again, a few seconds before midnight."

Images and numbers and bright white lights blossomed over a map of the entire world, faster and faster, until it was impossible to follow.

Suddenly the screen went blank, and turned a rich hue of lavender.

Rencke sat back in his chair. "My telephone here is secure. I've set up a backscatter encryption device that'll work both ways. Whatever telephone you use will be encrypted as well."

It was starting again as McGarvey knew it would. There were always alternatives to war, to acts of terrorism, to assassinations. Problem was nobody thought of them until afterwards.

"I haven't played fair with you, Mac," Rencke said. "I knew that you'd met with Yemlin, and I knew that you would be coming out here to see me."

"How?" McGarvey asked.

Rencke brought up another program. "You're my friend, so I keep track of you. When your name pops up somewhere, my snoopy systems take note."

The CIA's logo appeared on the screen, followed by the Directorate of Operations designator, and then Paris Station.

The text of a message sent to Langley from Tom Lynch came up.

"They know that you met with Yemlin," Rencke said, as McGarvey stared with disbelief at the name of the addressee. "The SDECE managed to pick up a portion of your conversation, and they handed it over to Lynch. They knew that you were asked to assassinate someone for the Russians. They don't know who. Their only concern is that it doesn't happen on French soil."

"Is this a fucking joke?" McGarvey demanded.

"What?" Rencke asked confused.

McGarvey stabbed a blunt finger at the screen. "Howard Ryan is the deputy director of operations?"

"I thought you knew."

McGarvey stepped back a pace. It was like the old Santiago days all over again. Everything changed, yet nothing changed.

"I'll keep in touch," he said at last.

"I'll be here, Mac," Rencke said. "Just watch yourself, will ya. But it's really good news about your parents."

TEN

Paris

McGarvey returned his rental car to the agency downtown, and
walked a few blocks over to the Gare St-Lazare where he got a
cab. The early evening was still pleasantly warm and the parks and sidewalk
cafés were jammed with people. Under normal circumstances he and Jacqueline would have gone out to dinner this evening. Thinking about it deepened
his already dark mood.

Howard Ryan was a pompous ass, who nevertheless had done a good job
for the CIA as its general counsel. He knew his way around political Washington, and during his tenure the Agency maintained the best relationship
it'd ever had with the Congress.

But as a spy he was a meddling fool who didn't know what he was doing.
Eighteen months ago he'd nearly gotten himself killed by an East German

gunman because he'd barged into a situation he knew nothing about. McGarvey had even saved his life after Ryan had shot him in the side.

Afterward Roland Murphy had actually apologized for the man, but McGarvey never dreamed that Ryan would be promoted to deputy director of operations. It was insanity, and he felt sorry for the poor bastards who had to work for him. Their lives were in danger. He wondered how many of them would have to be killed before someone finally saw the light and sent the lawyer back to New York. It was a chilling thought.

Another part of McGarvey was already beginning to work out the logistics of assassinating Tarankov, however. The odds against success were not very good. Maybe even worse than a thousand-to-one.

Killing someone was very easy, even someone as heavily guarded as a political figure. Rabin's assassin had simply walked up to the Israeli leader and pumped three bullets into his back, and one of the best security services in the world had been unable to prevent it.

The hard part was getting away afterward.

He paid off his cabby a block from his apartment and went the rest of the way on foot as he usually did. Out of long habit he scrutinized the traffic, studied the parked cars and scanned the rooflines for a sign that someone was interested in him. But there was nothing out of the ordinary tonight.

Lights were burning in his apartment windows. He stopped in the shadow of a doorway across the street and watched to see if he could detect any movements. Jacqueline had not officially moved in with him yet, but often she spent nights at his apartment. A few of her things were hanging in the armoire, and in the bathroom. Had their relationship continued to develop it would only have been a matter of time before she gave up her apartment. She'd been hinting about it for the last week or so.

He figured that she'd be worried about him now, and would be watching the street. But she didn't come to the window, and after five minutes McGarvey went up.

Only one light was on in the living room, and the bedroom door was ajar, the television playing inside. The air smelled of mentholated spirits.

"Jacqueline?" McGarvey called softly, as he moved across the room taking care to stay out of a sightline through the window.

"In here," she answered, her voice husky.

McGarvey pushed open the door and went in. Jacqueline was propped up in bed, a bottle of mineral water and some medicine bottles on the nightstand. "Are you okay?"

"No," she said. "I feel like *merde*. I've got a fever, my head is about to explode and every bone in my body aches. Anyway, where have you been all day, I've been worried about you."

McGarvey went to her side and felt her forehead. Her skin felt clammy. "You *are* sick," he said. He picked up the medicine bottles, which contained French over-the-counter cold and flu drugs. "Have you been here all day?"

"Yes," she said. "And I wanted some sympathy. Where were you?"

"Shopping," he said, giving her a wistful smile.

"Oh? What'd you buy?"

"Nothing much. Too many people, and I wasn't much in the mood."

"Are you still in your black ass from the weekend?" she asked. "If you are, I wish you'd get out of it. You're not very much fun to be around when you're like this."

McGarvey went to the writing desk, and inspected his failsafes on the cabinet beside it. They'd not been tampered with. He could feel Jacqueline's eyes on his back. "Printemps was very busy today," he said. He unlocked the cabinet and took out his Voltaire manuscript.

"What time were you there?" she asked.

"About two-thirty." McGarvey brought the manuscript back to the bed and handed it to her. "Unless you're a Voltaire fan this may be a little dry."

She was watching him, trying to gauge his mood.

"I saw a couple of people I knew."

"Who's that?" she asked calmly.

"You, of course. And Colonel Galan. I didn't know that he was an agent runner, I thought he was a desk jockey running R-Seven."

She set the manuscript aside. "How long have you known?"

"I suspected something from the beginning," he said.

"Yet you let me make a fool of myself," she flared. She tossed the covers back and got out of bed. She was wearing nothing but one of his shirts.

"At first it didn't matter, but then I started to care for you and I didn't want you to go."

She'd started toward the bathroom, but she stopped. "Is that why you followed me today?"

"Something's come up . . ."

"You met with the Russians on Saturday and they want you to kill someone for them," she blurted. She'd expected him to react, but when he didn't her eyes narrowed. "You know about that too?"

He nodded.

"How?"

"It's what I do, Jacqueline. It's my business."

She nodded warily. "Don't fool around, Kirk. Colonel Galan is a tough man. The Service doesn't care what you do outside France as long as it doesn't involve one of our citizens. But we take a very harsh stand on criminal acts inside the country."

She was a pretty woman, and bright. He was going to miss her even more than he first thought he would.

"You could be brought in for questioning," she said.

"Yes, I could," he replied evenly.

"I don't think Langley would interfere."

"Probably not."

"You'd be kicked out of France. Permanently."

"I've done nothing wrong."

"Mon cul!" Jacqueline swore. She ripped off his shirt, tossed it at him, and making no effort to hide her nakedness, strode across the bedroom to where she'd laid her clothes and got dressed.

"Don't forget your things in the bathroom," McGarvey said.

"Are you kicking me out?" she demanded.

"No, but you're leaving."

She stared at him for a long moment, her eyes glistening, then went into the bathroom, tossed her perfumes and lotions into a cosmetics bag, and came out. "What shall I tell Colonel Galan?"

"Whatever you'd like. But tell him the truth because he's heard everything."

Her eyes narrowed.

"There are three bugs. One in the living room, one in the bathroom and one in the wall over the bed."

Some color came to her cheeks. "Take care of yourself, Kirk."

McGarvey nodded. "You too, Jacqueline. *Je t'embrasse.*"

"Je te l'aussi."

After she was gone, McGarvey sat by the window in the living room while he smoked a cigarette and looked down at the busy street. For the most part he'd managed to put thoughts about his parents in the compartment of his mind that he rarely visited. The pain was very great; at times so great he couldn't stand it. If what Yemlin had told him was true, he would be relieved of a burden he'd carried with him all of his adult life. After his parents had died in an automobile accident he'd discovered what he thought was proof that they'd spied for the Russians. It had nearly killed him. But now he was being given a reprieve.

A bus lumbered by on the street below, trailing a cloud of blue exhaust. He'd wanted to talk about this with Jacqueline, but of course that was impossible, considering what she was. A relationship, any sort of a relationship, was the bane of a spy's existence. A woman was excess baggage, and he'd always thought of them in that vein, which he supposed was one of the main reasons he'd never been able to sustain a relationship. It was an either/or situation, and he seemed incapable of giving up his profession. At least for now.

When he finished the cigarette, he turned off the television and switched on the stereo to Radio Luxembourg which beamed popular music all over Europe. He turned the volume up so that he could hear it in the kitchen while he fixed a three-egg cheese omelet and made some toast in the oven.

He took his time, setting a place at the small table and opening a bottle of white wine. He hadn't eaten much all day, and the food tasted good. When he was finished he read the morning's *Le Figaro*, then washed up and put away the clean dishes.

Jacqueline's case officer would have notified Colonel Galan as soon as

McGarvey returned to the apartment. He would also have notified the colonel when Jacqueline left.

McGarvey glanced at his watch. If they were going to bring him in for questioning tonight they'd be showing up within the next hour or so.

Starting in the living room he cleaned the apartment from top to bottom, making no effort to mask the noises of what he was doing. In effect he was cleansing the place of Jacqueline's presence. He'd found out she was a SDECE spy sent to watch him, and he was ridding himself of her.

In the bedroom he tossed out the few remaining traces of her, including the mineral water and medicines on the nightstand. He did the same in the bathroom, scrubbing out the shower and the toilet, and cleaning the sink and mirrors.

When he was finished he took the garbage downstairs and stuffed it in one of the cans in the back alley.

Back in the apartment he sat by the window again and had another cigarette and glass of wine, cleansing his mind, as he had his apartment, of her. In effect she was a prostitute. Her pimp was the French Secret Service, and her john was McGarvey. He'd known that from the start. But as with Marta Fredricks, his watchdog in Switzerland a few years ago, he'd come to have a genuine feeling for Jacqueline despite himself. A feeling, he told himself firmly, that could go nowhere.

Marta had lost her life chasing after him. He was glad now to be rid of Jacqueline, at least in that respect. She would be a lot safer away from him.

Nobody was coming tonight, he decided finally. They weren't going to arrest him, they were simply going to watch him.

He went in the bathroom and urinated. When he was done he got up on the edge of the tub and carefully lifted the mechanism and false bottom out of the overhead gravity tank, causing the toilet to flush. He pulled out a flat, plastic-wrapped package from inside, and as the last of the water ran out of the tank, replaced the mechanism so that the tank would refill normally.

He opened the package on the bed and took out his Walther PPK, two spare magazines of ammunition, a silencer disguised to look like a small flashlight, ten thousand dollars cash in American money, British pounds and Swiss francs, a spare set of identity papers, a small plastic squeeze bottle containing hair coloring, and a set of light blue contact lenses.

These last he took back into the bathroom, where he cut his hair short with his electric razor, careful to rinse all the hair down the sink, then colored it a light gray. He put in the contact lenses, and when he was finished he looked like a somewhat older man, which matched the photographs in his false papers.

He took a long, hot shower, made certain that the bathroom was clean, then got dressed in a nondescript pair of slacks, turtleneck and leather jacket. He stuffed the plastic package and half-full hair coloring bottle, his laptop computer and a few extra items of clothing into an overnight bag which he set by the front door. He quickly checked the apartment one last time to make sure everything was shut off, then let himself out, silently closing and locking the door behind him.

He took the stairs two at a time to the top floor, where from a window at the end of the corridor he studied the shadows in the alley.

Five minutes later, certain that no one was down there, he climbed out onto the fire escape, and scrambled down to the alley and headed away, not at all sure when or if he'd ever be back.

Paris
The Left Bank

The Hôtel Trois Frères was a half-block off the Rue Vaugirad near the Gare Montparnasse. It was small, but clean, and catered mostly to European travelers on a budget who wanted peace and quiet in the middle of Paris for a reasonable price. The back rooms looked down on a pleasant terrace with a small fountain that ran all night. In the morning the hotel served a continental breakfast next door at a patisserie. It served wine in the evening from six until seven. Everyone, staff and guests, was polite but reserved. Europeans were not as a rule as snoopy as Americans.

McGarvey checked in under the name Pierre Allain, a political writer from Spa, Belgium, with the spare passport and credit cards he kept in reserve.

A lot depended on Jacqueline, her control officer and Colonel Galan. Galan had asked for help from the CIA. But when Ryan started to push there was no telling how the French would react. They wanted information, but they might resent interference. The French were sometimes touchy on the subject. Officially the CIA did not maintain a presence in France. It was a fiction that everybody could live with. Unless somebody started to get too aggressive.

The SVR, which was the foreign intelligence gathering arm of the new Russian secret service, also maintained a station here. McGarvey was not a hundred percent convinced that Yemlin had been able to mask his true purpose for coming to France. So it was possible that the Russians would be looking for him as well.

Before he went to bed for a troubled night of sleep, he disassembled his gun, wiped it down, then reassembled and loaded it.

For better or worse, he was back in the field, no longer a civilian. Anyone could be gunning for him.

In the morning over breakfast he scoured *Le Figaro* for any mention that the police were looking for him, then walked a dozen blocks over to the Boulevard St-Michel on the east side of the Jardin du Luxembourg where he called his apartment from a pay phone. When his answering machine kicked in, he entered the code to retrieve any messages. There were none.

Next he entered a three digit code which monitored noises in the apartment for thirty seconds. The place was silent. They weren't coming after him yet. But they would be if for no other reason than to ask him some questions.

He spent the next few hours before lunch shopping at the big department store, BHV, across from the Hôtel de Ville, where he bought a sport coat, a couple of shirts, a couple of pairs of slacks, and a few other items.

Dropping his purchases back at his hotel, he had a light lunch at a sidewalk café, then went over to the Bon Marché, the left bank's only department store, where he picked up a sturdy leather suitcase. He paid for his clothing with the Allain credit card, but paid cash for the suitcase. A visitor from Belgium might buy a sport coat and slacks in Paris, but it was less likely that he would buy a suitcase. It would be presumed he came with one.

Before he went back to his hotel, he called his apartment again. Jacqueline was on his answering machine.

"Don't hang up, Kirk. I want to talk to you. Hit five-six and your call will be rolled over to me—"

McGarvey hung up. He'd made the opening move, and they were countering. The next few days would see how serious they were.

He went back to the hotel, where the desk clerk, a pleasant looking woman in her early forties, flashed him a smile.

"Monsieur Allain, it is rare to see a man who enjoys shopping as much as you do."

The woman was flirting with him, he decided. "Not really, Madame, it is necessary. For the children, you know. And for my wife. They expect me to send them something from Paris."

She lowered her eyes. "Do you travel much, then?"

"Too much. I miss them."

The woman's eyes went to his left hand, and she smiled. He wore no ring. "Have a pleasant afternoon."

"And you, Madame," McGarvey said, and he went up to his room on the third floor where he laid the package containing the suitcase on the bed.

It was unlikely that the SDECE would get onto his Allain identity very quickly. Though every hotel registration card was collected by the police each night, there simply were too many visitors to Paris for all the cards to be thoroughly checked. As a safeguard, however, he could seduce the desk clerk, and have her include a registration card in the next bundle that showed he'd checked out.

Something to be considered, he thought. But it wasn't necessary just yet.

He unwrapped the suitcase, took all the tags off the new clothes, then packed them in the suitcase, which he rewrapped and addressed to Madame Suzanne Allain in Spa. He took the package downstairs and laid it on the desk so the woman could see the address.

"Could you tell me where the nearest post office is," McGarvey asked.

"We could take care of it for you."

"It's better if I do it myself. It has to be insured."

"Of course," the woman said, and she gave him directions to a post office a half-dozen blocks away.

McGarvey walked a few blocks from the hotel, unwrapped the suitcase and discarded the packing paper in a trash container, after first marking out the address. Then he took a cab to an Avis agency near the Gare de Lyon where he rented a mid-sized Renault for two weeks, paying extra for international insurance. He placed the suitcase in the trunk, and drove back to a car park that was attended twenty-four hours per day a few blocks from his hotel. He paid Avis with the Allain credit card, and paid cash for the car park.

Before he returned to his hotel he telephoned his apartment again, and got the same message from Jacqueline, but the place was still quiet.

He got back in time to have a couple of glasses of wine with a few of the guests in the lobby. The desk clerk, whose name was Martine, served them.

"Did you mail your package?" she asked.

"Yes, thank you."

"Have you made dinner plans for this evening?" She smiled. "There are several good restaurants nearby that I could recommend."

"Unfortunately I have to meet with some editors this evening, and then make an early evening of it."

"Too bad," she said, flashing him another seductive smile.

"Yes," he said. "Too bad."

McGarvey got his laptop computer from his room, and walked a few blocks to a pay phone near a metro station where he telephoned Otto Rencke.

"Hi ya, Mac," Rencke said.

"How'd you know it was me?" McGarvey said. His voice was scrambled in the handset. Rencke was using his back scatter encryption device.

"Somebody calls me from a pay phone in the middle of the Left Bank on this number it's gotta be you. Did you move out?"

"Yeah."

"You're taking the job, then?"

"I'm thinking about it," McGarvey said. "Has Langley responded to the SDECE's query on me?"

"Not yet, but I'm sure Ryan is working on it. You got your laptop with you? I've got everything you're going to need ready to download to you."

"How long will it take?"

"Ninety seconds."

"Okay, let me set it up."

"Mac?" Rencke said. "Remember what I said. Watch your ass, 'cause I think this is going to be a humdinger."

"Thanks."

"I'll be here when you need me."

McGarvey opened the computer and laid the telephone's handset beside it. A moment later, the computer screen lit up, and data began to flow from Rencke's computer into his.

ELEVEN

Paris
The Left Bank

In his hotel room McGarvey spent the next two days studying the material that Rencke had downloaded from his computer files. Besides the probability program which he'd developed to predict the outcome of a coup by Tarankov, Rencke had sent a complete dossier on the Tarantula, the people he surrounded himself with, and the armored train he used to make his strikes.

A number of things became very clear almost from the start of his studies, the first of which was Tarankov's intelligence. Although he had the brute strength and the unshakable determination of a Stalin or a Hitler, he was not a stupid man. In fact he was brilliant, something even his enemies begrudgingly admitted. Which meant he wasn't running around the countryside hoping that by some miracle the people would rise up and put him in power. He had a plan. A definite timetable.

If he wasn't stopped he would manage to take over the entire country with two hundred commandoes, his East German wife and Leonid Chernov, a former KGB Department Viktor assassin whose name McGarvey had never heard.

On Thursday night he called Rencke from a pay phone several blocks from the hotel.

"Have you tried calling your answering machine in the past thirty-six hours?" Rencke asked as soon as he picked up the phone.

"No."

"Don't. Langley sent the SDECE the information on you they wanted, and it's got them shook up. In their view you're a very dangerous man whom they would like very much to talk to right now. They put an automatic trace on your phone line. At this point they don't know if you're in Paris or not, but if you call from the Left Bank they'll be down there in minutes."

"Are they watching the airports?"

"Yup. And the train stations. But the border crossings haven't been alerted yet. You could get out that way. Either that or use a disguise."

"Have they issued a warrant for my arrest?"

"The street cops haven't got a warrant, I don't know about the Service," Rencke said. "You gotta understand, Mac, that to this point all my knowledge about the French is second hand. I can tap into the CIA's computers, and I can play with the French phone system, but I can't do much about the SDECE. They've got computers, don't get me wrong. But they're smart enough to know that they have to treat the really important stuff manually. The old fashioned way. If you want to know what they're doing you have to break into one of their offices and steal their paper files. It's almost un-American."

"Is anybody making any guesses who Yemlin wants me to kill?"

"Not yet. Leastways they've put nothing in their computers that I can find. But this morning Lynch sent a second query about you to Ryan. The French can't find you and they'd like the CIA to help."

"Have they ordered my expulsion from France?"

"It doesn't sound like it. They just want to talk to you, that's all."

"How about you? Has your name come up?"

"Knock on wood, but not yet," Rencke said laughing. "I still have my super virus in place and the silly bastards don't suspect a thing. But if they push me the CIA's entire computer system will crash, and crash good. Maybe *for* good."

"You'd do it, too."

"Why not? I've had to start over. It's good for the soul. Maybe they wouldn't be so arrogant, because good old Rick Ames didn't teach them a damn thing."

"I need some more information," McGarvey said.

"Leonid Chernov," Rencke said matter-of-factly. It was as if he could read minds. "You've got the whole enchilada, which worries me too. You're going to have to go head-to-head with him, but nobody knows anything about him. Not the CIA, nobody."

"How about the old KGB computer files?"

"Ha," Rencke said. "You ever try running through maple syrup on a cold day, Mac? It'd be easier than trying to wade through the mess they've created for themselves."

"It's a big organization, Otto. Some of their systems must be up and running."

"Without a central director, or a specific CPU for me to start from, I'd have to initiate a program search for every possible telephone number combination in Moscow. I could do it, but it might take a while. Maybe fifty years, give or take a decade."

"What if I get you a number?"

"Then we're in. Leastways through the first portal. Do you think Yemlin will hand over the keys to the castle just like that?"

"Won't hurt to ask," McGarvey said. "Keep your ears open, Otto, I'm going to be out of town for a couple of days."

"Will do, Mac. Good luck."

The desk clerk Martine was waiting for him in his room when he got back. She'd brought a bottle of wine and two glasses, and was propped up in bed, her shoes off, her silk blouse unbuttoned.

"You come as something of a surprise," McGarvey said, masking his irritation.

"You've been working entirely too hard, Monsieur," she said, and she giggled. She was tipsy.

McGarvey put his laptop on the writing table and glanced at his overnight bag. It had been tampered with, but he didn't think that the woman was a spy. She simply found him attractive and wanted to seduce him. And she was nosy.

"I am married."

"You don't wear a ring. And when you opened your wallet to withdraw your credit card I saw no photos of your wife or children." She smiled coyly at him over the rim of her wine glass, and shifted on the bed, parting her shapely legs. "You don't carry much clothing for a man who travels so much."

If she'd been in his overnight bag, she'd seen the spare magazines of ammunition. She wouldn't have recognized the silencer for what it was, because it was disguised as a working flashlight. But she knew that he wasn't a writer.

"What do you expect me to do?"

She set her wine glass aside. "Make love to me," she said huskily. "Dangerous men excite me. And from the moment I saw you I knew you were such a creature. Maybe you are a policeman here on a secret investigation. Or perhaps a private detective. Maybe even a spy."

McGarvey took off his jacket, then poured a glass of wine for himself. He sat on the edge of the bed and brushed his fingertips across her lips. She shivered.

"What will the management do if they find out that you're snooping around and trying to seduce the guests?"

"They'd certainly fire me. That wouldn't be so good. I'm not a wealthy woman."

McGarvey smiled. "Then we both have a secret to keep." He took a drink of his wine, and then opened her blouse and kissed the tops of her breasts.

She arched into him, a soft moan escaping her lips. "Don't hurt me," she cooed. "Not too much."

En Route To Helsinki

McGarvey checked out of his hotel around eight in the morning after securing his gun and two spare magazines of ammunition in a special compartment of his fake laptop computer that Rencke had designed and constructed for him. The compartment was shielded with sections of lead foil that appeared to airport security scanners as electronic circuitry. The computer would have to be completely stripped down to reveal what it contained. If it was turned on, the screen would light up with a convincing display. But that's all it would do. Instead of innards, the device only contained his weapon and spare ammunition.

He walked over to the car park, retrieved his Avis Renault, and was on the busy N2, heading north, past Le Bourget Airport by 9:00 A.M., the morning extremely pleasant.

Sometime over the past two days he had made his final decision to go ahead with the assassination of Tarankov, though he'd known that he would probably do it after Rencke had shown him his probability program. He no longer maintained any self-doubts, nor was he going to beat himself up over the decision. Second thoughts would come much later; in the night when he would see the faces of every person he'd ever killed, Tarankov's would be included.

He only had the vaguest idea how he was going to do it, and get away. But he knew from long experience that the solution would come to him in due time, and that he would recognize it when it arrived. He also knew that before such a solution became evident he was going to have to do more research. A lot more.

The truck stop on the outskirts of Maubeuge, where he stopped to have a quick lunch, was smoky and noisy, but the food was very good as it was at most French waysides.

By noon he was across the border into Belgium, the customs officer waving him through when McGarvey held up his Belgian passport, and seventy minutes later he was parking his car in the long term ramp at Brussels' Zaventem National Airport on the northeast outskirts of the city.

His bags were passed through airport security without a problem, and he got lucky with a Finnair flight departing at 3:00 P.M. He wanted to avoid, as much as possible, using his Allain papers in Belgium, because under any kind of questioning by the local authorities it would be obvious that he was not a Belgian. But the clerks at Finnair had no reason to question his nationality.

Because of the time difference it wasn't until 8:00 P.M. when he landed at Helsinki's Vantaa Airport, the weather here overcast, blustery and sharply colder than in Paris. He was passed through customs with no delay, though the officer did take an interest in his computer. By 9:30 P.M., he'd checked into the Strand Inter-Continental Hotel next to the old city downtown on the waterfront, and was dining on an excellent grilled salmon, with a very good bottle of French white wine.

Afterward he went down to one of the pay phones in the soaring atrium lobby, and direct-dialed Viktor Yemlin's apartment in Moscow. A noisy group of Russian businessmen were drinking and laughing around the fireplace across from McGarvey. The women with them were all young and expensively dressed. Even from a distance it was easy to determine that they were probably very high-priced call girls. The men were Russia's new millionaires; the women its entrepreneurs.

Yemlin answered his telephone on the third ring. *"Da."*

"Hello."

Yemlin didn't reply for several seconds. Music played in the background. "I think you have the wrong number. You want 228–0712." He broke the connection.

McGarvey hung up, and walked across the lobby to the bar where he ordered a cognac and lit a cigarette. Yemlin's line wasn't secure. The number he wanted to use was probably located some distance from his apartment. Possibly a pay phone. The FSK couldn't monitor every pay phone in the city, but given a little time, say a half-hour, they could isolate a specific number and tap it, which meant Yemlin would be standing by no later than fifteen minutes from now.

The cocktail waitress serving the group by the fireplace came back to the bar to order another round of drinks. She glanced at McGarvey, who smiled.

"Sounds like they're having fun," he said in English.

"They're Russians," she replied disdainfully. "I'm trying to get them to move their party up to the pool."

"Aren't they tipping very well?"

"Just fine," she said, smiling a little. "I'm just hoping they'll all drown up there."

"Good luck."

The bartender came to fill her order, and fifteen minutes later McGarvey went back to the pay phone and called the Moscow number.

Yemlin answered on the first ring. He sounded out of breath. "This is 228–0712," he said.

"Who is monitoring your home phone?" McGarvey asked.

"Possibly no one, this is just a precaution. Are you here in Moscow?"

"I'm in Helsinki. How soon can you get here? We need to talk."

"Are you taking the . . . package?"

"How soon can you be here?" McGarvey repeated evenly. He could hear the strain in Yemlin's voice.

"I'll take the morning flight. I can be there by noon."

"Will you be missed?"

Yemlin's laugh was short and sharp. "No one misses anything here any-more. Where do you want to meet?"

"Kaivopuisto. Enter from the southwest." McGarvey hung up, then went back to the bar where he had another cognac before going up to his room for the night. As he passed the Russian group one of them said something to the cocktail waitress, who dropped her tray, then spun around and rushed away. McGarvey didn't break stride, though he wanted to go over and punch the boorish, loud-mouthed bastard in the mouth.

Kaivopuisto

Helsinki's most elegant district on the waterfront was home to a number of foreign diplomats, and was maintained like a well-manicured park. On a pleasant day half of Helsinki took their walks here because it was so pretty. In the early days McGarvey had spent a month recuperating in Helsinki after an assignment that had gone bad in Leningrad. He'd often come down to the waterfront and he still remembered the area pretty well.

The day was raw. A chill wind drove spits of snow almost horizontally under a leaden sky. Still there were a number of people bundled up and walking through the district.

McGarvey had purchased a down-filled nylon jacket from a department store near the hotel, and by one o'clock, when Yemlin finally showed up, he wished he'd bought a warm hat and gloves as well. He tailed the Russian for ten minutes to make sure he'd come in clean, and then caught up with him halfway across the park.

"Did you know my parents?" McGarvey asked, falling in beside Yemlin.

"They were before my time, Kirk," Yemlin said. He was professional enough not to have reacted in an obvious manner when McGarvey suddenly showed up in disguise. "But I'd heard about them from General Baranov. He told me that it was a supreme irony that in some respects he had created you by planting false information about your parents being spies for us."

"You didn't give me much proof," McGarvey said. He'd destroyed the documents on Saturday before he went back to the apartment, and he had tried to put the news out of his mind.

"There is no more. Everything else died when you killed Baranov. No-body's around from those days who remembers anything. I'm sure there isn't much more in your own records beyond what Baranov planted. It was John Trotter's doing. But you knew that."

Trotter was an old friend who'd worked as Deputy Director of Opera-tions. In the end he'd betrayed them all, and his last act had been an attempt to kill McGarvey.

"Then you could be jerking me around here too, Viktor Pavlovich. You bastards invented the game."

"No," Yemlin said sadly, studying McGarvey's face. "But we were masters at it. We really didn't have much else. You know yourself that most of the West's estimates of our military and nuclear capabilities were inflated so that the Pentagon could justify its own budget."

It was true, McGarvey thought. And Tarankov, if he came to power, would start the cycle all over again.

"I believe in my heart, Kirk, that your parents were not the spies that you were led to believe they were. I don't know enough of the details to understand why Baranov ran that kind of an operation. I just know what he did. And if you'd thought about it then, you would have seen Baranov's touch. It was his style. A lot of us admired him."

They walked for a couple of minutes in silence. Deeper in the park they were somewhat sheltered from the wind, and there were even more Finns out walking on their lunch hours.

"This will be the last time we meet," McGarvey said. "I want you to make no attempt to try to communicate with me, or find me no matter what happens." McGarvey looked into Yemlin's eyes. "No matter what, Viktor Pavlovich, do you understand?"

"You're going to do it? You're going to assassinate Tarankov?"

"Yes."

"When?" Yemlin asked, his face alive with expression.

"Sometime before the June elections. Sooner if it looks as if he'll try a coup d'etat."

"You'll need help. I can pull enough strings in the SVR to supply you with information on Tarankov's movements."

"No," McGarvey said. "You're going back to Moscow as if nothing ever happened. You've never seen me, you've never discussed anything like this with me, and you will discuss this with no one."

"Impossible," Yemlin said, shaking his head. "Sukhoruchkin and Shevardnadze know everything."

"Then I'll call it off—"

"Please listen to me, Kirk. These men have just as much stake in this as I do. We've already laid our lives on the line. It was us three who discussed and approved hiring you to kill Tarankov. If you fall so do we. They have to be told. But I swear to you no one else in Russia, or anywhere else for that matter, knows what we've asked you to do. They haven't breathed a word, even hinted about it, to anyone. I swear it."

McGarvey thought about it for a moment. "You may tell them that I've accepted the job, but nothing else. Not that we met here, not my timetable, nothing. I won't go any further than that, because as you say, lives are on the line. And mine is more precious to me than yours. You'll either agree to this, or you'll have to find someone else."

"There is no one else," Yemlin said heavily. "I agree. What about money?"

"One million dollars," McGarvey said. He handed Yemlin a slip of paper with a seven-digit number written on it. "This is my account at Barclay's on Guernsey. British pounds, Swiss francs or American dollars."

"I'll have it there before I leave Helsinki today," Yemlin said. "What else?"

"The SVR must have a central data processing center that shares information with the FSK and the Militia."

"Of course."

"I want the telephone number."

Yemlin pulled up short, and his eyes narrowed. "Even if I knew that number it wouldn't do you any good without the proper access codes. Those I can't get."

"Nonetheless I want it."

"Assuming I can come up with the number, how do I get it to you?"

"Place an ad in the personals column of *Le Figaro* starting in three days. Say: Julius loves you, please call at once. Invert the telephone number and include it."

"I can't guarantee anything, Mac, but I'll do my best," Yemlin said. They started to walk again. "What about identity papers and travel documents? I can help with that."

"I'll get my own."

"Weapons?"

McGarvey shook his head.

"A safehouse in Moscow in case you have to go underground?"

They stopped again. "You've been in the business long enough to know that the bigger the organization, the greater are the chances for a leak. And right now the SVR and every other department in Russia is riddled with Tarankov's spies and informers. I'll work alone."

"I caught you once."

McGarvey smiled. "Yes, you did, Viktor Pavlovich. But things were different then. I was a lot younger, and the KGB was a lot better."

Yemlin agreed glumly. "In Paris you told me that the odds of success were a thousand to one against an assassin. What's changed your mind?"

"Nothing," McGarvey said. "If anything I think the odds are worse, and will get worse the longer we wait. If Tarankov takes over the government either by elections or by force, he'll be even harder to kill."

Yemlin looked down the broad boulevard the way they'd come. "As it is the aftermath will be terrible. I don't know if Russia will survive." His resolve seemed to stiffen and he turned back to McGarvey. "I do know that unless Tarankov is killed we will certainly not survive as a democracy."

"You're sure this is what you want?" McGarvey asked. "Because once we part here it will be too late to change your mind."

Yemlin nodded after a moment, and he shook McGarvey's hand. "Goodbye, Kirk. God go with you."

TWELVE

Washington

The National Press Club's main ballroom was all aglitter for the annual Person of the Year banquet, although the several hundred journalists and diplomats paid scant attention to the fine linen, silver and porcelain, they'd seen it before, often.

Word was out that President Lindsay would be given the honor this year (eighteen months late) for his international policies including the handling of the Japanese trade issues. For the first time since World War II the U.S. balance of trade with Japan was heading in the right direction. No one expected parity in the near future but Lindsay was taking the country in that direction.

It was a little before nine in the evening, and although the President and Mrs. Lindsay weren't scheduled to arrive until 9:45 P.M., dinner was winding down and dancing had begun.

Howard Ryan and his stunningly dressed wife, Evangeline, had just finished a dance and were heading back to the table they shared with Senate
Majority Leader Chilton Wood and his wife, J3 Admiral Stewart Phipps and
his wife and Bob Castle, political columnist for the *New York Times*, when
Ryan's assistant DDO, Tom Moore, and his dowdy wife Doris intercepted
them.

"You two cut a fine figure out there," Moore said.

"We're defined by our social graces," Ryan said pompously. He kissed
Doris on the cheek. "If your dance card isn't filled, put my name on it."

"Thanks for asking, Howard, but I have a feeling that Evangeline and I
are going to be deserted tonight," Doris said. She seemed resigned.

Ryan shot Moore a questioning look. His assistant was worried.

"Why don't you and Doris go back to our table and have another glass
of wine," Ryan told his wife. "Tom and I will join you ladies in a couple of
minutes."

"Don't strand us here, Howard," Evangeline warned, and she and Doris
headed back to the table. She did not share her husband's love for intrigue.

"This better be good," Ryan told his assistant.

"It's much worse than that, Howard. Believe me," Moore said. "My car
is in front. I suggest we go for a ride."

Ryan was annoyed. He wanted to see the President again, but Moore's
obvious agitation was worrisome. They walked outside, got into the assistant
DDO's car, and pulled away, merging with traffic on 14th Street.

"I just came from Langley," Moore said. "Farley Smith caught me as
Doris and I were leaving the house. He must have missed you by only a
couple of minutes."

Smith was chief of the CIA's archives section where the agency's most
highly classified records and historical documents were stored. He was working on deep background for Ryan's follow-up report to the President on
sending an envoy to Tarankov.

"What has he come up with?" Ryan asked.

"We've got trouble, Howard," Moore replied. "Not just the DO, but the
entire agency. If this breaks, the remainder of our careers will be spent on
the Hill answering some tough questions that'll make the Iran-Contra fiasco
look like a tempest in a teacup."

He stopped for a red light and looked over at Ryan. "What's the worst
thing you can think of that could happen to us in this operation? The absolute worst piece of information."

"Don't play games, Tom. Lay it out for me."

"Tarankov is ours. Or was."

Ryan was stunned. "What are you talking about?"

"In the seventies his code name was CKHAMMER," Moore said. The
CK digraph was an old CIA indicator that the code named person was a
particularly sensitive Soviet or Eastern bloc intelligence source.

"He spied for us?" Ryan asked, thunderstruck.

"While he was in the missile service. His parents ran into trouble with the KGB, and were sentenced to ten years in a Siberian gulag. They were friends of the Sakharovs. Our Moscow COS at the time, Bob Burns, assigned a case officer to see if Major Tarankov could be turned. He was, and until he was transferred out of the service he apparently provided us with some pretty good information."

"Then we have the bastard," Ryan said triumphantly. "We'll get a message to him to back off, or we expose what he was to the Russian people. It'll ruin him." Ryan had another thought. "Do we have proof? Photographs? Documents? Signatures?"

"Presumably, but it's all worthless, because there's more."

"What more can there be?" Ryan demanded. "The son of a bitch was a spy. His people can't trust him. Hell, we'll even offer him political asylum. We can dump him in Haiti, or maybe Panama where he'd be out of everyone's hair."

"Money. A lot of it. Moscow station had an open checkbook for a few years back then, because of the SDI thing. Word was that the Russians were way ahead of us on research. Farley is still digging, but he thinks that rumor may have gotten started on the basis of false information Tarankov sent us."

"Where are you going with this?"

"Over a nine year period we gave Tarankov, and a supposed network of spies under his direction, more than seventy million dollars. All of it black, none of it authorized by, or even known about on the Hill or the White House."

"He used the money to buy that goddamned train."

"It would appear so."

"Nothing has changed—"

"We can't send an envoy to Tarankov. He'd just laugh in our faces. Imperialist bastards who tried to buy Russia for seventy million. It would backfire on us. It would set our foreign policy back a hundred years."

They came around the corner on K Street a block from the National Press Club.

"We have to move very carefully, Howard," Moore said. "Tarankov must be arrested and put on trial as soon as possible. Before the June elections."

"Our involvement will come out in any trial."

"It won't matter," Moore interjected. "As long as we're not involved with him now we can deny everything. Tarankov will come out sounding like a desperate man clutching at straws."

"The President wants to send me as the envoy."

"You'll have to convince him differently. We cannot be seen interfering in Russian internal affairs. It would do us a great deal of damage."

Ryan had another thought. "Who else knows about this?"

"Nobody. And Farley had the good grace not to mention sending this upstairs to the director's office."

"Murphy has to be told."

"That's your job, Howard."

Damned right, Ryan thought. "And your job is to keep a lid on this thing. I want you to convince Farley that I mean business. If so much as a hint of this comes out of his office I'll nail his ass to the barn door."

"Of course."

"Where's the file at this moment?"

"In my safe."

"I want it on my desk at eight sharp. I'll see the general at nine. He's due back from New York sometime tonight."

CIA Headquarters

It was a few minutes before nine when the Deputy Director of Central Intelligence Lawrence Danielle called Ryan's office. "We're here, are you ready?"

"I'm on my way," Ryan said. "Has Technical Services scanned his office?"

"They just left."

He checked his pocket watch, buttoned up his coat and took the Tarankov file recovered in a D.D.O. EYES ONLY gray folder with a blue border on each page up to the seventh floor. He'd had a sleepless night worrying about what he would to have to face this morning. And reading the material Moore had brought over, he decided that his assistant had not exaggerated.

Ryan's specialty, among others, was turning negatives into pluses. This time, however, he was out of ideas except one, and that was when the play got too hot you always handed the ball over to someone else. It was one of his axioms for survival.

Roland Murphy was having coffee at his desk while he watched the 9:00 A.M. news reports from CNN and the three major news networks on a multiscreen TV monitor, as he did every morning. He was a large man with prizefighter's arms and dark eyebrows over deep-set eyes. He was one of the toughest men ever to sit behind that desk, and no one who'd ever come up against him thought any differently.

With him were the aging, but still effective, Danielle who'd been in the business for more than thirty years; the dapper dresser Tommy Doyle, who was Deputy Director of Intelligence; and Carleton Patterson, the patrician New York lawyer whom Ryan had recommended to take over as general counsel.

Murphy's eyes strayed to the file folder. "Has something happened overnight, Howard?"

"In a manner of speaking, General," Ryan said, closing the door. "I suggest that you ask not to be disturbed, and that you shut off the tape recorder."

Murphy's eyebrows rose, but he called his secretary and told her to hold everything until further notice, then opened a desk drawer and flipped a switch. "We're clean and isolated," he said. "You have our attention."

Ryan sat down in the empty chair and laid the file folder on the edge of Murphy's desk. Nobody made a move to reach for it. "The President must be convinced not to send an envoy as I originally suggested to speak with Yevgenni Tarankov."

Murphy studied Ryan's eyes. "If you feel that strongly about it, we'll send someone else. I don't think that will be a major stumbling block."

"No, Mr. Director, we can't send anybody to see him, unless or until he becomes President of Russia by whatever means. To do so would irreparably harm the United States, and this agency specifically. Something has come up."

"Who knows about this?" Patterson asked softly.

"Tom Moore and Farley Smith."

"Archives?"

Ryan nodded.

"No one else on your staff, or Smith's staff knows anything?" Patterson asked.

"That's correct."

"What is it, Howard? What dark secret have you stumbled upon?" Danielle asked.

"I've come up with incontrovertible proof that in the seventies and early eighties Tarankov spied on his own government for the United States. Specifically for a case officer working out of Moscow Station under Bob Burns."

"I'll be damned," Doyle said.

Murphy and Danielle exchanged glances. "It was before my time, Lawrence," Murphy said. "Did you know anything about it?"

"No. It must have been a soft operation."

"His code name was CKHAMMER," Ryan said. "Someone thought he was important."

"I didn't know anything about it, Howard," Danielle said mildly, but there was a dangerous edge to his voice. He'd played this game so often that he was a master at it. "What's your point?"

"His operation was called LOOKUP, and over nine years we paid him nearly seventy million dollars for SDI information. All of it black. Money he used to buy the armored train he's terrorizing the countryside with. It makes for some disturbing possibilities."

"That puts a hell of a spin on the situation over there," Murphy said. "How do you see it?"

"We certainly can't open a dialogue with him now," Ryan said. "It could backfire in our faces. He'd accuse us of trying to bring down Kabatov's government."

"He's one of us," Doyle said.

"Not any longer," Ryan shot back. "But if Kabatov is successful in arresting him and bringing him to trial we'll be out of the woods."

"He wouldn't use his relationship with us as a defense, that's for damned sure," Murphy said. "But he could end up asking us for asylum."

"Which we'd deny him," Ryan said.

"Doesn't say much for how we treat the people who've worked for us," Danielle suggested.

"Tarankov is no friend of ours," Ryan replied sharply. "He never was. In those days we were helping a lot of questionable people. Batista then Castro, Noriega, Marcos. It's a big number, and most of the decisions were poorly thought out. It gave us a bad reputation which we're just beginning to live down. If the truth came out about our involvement with Tarankov it would push back the clock, and no one would come out smelling like a rose."

"I'll have to brief the President—"

"No, sir," Ryan interrupted. "I think that would unnecessarily complicate matters. Let me work up a new proposal showing why sending an envoy to Tarankov isn't such a good idea after all. He wasn't all that keen on it in the first place."

"You'll come out with egg on your face for waffling," Murphy warned.

"Better me than the agency."

Danielle gave him an amused look of barely concealed contempt. "I'd like to see that proposal before we kick it over to the White House."

"We'll all take a look," Murphy said, before Ryan could respond. "The President will have to be convinced that we must support Prime Minister Kabatov's government."

"At all costs," Ryan said. "It's our only course."

"Is any of that file in the computer?" Danielle asked.

"No," Ryan said. "Smith got this from the warehouse. It's the only copy."

"How about cross-references?"

"He's pulling them now."

"When he's dug everything out, we'll put a fifty-year seal on the material," Danielle said.

"We'll destroy the files," Ryan said.

Danielle shook his head. "We've done questionable things, Mr. Ryan. But we don't destroy records, because in the end we're accountable to the public."

"No—" Ryan said.

"I have to overrule you on this one, Howard," Murphy said. "Lawrence is right. We'll let the historians struggle with it fifty years from now, but we won't alter the record."

"As you wish, Mr. Director," Ryan said darkly.

"Then we all have work to do. I suggest we get to it."

Tom Moore came over when Ryan got back to his office. "Did they go for it?" he asked.

"They didn't have any choice," Ryan replied harshly. "As soon as Smith is finished with his search, I want everything hand-delivered to me."

"Are we going to destroy it?"

"No. It's going under a fifty-year seal."

"Just as well," Moore said.

"In the meantime I'll put something together for Murphy to take over to the White House. I'll need comprehensive reports on Kabatov's government, on Yeltsin's assassination, and a sanitized version of Tarankov's background."

"Will do."

"I'll need it yesterday, Tom."

"I'll get on it right away," Moore assured him. He turned to go, but stopped at the door. "This business with the French and McGarvey doesn't want to go away. How far do we want to take it?"

Ryan's stomach knotted up, and he absently touched the scar on his chin. "Maybe it was McGarvey who killed Yeltsin. I wouldn't put it past the bastard."

"The timing is wrong. But the French are worried that the Russians have hired McGarvey to kill someone in France."

"Arrest him, and put him on a plane back here. We'll pick him up at the airport."

Moore shook his head. "That's just the problem. They can't find him. Seems as if he's gone to ground."

Ryan looked up at his assistant deputy director with renewed interest. Hate for McGarvey still burned very hotly in his gut. "Has he broken any French laws?"

"Presumably not. They merely want to talk to him. He was living with a French intelligence officer who was keeping tabs on him, but he kicked her out and disappeared."

Ryan could sense trouble. It was McGarvey's pattern. When he was given an assignment the first thing he did was drop out of sight. The son of a bitch was back in the field. He still hadn't learned his lesson.

"We need to give them all the help we can. Have Tom Lynch do what he can for them. But it's a safe bet that some Russian has hired him to kill someone. Probably a mafia thing. Or, maybe he's even decided to work for Tarankov, and is stalking Prime Minister Kabatov. With a man like McGarvey anything is possible."

"I'll call Lynch and talk to him personally," Moore said.

"Wait," Ryan said. He'd had another thought. "Correct me if I'm wrong, but didn't we hire Elizabeth McGarvey as a translator over my objections a few months ago?"

Moore shrugged. "Is she some relation?"

"His daughter," Ryan said. "Find out if she's on the payroll. Maybe we'll borrow her for this one." Ryan smiled. "Who better to find a father, than his daughter?"

"Isn't that a little extreme, Howard? She's done nothing to harm the Agency has she?"

"We're not going to harm her," Ryan replied, holding his anger in check. "I'll simply explain to her that we'd like to speak to her father, but that he's gone to ground. We'd like her help getting a message to him. Nothing more than that, Tom."

THIRTEEN

Moscow

McGarvey's train pulled into the old Leningrad Station at precisely 8:55 in the morning, and he took his two bags inside where he had a glass of beer, some black bread and caviar at the stand-up counter.

Customs, crossing the border from Finland, was much less stringent by rail than by air. Russian officers had come aboard outside Vyborg in the early evening just after supper to check tickets, passports and luggage. The train was full and they wanted to get back to their own meals, so they didn't spend much time opening baggage, though they admired McGarvey's computer, and even switched on his silencer disguised as a flashlight. It was bulky, but it worked.

He'd booked a private sleeping car, and after they'd passed through St. Petersburg he went to bed and had a reasonably restful sleep, though being back in Russia again put him on edge. It was tradecraft. In the old days this was called being in "badland," where even a small mistake could cost you your freedom or your life.

There was nothing pretty about the station. It had been built during the Stalin era, and although it was very large and always busy, it was drab and gray. Lenin's railway car was on permanent display track side, and in the vaulted arrivals hall a huge area had been set aside for booksellers to display their wares. They had a lot of traffic this morning. The last time McGarvey had been here there'd been more KGB officers than customers, but now everything was different. If anything, the people looked even more drab and depressed than they had under the old Communist regime, but they didn't have to constantly look over their shoulders.

Even the food had been better, McGarvey thought, finishing his watery beer, though not by much.

He picked up his bags, bought a Moscow guidebook in French from one of the foreign currency shops, and made his way through the crowds to the taxi stands out front.

The weather was horrible, twenty degrees colder than Helsinki and snowing, though it wasn't as windy. Big piles of filthy snow were everywhere, and the people on the streets were sullen. Traffic was monumental. No one paid any attention to stop lights or speed limits. Pedestrians surged across the broad Komsomol Prospekt at irregular intervals forcing the traffic to a standstill by the sheer press of bodies. Soldiers seemed to be everywhere, many of them in shabby uniforms, and many of them drunk despite the early hour.

Reading about conditions here and seeing television reports on the situation did not convey the true nature of what Moscow, and presumably the rest of Russia, had become. Even the most casual observer couldn't help but see that the country was ripe for revolution. The problem was no one had any idea which way it would go when it came.

McGarvey took a cab to the newly refurbished Metropol Hotel on Marx Prospekt downtown. The Strand Inter-Continental in Helsinki had called ahead and reserved a room for him for three days. The brawny, mean-looking cabby was in a foul mood and cursed everybody and everything in his path, cutting off drivers, nearly running over pedestrians, and even pulling up on the sidewalk at one point to get around a traffic snarl.

When they pulled up at the hotel he demanded a hundred dollars from McGarvey who told him in French that he didn't understand. The driver switched to guttural French and demanded 500 francs.

"Ce n'est pas possible," McGarvey said and he handed the driver a hundred-franc note.

For a second the man didn't seem to comprehend what was happening, but then his face turned red. "Fuck your mother," he swore in Russian, and he snatched a machete off the seat beside him.

Before he could swing it around, McGarvey smashed the side of his hand into the cabby's collar bone at the base of his neck, then clapped the palms of his hands over the man's ears.

The cabby reared back, screaming in pain. He dropped the machete and clutched at his head.

"*Merci,*" McGarvey said pleasantly. "*Au revoir.*" He climbed out of the taxi, got his bags and walked into the hotel lobby leaving the cabby screaming obscenities in the driveway, and the doorman completely indifferent.

The turn-of-the-century hotel had been completely redone a few years ago and was good even by western standards, though the service was somewhat indifferent. It took the pock-faced clerk fifteen minutes to find McGarvey's reservations under the name Pierre Allain, and another twenty minutes to run his credit card through the terminal. There was no bellman, so McGarvey took his own bags up to his old-fashioned but very well furnished room on the ninth floor. It had a spectacular view of the city looking toward the Kremlin's walls and towers. A couple of minutes later a bellman in uniform showed up. He closed the curtains that McGarvey had opened, then opened them again, turned on all the lights in the room and the bathroom, flushed the toilet and checked the waterflow in the sink and tub, then turned on the television full blast, and held out his hand for a tip.

McGarvey gave the man a few francs.

"Thanks," he said in English. "You speak English?"

"A little."

"That's good. Anything you need, anything whatever, you just call me. Name's Artur. Women, coke, maybe you Belgians like little boys? Call me, you'll see."

"I'll keep you in mind, Artur."

The bellman gave him a long, appraising look, then left the room.

McGarvey locked the door, then searched the room for bugs, but he didn't find any. Either they weren't there because the successor to the KGB didn't care, something he doubted, or they'd been buried in the walls when the hotel was refurbished. The main thing was there were no hidden closed-circuit television cameras.

He opened his laptop, and removed the bottom panel, revealing his pistol and spare magazines. He pocketed one of the magazines, then tested the Walther's action, stuffed it in his belt at the small of his back, and reassembled the computer.

McGarvey had purchased a pair of gloves, a Russian fur hat and a pair of warm hiking shoes from the department store around the corner from his hotel in Helsinki. He changed into the heavier shoes, stuffed the Moscow guidebook in his coat pocket and left the hotel.

Killing Tarankov and getting away presented a number of challenging problems, not the least of which was the when and the where. The man and his entourage were constantly on the move. And whenever he roared into a city he was immediately surrounded by thousands, sometimes even tens of thousands of adoring people. He was worshiped like a god, and his people took full advantage of this fact, in effect using the crowds as a buffer against any would-be assassin. It was the reverse of how other security services operated. But it worked.

On the way from Helsinki, McGarvey had figured out the second half of that problem. The where would be here in Moscow, because if Tarankov meant to take over the government, it was here he'd have to come. Terrorizing every other city in Russia would and already had taken him a long way. But Moscow had always been the center of Russia. Even when the governments before the revolution were housed in St. Petersburg, Moscow was still the heart and soul of Russia. Holy Moscow. With the breakup of the Soviet Union nothing had changed in that respect.

And Moscow had its center, Red Square.

McGarvey stood in front of the big department store G.U.M. and stared across the broad square at Lenin's Tomb at the base of the Kremlin. He'd been here during his tenure at Moscow Station early in his career, and on several occasions since. He'd last been here eighteen months ago. And in that short time the city had gone sharply downhill, though traffic was worse. The entire nation was starving to death, but cars were everywhere, Russian built Ladas and Zhigulis, plus a surprisingly high number of Mercedes and BMWs. What little middle class there'd been before the breakup of the Soviet Union was almost completely gone now, leaving Russians stratified into the very poor or the very rich. There was no in between.

The system had failed, completely and miserably, and yet this morning despite the horrible weather the line in front of Lenin's Mausoleum was as long as it had ever been. Young people looking for something to believe in, and old people who knew what they believed in and desperately wanted to regain the old ways.

Lenin's Mausoleum and Red Square, free of anything but pedestrian traffic or official vehicles, seemed to be the only constants left in Moscow. The only bits of the old days that had remained, by outward appearances, the same.

He walked across the square where he bought a bouquet of wilted flowers from an old babushka at a kiosk, and joined the line for Lenin's tomb in front of the red brick History Museum opposite the entrance to the Alexandrovsky Garden. It took about twenty minutes until he got to the doors. Since he was obviously a foreigner, he had to show his passport. The people in line behind him stopped a respectful distance away as he approached Lenin's embalmed body in its glass-topped coffin, studied the corpse's surprisingly intact features, then laid his flowers with the others on the marble floor. As he turned to leave, one of the uniformed guards came over, smiled sadly, and shook his hand.

"*Merci, monsieur,*" he said gently.

"He was a great man. Many of us in Belgium admire what he stood for,"

McGarvey said humbly. He glanced toward the broad marble stairs at the back. "It would be an honor to be allowed to stand on the balcony where so many great men have watched the May Day parades. Is it permitted?"

"For you we will make an exception," the guard replied. He led McGarvey up to the wind-swept balcony.

When Tarankov made his triumphal entry to Moscow it would be to this place. McGarvey looked out across the square, apparently lost in a vision of what it would be like to stand in front of the soldiers and tanks and rockets parading through the square while a million people watched. Overcome with emotion, he turned away and raised his eyes to the heavens. The Kremlin's brick walls rose above the mausoleum. McGarvey measured the firing angles and distances for a shooter placed somewhere on the wall above, and decided the shot would be an easy one. The problem would be getting away afterward. It would be difficult, perhaps even impossible.

"Thank you," he said turning back to the guard. "Perhaps someday you will have greatness returned to you."

The guard bridled, but then nodded. "We will, and sooner than those fools inside realize."

Back outside, McGarvey turned left and walked up the hill to the Sobakina Tower pedestrian gate at the northern corner of the Kremlin, bought a ticket for the grounds and, taking out his guide book, went in. The walls beneath the one-hundred-eighty-foot tower were twelve feet thick to hide a secret well and a passageway out of the fortress into the Neglinnaya River which flowed underground. He'd considered that a possible escape route. But access to the passageway was through a series of heavy steel gates in the tower, that on the day Tarankov made his triumphal entrance into Moscow would likely be heavily guarded. It would be possible to take out the guards and blow the gates. In the noise and confusion of Tarankov's appearance such activities might go unnoticed. But if he became trapped in the river passage it would be a simple matter for the authorities to wait at the Moscow River outlet for him to appear, and he would be captured. It would be impossible to take the underground river upstream.

But the Kremlin still intrigued him, because no one would expect Tarankov to be shot from behind. The problems here were threefold; getting past the heavy security, making the shot unobserved, possibly from the top of the Kremlin wall directly above and behind the speaker's balcony atop Lenin's mausoleum, easy if the only consideration were sight lines, and making good his escape for which he wanted several options. He didn't think he could rely on one escape route no matter how foolproof it seemed.

The few people wandering around the Kremlin paid him little attention as he sauntered past the Arsenal to the Senate Building, which backed the wall directly behind Lenin's tomb, to his left. From time to time he stopped, read from his tour book then looked up, as if he were trying to orient himself, while he studied the top floors of the building. The Senate was one of the few buildings in the Kremlin that were closed to the public. But with the proper credentials it would be possible to gain entrance to the building. He might be able to make his way to the roof from where a shot at Tarankov's back would be possible. Assuming that guards would not be placed on the roof against just such a possibility, he would still be faced with his escape after the kill.

Once Tarankov was down and the direction of the shot established, which might only take seconds, the Kremlin would be sealed. His only hope at that point would be blending in until the confusion subsided and the gates were once again open. It would mean he'd have to come up with foolproof documents and a rock-solid disguise—a shaky proposition at best. It left him no options, unless he had a set of papers and a disguise other than the one he used to gain entrance, or an alternate route over or beneath the walls.

There was something about this place that struck him more like a prison than the seat of government. It was a fortress which protected itself not only from without, but from within.

He looked at the problem from another direction as he continued past the Supreme Soviet building and headed toward the Spassky Tower gate which opened onto Red Square. If his objective was to get inside the Kremlin to assassinate someone, he would face the same problem: that of breaching the heavily guarded walls. He would have to come up with several alternatives to get inside, and then more options for getting out.

Stopping a moment to consult his guide book again, he studied the area between the Supreme Soviet and Senate buildings and the wall from which the Senate Tower rose. Lenin's Tomb was just on the other side. He made his decision. The Kremlin's walls, since they'd seen the last of Napoleon in 1812, had withstood every assault except those of a political nature. As intriguing as the possibility was taking Tarankov by surprise from behind, he dismissed it. He would kill Tarankov while the man made his speech atop Lenin's Mausoleum, but it would have to be done from outside, somewhere around Red Square, somewhere within a range that would give him a reasonable shot. Say two to three hundred yards.

McGarvey walked through Spassky Tower Gate back out to Red Square, snow now falling in earnest. The wind had picked up so that visibility was restricted. But rising out of the swirling snowstorm less than three hundred meters away were the fantastical shapes and colors of the domes of St. Basil's Cathedral. The building was to Russia what the Eiffel Tower was to France, a symbol of the nation's ties with the past. Turning, he studied the line in front of Lenin's Tomb and the speaker's balcony above. Tarankov would come here not only to face the million people who would crowd into Red Square, but also to face Russia's past. St. Basil's.

Pocketing his guidebook, McGarvey made his way across the square to the main entrance of the church where he bought a ticket and went inside the antechamber which housed a museum. A dozen people, some of them foreigners, studied the displays which depicted the history of the cathedral and the story of its construction. A cutaway model showed the layout of the entire structure which consisted of nine main chapels—the tall slope-roofed one in the middle, four big onion domes on the four corners and four smaller ones in between. All of the chapels were linked by a elevated gallery, and all of the chapels had exits that led either out onto Red Square or into the rest of the cathedral complex and a small garden.

The church was built on bedrock at the south end of Red Square, its foundations driven deep underground in an area honeycombed with subterranean rivers all flowing down to the Moscow River. The lower levels held crypts which in the late seventeenth century were used to house Russia's state treasury. Like the Kremlin, St. Basil's had also been a fortress of sorts, with its own dark secrets and underground passageways and escape routes.

McGarvey left the museum and walked into the main tower which was a forest of scaffolding rising one hundred and seven feet into the darkness. Directly above were the covered galleries connecting the other eight chapels, and at the rear were iron gates which led below to the crypts. Two old women stood near the front of the main chapel, their heads bowed in prayer.

On the day Tarankov arrived in Moscow, St. Basil's would be closed. The church had become too great a symbol of Russia's deeply religious past for it to remain open when he was giving his message for the future. There could only be one god in Holy Russia, and the Tarantula meant to be that god.

McGarvey climbed the stairs to the gallery on his left, and followed it around in a large circle to each of the other eight chapels, descending into each where he searched for and found the various ways outside.

Two hours later he was back in the main tower where he studied the locks leading into the crypts. They were massive, but made out of soft iron and could easily be blown by a very small amount of plastic explosive, or cut with bolt-cutters.

He looked up through the scaffolding. There would be no problem climbing to the top, where from one of the openings he would have a clear shot at Tarankov standing on the balcony above Lenin's Mausoleum.

From that point he would have a couple of minutes to make his way down out of the tower, where, depending on how organized the authorities were, he could descend into the crypts and make his escape through one of the underground passages, or make his way through one of the chapels and outside where he could lose himself in the confusion.

He had the where. Next he needed the when.

FOURTEEN

Moscow
The Kremlin

Viktor Yemlin sat across the broad conference table from Yuri Kabatov, who'd been appointed interim president, and Yeltsin's former chief of security Lieutenant-General Alexander Korzhakov, watching both men read copies of his overnight report. He'd been summoned to the office of the director of the SVR late last night where he'd been ordered to prepare a briefing for the president on the West's reaction to their concocted story about Yeltsin's death.

McGarvey was right, of course. The Americans did not believe the story. But to this point they continued to maintain the position that they did. President Lindsay was scheduled to attend the state funeral on Friday, and the western news media continued to report on Yeltsin's life, all but ignoring any references to Tarankov and the incident at the Riga Nuclear Power Station in Dzerzhinskiy. Yemlin used to admire the honest relationship the CIA apparently had with the President and Congress, until he'd come to learn that truth was highly subjective and depended on the political mood of the government body being reported to. Presidents of the United States and of Russia were alike in that they were mere men in difficult positions who wanted to hear what they wanted to hear.

He'd spent all night gathering the latest information from the analysts and translators in the various departments of the North American Division. By one in the morning it was 5:00 P.M. in Washington, and the first of the dailies from the Russian Embassy on 16th Street were coming in, along with the first late afternoon reports from the Russian delegation to the United Nations. As he'd learned to do, Yemlin refrained from any speculation. He merely presented the facts as they came to him, placing them in an outline that supported what Kabatov's new government wanted to believe.

By 6:00 A.M., he'd finished his first rough draft report, which ran to sixty-eight pages, with another three hundred pages of translations, mostly of articles that had appeared in the early editions of the *New York Times* and *Washington Post*.

By 8:00 A.M., the translations of ABC's, NBC's, CBS's and CNN's 11:00 P.M. news reports came across his desk, and he included them in his final report which was finally ready at 10:00 A.M., exactly one hour before he was scheduled to arrive at the Kremlin.

General Korzhakov finished first, and closed the report. He stared at Yemlin, his dark eyes burning, his thick lips pursed until President Kabatov also finished and looked up.

"The fiction seems to be holding," Kabatov said.

"It would appear so, Mr. President," Yemlin said tiredly. He was too old for all-night sessions. His eyes burned, his throat was sore and he felt as if he couldn't go on much longer before he had to get some rest.

"In any event it's in their best interest to go along with us so long as our problems remain internal," Korzhakov said, his voice flat and unemotional. "Has the SVR given thought to that? Because I'm sure that the CIA is watching us closer than ever."

"My division's efforts are directed toward North America, General," Yemlin said, after a careful moment. "We have detected no outward indications that the CIA or FBI have begun to take a more active role against our diplomats in Washington or New York." He shrugged. "As for internally, that is a matter for the FSK. General Yuryn could best address the issue."

"You're both still the KGB," Korzhakov burst out, angrily. "You communicate with each other."

"To this point, on this issue, my division has been given nothing. I assume that the service has managed to place an agent aboard Tarankov's train. But no one has said anything to us."

Korzhakov and Kabatov exchanged a glance, and the Russian president sat back, content to let his chief of security continue.

"Apparently there have been difficulties. The man they sent was found

last night—what was left of him—in a taxi parked in front of the Lubyanka."
Korzhakov ran his fingers through his thick black hair. "There is a leak at
high levels."

"It was expected."

"General Yuryn suspects that you may know something about it."

"My division—?"

"You personally," Korzhakov said bluntly. He opened a file folder. "On
the evening of 23 March you and Konstantin Sukhoruchkin took off aboard
an Air Federation passenger jet on a flight plan to Volgograd. In fact it is
believed that you flew to Tbilisi." Korzhakov looked up. "Can you tell us
the nature of your trip?"

Yemlin was stunned, but he was professional enough not to let it show.
In this business you always planned for the worst for which a partial truth
was sometimes more effective than a well-crafted lie. "We went to see Eduard Shevardnadze."

"You admit it?" President Kabatov demanded, rousing himself.

"*Da.* President Shevardnadze is an old friend, whose opinion I value
highly. I was troubled after President Yeltsin's assassination, as was Konstantin. We wanted some advice."

"In regards to what?" Korzhakov asked.

"Tarankov's chances for becoming President of Russia and starting us
back to the old ways," Yemlin said. "It would destroy us."

"I agree with that much at least," President Kabatov said. "But Shevardnadze is no friend of Russia's."

"I'm sorry, Mr. President, but he is not our enemy. Georgia has just as
much to fear from Tarankov as we do."

"What was his advice?" Korzhakov asked coolly.

"He gave none," Yemlin said heavily, letting his eyes slide to the dam-
nable file folder.

"Did you tell him the truth about Yeltsin's murder?"

"Yes," Yemlin said looking up defiantly.

"Traitor—"

"*Nyet*," Yemlin interrupted sharply. "I love Russia no less than you, Comrade General."

"What were you doing in Helsinki yesterday?"

Yemlin was glad that he was seated. He didn't think his legs would support
his weight. "Shopping," he replied. "I'm no traitor, but I'm no idealist either."

"Were you shopping in Paris last week as well?" Korzhakov asked after
a moment.

Yemlin forced himself to remain calm. If they knew anything substantive
they would have arrested him by now. This was General Yuryn's doing. He
was caught in the middle of a factional fight that had been brewing since
the KGB had been split into the internal intelligence service and the external
service. Yeltsin's murder was a catalyst that the SVR had planned using
against General Yuryn. The wily old fox was simply fighting back.

"Among other things," he said.

"What things?"

"As you probably know I own a small apartment in Paris."

"Do you have a mistress there as well, whom you're supporting?"

Yemlin refused to answer.

"A bank account, perhaps?" Korzhakov suggested. "You crafty old bastard, have you been salting away money in foreign banks all along?"

"No. Nor is that why you called me here today," Yemlin said looking into President Kabatov's eyes. Sudden understanding dawned on him. They were frightened, and they were clutching at straws. "I will not accept blame for the failures of the FSK or the Militia not only to protect President Yeltsin, but to arrest Tarankov."

Korzhakov flared but said nothing.

"Mr. President, if our government is divided, if we fight amongst ourselves, Tarankov will win," Yemlin said trying one last time to convince them that nothing less than the nation was at stake. "We're trying to become a nation of laws. That means laws for everyone, from kulaks to presidents."

"You've spent a lot of time in the West, Viktor Pavlovich. Is that what you learned?" Korzhakov asked. "Because if it is, then you are a naive man."

"I'm an old man who has given his life in service to his country. I would like peace now."

"Thank you for your report," Korzhakov said abruptly. "We'll expect to be updated should anything significant occur."

"Very well," Yemlin said. He rose and went to the door.

"Viktor Pavlovich," President Kabatov said. "We are not the enemy. Nor do we believe you are. But you have an enemy in General Yuryn. A powerful enemy. Take care of yourself."

"Thank you, Mr. President. I will."

Yemlin paused at the head of the broad granite stairs in front of the Senate Building, letting the sharp wind and harsh snow beating against his body clear his head. He was so mentally and physically tired that he felt detached, as if his skin didn't fit, and his feet weren't his own.

Russians loved intrigue. It was in the national spirit, as chess and poetry were, and he was just as guilty as the rest of them for deriving pleasure from playing the game. But in this instance they weren't talking about a mere intelligence coup. This time the future of Russia was at stake, and for one frightening moment he wished that he could recall McGarvey, or more accurately he wished that he could justify such a move to himself. But he could not.

Someone touched his elbow and he looked up, startled, into the sharply defined features of Moscow Mayor Vadim Cheremukhin.

"Viktor Pavlovich, you look like a man who could use some cheering up," Cheremukhin said. His face was flushed and even in the wind Yemlin could smell vodka on the man's breath.

"A good night's sleep."

"Time enough for that for both of us soon, hey?" Cheremukhin said. He was of the old school like Yemlin, but less of a moderate, although behind Kabatov he was among the most important men in Russia today. "Come on, we'll dismiss your driver and take my car over to the club. What you need is a steam bath, a rubdown, some good champagne and caviar, and then maybe a girl. You can sleep afterward."

Cheremukhin's private club, the Magesterium, had been constructed for his predecessor Yuri Luzhkov who'd complained that he had no place to go after hours. The Mafia had built it, along with a lot of other clubs throughout the country, for the new elite after the Soviet Union had disintegrated. Gangsters, movie stars, businessmen and politicians all had their own private sanctuaries that stressed physical security along with booze, women, casinos, and rat-races through neon-lit mazes. Anything went at the clubs; from drugs to little boys and from S&M to any other kind of kinky sex imaginable, and some that wasn't imaginable. The Magesterium provided all of that, plus good food, quiet rooms, subservient service, mostly from black African students recruited from Patrice Lumumba University, an excellent library and oak-lined conference rooms, reading nooks, a movie theater and a computer learning center.

"I think not," Yemlin protested. He'd been to some of the clubs, the Magesterium included. He found them to be too frantic for his own tastes. A symbol of some of what was wrong with Russia.

"Nonsense," Cheremukhin said. He waved Yemlin's driver off, and his Zil limousine slid in behind it. He took Yemlin by the arm and guided him down the stairs and into the back seat for the short ride over to the club.

Yemlin was too weary to fight him. A glass of champagne, a steam bath and a rubdown would be nice. Afterward he would make his own way home. He knew a number of men who'd succumbed to the club scene, their lives centered around their evenings like a drug addict's around his needle. He wasn't one of them.

"The center holds," Cheremukhin said, as they passed through Spassky gate into red square, and turned right down toward the river past St. Basil's.

Yemlin wasn't sure he'd heard Cheremukhin correctly, and was about to ask what he said, when out of the corner of his eye he spotted a familiar figure, and his blood froze. It was McGarvey crossing Red Square. He fought the overwhelming urge to turn around and look back, or let slip an outward sign that he'd just been shaken to the core. McGarvey here in Moscow. Already. It didn't seem possible.

"It's guys like you who're keeping everything together," Cheremukhin said. "Kabatov doesn't have a clue, and Korzhakov is almost as bad a prospect as Tarankov. But at least we've gotten rid of Yeltsin."

Yemlin focused on the Mayor. "What do you mean?"

"Haven't you heard?"

Yemlin shook his head. "I don't know what you're talking about."

"I thought that's why you were in the Kremlin. Didn't Kabatov send for you to ask your opinion? He's worried about the Americans, he doesn't know how they're going to take it."

"Take what?"

"Kabatov has been appointed chairman of the Communist Party. The center holds. He doesn't know what he's doing, but this time I think he's stumbled onto something. If we take over the Communist Party, Tarankov will have nowhere to go. It's what the Americans call an end run."

Yemlin's head was spinning. If McGarvey killed Tarankov the problem wouldn't be so acute. In the confusion and panic that would follow no one would take notice of Kabatov's stupid move. But he did not have the luxury of that assurance, nor could he let on even if he did. "Kabatov is a fool," he stammered.

"Agreed, but he can be controlled."

"By whom?" Yemlin responded angrily. "Tarankov will use it as further proof that democracy has failed. It might even force him to make his move sooner than the June elections."

Cheremukhin eyed Yemlin critically. "I see what you mean, but I don't agree with you. The Party is winning elections again because it's what the people want. But it's not the old Party."

"Kabatov is now President and Prime Minister of Russia as well as Party Chairman. Tarankov only has to topple one man to control everything. We've done his ground work for him. I'm sure he's quite pleased."

"He'll be arrested."

"Don't be a fool," Yemlin shot back before he could stop himself.

Cheremukhin's eyebrow rose. "Do you know something that we don't, Viktor Pavlovich?"

"No," Yemlin said. "But trying to arrest the Tarantula cost Yeltsin his life, and I don't think that Kabatov fully understands what he's up against."

"Some of us do, believe me," Cheremukhin said darkly.

"I hope so," Yemlin replied, distantly.

It was before noon, and the snowstorm had intensified, snarling traffic in the ordinary lanes. Cheremukhin's limousine sped across the river on the Great Stone Bridge in front of the Rossiya Hotel, the official lane empty in both directions. Yemlin had to fight the urge to turn and look over his shoulder at Red Square which in any event had already disappeared. It had begun. McGarvey was in the field. In the heart of Moscow staking out his killing field. Yemlin had a fair idea what McGarvey might be planning. But if Tarankov managed to get this far they might have already lost.

"We would like your help with this," Cheremukhin said. "You know a lot of people. I'm sure that you even know some of Tarankov's supporters in the SVR and FSK. There has to be a way."

"I'll do what I can."

"If you prefer not to work with Kabatov I'll do whatever I can to help. I have connections too. Just say the word and I'll pull strings."

"For now you can keep an eye on Korzhakov. I want to be informed when they plan on making their move against Tarankov."

"It won't be in Nizhny Novgorod, I can tell you that much," Cheremukhin said. "But I'll see what I can come up with. Kabatov trusts me."

The limousine pulled through the gates onto the private grounds of what once was a sewing machine factory. The parking lot was half-filled with Zils and Mercedes SELs. Guards dressed in American Marine combat fatigues and armed with M16 assault rifles were everywhere. The driver pulled up to the front doors, and they were escorted inside to a large reception area that looked like the lobby of a luxury resort hotel. Cheremukhin handed him over to a beautiful young black woman wearing a skimpy bikini beneath a transparent gauze jacket.

"Renée, I would like you to meet my friend Viktor. He is to be given anything he wants, and you'll put it on my tab," Cheremukhin said.

The young woman lit up in a smile as she took Yemlin's arm. She smelled of cinnamon and some other spice, her accent very charming. "My pleasure to meet you, Viktor."

"Start with some champagne, a bath, then a rubdown," Cheremukhin grinned. "After that, who knows? But he's tired, so he needs some peace and quiet."

Yemlin felt as if he were on the verge of collapse. So much had happened in the past week that he was in sensory overload. He wanted to sleep.

"Enjoy," Cheremukhin said, and he left.

"That Vadim is a good guy," Renée said innocently. "Whatever he says around here goes. So you just leave it to me, Viktor, okay?"

"Okay," Yemlin mumbled, too tired to do anything but go with the flow.

She led him down one of the thickly carpeted corridors, the lighting subdued. Soft music played from hidden speakers and she chatted like a magpie about everything from Paris fashions to the wonderful people she'd met since coming to the university. At one point he stumbled and she pulled him up, and put his arm around her thin shoulders, his fingertips brushing her breasts.

"Silly me going on like this while you, poor man, are nearly dead on your feet," she cooed. "But I have just the thing for your tired bones. You'll see. Just what the doctor ordered."

Although the club was busy there wasn't a hint of noise or activity back here. Renée brought him into a three-room suite luxuriously furnished, and led him immediately into a palatial bathroom with a huge sunken tub filled with steaming, scented water.

A moment later a young man dressed only in a white swimming suit came in behind them with a bottle of champagne and one flute.

Yemlin stepped back.

"Here's Valeri to help us," Renée beamed. "Isn't he just beautiful? We call him the little doll."

Yemlin had never seen a more handsome man, not even among the

American movie stars. In his mid-twenties, his athletic body was slightly tanned, his facial features perfectly proportioned, his eyes startlingly blue, and his teeth gleaming white.

"Renée exaggerates," Valeri said, smiling. His voice was deep, his Russian cultured. "But she's cute. Would you care for a glass of wine while you're in your bath, Mr. Yemlin?"

Yemlin said nothing.

The girl tittered. "Valeri is just a masseur. He doesn't bite."

Yemlin smiled despite himself. For a moment he'd been star-struck like a silly old lady. "Sure. And after my bath and rubdown, I want to get a few hours sleep." He looked at the girl. "Alone."

"Oh pooh," Renée said, and she helped him undress as Valeri poured a glass of champagne.

The bath water was a perfect temperature. The heat seeped into Yemlin's bones, and he sighed in contentment. Renée got undressed, her breasts high and firm and she got into the tub with him, and started on his broad back with a Finnish scrub sponge. Valeri handed him the champagne then went into the bedroom where he laid out his oils and lotions beside a low, towel-draped massage table.

The champagne was Russian, sweet and cold, just as he liked it, the bath soothing, and Renée's ministrations wonderful. After a few minutes Valeri refilled his glass, and Yemlin began to feel like he was drifting, the sensation wonderfully comforting. He was in a safe haven where for the first time since he could remember he felt warm, and secure.

When he was finished, Renée and Valeri helped him out of the bath, dried his body with warm towels, and led him to the massage table, where he lay down on his back.

Renée left, and Valeri began massaging Yemlin's neck and shoulder muscles with an incredibly strong, but gentle touch, his hands slippery with warm oils.

Yemlin watched the young man for several minutes before realizing he was naked. Muscles corded down his back, and rippled his firm buttocks. When he straightened up, Yemlin saw that his penis was large and semi-erect. He knew that he should be embarrassed, but the boy was so handsome that watching him was like watching an erotic movie, and Yemlin began to respond despite himself.

"That's better, Viktor," the young man said, gently massaging Yemlin's inner thighs, his finger tips flicking around Yemlin's anus.

The effect was galvanizing. Yemlin had not felt anything like it since he'd had a prostitute in Tokyo. A groan of pleasure escaped from his throat.

Valeri's lips closed around Yemlin's penis, the sensation incredible. He could do nothing but lie back as the young man took him deep into his mouth. It was like nothing he'd ever felt, pleasure building and rising in waves. He'd been a thirty-five-year-old man before that Tokyo prostitute had done such a thing for him, and right now the pleasure was every bit as good, even though he felt a pang of guilt at the back of his mind for having it done to him by a man.

And then he was coming, as he'd not come for many years, the intense feeling of relief coursing through his body like nothing else could.

His lotion-filled hand was on Valeri's rigid penis now, the young man's lips next to his head, cooing, and whispering softly.

"Paris was wonderful, Viktor. Just like now. Was it with your mistress?"

"McGarvey," Yemlin murmured.

"Her name is McGarvey?"

"No, Kirk," Yemlin mumbled. He wanted to return the pleasure the young man had given him. "Kirk has agreed. He's here."

"In Moscow?"

"Yes, he's here."

"Why, Viktor? Why is Kirk McGarvey in Moscow?" Valeri whispered.

"To help us. To save the Rodina."

"How?"

"To kill the Tarantula. Kill Tarankov. It's the only way."

"That's very good, Viktor," Valeri cooed. "Very good. Now tell me about Kirk McGarvey. Tell me everything."

FIFTEEN

Moscow

McGarvey spent the afternoon in the lobby of the Metropol Hotel sipping mineral water and scouring a dozen of the newspapers and news magazines published in Moscow for anything pertaining to Tarankov.

As he suspected there was plenty of coverage about President Yeltsin's heart attack, but none of the articles offered any speculation on the real cause of his death. No one was making a connection between the attack on the Riga nuclear power station in the Moscow suburb of Dzerzhinskiy and the bomb blast in Red Square. Nor did any of the articles on the power plant explosion mention Tarankov's name. In fact most of the articles reported that the attack had been staged by so far unknown terrorists or dissidents, who possibly were disgruntled workers at the plant.

Russia's capacity for self-inflicted delusions was almost as great as the nation's capacity for suffering. If you're hungry read a cookbook. But read it alone, because your neighbors might see it and want to come to your house for a meal.

Novy Mir, the magazine that had serialized Solzhenitsyn's *Gulag Archipelago*, however, reported, in a two paragraph piece buried in the middle under a column headed "Upheavals," that General Yevgenni Tarankov gave a speech recently in Dzerzhinskiy, and was scheduled to speak again tomorrow in Nizhny Novgorod, a city about three hundred miles east of Moscow that under the Soviet rule had been renamed Gorki.

It was Russian doublespeak. Anyone in the know reading the article would immediately understand that the magazine suspected the attack on the Riga power plant had been staged by Tarankov. By reporting his next speaking engagement, the magazine was practically daring the government to do something about it.

Considering the liberties that Russian journalists had been taking for nearly ten years, the lack of coverage Tarankov was getting bespoke the seriousness with which his campaign was being taken. Everyone in Moscow was frightened to death that if and when Tarankov took over he would purge every newspaper or magazine that had given him bad press.

McGarvey's guide book provided the information that the most convenient train to Nizhny Novgorad left at 11:10 P.M. from the Yaroslavl Station arriving overnight just before 7:30 A.M. But taking the train presented two immediate problems. The first was that going there just now as a foreigner would be dangerous. If Tarankov's people were as well organized as McGarvey thought they must be, the airport and train stations would probably be monitored for any suspicious people. He did not want to blow his Belgian cover yet. It would provide a solid track that would mysteriously disappear should the need arise.

The second problem was his hotel room. In Russia if you checked out of your hotel you had only two choices. You either checked into another hotel or you left the city.

In one of the newspapers he'd read an article about the prostitution rings that operated out of several of the hotels in Moscow, using women from the former East Germany and Poland. The Metropol was not one of them, but McGarvey circled several of the hotel names in the article, underlining one of them several times as if for emphasis. His bellman Artur had gone through his things. Nothing was missing yet, but he would be sure to see the newspaper with the circled articles and believe that McGarvey hadn't simply abandoned his room.

Leaving everything behind except for his money, his gun and the clothes on his back, he emerged from the hotel a few minutes before 5:00 P.M., the afternoon dusk already deepening in the still falling and blowing snow. Two blocks away he found a cab to take him out to the flea market at the Dinamo

Stadium beyond the outer ring road near the Frunze Central Airfield. The going was difficult but the driver didn't seem to mind. He kept slyly looking at McGarvey's image in the rearview mirror.

The stadium's parking lot was huge. Despite the horrible weather hundreds of entrepreneurs sold everything from Kalashnikov rifles to western currencies from stalls, or from the backs of their cars or trucks. Barrels filled with burning trash or oily rags lent a surreal air to the place. Perhaps a thousand people wandered from stall to stall. Some huddled around the wind-whipped flames. Still others, many of them well dressed and accompanied by armed men, lugged their purchases back to Mercedes and BMWs parked at the fringes, and guarded by other armed men.

"This is not such an easy place," his driver said pulling up. "Maybe you could use some help."

McGarvey held up a British hundred-pound note. "I collect military uniforms. Identity cards. Leave orders, pay books. That sort of thing."

"I know a guy who has that stuff," the cabby said, reaching for the money. But McGarvey pulled it back.

"I don't want any trouble. I want to buy a few things, and then I want you to bring me back downtown to the same place you picked me up."

"You need some muscle. Five hundred pounds."

"A hundred now and another hundred when we get back to the city."

"I don't want any bullshit," the driver protested as he reached for something in his jacket.

McGarvey pulled out his pistol, jammed the barrel into the man's thick neck, and pulled the hammer back. *"Don't fuck with me, I'm not in the mood,"* he said in guttural Russian.

The driver froze, his eyes on McGarvey's in the rearview mirror.

"You can either make an easy two hundred pounds, or you can try to take everything I have."

The cabby shrugged and laughed nervously. "Your Russian is pretty good, you know. Where'd you pick it up?"

"School One," McGarvey said. It was the KGB's old spy training school. One of the best in the world.

"Okay," the cabby said, blanching. "No trouble."

McGarvey uncocked his gun, stuffed it in his pocket and gave the cabby the hundred pounds.

They drove around to the west side of the vast parking lot where the cabby led McGarvey to a ring of a half-dozen army supply trucks and troop transports. Within a half-hour McGarvey bought a canvas carryall and an army corporal's uniform, including greatcoat, olive drab hat, gloves and cheap leather boots. He also bought the identity papers and leave orders for Dimitri Shostokovich stationed at Zakamensk in the far southeast along the Chinese border. The burly entrepreneur who sold him the lot for a hundred pounds stamped the current dates on the orders, and flashed McGarvey a gold-toothed grin.

"The photographs don't match, but no one will look very closely," he said. His breath smelled like onions and beer. "You've got eleven days until you're AWOL. But nobody gives a fuck about that either." He stuffed everything into the carryall.

Several men came into the circle of trucks and stood around one of the barrels of burning rags.

"Time to go," McGarvey's driver warned.

McGarvey reached his hand into his coat pocket and partially withdrew his gun. He looked directly into the salesman's eyes. "I don't think those gentlemen mean us any harm."

"No," the salesman said after a moment. "But if there is nothing else you wish to buy, perhaps it is time to go. Unless you would like some help with your . . . project."

"What project would that be?" McGarvey asked easily.

The salesman motioned toward the carryall. "Maybe you yourself are a businessman. I have certain connections."

McGarvey seemed to think about it for a moment. "How do I find you?"

"I'm here every night. Just ask for Vasha."

"The . . . project could be big. Maybe you couldn't handle it."

Vasha licked his lips. "You might be surprised."

McGarvey picked up the carryall. "I'll keep you in mind."

"Okay, you do that."

On the way back into the city the cabby once again kept looking at McGarvey's image in the rearview mirror. He sensed that some kind of a deal was going down and he was hungry. He wanted to be a part of it.

"I know this city. I could take you anywhere you want to go," he said hopefully. "Nobody can watch their own back one hundred percent. I've got good eyes and plenty of guts. And I've got some pretty goddamned good connections. I brought you to Vasha with no trouble."

"What's your name?" McGarvey asked.

"Arkady."

"How can I reach you? Day or night?"

Arkady snatched a business card from a holder on the dash and passed it back. "How do I reach you?"

"You don't," McGarvey said. The cabby's name was Arkady Astimovich and he worked for Martex, one of the private cab companies in the city. "We'll see how you do this time, Arkasha. Keep your mouth shut like you promised, and I might have something for you."

"What about tonight?"

"No. And don't try to follow me. A little bit rich is better than very much dead. Do you understand?"

They pulled up at the curb a couple of blocks from the Metropol near the Moscow Arts Theater. Traffic was heavy tonight. The driver stared at McGarvey's reflection for a few moments. "I understand," he said.

McGarvey handed him the second hundred pounds, got out of the cab and disappeared into the blowing snow and crowds with his canvas carryall.

He ducked into the shadows of a shop doorway just around the corner, and waited for five minutes, but the cab never showed up. Astimovich was hungry, but apparently he was also smart.

Hefting his carryall, McGarvey walked down to the metro station on Gorki Street and bought a token for a few kopecks. Just inside he studied the system map which showed the stop for the Leningrad, Kazan and Ya-roslavl Stations was Leningradskaya. He put his token in the gate, and when the light turned green he descended to the busy platforms. It took him several minutes to figure out which train was his, and he got aboard moments before the doors closed. There were less than a dozen people aboard the car, among them four roughly dressed young men, whom McGarvey took to be in their twenties. They eyed him as he took a seat by the door, the carryall between him and the window.

He had no illusions about what Russia had become, but since his arrival in Moscow this morning the only cop he'd seen was the one directing traffic near the hotel. In the past the Militia seemed to be everywhere, including the metro stations. But Moscow, and presumably the entire country, had sunk into an anarchy of the street. The only faction with any real power was the Mafia and the armies of private bodyguards. Street crime was not completely out of hand yet because businessmen and shopkeepers paid protection money called *krysha*, which literally meant roof. Without it you were either a nobody or you were dead. And the Militia might come if they were called.

At the next stop a couple old women got aboard, spotted the four young men, and immediately stepped off. A couple of the other passengers also got out, and the remainder kept their eyes downcast.

Three stops later all the other passengers got off the car, leaving only McGarvey and the four men, who got up and languidly took up positions at the front and rear doors. They didn't speak nor did they make any effort to approach McGarvey, but they watched him.

The public address system announced the next stop was Leningrad Station, and as the train slowed down McGarvey got up and went to the back door. One of the young men grinned, showing his bad teeth. He started to say something when McGarvey smashed the heel of his heavy boot into the man's right kneecap, the leg snapping with an audible pop.

He went down with a piercing scream. The second man shoved him aside with one hand while fumbling in his ragged coat pocket with his other.

Before he could pull out a weapon, McGarvey smashed him in the face with a roundhouse right, his head bouncing off the door frame. McGarvey pulled him forward, off balance, and as he doubled over, drove a knee in the man's face.

McGarvey pulled out his gun, and brought it up as he swiveled around in one smooth motion to face the other two men charging up the car toward him. "*Nyet*," he warned.

The two men pulled up short, angry and confused and a little bit fearful. In a matter of seconds the man they'd targeted to rob had taken out two of their friends, and now held a gun on them as if he knew what he was doing.

The train came to a halt, the doors slid open, and McGarvey stepped off, pocketing his gun before anyone on the crowded platform could see what was going on. He headed directly for the escalators to the street level.

There was a commotion on the platform behind him, but he didn't think the other two men would be coming after him. They'd be getting their two injured friends out of there before someone else moved in and took advantage of them.

Yaroslavl and Leningrad Stations were directly behind the metro entrance, separated from each other by a large brown brick building where advanced reservation train tickets were sold to Russians. Only tickets that were to be used within twenty-four hours were sold from the train stations in a complicated system that separated foreigners from Russians, and Russian civilians from veterans and active duty soldiers. Even most Russians didn't understand the system, and sometimes the lines were endless.

McGarvey ducked around the corner and crossed the street where in the darkness behind the advanced ticket building, he changed into the army uniform, stuffing his civilian clothes into the carryall. The uniform stank of sweat and mildew and dirt, and the greatcoat with corporal's chevrons was stiff with grease and mud. The boots were cheap, worn down at the heels and extremely uncomfortable. He pocketed his gun, and the identity and leave papers, and pulling his filthy fur hat down over his eyes, made his way back to the Yaroslavl station. Tickets for veterans were sold from two windows upstairs, and although the station was extremely busy this evening, he got lucky and only had to wait in line for an hour and a half. No one paid him the slightest attention. He could have been invisible.

He paid for a round trip fourth class, or hard class, ticket to Nizhny Novgorod, which on the timetables was still listed as Gorki, from a surly old woman, a cigarette dangling from the corner of her mouth. She barely looked up at him, but she didn't start working on the tickets until McGarvey had passed his money thorough the narrow opening.

Downstairs in the cavernous arrivals and departures hall, McGarvey bought a couple bottles of cheap vodka, a few package of Polish cigarettes, and a package of greasy kielbasa sausages, a loaf of dark bread, some pickles, a couple of onions, a large tomato and one bottle of mineral water. All of these he stuffed into his carryall, then headed down to wait for his train. He cracked the seal on a bottle of vodka, took a deep drink, and sat on his carryall in the middle of the huge crowd waiting for the train.

It took him a few minutes, listening and watching, before he began to pick up an undercurrent of excitement. Something rare for Russians. All these people were going to Nizhny Novgorod for the same reason. To see Tarankov. The Tarantula. Their savior. And they were excited about it.

SIXTEEN

CIA Headquarters

Elizabeth McGarvey looked up from her computer screen, the Cyrillic letters of the Russian language blurring in her vision. It wasn't 5:00 P.M. yet which meant she had another half-hour of this crap before she could get out of here. She got up and walked past the rows of the translator's stations to the women's room, where she dampened a paper towel, daubed her face, and looked into the mirror at her bloodshot eyes, and pale complexion. She was only twenty-three, and already she was taking on what her co-workers called the archival pallor. The only light that ever shined on them fifty hours a week came from fluorescent tubes in the ceilings, and monitors they sat in front of. She was in love with the idea of working for the Central Intelligence Agency, but bored out of her skull with translating foreign broadcasts—mostly Russian these days—for the analyst geeks up on the fourth floor. But she was still too new to ask for a transfer to the Directorate of

Operations, and she was already getting the impression that being her father's daughter put her at a distinct disadvantage so long as Howard Ryan was DDO. She brushed her long blonde hair, touched up her lipstick and went back to her console.

Over the past three or four days the analysts had demanded information about the ultra-nationalist General Yevgenni Tarankov. Though nothing official had filtered down to them in the Foreign Broadcast Information Service, it didn't take a genius to figure out what was happening. Tarankov had probably hit the Riga nuclear power station in Dzerzhinskiy—she'd seen a brief mention about him in *Novy Mir*—and it was also possible that he'd been involved with the incident in Red Square the next morning in which Yeltsin had died. But his death didn't make any sense to her. If Tarankov was behind the explosion in Red Square Yeltsin would have been the direct target. There was no other reason for such an attack. If that was the case, and Yeltsin had died in the blast, and not of a heart attack as the Russian media was reporting, it meant the Kremlin was lying for some reason.

Elizabeth brought up the transcripts for the past seventy-two hours of on air broadcasts of the official Russian news agency, transferred the entire block of material into the RAM section of a recognition program she'd been working on for the past couple of weeks, and asked the computer to search for three pieces of information. Yeltsin's movements, Tarankov's appearances, and the routine informational news releases issued by the offices of the President, Minister of Defense and the mayors of Moscow and St. Petersburg over that period. They were the most powerful men in Russia. And they had the most to lose if Tarankov won in the June elections.

Her boss, Bratislav Toivich, came over as the program began to run. He was a Lithuanian who'd immigrated to this country in the late fifties as a young man, but he'd still not lost his accent, or his rigid hatred for the Russians. He was a thick-waisted man who smoked constantly, and always had a hangdog look as if he'd just received some terrible news. No one had ever seen him smile. But he was brilliant, he was fair, and he was kind. Everyone loved him.

"Are you writing love letters now?" Toivich asked pulling up a chair beside her.

"The company doesn't give me the time for a love life."

"Aren't there any good men in Washington these days?"

"None that I've met."

Toivich studied the blocks of text rapidly shifting across the screen. "What are we looking for here? This is your new program?"

"Yes," Elizabeth said. She turned to him. "Yeltsin's heart attack doesn't make any sense to me."

"Dzerzhinskiy could have been the straw that broke the camel's back. He's had health problems for years."

"Agreed. But no one is making a big deal out of the car bombing in Red Square. That in itself is kinda weird. You'd think they'd be all over it, Mr.

B. The Communists should be screaming bloody murder. They've been predicting this sort of thing all along. It's the moderate reformers' fault."

"Maybe it is," Toivich suggested.

Elizabeth was shocked. "I can't believe you said that."

"As far as I'm concerned the dirty bastards can wallow in their own filth, they deserve it. But what's happening in Russia now was expected. In any change, especially such a big change, anarchy always follows. How they come out of it will be a measure of their strength."

"You think Tarankov has a chance?"

"Let's put it this way, my little *devochka*. He hasn't one chance in a million of failure. The military is behind him, and so is the FSK."

Elizabeth looked at her computer screen. "It'll be worse than before."

Toivich shrugged. "In that case we'll deal with the situation just like we've dealt with every other crisis. We'll play catch up."

"Was it all a wasted effort?" she asked sincerely. There were so many things that she did not understand yet. She wished her father were here at her side to talk to. But he'd go ballistic when he found out his only daughter was working for the Company. She wanted to get into operations training at the Farm first, before she broke the news to him. She wanted him to be proud of her, something her mother never could be.

Toivich's face darkened. "Don't ever say that again," he said harshly. "A lot of good people gave their lives to fight the bastards. And if you don't understand that, you of all people, then you don't belong here."

Elizabeth was instantly contrite, though in a hidden compartment at the back of her head, she wanted to lash back. If we'd done such a hot job defending the faith, then why were there more troops under arms worldwide than at anytime since the Second World War? Why was everything going to hell in Russia? Why had the world become such a dangerous place? Who was kidding whom?

"Sorry," she said. "I didn't mean it the way it came out."

"Your daddy would take you over his knee if he heard you talking nonsense like that," Toivich said. "Have you talked to anybody about this program?"

"Nobody other than you."

"Well, shut it down for tonight. They want to talk to you upstairs right now."

Elizabeth's eyes narrowed, her stomach fluttered. "Who wants to see me, and about what?"

"Mr. Ryan's secretary called, but she didn't say why," Toivich said.

Elizabeth's temper flared, but Toivich held her off before she could blurt out anything.

"Ryan's problem is with your father, not you. And that's a subject you're supposed to know nothing about, so keep your temper in check," Toivich said. "If he tries to pull anything with you he will be stepped on, I promise you. Nonetheless he's still Deputy Director of Operations. And if you ever want to get over there you'd better learn something your father never learned. Politics."

"Bullshit," Elizabeth said sharply.

"I'm from the old school, Elizabeth, which means I'm not very politically correct. Where I come from young ladies don't use words like that. Maybe next time I'll wash your mouth out with soap." He looked indulgently at her. "Would you like me to come up there with you?"

"No thanks, Mr. B. You might be from the old school, but I'm from the new. My dad taught me to fight my own battles."

"I'll be here when you're finished if you want to talk."

"Thanks," Elizabeth said. She shut down her program, and took the elevator up to the sixth floor where she was directed by a civilian guard through the glass doors at the end of the corridor.

The Deputy Director of Operations' secretary, a dowdy old woman, her silver gray hair up in a bun, looked up when Elizabeth came in.

"I'm Elizabeth McGarvey, Mr. Ryan sent for me?"

"Yes, dear, just a moment please," the older woman said, pleasantly. She got up and went into Ryan's office. A moment later she came back. "You may go in now."

Elizabeth nodded and as she passed, Ryan's secretary whispered something to her that sounded like, "His bark is worse than his bite," and then she was inside.

Howard Ryan and another older, more serious looking man got to their feet, and Ryan came around his desk, a phony smile on his face.

"Ms. McGarvey, it's a pleasure to finally meet you. I'm Howard Ryan, Deputy Director of Operations." They shook hands. "I'd like you to meet my assistant DDO, Tom Moore."

"Sir," Elizabeth said, shaking Moore's hand. His grasp was like Ryan's, limp and damp. Just like her father had told her.

Ryan motioned for them to have a seat, and he went back behind his desk. "I was absolutely delighted when I learned that we had a second generation McGarvey working for us," he said. "What made you decide on the Agency as a career? It was your father's doing I'll bet. He must be very proud of you."

"I've admired my father for as long as I can remember," she said, careful to keep her tongue in check.

"Then you and he must have had long talks about his work for us."

"Only in the most general of terms, Mr. Ryan. He believed very strongly in what he was doing. So do I."

Ryan chuckled. "I guess we can skip the brainwashing sessions on this one, Tom," he said to Moore. "She's already been well indoctrinated."

"How is your father these days?" Moore asked. "We understand that he's back in Paris."

"He's doing fine," Elizabeth said. She hadn't talked to him in more than six months, in part because she didn't want to let slip about her new job.

But in part because she'd all but begged him to stay in the States eighteen months ago after all the air crashes. He'd had something to do with the investigation, she was certain of it, though he'd told her nothing about it. At the time she'd felt vulnerable, and wanted him nearby. When he left she'd been angry.

"Have you talked to him recently?" Ryan asked. "Has he come here to Washington to see you and your mother?"

"No."

Again Ryan exchanged a look with Moore. "Good heavens, you haven't had a falling out with your father, have you? That would be terrible. He isn't upset that you're working for us is he?" Ryan spread his hands. "I don't mind telling you, since you're one of us now, that your father and I have had differences of opinion. Some of that unfortunately came to an ugly head about a year and a half ago. But that in no way negates my sincerest admiration for the man and what he's done for this agency. For his country. Even the President speaks of him fondly."

"No, sir, there's been nothing like that," Elizabeth said, wondering where he was taking this. "We're still pals."

"Still pals," Ryan said to Moore, who chuckled and looked approvingly at her.

She wanted to ask them if their parents had any children who'd lived, but she bit her tongue. Politics, Mr. B. called it. Bullshit, she thought.

"Well, we'd like to talk to him, and we thought that you might help us."

"Call him at his apartment in Paris."

"We tried," Moore said. "He's gone. We thought maybe he'd contacted you in the past few days."

Elizabeth's stomach was hollow. Something was going on that had driven her father to ground, and it was important enough for the CIA to resort to this tactic.

"Mr. Ryan, my father did mention your name once or twice over the past few years, but like I said only in the most general of terms. But I know my father well enough, and I've worked for the CIA long enough, to understand that something is going on that you need his help for." Elizabeth tried to read something from their expressions, but she couldn't. Moore seemed vapid, and Ryan seemed calculating.

"That's not quite the truth. . . ."

"He's gone to ground, you want to talk to him, but you can't find him," Elizabeth said. "And I suspect even if you did get a message to him there's a good chance he'd ignore it. Especially if he's working on something that he considers important."

"You're a very astute young woman," Ryan said after a few moments of silence. "Actually it's the French SDECE who would like to speak with your father."

"About what, Mr. Ryan?"

"That's not relevant to your purposes at the moment."

"Bullshit," Elizabeth said, unable to contain herself any longer. "You didn't call me up here to chat about my health. You want me to find my father for you."

Ryan closed his eyes. "Christ," he said half under his breath. When he opened his eyes again his expression and body language were flatly neutral, as if he'd pulled on a new skin. "We want you to tell him that the French intelligence service wish to speak with him. He can meet them at our embassy. But he's broken no French laws, nor is he a fugitive from French justice. No warrant has been issued. They just want some information from him. Nothing more."

"About what?" Elizabeth shot back.

"Don't play hardball with us, young lady," Moore said. "You'll find yourself on the outside looking in."

"If you want to fire me, go ahead and do it. But if you want my help, don't tell me lies. It's the thing my father hates the most. And I inherited the trait."

"Tom spoke out of turn, Ms. McGarvey. We don't want to fire you. As a matter of fact I called you up here this afternoon to offer you a job in Operations. We've got a class starting at the Farm the first of June. If you're interested."

"First I bring you my father."

"Good heavens, I don't know what you think we are. Fools, perhaps. Opportunists, maybe. But we're not the enemy, Elizabeth. I'm offering you a job in Operations. You can take it or leave it. Frankly I think you'll turn out to be a bigger pain in the ass than your father, but I think you have the potential of being almost as good as he was."

"Don't try to tell me—"

"Please hear me out," Ryan cut her off. "I can show you your personnel file, if you want to see it. When you were evaluated for employment all three of your interviewers recommended Operations. In part because of your abilities, and in part, I have to admit, because of what your father has done for us." Ryan studied her for a moment. "Now that is a fact, believe it or not. In the meantime we want to get a message to your father for the French. Nobody can find him, and I think you're well aware that when your father wants to hide himself he's very good. Possibly the best there ever was. At this moment we and the French have exhausted every means at our disposal short of an all out manhunt. Now that's something very dangerous. People could get hurt. So we turned to you because you know your father probably better than anyone else, and if you should happen to show up on his doorstep his first reaction won't be to escape out the back door, or shoot. We want your help."

"What do the French want to speak to him about?" Elizabeth asked.

"Will you help us?" Moore asked.

"Not until you tell me why the French are interested in my father."

"Under the circumstances her request is reasonable, Howard," Moore said.

Ryan seemed to consider it for a moment, and Elizabeth had the feeling she was being set up.

"Will you accept an immediate transfer to Operations?" Ryan asked. "Independent of whether you help us out with this assignment?"

"What would my job be?"

"Special field officer in training," Ryan answered, vexed. "But if you work for me it won't be so easy as translating. I'm not an easy man to work for."

She wanted to tell him that sudden flash of truth was refreshing, but she held her tongue. "Okay."

"Welcome aboard," Moore said.

"My boss will have to be told."

"We'll take care of it," Moore promised.

Ryan selected a file folder from a pile on his desk. "You're to consider this matter highly confidential. You'll speak about it with no one outside of this room without prior permission, or face prosecution under the National Secrets Act. Do you understand?"

"Yes, sir," Elizabeth said. Don't sell your soul for expediency, her father had cautioned her once. But don't turn your back on whatever works. She was in!

"Does the name Viktor Yemlin mean anything to you?"

"He's head of the Russian SVR's North American Directorate."

Ryan's eyes lit up. "How do you know this?"

"We're running programs for the DI on the current situation in Russia, his name came up. Until a few years ago he was the KGB's *rezident* here in Washington."

"Your father never mentioned his name?"

Elizabeth searched her memory. She shook her head. "Not that I can remember."

"They know each other," Ryan said.

"Considering the work my father did, I'm not surprised."

"What work is that?" Ryan asked, a flinty look in his eyes.

"He never discussed assignments, Mr. Ryan, if that's what you mean. But my father was employed by the Company for a number of years. He would have been of great interest to Yemlin. I'm just saying that the connection between them wouldn't be unusual."

"Comrade Yemlin showed up in France last week. He was followed to a meeting with your father at the Eiffel Tower. The French managed to overhear a part of their conversation and it worried them sufficiently to contact our Paris Chief of Station for help. Specifically they wanted to know if your father was currently on assignment for us. We told them no."

Ryan was in his formal mode, speaking like a New York attorney. It bugged Elizabeth. She wanted him to quit beating around the bush and tell it straight. But again she held her tongue.

"Were you aware that your father is seeing a woman in Paris?" Moore asked.

Elizabeth smiled despite herself. "I'd be surprised if he wasn't."

"Her name is Jacqueline Belleau and she works for the French secret service."

"To spy on him," Elizabeth flared.

"Frankly, yes," Ryan admitted. "Your father met with Yemlin on Saturday. On Monday he kicked Ms. Belleau out of his apartment and disappeared."

"Maybe he found out what she was, and he just got rid of her. I would have in his shoes."

"It's the timing that has the French most worried," Ryan said. He slid the file folder across to Elizabeth. "That's a transcript of what the French were able to monitor."

Elizabeth reached for the file folder.

"Before you read that, I have to ask you something, Ms. McGarvey," Ryan said, his tone suddenly gentle. "Did you know your grandparents, on your father's side."

The question took her by surprise. "No. They were killed in a car accident in Kansas before I was born. But I saw photographs, and my father used to talk about them. He was very close to them."

"I don't know of any other way to put this, except to tell you the way it was. Until recently this agency believed that your grandparents were spies for the Soviet Union."

"Crap," Elizabeth said.

"Yes, indeed, it was crap, as you put it," Ryan said. "An internal audit team is working to clear their names, but it's something your father might not know yet."

Elizabeth's throat was tight, and her eyes smarted. "My father believed that grandma and grandpa were spies? Is that what you're saying?"

"Unfortunately, yes," Moore said. "It was apparently some kind of a Soviet disinformation plot to discredit him."

Sudden understanding dawned on Elizabeth. "Around the time of Santiago?"

Ryan stiffened, but said nothing.

"It would seem so," Moore said. "Amends will be made, believe me. But it's a burden that your father has carried for a long time. Too long a time."

Elizabeth was confused. She didn't know how she felt, or even how she should feel, except that she was so terribly sorry for her father that she wanted to cry.

"It's made your father, shall we say, vulnerable in certain situations," Moore continued in his patronizing tone.

"Angry would be closer to the truth," Elizabeth shot back.

"Yes, angry."

Elizabeth opened the file folder and read the single page of transcript. She could hear her father's voice, almost feel his presence in the few lines, and the ache in her heart deepened. She looked up finally, squaring her shoulders, stiffening her resolve. She was a McGarvey. Strong. Resolute. "Sometimes it's all we have, Liz," her father told her a few years ago in Greece. They were in trouble, and he wanted to comfort her, and yet make her aware of the truth.

"We have no idea what Yemlin wants your father to do for the SVR," Moore said. "But the French are worried that—"

Ryan interrupted. "The French are concerned that whatever Yemlin wants will involve a French citizen, or possibly someone on French soil."

Elizabeth's head was spinning again. She'd seen her father in action, and she'd heard enough dropped hints downstairs over the past few months, to figure out what his job had been. Or at least a part of it. Her father killed people. Bad people. Horrible people. But he had been a shooter for the CIA in the days when the Company denied such hired guns existed. Her mother would be aghast if she knew, although Elizabeth thought her mother probably had an idea at the back of her head. But they never talked about it. Never.

A thought flashed in her head like a bright flare, and she had all she could do to keep it from showing on her face. Yemlin had come to ask her father to assassinate someone. Someone not in France, but in Russia. Someone who was tearing the country apart. Someone who could conceivably embroil all of eastern Europe in a war. Someone who had the complete attention of the CIA.

Yemlin had asked her father to assassinate Yevgenni Tarankov, and her father had probably accepted the assignment otherwise he would not have gone to ground.

"All right," she said.

"Ms. McGarvey?" Ryan asked.

"I'll find my father and get the message to him, but I'll do it completely on my own. If my father gets the slightest hint that the agency is following me, or that he's being set up, nobody will find him. And if I find out that I'm being followed I'll tell my father everything, which will make him mad." She flashed Ryan and Moore a sweet look. "You probably already know that when my father is angry you don't want to be around him. He sometimes tends to take things to the extreme."

"We'll stay out of your way, Ms. McGarvey, you have my word on it," Ryan said. "As of this moment you are operational. Tom will set you up with a codename, contact procedures, travel documents and money, everything you'll need." He sat forward. "Time is of the essence. Because if your father takes the Russians up on their offer, he'll either be arrested and jailed, or killed. Something I most sincerely assure you, young lady, that no one in the Agency wants to happen."

SEVENTEEN

Nizhny Novgorod

McGarvey's train arrived at the main railway station on the west bank of the Volga River a few minutes after seven in the morning, and he walked across the street to a small workmen's café crowded with roughly dressed factory workers and a few shabbily attired soldiers. The snowstorm had ended sometime in the middle of the night, and the sun shone brightly. A blanket of snow made the city of 1.5 million seem almost pretty. The upbeat mood of passengers aboard the train was matched by the festival atmosphere of the town. No one seemed to be working today, everybody seemed exuberant, expectant. Banners with Tarankov's name and likeness, or plain banners with a stylized design of a tarantula spider, hung from the front of the railway station, and from utility poles on the broad avenue leading across the river toward the Kremlin whose walls rose from the hill overlooking the city center. They fluttered and snapped in the fresh breeze that carried with it odors of river sewage and factory smoke. Like most Russian cities, Nizhny Novgorod stank, but it was better than some places.

His hard class car had been so packed with bodies last night that there'd been no room to sit down, not even on the drafty connecting platform. What little sleep he'd managed to get had been done standing up. Combined with the effects of stale air, too many cigarettes, and too much vodka—everybody on the train was drunk even before they'd left Moscow—McGarvey felt like he'd been on a seven-day binge. Catching a glance at his reflection in the dirty window of the café, he looked as if he hadn't bathed or slept in a week. It was exactly the effect he wanted to achieve, because now he fit in. Now he was part of the scenery. No one to give a second notice to. No one threatening. Just another corporal too old for his rank, with obviously nowhere to go, and no hope, except for Tarankov.

He bought a plate of goulash and black bread for a few roubles, and found a place in the corner at the end of a long table, where he sank down gratefully on the hard bench. Keeping his eyes downcast he ate the surprisingly good food, while he listened to what the men around the table were talking about. They all worked the night shift at the MiG factory on the eastern outskirts of the city, and they'd come down here after work to catch what they were calling "the Tarantula's act." They were all cynical, as only Russians could be, nonetheless their oftentimes heated discussion about Tarankov was tinged with a little awe, and even hope. It was about time somebody came along to get them out of the mess that Gorbachev started, and that the drunken buffoon Yeltsin had worsened. They'd lost the southern republics and the Baltics, and they'd also lost their dignity as a nation. Russians were taking handouts from foreigners just so they could have a hamburger at the McDonald's in Moscow. AIDS, crack cocaine and the Mafia were direct imports from the west.

"Sonofabitch, but even our soldiers are starving in the streets," one of the workmen shouted. "Just like this sorry bastard."

McGarvey looked up. The men around the table stared at him with a mixture of pity and anger.

"Where the hell did you serve, Corporal?" one of the men asked.

"*Yeb vas*, Afghanistan," McGarvey mumbled, and he went back to his food.

"He's goddamned right. Fuck your mother," the man said.

Someone slammed a not-so-clean glass down in front of McGarvey, filled it with vodka, and they went back to their discussion, this time about the drunkenness in what was once the greatest military in the world. Officers lived in tarpaper shacks, and enlisted men were billeted in tents or simply allowed to roam the streets between duty assignments. The situation wasn't quite that bad, but Russians loved to wallow in self-pity, and loved even more to exaggerate their problems.

After his breakfast and a second glass of vodka from the factory workers at his table, McGarvey wandered outside where he bought a half-liter of vodka from one of the street kiosks that were springing up around the railway station, and down the broad Ploshchad Lenina that led past the Tsentralnaya Hotel and across the river into the city proper. More people streamed into the area, so that for several blocks in every direction around the railway station, and along the boulevard across the river, crowds were amassing, their collective shouts and laughter rising like the low hum of a billion cicadas.

He stood to one side of the square where he had a good view of the switching yard and passenger platforms a hundred yards to the west, and the boulevard into the city. A few stragglers crossed the street, but for the most part the thoroughfare was kept perfectly clear, although there were no traffic cops or Militia officers to restrain the crowd.

The effect was strange, and unsettling to McGarvey. It was as if Tarankov's presence were strong enough that his people automatically cleared a path for his triumphal entry to the city. Parishioners did not block the aisle out of respect not only for the ceremony, but for the priest. The same deference had been accorded Stalin in the late forties and fifties. He had saved the country from the Nazis. Now Tarankov promised to save the nation from oblivion. The people loved him for it.

A huge roar went up from the crowds lining the bridge a half-mile to the south. People streamed out of the railway station and cafés and hotels as the commotion approached like a monster wave.

An open army truck appeared on the crest of the bridge, and for the first minute or so McGarvey thought the Militia might be on its way after all. But there was only one truck, moving slowly, the people along the route reacting as it passed.

A buzz of excitement suddenly swept through the tens of thousands of people around the railway station, rising in pitch as the truck came closer, and they could see the half-dozen men and two women dressed in civilian clothes in the back. They were obviously prisoners. Four men dressed in blue factory coveralls and armed with Kalashnikov assault rifles, stood in the back of the truck with the eight unarmed passengers.

Somebody beside McGarvey suddenly began jumping up and waving his fist in the air. "Death to the traitors!" he shouted. "Death to Lensky! Death to the traitors!" Viktor Lensky was the mayor.

Others in the mass of people took up the chant that soon rose to a deafening roar, as the truck pulled up in the square across from the railway depot.

The guards jumped down from the back of the truck, and made their prisoners climb down and line up in a row beneath one of the tarantula banners flapping in the breeze. None of the civilians wore overcoats or hats despite the cold. They looked frightened.

The mood of the crowd was turning ugly, but although people shouted curses and taunts at the prisoners, they made no move to go after them. But the air of expectation was even greater now than before. More people streamed in from the city, choking the main boulevard, as if they no longer expected Tarankov to need the route into the city. Whatever was going to happen, they expected it would happen down here by the railway station.

According to what Rencke had pieced together, Tarankov's usual method was to charge up to a city's train depot, send several of his commando units ahead into the city to arrest the mayor and other city and federal administrators, and rob the banks. While that was going on, Tarankov and his personal guards and inner cadre made their way slowly into the main square, while he harangued the crowds, inciting them into a fever pitch of bloodlust. At the right time the prisoners were gunned down, the money stolen from the banks was distributed to the people, and in the confusion Tarankov and his commandoes made their way back aboard their train and roared off. So far they'd met no resistance from the Militia or from the military.

But this time something was different. For whatever reason the people knew that Tarankov wouldn't be going into the city center, so they'd rounded up as many apparatchiks as they could—McGarvey figured that the smart ones had already fled the city or hidden themselves—and brought them down here to be executed.

Perhaps the military had set up an ambush downtown, meaning to trap Tarankov and his forces from returning to the safety of their heavily armed train. But if that were the case they would have to shoot into the people, because Tarankov would certainly not hesitate to use the crowd as a shield. A massacre of innocent civilians would severely damage Moscow's already tenuous hold on the nation. They would be playing directly into Tarankov's hand.

The railroad line came from Moscow in the west, and Kazan in the east. McGarvey shaded his eyes and searched the sky in both directions finally picking out a half-dozen tiny specks in the air to the southwest. They were flying low and in formation. Too slow to be jets, McGarvey figured they were probably helicopter gunships. If they were hunting Tarankov, trying to prevent him from even getting close to Nizhny Novgorod, they would concentrate on the locomotive. Once it was destroyed or derailed, Tarankov and his commandoes could be surrounded and wiped out in the countryside where civilian casualties would be limited.

It was a good tactic, but Tarankov had survived long enough to anticipate something like this happening. The intelligence reports Rencke had pirated warned that Tarankov's people were not only highly trained and motivated special forces officers, they were equipped with state-of-the-art radar and radar tracking weapons, including close-in weapons systems, rapid-fire cannons, and probably magazine-launched surface-to-air missiles, that Rencke thought might be based on the Russian Navy's SA-N-6 system, which was good out to a range of seventy-five nautical miles, accurate enough to shoot down helicopter-launched missiles or even cruise missiles, yet compact enough to easily be carried aboard a train.

For the next five minutes nothing happened, although the helicopter formation seemed to be getting closer. If they were Mi-24 Hinds, which

McGarvey figured they probably were, he estimated their distance at three or four miles.

A man in blue coveralls standing nearby, noticed McGarvey watching the sky and the shaded his eyes and looked up. When he spotted the gunships he pointed. "It's the army!" he shouted.

At that moment the helicopters suddenly broke formation. An instant later three contrails rose up from the ground, and in seconds three of the helicopters exploded in mid-air. The other three turned away from the action.

The man in the blue coveralls got the attention of the people around him, and excited shouts began to spread outward like ripples in a pond as others spotted the battle in the sky to the southwest.

For a minute or two it looked like the three remaining helicopters had broken off for good, but then they swung around in a large arc and headed back.

Now Tarankov's train came into view between the low hills that swept down to the river. It was moving very fast, and the crowds on the south side of the station who could see the action shouted back what was happening. Tens of thousands of people tried to push their way to the back of the terminal building so that they could see what was unfolding, but they were blocked by the press of bodies.

One of the helicopters fired a pair of missiles that streaked directly toward the locomotive, but at the last second they exploded in mid-air short of their target.

An instant later another of the helicopters went up in a ball of flame on the tail of a rocket launched from the train.

A cheer rose up from the crowd.

This time the remaining two Hinds turned tail and headed off. For a full ten seconds it seemed as if they would make good their escape, when a pair of rockets were launched from the train, and blew them out of the sky.

Another huge cheer spread across the vast mob, people hooting and shouting and whistling and clapping. The Tarantula had been tested and he'd proved himself. He was invincible. He had power and justice on his side. He was not only for the people, he was of the people. He was father to the Rodina—to Mother Russia—and the crowd was delirious with excitement.

People were everywhere. On the streets, along the tracks, on the roofs of every building for as far as McGarvey could see. And still more people streamed out of the city to catch a glimpse of the first hero Russia had known since Papa Stalin. But the Tarantula was even better than Stalin, because he was coming from adversity with Moscow and the entire world against him.

McGarvey continued searching the sky to the west and southwest, but nothing else was up and flying, and within minutes Tarankov's train would roar into the outskirts of the city. If the military wanted to stop Tarankov they'd either badly underestimated the firepower aboard his train, or overestimated the skill of their helicopter pilots and the effectiveness of the Hind's weapons. It seemed more likely to him that whoever had ordered and engineered the attack had done so only for show, which placed them on Tarankov's side. It would have been relatively easy for a pair of MiG-29 Fulcrums to stand well off, illuminate the train with their look-down-shootdown radar systems, and accurately place a half-dozen or more air-to-surface anti-armor missiles on the target before the train's radar systems had a chance to react to the attack. But the Tarantula had spun his web very well. He had friends in high places.

The people began to fall silent, until in the distance they could hear the distinctive roar of Tarankov's incoming train, its whistle hooting in triumph.

McGarvey slowly edged his way through the crowd along the south side of the square until he was in position about thirty yards from where the eight prisoners stood shivering in the frigid wind that funneled down the hills and across the broad river. They looked resigned. All the fight had gone out of them. Tarankov was coming, and they were being held captive not only by their armed guards, but by the tens of thousands of people surrounding them, and by their own fear. Nizhny Novgorod had become a model for free enterprise over the past half-dozen years, and within the next half hour or less they were going to pay the price for their successes with their lives, and they knew it.

A broad section of the loading platform about fifty yards west of the terminal had been cleared of people, and McGarvey realized that he'd suspected all along. Tarankov had his front men here. The demonstration was too well organized, the boulevard had been kept clear for too long, and now the loading platform free of people, bespoke good planning. Yet if Tarankov's people were here they were well blended with the crowd, because McGarvey was unable to spot them, or any unified or directed effort.

The armored train came around the last curve before the depot, and sparks began to shoot off its wheels as it slowed down, its rate of deceleration nothing short of phenomenal, the roaring, squealing noise awesome.

Even before it came to a complete halt, big doors in the sides of some of the armored cars swung open, hinged ramps dropped down in unison with a mind numbing crash and a dozen armored personal carriers shot off the train, their half-tracks squealing in protest as their treads bit into the brick surface of the loading platform.

Within ten seconds the APCs had taken up defensive positions around the depot and the square, leaving a path from the rear car of the train to the prisoners who stood frozen to their places by the sheer spectacle of Tarankov's arrival. Two hundred well-armed troops, dressed in plain battle fatigues, scrambled out of the troop carriers, and moments later a collective sigh spread across the crowd.

A man of moderate height and build, also dressed in battle fatigues, appeared on the rear platform of the last car. He paused a moment, then raised his right fist in the air.

"COMRADES, MY NAME IS YEVGENNI TARANKOV, AND I HAVE COME TODAY TO OFFER MY HAND IN FRIENDSHIP AND HELP." His amplified voice boomed across the crowds from powerful speakers mounted on the train, and on each of the APCs.

The people went wild, screaming his name, raising their right fists in salute, waving banners and posters with his picture. Old women and men, tears streaming down their cheeks, pressed forward, calling his name, begging for him to see them, to hear their pleas. It reminded McGarvey of a revival tent meeting his sister had taken him to when he was a boy in Kansas. He half expected to see people on crutches and in wheelchairs making their way to Tarankov's side so that he could heal them with his touch. In effect that's what they were asking him to do here today. Heal the nation with his touch. Right the wrongs they'd endured for so many difficult years.

Tarankov was joined by a dark haired woman and a tall man, both dressed in plain battle fatigues. The three of them stepped down from the train, and headed through the ranks of APCs and commandoes into the square.

"OUR COUNTRY IS FALLING INTO A BOTTOMLESS PIT OF DESPAIR. OUR FORESTS ARE DYING. OUR GREAT VOLGA AND LAKES HAVE BECOME CESS-POOLS OF WASTE. THE AIR OVER THIS GREAT CITY OF GORKI IS UNFIT TO BREATHE. THE ONLY FOOD WORTH EATING FILLS THE BELLIES OF THE AP-PRARATCHIKS AND FOREIGNERS HERE AND IN MOSCOW. OUR CHILDREN ARE DYING AND OUR WOMEN ARE CRYING OUT FOR HELP, BUT NO ONE IN MOS-COW CAN HEAR THEM. NO ONE IN MOSCOW WANTS TO HEAR THEM."

A silence descended over the people, as Tarankov strode into the square, his amplified voice continuing to roll over them.

"OUR HEALTH CARE SYSTEM IS BANKRUPT. OUR MILITARY HAS BECOME LEADERLESS AND USELESS. HOOLIGANS AND PROFITEERS EAT INTO US LIKE A CANCER GONE WILD. AIDS AND DRUGS AND MINDLESS MUSIC ROT THE BRAINS OF OUR CHILDREN."

As Tarankov and his group approached the prisoners, McGarvey worked his way closer to the edge of the crowd so he could get a better look. The Tarantula was not a very imposing figure. He could have passed as any ordinary Russian on the street, or in a factory, except that his fatigues were well pressed, his boots well shined, and his face alive with intelligence and emotion. It was obvious, even at a distance, that Tarankov was no charlatan revival preacher. He was a man who truly believed that he had the answers for his people, and that he was the one to lead them out of what he was calling a cesspool of hopelessness imposed on them by the western powers.

"MOSCOW . . . HOW MANY STRAINS ARE FUSING IN THAT ONE SOUND, FOR RUSSIAN HEARTS?"

A cheer went up from the crowd.

"WHAT STORE OF RICHES IT IMPARTS! I WILL GIVE YOU MOSCOW! I WILL GIVE YOU RUSSIA!"

The crowd roared its approval, chanting his name over and over.

"I WILL RETURN YOUR PRIDE, YOUR HOPE, YOUR DIGNITY! I WILL RETURN THE SOVIET UNION TO YOU!"

Again the crowd cheered wildly. They held up his picture and posters with his name or the tarantula symbol, and chanted his name.

The attractive woman beside him was his East German wife Liesel. Rencke had come up with one photograph of her taken while she was at Moscow University. She had held her good looks, and her figure was still slight. She was beaming at her husband with such a look of open admiration and adoration that whoever loved Tarankov, had to love her.

"IT IS BETTER TO LOSE A RIVER OF BLOOD NOW THAN THE ENTIRE COUNTRY LATER, EVEN IF IT IS RUSSIAN BLOOD," Tarankov shouted. He stopped a few yards in front of the prisoners, unbuttoned the flap of his holster and pulled out his Makarov pistol.

"WE WILL ONLY SPILL THE BLOOD OF TRAITORS." His voice boomed across the square.

He was wearing a lapel mike, which broadcast his voice back to a central amplifier probably aboard the train, which in turn sent it out to the loudspeakers. It was a clever bit of stagecraft.

"LOOK AROUND AND YOU WILL SEE WHAT THEY HAVE DONE TO YOU. IT IS TIME FOR A CLEAN SWEEP BEFORE WE ALL CHOKE ON THE FILTH."

The man beside Tarankov stood a full head taller than his boss, and unlike Liesel he wasn't looking at Tarankov with adoration. Instead his eyes continually swept the crowd. It was obvious that he was a professional who had no illusions about Tarankov's safety. No one was immune from assassination, and he knew it.

His gaze landed on McGarvey and remained for a moment. McGarvey raised his right fist in salute, and shouted Tarankov's name with the chanting crowd, and the man's eyes moved away.

McGarvey had no doubt that he was Leonid Chernov. And in the brief moment that Tarankov's right hand man had looked at him, McGarvey had the uneasy sensation that an old enemy of his had come back from the pauper's grave in Portugal. His name was Arkady Kurshin, and he'd been General Baranov's right hand man a number of years ago. Because of Kurshin, McGarvey had lost a kidney, and had nearly lost his life. No man before or since had been as dangerous an enemy. But at this moment, McGarvey thought he'd just looked into the eyes of Kurshin's equal, and a slight shiver played up his spine, a little tingle reached up from his gut chilling him like a fetid breeze coming from an open grave.

"WHEN OUR STRUGGLE IS OVER, I PROMISE THAT I WILL RAISE A BRONZE STATUE WITH MY OWN TWO HANDS IN DZERZHINSKY SQUARE OF A YOUNG RUSSIAN SOLDIER, HIS RIFLE RAISED OVER HIS HEAD, AND HIS FACE TURNED UP TO HEAVEN IN HOPE."

McGarvey moved a few yards away, and a little deeper into the mob. When he caught a glimpse of Chernov again the man was looking directly at the spot where McGarvey had been standing. Chernov suspected something. But he didn't know yet, he couldn't know.

"TRAITORS TO THE PEOPLE," Tarankov shouted. "ALL OF YOU." He raised his pistol and shot one of the prisoners in the forehead, driving the older man dressed in a business suit backward, his head bouncing off the pavement, blood splashing behind him.

One of the women screamed, and Tarankov shot her twice in the chest, knocking her off her feet.

In the next seconds a half-dozen of Tarankov's commandoes opened fire on the remaining prisoners who madly tried to scramble out of the way, cutting them down before they could get more than a step or two.

When the firing stopped, the crowd went totally wild, cheering and hooting in a frenzy of bloodlust, that seemed as if it had the power to continue unabated for hours if not days.

Tarankov holstered his pistol, then turned to his people and raised his hands. Almost immediately the crowd fell silent.

"I HAVE A VISION FOR THE FUTURE OF THE RODINA WHICH I WILL SHARE WITH YOU TODAY, COMRADES," he began.

McGarvey glanced over at Chernov who was staring at him, and he let all expression drain from his face except for one of love and admiration. Tarankov was his hope too.

But one thing was certain. Tarankov was not going to wait until the general elections in June to take over the government. He would almost certainly make his move much sooner than that, and McGarvey had a good idea exactly when that would be.

EIGHTEEN

Chevy Chase, Maryland

Pulling into the driveway of her mother's two story colonial across from the country club at 9:00 A.M., Elizabeth felt like death warmed over, yet she was more alive than she'd ever been. She was working for Operations, and if everything went right she'd soon be working with her father. It couldn't have been better, though she had to find him first, and keep Ryan's goons away from him until they figured out what their next moves would be.

It had been after midnight by the time she was able to go home and then she hadn't got much sleep. They'd set her up with a false passport and a complete legend under the name Elizabeth Swanson, from New York City. Her contact procedures were direct to Tom Moore on a blind number. When she went to France she was supposed to report to the COS Tom Lynch.

Between photo sessions and briefings, Elizabeth had managed to get back down to her own computer console. Toivich was gone for the evening, and no one else in the section had been told yet that she no longer worked for the DI. With her new operational designation it only took fifteen minutes to get into the archival section for former personnel where she called up her father's extensive file. Within the first five minutes of reading, her mouth had dropped open and stayed there until she was called back upstairs around ten.

Her father was James Bond personified. He'd been everywhere, done everything, and had accomplished in spades every single assignment he'd ever been given. Four presidents had given him secret citations, and every DCI and DDO, except for Ryan, gave him glowing marks. If she'd read correctly between the lines, her father had literally saved the country from war in the Pacific eighteen months ago. Before that he'd saved Los Angeles and San Francisco from a nuclear attack by a Japanese terrorist. Although he'd not been on the Company's payroll for years, it seemed that each time the CIA got itself into a jam, they called on her father to help them out.

He'd been wounded numerous times, had lost a kidney in one operation, and Phil Carrara, a former boss who had himself been killed in the line of duty, had written that more than any other person in the CIA, McGarvey had done the most to help win the Cold War, a sentiment even President Lindsay wholeheartedly endorsed.

Several times during her reading, she had to choke back tears. Her father had given his entire life to his country, but in public he was a nothing, and in private Howard Ryan, the third most powerful man in America's intelligence community, despised him. On top of that he thought that his parents had been spies. A shame that he'd carried with him for all of his adult life.

There was so much that she wanted to say to him, so many things she wanted to tell him, so much she wanted to know, but none of it mattered one whit to her. The only thing that mattered was that she loved him with all of her soul. More now than when she was a little girl and fantasized about him and her mother getting back together. So much that she could hardly contain herself from bubbling over.

Her mother, wearing a white bathrobe, her hair bundled up in a towel, opened the front door of the house and beckoned to her.

Elizabeth got out of her car and hurried up the walk to her mother, and pecked her on the cheek. "Hi, Mother."

"What are you doing here in Washington, and why didn't you come right in? Why were you sitting there like a lump on a log?" Kathleen McGarvey demanded. She was almost as tall as her daughter, and even more beautiful in a classic sense. Her neck was long, her features sharply defined, her lips full, her high cheekbones delicately arched, and her eyes brilliantly green. Although she was nearly fifty, she could have passed for a haute couture fashion model anywhere in the world. Her beauty was timeless, like Audrey Hepburn's and Jackie Kennedy's had been.

"I was trying to figure out the best way of telling you what I have to tell you. There's so much of it, I don't know where to start."

They went inside, and Kathleen gave her daughter a sharply appraising look. "Good heavens you're not pregnant, are you, dear?"

"No, Mother, I'm not pregnant. But if I were I'd be at an abortion clinic, not here. I'm not ready to have kids."

Kathleen patted down a strand of her daughter's hair. "No, I don't expect you are ready," she said wistfully. "Nor am I quite ready to become a grandmother. Now, when did you get into Washington?" she asked as they went into the kitchen.

The coffee was ready, and Elizabeth got them a couple of cups. "About six months ago."

"Oh?" Kathleen said, pouring the coffee.

Elizabeth perched on one of the stools at the counter across from her mother, and sipped her coffee. She could have used a cigarette, but that was something she definitely wasn't ready to tell her mother. "I got a job here in town, but I wanted to wait until I was sure it was going to work out before I told you about it."

Kathleen sipped delicately at her coffee. "Would you care for something to eat, Elizabeth? I could warm up some cinnamon rolls, you like those."

"Just coffee, Mom."

"Mother," Kathleen corrected automatically. She didn't like abbreviations or diminutives. Elizabeth, not Liz. And Kathleen, not Katy. It was a habit she'd never been able to break her husband of.

"Sorry," Elizabeth mumbled, lowering her eyes.

"I see," Kathleen said. "Look at me please."

Elizabeth looked up.

"I'm not going to like what you're going to tell me very much, am I?"

"Probably not. I'm working for the Central Intelligence Agency. In the Directorate of Operations, just like Daddy."

Kathleen's composure slipped a little, but she brought it back. "Your father has done very good, even great things for his country. I'm sure you know that. But do you know exactly what his job was?"

"Yes, I do."

"Then I only hope for your sake that you don't exactly follow in his footsteps, Elizabeth. But I'm sure that you will do very well at whatever it is they want you to do." It was a brave speech, but Kathleen had to turn away, her eyes glistening.

"I'm sorry, Mother. But it's something I've wanted to do for a long time."

"I would have thought that after Greece you would have changed your mind."

Four years ago Elizabeth and her mother had been kidnapped by an organization of former East German intelligence officers who wanted to force McGarvey into a trap and kill him. But her father had beat them all. The experience had nearly destroyed her mother.

"Greece made me want it even more."

"I see," Kathleen said, once again facing her daughter. "So you came this morning to break the news to me, is that it? Or is there more?"

"I came to ask for your help. I'm trying to find Daddy."

"He's in Paris at his old apartment."

"He's gone. We think he's in hiding."

Kathleen's face turned white. It wasn't the reaction Elizabeth had expected. "Howard Ryan wants to find him, and that miserable, fucking son of a bitch is using you to do it."

Elizabeth was shocked to the bottom of her soul. Never in her life had she heard her mother utter a swearword, let alone a combination like that. Her mouth dropped open for the second time in the past twelve hours.

"Close your mouth, dear," Kathleen said, and she picked up the telephone.

"Who are you calling?"

"Roland Murphy. And if I don't get satisfaction from him, I'll call Jim Lindsay."

"Mother, you can't call the DCI and you can't call the President. I volunteered for this assignment, and I'll do it with or without you. But Daddy needs my help and I'm going to give it to him. His life could depend on it."

Kathleen put the telephone down. "Listen to me, darling. I know Howard Ryan. He's a pompous ass, but he's a powerful pompous ass who is an expert at manipulating people. He has a grudge against your father, and he means to use you to get back at him."

"I didn't think you knew that much about Daddy's career."

"I'm not stupid, Elizabeth. I hear things and I see things. But just because I cannot live with your father, doesn't mean I stopped loving him."

Elizabeth's throat was tight, and her stomach hollow. "Why," she asked softly.

"I cannot live with an . . . assassin."

"Why didn't you tell me that you still loved Daddy."

"You weren't ready," Kathleen said. She studied her daughter's face. "I'm not certain you're ready yet. But Howard Ryan is a dangerous man, darling."

"All the more reason for me to find my father as soon as I can. I have to warn him."

Again Kathleen studied her daughter's face. "You are your father's daughter. Stubborn."

"You dig your heels in too, Mother."

Kathleen smiled wanly. "If he's gone into hiding he won't be out of touch. He always arranges for a contact who can keep him informed with what's happening on the outside. He told me that one of his worst fears was dying alone and being buried in an unmarked grave somewhere."

"What did you say to him, Mother?"

"I told him to get out of the service, of course."

"What would you tell him now?"

"The same thing, Elizabeth. The same thing I'm telling you. The Cold War is over. We won it. There's no compelling reason any longer to maintain such a large intelligence service."

Elizabeth wanted to hate her mother, but she could not. She couldn't even feel sorry for her, because from her mother's point she was correct. She decided not to say anything about Grandma and Grandpa.

"Until last year your father was involved with a woman here in Washington. She's a lobbyist for the airline industry. Her name is Dominique Kilbourne. She might know something."

"Was she involved with Daddy's last assignment?"

"I believe so."

"Will she know who I am?"

Kathleen smiled. "I can't imagine your father *not* talking about you."

"One more favor, Mother," Elizabeth said. "I'd like to borrow one of your credit cards for awhile. I want to get to Paris without leaving a track."

Kathleen hesitated.

"I'll pay you back, Mother, I promise."

"Of course I'll give you one of my credit cards. It's not that, darling. You're my only child and I want you to be safe."

"None of us are safe, Mother."

"Your father says that."

"I know," Elizabeth said.

Elizabeth called the reference desk at the public library from a pay phone and had the woman look up the address of Dominique Kilbourne's office in the list of registered lobbyists. It turned out to be an entire floor of a solid five story building off Thomas Circle, a few blocks from the Russian Embassy.

It was past 11:30 A.M., by the time she presented herself to the receptionist.

"Do you have an appointment?" the woman asked.

"No. But I just need a few minutes of her time. It's important."

"I'm sorry, but Ms. Kilbourne's schedule is completely full today and for the remainder of the week." The secretary touched a few keys on her computer. "I can fit you in next week. Wednesday at two in the afternoon."

"Tell Ms. Kilbourne that Elizabeth McGarvey is here."

Something crossed the secretary's expression. "Just a moment, please," she said, and she got up and went inside.

Elizabeth stepped around the desk so that she could read the computer screen. Dominique Kilbourne's schedule was tight. She was scheduled to be at lunch with a congressional group at the Senate dining room in twenty-five minutes.

The receptionist returned a minute later. "She'll see you now. It's the last door at the end of the hall."

Elizabeth didn't know what to expect, but she wasn't disappointed. Dominique Kilbourne was pretty, with a pleasantly narrow face, short dark hair, coal-black eyes and a slight figure. She looked like a decisive, take-charge woman.

"Thank you for agreeing to see me, Ms. Kilbourne," Elizabeth said.

Dominique motioned her to a seat in front of a starkly modern brass and glass desk. The office was of moderate size, but extremely well furnished, with a couple of Picasso prints on the walls, a large luxurious oriental rug on a marble tiled floor, and large windows with a good view toward the White House. "You come as something of a surprise."

"I'm trying to locate my father. My mother thought you might know where he is."

Dominique stiffened. "The last I heard your father was going to Paris. That was more than a year ago. Beyond that I can't help you, or your mother."

"I'm sorry, I didn't mean to have it come out like that. This has nothing to do with my mother. I simply want to find my father, and I was hoping that you might know something."

"I'm sorry, Ms. McGarvey, I don't," Dominique said. She picked up her telephone. "Sandy, get me a cab, please. I'll be leaving in a minute or two."

"Ms. Kilbourne, I work for the Central Intelligence Agency. I think I could get an FBI Counterespionage unit down here to bring you in for questioning about a national security matter."

"Go ahead," Dominique said, unperturbed, hanging up.

"I work for Mr. Ryan, and I think he could pull a few strings."

"Howard Ryan is an ungrateful son of a bitch whose life your father saved," Dominique blurted angrily. "I was there, I saw it. So you can go back to Langley and tell him that if he wants to find Kirk McGarvey he can do it on his own. I certainly won't help him. Or you."

Elizabeth was a little embarrassed, but she didn't let it show. "I don't know why I should be surprised by your reaction, Ms. Kilbourne. My father has terrible luck with women, but the ones he's attracted to are as strong willed as they are beautiful."

"Thank you for the compliment, if that's what it is, but I still can't help you," Dominique said coolly. "Now if you'll excuse me I have a luncheon appointment."

Elizabeth glanced at the wall clock. "You have fifteen minutes to get to the Senate dining room, so you should have Sandy call over there and tell them you'll be late for lunch because something else has come up. It's a family emergency."

"Get out of here."

"You're going to help me find my father for the same reasons I have to find him before Ryan does. You're in love with him, or at least you were."

Elizabeth had been guessing, but Dominique reacted as if she'd been shot, some of the light fading from her eyes.

"My father has a habit of walking out on the people he loves most, not because he wants to be mean, but because he wants to protect us. Being around him can be dangerous."

"You're telling me."

"This time his life is on the line. I have some information that he has to have. Without it he could be walking into a trap."

"Your father is an amazing man," Dominique said.

"Yes, he is, Ms. Kilbourne," Elizabeth said. "But he's just that. Only a man. Will you help me?"

Dominique thought a moment, then picked up the phone again. "Sandy, cancel that cab. Then call Senator Dobson and give him my apologies, but I won't be able to have lunch with him today. See if we can reschedule for later in the week." Dominique looked at Elizabeth. "Everything is fine. But cancel my appointments for the remainder of the afternoon as well."

"All that isn't necessary," Elizabeth said when Dominique hung up. "I don't need your entire afternoon."

"I do," Dominique said bitterly. She went to a sideboard where she opened a bottle of white wine from a small refrigerator, poured two glasses, and brought them back.

"Thank you, Ms. Kilbourne," Elizabeth said, taking one of the glasses.

"We better start using first names, otherwise it's going to become awkward," Dominique said. She gave Elizabeth a bleak look. "I can see a lot of your father in your face, and in your voice. But I thought you were working for the United Nations."

"I just started with the Company about six months ago. My father doesn't know yet."

Dominique managed a faint smile. "I have a feeling he'll go through the roof when he does find out."

Elizabeth couldn't help but laugh. "I think you're right. But first I have to find him."

Dominique's face had sagged, but she picked herself up. "You father hurt me very much."

"I'm sorry."

Dominique waved her off. "It has nothing to do with you, except that he said the same thing to me last year that you just said. Being around him is dangerous. There are a lot of people from his past who could be gunning for him. There are a lot of old grudges on both sides of the Atlantic. Now you."

"Have you heard from him in the past year?"

"No."

"That's not like him."

"When we parted we had some angry words. I told him that I would either have all of him, or I wanted nothing."

"With my father that was a mistake, if you loved him."

"I don't need some twenty-year-old giving advice to the lovelorn, even if she is a McGarvey," Dominique flared. "You've apparently inherited his manipulative trait as well."

"I didn't come here to be your friend," Elizabeth said harshly. "Although that would have been nice. How can I reach my father?"

"What has he done?"

"I can't tell you that, except to say that it's vitally important that I see him."

"Is it the Russians?" Dominique demanded. "Has Viktor Yemlin popped up looking for his quid pro quo?"

"What are you talking about?" Elizabeth asked sharply, trying to hide her surprise.

"If you're going to play in your father's league, you'd better do your homework first. Yemlin is an old adversary who helped your father out last year. One thing I learned about the business is that nobody does anything for nothing. Your father expected he would show up sooner or later."

"I can't answer that," Elizabeth said.

Dominique started to say something, but Elizabeth overrode her.

"It may sound melodramatic, but the less you know the better off you'll be. Now I'll ask you once again, how can I reach my father."

Dominique turned away. "I don't know," she said. "At least not directly. But he did mention the names of two men he trusted with his life. One of them was Phil Carrara, who was killed. And the other was Otto Rencke, apparently some computer expert who's a black sheep. There was something about Twinkies, but I don't remember all the details."

"Is he here in Washington?"

"He was. But he's in France now. Not in Paris but somewhere nearby."

"Did my father give you his phone number, or e-mail address? Anything like that?"

"No," Dominique said. "But apparently Rencke worked for the CIA once upon a time. He's supposed to be a genius whom everybody is afraid of. But if anybody would know how to get in touch with your father it would either be Rencke, or Yemlin. Beyond that I don't know anything, because if one of them had come to me trying to find your father I would have given them your name. Your father told me that there was only one woman in his life who he loved unreservedly, and who loved him the same way. It was you."

"A father-daughter prerogative," Elizabeth mumbled, masking her sudden emotion.

"He's a more complicated man than I thought, isn't he," Dominique said desolately.

"You can't imagine," Elizabeth replied.

NINETEEN

Moscow

The overnight train back to Moscow was just as crowded as the train out, but if anything the passengers were in even higher spirits than before. They'd seen Tarankov's magic with their own eyes. The blood of the revolution had been spilled in Nizhny Novgorod just as it had in other cities. Their only disappointment was that they'd come away without the money they'd expected. Tarankov's troops never left the vicinity of the railway station, and had not robbed any banks for the people.

"Ah well, maybe it was just a lie," an old man said philosophically. "But killing those bastards was real."

"Wait until he returns to Moscow, then those bastards in the Kremlin will see what a real man is like," another one voiced the generally held opinion. "Then the trains will run on time again, and we'll have food that we can afford back in the shops."

McGarvey had gotten aboard early enough to find a spot in the corner where he curled up, a half-empty bottle of vodka between his knees, as he pretended to sleep, the conversations swirling around him. At one point someone eased the vodka bottle from his loose grip, and then he dozed until they pulled into Yaroslavl Station around 6:30 of a dark gray morning.

After the grueling night the passengers who got off the train were still drunk or hung over, their excitement dissipated, and they wandered away heads hung low, quietly as if they'd just returned from a funeral and not a revolution.

McGarvey found a toilet stall in the nearly deserted arrivals and departures hall, where he changed back into his civilian clothes, stuffing the filthy uniform into the carryall with the last of the greasy sausage and bread.

Someone came into the restroom and used the urinal trough.

McGarvey waited until he was gone, then emerged from the stall leaving the carryall behind as if he'd forgotten it, and out front caught a cab for the Metropol.

The trip to Nizhny Novgorod had made a number of things clear to McGarvey, among them that Tarankov's security was extremely effective. His armored train was a well armed fortress that even a half-dozen attack helicopters had been unable to stop. And once he arrived in the city, his commandoes had set up a defensive perimeter that would have taken a considerable force to penetrate. A lot of civilians, which were Tarankov's major line of defense, would have been killed in the battle, something at this point that the Kremlin could not afford to do.

Whatever lingering doubts McGarvey might have had about Tarankov's time table had also gone out the window in Nizhny Novgorod. On May Day Tarankov's train would roar into Moscow, and he would swoop into Red Square at the head of his column of commandoes with more than a million people screaming his name. It was the one day of the year that no Russian could resist celebrating. Whatever forces the Kremlin would be able to muster, if any, by that late date, would not be sufficient to stop him.

In May Tarankov would ascend to the same throne that Stalin had held unless he were killed.

Despite yesterday's events, which nearly everyone in Moscow must have heard about in news reports or by word of mouth, nothing outwardly had changed. Although seeing the city through new eyes, McGarvey felt an underlying tension even in the traffic and in the way the cabby drove. Moscow was holding its collective breath for the elections in less than three months. It was as if Russians were resigned to another great upheaval.

The cabby dropped him off at his hotel around 8:00 A.M., and he went straight upstairs to his room where Artur the bellman intercepted him as he got off the elevator.

"You look like hell. You must have had a good time."

"Not bad," McGarvey mumbled pulling out his key.

Artur snatched it from him, preceded him down the corridor and unlocked his door with a flourish. "The floor maid was worried. She wanted to report you downstairs, but I told her to mind her own fucking business. You want a hair of the dog. I got some good Belgian brandy for you."

"No thanks," McGarvey said. "I'm going to Helsinki tonight. My train leaves from Leningrad station a little after six. But right now I want some sleep, and I don't want to be disturbed until three. Then I'll want a bottle of white wine, and something to eat. At 4:30 I want a cab driver by the name of Arkady Astimovich to pick me up. He works for Martex. Do you know him?"

"He's a shit asshole, but I know him."

McGarvey pulled out a fifty-franc note. "I want Arkady here by 4:30."

Artur grabbed the money. "Anything you say. But just watch your back with that one. He's in the Mafia's pocket."

His room had been searched, but nothing was missing, nor did it appear that his laptop computer had been tampered with. After a shower he went to bed, but sleep was a long time coming. He knew the approximate when of the kill, as well as the where. Thinking about the cab driver Arkady, the Mafia entrepreneur Vasha, and the bellman Artur he had a glimmering of the how not only of the kill, but most importantly of his escape. He slept, finally, dreaming that he was climbing through the scaffolding inside the main dome of St. Basil's while Tarankov's right hand man Leonid Chernov was in the crowd of a million people in Red Square looking up at him.

CIA Headquarters

It was past 9:00 P.M. in Washington when Elizabeth brought up a photograph of a good-looking woman on her computer screen. She had been assigned a cubicle in DO territory on the fourth floor, and a computer terminal with a designator that allowed her access to a broad range of files in the CIA's vast database. She'd reported to a somewhat disinterested Tom Moore that she was making some progress, but that it might take longer than she thought to find her father. Background noise, her father called it. Like soft music to lull someone asleep while you did the real work.

This afternoon she had the Company's travel section book her an evening flight for the next day to Paris under her Elizabeth Swanson identity. It gave her another twenty-four hours plus to finish up here in Washington. Meanwhile, on the way back to her apartment, she stopped at a pay phone and telephoned a travel agency booking a late shuttle flight to New York's Kennedy Airport, where she would stay at the Airport Hilton, and take the Air France Concorde to Paris under her own name, but using her mother's credit card. The simple subterfuge would give her an evening and a full day in Paris before she was missed. Hopefully it would be enough time to find her father.

She packed a bag which she locked in her trunk, and came back out to Langley. No one at the gate or upstairs in Operations thought anything of it. She was McGarvey's kid on a special assignment for Ryan. She had a lot to prove so she was doing her homework after school.

Jacqueline Belleau's photograph and brief file, marked confidential, were in the French section of identified SDECE agents. She was forty, born in Nice, educated at the Sorbonne in languages and modern political history, and was recruited by the SDECE ten years ago. She'd started her career in the secret service just as Elizabeth had, as a translator. She'd spent two years working from the French delegation at the United Nations in New York. No mention was made of her specific assignment, but she was recalled to France after her lover, who worked for the Canadian delegation, committed suicide by flinging himself into the East River one early winter evening. The young man was a nephew of the Canadian Prime Minister, who was pragmatic enough to understand that such things happen. Nevertheless everyone seemed to agree that it would be for the best if Mademoiselle Belleau returned to her side of the Atlantic without delay. Her continued presence was deemed too embarrassing for the Canadians.

The photograph was an official one, possibly her UN identification picture, and she looked stern. Nevertheless in Elizabeth's estimation she was beautiful. Just the kind of woman her father was attracted to.

Elizabeth smiled sadly. Her mother, Dominique Kilbourne, and this French woman could have been cut from the same cloth. Slender, narrow pretty faces, high cheekbones, expressive eyes. They all had a sensuousness to them that reminded Elizabeth of the photographs she'd seen of her grandmother, who'd been a beauty in her day. It gave Elizabeth another understanding of her father, and her heart ached a little for what could have been. Most of her life she'd dreamed that someday her mother and father would somehow get back together. Even now, she found she wished for such an impossible reunion. "Too much water under the bridge," her father would say. She could hear his voice.

The file gave Mademoiselle Belleau's address on the Avenue Felix Faure in the 15th Arrondissement, on the opposite side of Paris from her father's apartment off the Rue La Fayette in the 19th.

Elizabeth thought about taking a printout with her, but decided against it. In the unlikely event that French customs searched her bags, it wouldn't go for her to be carrying the dossier of a French secret intelligence officer. Too many questions would be asked, especially by Ryan and Moore. Specifically, why hadn't she been traveling under her Elizabeth Swanson identity.

She canceled the file, backed out of the program, then shut down her terminal, and sat back in her chair. Her eyes burned from a lack of sleep and from staring at computer screens. Although she went out on dates she'd avoided becoming involved with anyone specific. A mistake? she wondered. Speaking to Dominique Kilbourne and seeing Jacqueline Belleau's photograph brought her a sharp image of her father being caressed by them. She wished she had someone to caress. Someone she could share her inner fears with. Someone to love. Someone in her bed.

Elizabeth shut off the lights and went downstairs to the nearly deserted cafeteria for a cup of coffee and a smoke. Toivich was seated alone in a corner reading a newspaper. Elizabeth brought her coffee over to him.

"Mind some company, Mr. B?" she asked.

Toivich looked up. "My little *devochka*, it's late."

Elizabeth sat down across the table from him. "I wanted to apologize for not taking the time to let you know that I was transferred to Operations."

"I was told. But I don't think Mr. Ryan would approve of you sneaking back down to your old console for a little night work."

"I have my own terminal in DO now."

Toivich clucked. "I'm not talking about tonight. You know what I mean. But I can't blame you. A daughter has the right to know about her father, especially when she's been assigned to find him."

Elizabeth looked sharply at him. "What have you heard?"

"Enough to know that you should take great care that you don't try to be a wild west cowboy like your father."

Elizabeth started to protest, but Toivich held her off.

"Your father was the very best. Still is, I suspect. If he's gone to ground for some reason there will be a great many people interested in him, and therefore you. Some of them very bad people you've not been trained to deal with." Toivich looked into her eyes. "Genetics is important, but so is education and experience. And luck."

"Why does Howard Ryan hate my father so badly?"

"Mr. Ryan is the quintessential corporate man. Your father on the other hand is a maverick. Each time he pulls off one of his coups, it makes Mr. Ryan look like the fool he is."

"He's jealous of my father, is that it?"

Toivich shrugged. "That and a little fear, perhaps. Ryan wants to become DCI, and he has an excellent chance of taking over when the general steps down. And maybe Ryan would be the right man for the job. It would keep Congress off our backs because Ryan is also the consummate politician. But so long as your father continues to do what he does best, he's a thorn in Ryan's side. He's become Mr. Ryan's *cause célèbre*."

"I see."

"By sending you he means to flush your father out of hiding, which will happen because your father will drop everything to protect you from harm's way."

"But I'm not in any danger. My father is."

"That's just the point, Elizabeth, you probably are in grave danger. Especially if you start playing by your own rules. If you cut your support system before you reach your father, nobody might get to you in time if you get into trouble."

Elizabeth said nothing. She'd not lost her determination to find her father and warn him, but she was frightened now.

"Think about it."

"Am I being followed, Mr. B?"

Toivich shrugged again. "Probably."

"What if I don't want to be followed?"

"If you don't do anything that you're not supposed to do, it won't matter."

"I need to get to Dulles by eleven, and I don't want anybody to know about it."

"You just told me."

Elizabeth flashed him a smile.

Toivich shook his head. "Where are you parked?"

"Out back in D."

"They'll be waiting at that door. I was just about to leave. We'll go out the front and I'll drive you around to your car. But it won't take them long to figure that out, so you won't have much of a head start."

"It's all I need. Thanks, Mr. B."

Moscow

"How did it go?" Arkady Astimovich asked on the way over to the Leningrad Station.

"I think I'm going to be a rich man," McGarvey replied. He sat in the front seat with the cabby. "But I'm going to need some help."

"I told you that I've got some goddamned good connections in this city."

"The Mafia?"

Astimovich glanced over at him, and nodded warily. "You gotta deal with them if you want to survive in this town. It'll be expensive, but damned well worth it."

"How much are you paying?"

"Plenty," the cabby said. He laughed. "Everybody pays. My brother-in-law is a big deal son of a bitch at the Grand Dinamo, and still I pay."

"I don't have a problem with that. But when the time comes I don't want to deal with some kulak."

"My brother-in-law knows what he's doing," Astimovich said. "What kind of business are we going into, boss?"

"I'll let you know when I get back."

"When's that?"

"A few weeks. Maybe a little longer, maybe a little sooner."

"What do you want me to do in the meantime?"

"Keep your mouth shut."

They pulled up in front of the busy Leningrad Station, traffic heavy as usual. The snow had finally stopped but the temperature had plunged. Everything looked dirty.

"Three weeks is a long time," Astimovich said sullenly. "How do I know you're coming back?"

"Because we're going to make some money," McGarvey said. He peeled a thousand francs from a thick bundle of bills and handed it to the cabby. "Let's call this a down payment, shall we?"

"*Spasiba*," the cabby said, pocketing the money.

"Do as I say and you'll be a rich man. Cross me and I'll kill you. I've got connections now in this town too."

"Okay, boss. You'll see everything will be hunky-dory."

McGarvey got his bag from the back seat of the cab and disappeared with the crowds inside the railway station. He waited by the front doors for a few minutes to make sure that Astimovich wouldn't try to follow him, then went to the stand-up restaurant and had a glass of beer and a meat pie. In three days he had learned what he needed to know about Tarankov and conditions in Russia. He felt that his odds had greatly improved from the thousand-to-one he'd told Yemlin. But there was still a long way to go, because he wouldn't go through with the assassination unless he could improve his chances to at least fifty-fifty.

His overnight train for Helsinki was scheduled to arrive in the Finnish capital shortly before 9:30 A.M., giving him ninety minutes to make his Finnair flight to Brussels where he would pick up his Avis Renault and drive back to Paris.

He was leaving Russia several thousand francs poorer, but if the million dollars had been deposited in his Channel Islands account as Yemlin promised it would be, then money would not be a problem. Nor would it have been in any event. The investments he'd made over the past twenty-five years, starting with the proceeds from the sale of his parents' ranch in Kansas, had done well. He was not a wealthy man, but he was independent. His demand for money from Yemlin had only been done to insure that the Russian was serious. Money was something they understood almost better than any other concept.

Gathering his bag, he left the restaurant and walked through the terminal to the trackside gates where he had to show his ticket and passport. Outgoing Russian customs wouldn't occur until Vyborg, but his gun was tucked safely away in his laptop computer, and Russians these days were more interested in what was being brought into the country than what was being taken out.

TWENTY

Paris

A few minutes past 5:30 P.M., the Air France Concorde SST from New York, touched down at Charles de Gaulle Airport with a tremendous roar, its needle nose drooping like some gigantic insect. Of the 143 passengers, Elizabeth McGarvey was one of the last off, letting her seat partner, an extremely boring attorney from New Jersey, precede her. During the four-hour flight across the Atlantic the man had done everything within his power to convince her to meet him at his hotel for drinks tonight. At first his attentions had been flattering because he was reasonably good looking. But then he'd become funny and finally annoying. But she didn't want to attract any attention so she'd quietly gone along with him, even taking down his hotel number. But she refused to ride into the city with him or even get off the plane together because her father, who was insanely protective of his daughter, would be meeting her, and she didn't want to cause a scene, to which the lawyer agreed wholeheartedly. By the time she got off the plane she was in an extremely bitchy mood.

She taped the Elizabeth Swanson passport and identification papers to her midriff between the bottom of her bra and the top of her panties. She didn't think that even a Frenchman would dare pat her down. And unless authorities were expecting her, there'd be no reason for the customs officers to become suspicious.

"The purpose of your visit to France, Mademoiselle?" the young passport control officer asked from his booth.

"Pleasure," Elizabeth replied curtly.

The officer stamped her passport indifferently, and she walked back to customs. She'd flown Air France, not a foreign carrier, so she'd arrived at Aérogare Two which was only for Air France and therefore uncomplicated. This evening the terminal was practically deserted.

There was no sign of her seat-mate when she picked up her bag and headed for the RIEN A DECLARER line. The customs official smiled at her and passed her through with a wave, and she was in France. It had been easy.

Upstairs in the main terminal she got a couple of thousand francs from the ATM using her mother's credit card, then went back downstairs again and outside to the cab ranks.

"Good evening, Mademoiselle," the cabby said.

"L'Hôtel Marronniers sur la Rue Jacob dans la Rive Gauche, s'il vous plait," she said, sitting back.

"Oui, Mademoiselle," the driver replied respectfully.

As they pulled away from the curb, Elizabeth took a cigarette out of her purse, lit it, then cracked the window by a couple of inches.

"Pas d'fumer, Mademoiselle," the driver said sternly over his shoulder.

Elizabeth ignored him.

"Mademoiselle, please no smoking," he said, looking at her reflection in the rearview mirror.

She stared out the window, totally ignoring him, as she slowly uncrossed her legs giving him a good view up her short skirt, and then sat back even farther so that her skirt hiked almost up to her panty line.

The driver stopped complaining, but from time to time he glanced in the rearview mirror, and she rewarded him with a couple more looks up her skirt, which seemed to make him happy.

She and her mother had spent a few days at the small, but pleasant Hôtel Marronniers on the Left Bank a few years ago after she'd finished school in Bern. She thought it unlikely that anyone on the staff would re-member her, but even if they did it wouldn't matter, because she wasn't here illegally, nor had she committed any crime on French soil.

Her father was here someplace, she thought as they crossed the river and got off the ring highway at the Quai Marcel Boyer above the Pont National. Paris was his home of choice, he'd explained to her, because for the most part the people were civilized, they minded their own business, and their food and wine were the best in the world. Besides, where else would a Voltaire scholar feel more at home than in France?

Rush-hour traffic was thinning out by the time the cabby dropped her off in front of the hotel that was hidden behind a courtyard. She went inside, showed her passport and booked a room for a week, and paid for it with her own credit card. It would take twenty-four to thirty-six hours for her presence to be known in Paris from her hotel registration. By then she would have either found her father or she would have checked in with Tom Lynch, so hiding her trail was no longer as important as it had been on the shuttle from Dulles to Kennedy, and the Concorde flight over.

She thought she recognized the old concierge behind his desk, but if he remembered her he gave no hint of it. The bellman helped her upstairs with her bag, and after she tipped him and he was gone, she flung open the windows and breathed the Paris air. No other city in the world smelled quite like this one, she thought. And especially this time, because she was in Paris on a secret mission. It was better than the movies, because it was real.

She took a quick shower, dried her hair, then dressed in a pair of blue jeans, a pretty white V-neck light sweater and a pair of black flats that matched her shoulder bag. She hid her Elizabeth Swanson papers under the bed, then went out.

It was dinner time, and she was famished. She sat down at a sidewalk café a couple of blocks from her hotel, where she had a half-bottle of Chardonnay, a small salad, a cheese omelette with pommes frittes and a café express afterwards.

She'd been on her own since college, first in New York, and for the past few months in Washington. But being here in Paris like this, was different. Vastly different.

The address of her father's apartment was across the river near the gares du Nord and de l'Est, in what until recently had been a rough workingman's neighborhood. But Paris was undergoing a renovation, and cruising past his building in a taxi Elizabeth could see why he liked this part of town. It was anonymous, with an easy egress from the city on the main Avenue Jean Jaurés, plus the two railway stations. There was a small park across the street from a pleasant looking café a half-block from his apartment.

She had the cabby cruise around the neighborhood, explaining that she wasn't quite certain of the correct address, while she looked for signs that her father's place was under surveillance: someone loitering across the street, a van with too many antennas parked on the street, the chance reflection of binocular lenses in a second story window. But if they were there, she couldn't spot them, and she had the cabby drop her off in front of the café.

Although the evening was starting to get cool, Elizabeth sat at an outside table where she had a coffee while she watched the neighborhood. Her father's apartment was on the third floor front, and the windows were dark. She hadn't expected to simply take a cab out to his apartment, knock on his door and find him at home. But seeing his darkened windows gave her a chill. She felt not so much on her own now, as she did alone, abandoned again like she'd been when she was a child.

She'd become spoiled over the past few years, having him a car-ride away when he lived outside Washington, or a telephone call away when he lived here. And she'd forgotten what it had been like without him for most of her childhood. She'd bounced from missing him so badly that she ached, to hating him so deeply that she dreamed once of shooting him in the head with a gun, then cutting off his arms and legs with a machete and using his parts to feed the sharks. The next morning she'd been so ashamed of her dream that she'd thrown up and managed to produce a fever so that her mother kept her home from school. She just couldn't face her classmates, almost all of whom had both parents at home.

Later when she'd come to learn at least in general terms what her father did for a living, she'd become so proud that she couldn't stop talking about him. Finally the school principal had called her mother in to ask her to stop Elizabeth's fantastical stories. They frightened the other students, and some of the teachers and parents. At any rate if her father really was a spy, Elizabeth shouldn't be so open about it. Her mother had been deeply embarrassed and for several months afterward Elizabeth was not allowed to speak her father's name.

A half-block away the Rue La Fayette was busy, but on this side street only a few cars and few pedestrians moved. It was a week night and most French families were at home eating dinner and watching television. Some new plane trees had been planted along both sides of the street, and although they were small, and their branches mostly bare, there were a few green buds on some of them. In ten or fifteen years this would be an extremely pleasant, and therefore expensive neighborhood.

Certain now that no one was watching her father's apartment building, Elizabeth paid for her coffee, and made the first pass on foot, looking through the windows into the empty ground floor vestibule. She crossed the street at the corner, and returned. She had to wait for a taxi to pass before she could cross back and she ducked inside the apartment building.

Her father's name was listed on a white card on the mailbox for 3A, and for a few seconds she hoped that she was on a wild goose chase. A radio or television was playing somewhere within the building, and she heard a woman's voice raised in what sounded like anger. A man barked a sharp reply, and the woman fell silent. She took the stairs at the back of the hall two at a time to the third floor where she held up for a full minute. This floor was quiet. No light shone from under either the front or rear apartment doors. Even the air smelled neutral, only a faint mustiness indicated the building was old. Again she hoped she was on a wild goose chase, and her father would come up the stairs behind her and be flabbergasted when he saw her standing in the darkness. But no one came up. She stepped out of the stairway to her father's apartment, hesitated a second longer, then rang the bell.

The door to the opposite apartment behind her opened, and she turned, catching the impression of a bulky man in shirtsleeves standing there with a gun in his hand.

The thought that she'd made a dreadful mistake coming here flashed through her head like a bolt of lightning. Moving on instinct she charged into the stairway and raced downstairs without a sound. If she could make it outside she had a fair chance of losing herself in the night. Among her talents were the 220 and 440-yard dashes for which she'd won trophies in high school and college. One of her coaches had even suggested training for the Olympics, but she hadn't been interested.

She reached the ground floor as the front door slammed open and several men in dark windbreakers barged into the narrow vestibule.

Turning, she started back up the stairs when the man from the third floor suddenly appeared, blocking the way.

Elizabeth turned again, this time into the muzzles of two very large pistols. She stopped and her entire body sagged.

"Shit," she said.

The flashing blue lights of several police cars were gathered on the street, along with a growing number of onlookers.

"Give me your purse, Mademoiselle," one of the gunmen said.

"*Je suis le fille de Monsieur Kirk McGarvey*," Elizabeth said, carefully handing her purse to the surprised plain clothes officer.

"What are you doing here, Mademoiselle McGarvey?" one of the other plain clothes officers asked. He was heavyset and very dark and dangerous looking.

"I came to see my father, naturally," Elizabeth replied. "Is this how you treat all your visitors to France?"

The heavyset man searched her purse, and examined her passport. "Your father is not at home."

"Evidently not."

"Where is he?"

"I thought he was here."

"Was he expecting you?"

"No," Elizabeth said. "Now if that's all, I'd like my purse and I'll go."

"I would like to ask you a few questions, if you'll come downtown with us. With no trouble, please."

"First I'd like to call my embassy."

"In due time, Mademoiselle," the heavyset man said. "If you cooperate we will not handcuff you."

Elizabeth stepped up to him. He towered a full head over her, and he looked dangerous, more like a street thug than a cop. "What am I being charged with, and who the hell are you?"

"You're being charged with nothing, yet. As for my name, I am Colonel Guy de Galan." He stepped aside for her. "Now, if you please, Mademoiselle?"

Elizabeth hesitated a moment longer. She still had twenty-four hours before Tom Lynch was expecting her. The French were looking for her father, but with luck they might buy her story and let her go, providing they did not find out what hotel she was staying at and search her room.

Out in the street several dozen people had gathered to watch what was going on. She searched the crowd for a familiar face, either her father's or Tom Lynch's whom she was sure she would recognize from the photographs she'd seen. But they were all strangers hoping to catch some interesting action.

Getting in the back of Colonel Galan's car she glanced up at her father's apartment, a bitter taste in her mouth. In less than forty-eight hours working for Ryan she'd managed to get herself arrested. It wouldn't look so good in her personnel file, but she didn't think that the Deputy Director of Operations would be very surprised.

TWENTY-ONE

Bonnières

McGarvey flipped off the Renault's headlights shortly before 10:00 P.M. as he approached Rencke's house, and stopped in the woods to make sure there was no danger.

It was good to be back in France, even if his stay was only temporary. The evening was cool, but it was sharply warmer than Russia or Finland and he was sweating lightly by the time he reached the edge of the trees overlooking the farmhouse.

He'd spent a reasonably restful evening aboard the train from Moscow to Helsinki, and even managed to get another two hours of sleep on the Finnair flight. By the time he reached Brussels he was well rested and made the 235-mile drive to Bonnières in under five hours, which included a leisurely dinner in an excellent bistro in Compiègne.

A thin curl of smoke rose from the chimney of the farmhouse, and a light shone from one of the windows. Nothing seemed out of the ordinary, nevertheless McGarvey settled down to wait for a full thirty minutes to see if anything developed. Even the most disciplined surveillance officers would do something in that time span to reveal themselves to a careful observer. Light a cigarette, cough, move a branch or a bush, key a walkie-talkie.

During the drive across France he had worked out more of the details of the first glimmerings of a plan that had come to him in Moscow. Getting into Russia would provide no real difficulty. But once Tarankov was down, getting back out again could be difficult unless his cover was airtight. When the authorities looked at him, he wanted them to see what they expected to see, and not an assassin. In fact, if all went well the Russia Mafia would actually help him get out and never know what they'd unknowingly done.

Something moved at the edge of the woods fifty yards to the left. McGarvey stood stock still behind the bole of a large oak tree, all of his senses alert.

The bushes rattled, the sound almost inaudible. Moments later a small white-tailed deer stepped into the clearing. It was a doe, and she was cautious, her nose up testing the air. She looked toward McGarvey then meandered the rest of the way down the hill, daintily skirted Rencke's solar panel arrays, and followed the far edge of the woods, finally disappearing toward the river.

McGarvey walked back to the car satisfied no one was watching the house, and drove the rest of the way down the hill. An excited Rencke was waiting for him at the front door, his hair a mess, his blue jeans dirty and his tennis shoes untied, the laces flapping as he hopped from foot to foot.

"Hiya, Mac. Tell me you were in Nizhny Novgorod and you'll make my day. I won't even complain that you didn't bring me any Twinkies this time. Tell me! Tell me!"

"I was there, and it's even worse than you thought," McGarvey said, preceding Rencke inside. He stopped in his tracks.

Most of the computer equipment was gone, or had been dismantled and packed in large boxes. Only one monitor still showed anything, and two partitioned suitcases were almost completely filled with super dense floppy disks. McGarvey felt a twinge of uneasiness.

"What's going on, Otto? Is somebody onto you?"

"Maybe the Action Service, I'm not sure," Rencke said brusquely. "But as of a few hours ago all the CIA circuits to Paris Station went blank except for routine housekeeping data after the French requested it."

"What was the last message sent?"

"It was an FYI to Lynch from Tom Moore, Ryan's assistant, that you would be in French custody within twenty-four hours."

McGarvey considered this news for a moment.

"Did he say how?"

"No. But it's getting flaky out there all of a sudden, know what I mean?

Somebody is taking this shit mucho seriously, and you're at the middle of it."

"Has anyone made the connection between me and Tarankov yet?"

"There's been nothing on any of the circuits. But I think they might be making the leap. Kabatov has asked for U.S. help, and it looks like Lindsay is about to give it to him."

It wasn't surprising. From what McGarvey had seen Kabatov's government was in serious trouble. "What kind of help?"

"NATO has been instructed to conduct exercises in Poland, and they're moving I don't know how many divisions up there now. All our air bases in Germany are on alert, and the Sixth Fleet has deployed from Naples. The sabres are rattling big time, Mac. Brings you back to the early sixties,"

"Have you got someplace—?" McGarvey began.

"That depends on you," Rencke cut in. "But I found a house with a garage up in Courbevoie. It's French yuppieville, and I don't think anyone would expect to find me there. Anyway, there's a telephone substation fifty meters from my backdoor, the N308 is a block away, and it's less than twenty minutes to downtown Paris. I should have been a real estate agent, don't you think?"

"How long did you rent it for?"

"A year, but more to the point, are you taking the job? Are you going to kill Tarankov?"

"Yes, and I'm going to need your help," McGarvey said.

"That's why I rented Courbevoie. Otherwise I was thinking that a winter in Rio wouldn't be all that bad."

McGarvey had to laugh despite the situation. "I don't think they sell Twinkies down there, Otto."

"They do, Mac, I checked. What do you think, I'm crazy or something?" Rencke's eyes were alive with excitement. "You saw him blow away those apparatchiks in Nizhny Novgorod, Mac? You looked into his eyes and saw—what?"

"I saw the killings, but it was Leonid Chernov who looked into my eyes."

Rencke was suddenly serious. "Bad shit, Mac, because he's gotta be the baddest dog of all. No records on him. Nada, unless you brought me the SVR's database number."

"Have you still got a secure outside line?" McGarvey asked.

"For the moment."

"Okay. Pull up today's *Le Figaro*. The personals column."

Rencke went to the one computer that was still running, and within a minute he was scrolling through *Le Figaro*'s want ads. "What are we looking for?"

"There," McGarvey said, stabbing a finger on the screen. *Julius loves you, please call at once. 277-8693.* "The telephone number is inverted. Add five to each number, and start over again past zero."

"All right," Rencke said. "It's 722-3148. Did Yemlin place the ad?"

"Yes."

"It could be traced, Mac. Do we want to trust it?"

"We don't have any other choice. I need more information on Chernov, because I think that I'll come up against him sooner or later. If he's what I think he is Tarankov has given him a free hand, and he'll probably have his own connections among the old KGB's Department Viktor people. It means he's dangerous and I'll probably have to kill him in order to get out."

Rencke looked at McGarvey with wonder. "You're really going to do it. You're going to assassinate the bastard."

"Yes, I am."

"Why?" Rencke asked.

"Because it's what I do," McGarvey replied. "And I'm getting paid one million dollars for the job. But Tarankov certainly won't be the first politician whose assassination didn't make any difference in the long run. But just now at this point in time Russia can go either way. Maybe I don't like the thought of having to fight a cold war all over again. Or have nuclear missiles pointed at us. Maybe by killing this one man I can save some lives. They were apparatchiks in Nizhny Novgorod. Probably corrupt and arrogant as hell, but Tarankov and his men executed them without a second thought. You predicted that if he gains power tens of thousands, maybe millions of people would die. I might be able to prevent that."

Rencke had become subdued, his face long. "It's something else too, isn't it Mac? It's about your parents."

"I guess," McGarvey said.

The house was suddenly closing in. He went out to the courtyard, and lit a cigarette. He had the fleeting thought that if someone was out there in the trees the flare of his match and the glowing tip of the cigarette would make him a perfect target for assassination. It was a thought he'd had from time to time. It would answer the ultimate question, as Rencke had suggested, of finding out what came afterward. And it would be a release from his dreams in which he clearly saw the faces of every person he'd ever killed. His sister in Utah had stopped speaking to him years ago, so his nieces and nephews had grown up without knowing their uncle. It was at times like these he missed the sense of family. His wife couldn't live with him, and he'd been frightened for the safety of every woman he'd ever known intimately. Lately he'd even tried to keep his daughter at arm's length for fear that she would come to harm's way. Yemlin showing up in Paris had shaken him more than he wanted to admit, because despite his expertise in the business he was just as vulnerable as any other man. This kill would be the ultimate for him, because although he knew in his heart of hearts that he would never be able to reduce the odds of success to fifty-fifty he was still going ahead with it. He wasn't invincible, but he didn't care because the prize was worth the risk.

"I never knew my parents, so I can only guess what you must be feeling,"

Rencke said from the darkness behind McGarvey. "But at least you had them when you were growing up. You had family. A sister, and then a wife and a daughter. No matter how bad it gets, you had that much, Mac. Which was more than I ever had. I don't even have my cats anymore. I've got nobody except for you."

McGarvey turned around. Rencke had extinguished the house lights and he stood in the deeper shadows beneath the eaves. He looked like the silhouette of a comic figure, except that it was painfully obvious from his words that he was hurting.

It seemed to McGarvey that he had given of himself for most of his life. He'd given himself to his country, which since Santiago didn't seem to care, or even want to know about him. He'd given everything he was capable of to women, but in the end they'd all rejected him for one reason or another. Because of his fears, of course, but because he was apparently incapable of giving them what they needed, on their terms. Elizabeth was the only exception, but she was young and she still idolized him. In time her eyes would be opened and though she might not reject him, she would at least keep him at arm's length.

He'd fared no better with men either. He'd looked up to his father, who he'd been told was a traitor. He'd looked up to John Lymann Trotter, a former DDO, who'd tried to kill him. He'd looked up to Phil Carrara, another DDO, who'd died trying to help him. And he'd looked up to CIA director Roland Murphy, who thought that at best McGarvey was a sometimes necessary evil.

"We're a couple of misfits, aren't we, Mac?" Rencke said. "You're an assassin and I'm a flake. But you know, it's sometimes the misfits who get the job done."

"If you're a misfit, Otto, I wish the rest of the world were misfits too," McGarvey said gently.

Rencke laughed. "That makes us family."

"Sure does. But until the job is done we're going to be a busy family and you're going to have to do exactly as I say."

"I'll do it, Mac."

"When can you take possession of your new house?"

"I signed the lease two days ago. It's mine right now. I just wanted to wait until you came back."

"We're going up there tonight. What we can't take with us, we're going to destroy, as if you'd suddenly left here and vandals broke in."

"It's rare in France."

"It's rare, but it happens. Maybe the brothers of one of your conquests in the neighborhood decided to get even. We'll let the local cops figure that out."

"If you'll help me we can be out of here within the hour," Rencke said.

"Okay. But I'm not going to tell you what I'm planning so that if something goes wrong you'll be able to get out. No matter what happens, if something starts to go bad you're going to run. To Rio if you want. If I come out okay, I'll find you. Are you all right for money?"

"I have plenty. Most of it outside of France."

"Once I start, you won't be able to contact me, so you'll have to set up a very secure number where I can reach you if I need information."

"Can do."

"We'll arrange a code phrase so that when you answer I'll know that everything is okay. Yemlin and his people might be the weak link. If he falls they won't know what I've planned, but they'll know that I'm coming. You're going to have to do what you can to get back into the CIA's computers. And hopefully the SVR's number that Yemlin gave us is a valid one."

"I'll say your daughter called and she's fine," Rencke said.

McGarvey had a sudden odd feeling, like butterflies fluttering inside his head.

"The code phrase," Rencke prompted. "I'll use that one if everything is okay."

McGarvey nodded. "That'll work. She'd be pleased if she knew."

"She's a pretty girl."

"When did you meet her?" McGarvey asked a little too sharply.

"It's okay, Mac. I've kept up with you and your family. I wanted to make sure everything was going okay. Your ex-wife is doing fine, but I'm glad she didn't marry that attorney puke. And Elizabeth's marks finally came up, and she was doing fine for the UN last time I checked." Rencke smiled. "Think of me as an uncle. When this is all over with, maybe you can ask her to write me a letter now and then. Maybe invite me to the wedding when she gets married." Rencke's face lit up. "I'd made a terrific godfather. I mean it'd be great, don't you think?"

McGarvey laughed and shook his head. "You are a flake, Otto, but you're my flake now."

Rencke laughed out loud and hopped from one foot to another.

"But if you ever touch her, you'll die," McGarvey said, trying to keep the grin off his face, but it only made Rencke laugh all the harder.

Gallows humor, McGarvey thought as he went inside and helped Rencke dismantle the equipment he needed, and destroy the rest.

TWENTY-TWO

Le Bourget

Elizabeth estimated that it was past one in the morning, and she was tired, hungry and just a little bit frightened. They'd taken her to what looked like an army post or police barracks somewhere on the outskirts of Paris, placed her in a small windowless room furnished with a steel table and three chairs, returned her cigarettes and matches, gave her a bottle of Evian and a plastic glass, and had left. But that had been hours ago, and now she was bored out of her skull and she had to pee.

She got up, smoothed her hair with her fingers, then lit another cigarette and perched on the edge of the table and stared pointedly at the small square of plastic imbedded in the wall. Behind it was either an observation port, or a closed circuit television camera. Either way, they were watching her, and they damned well knew that she knew it. It was irritating because they were treating her like a criminal, and when she finally showed up in Tom Lynch's office she'd have some explaining to do. At the very least she figured Ryan would fire her, and she didn't have much of a leg to stand on. But she wasn't going to give the French the satisfaction of watching her fall apart.

She stubbed out her cigarette in the overflowing ashtray, raised her middle finger at the plastic square and threw herself down on the chair.

"*Les salopards*," she swore softly.

The door opened and a kindly looking man with a wrinkled face and thinning white hair came in with a file folder, which he placed on the table. He pulled up a chair, and sat down across from Elizabeth.

"Good evening, *ma p'tite*. My name is Alexandre Lévy, and I would like to ask you a few questions, after which you will be free to leave. Someone will take you back to your hotel. I'm sure that you would like to have a hot bath, perhaps have a bite to eat and then go to bed. You must be exhausted."

"Why was I arrested?"

"Oh, good heavens, young lady, you're not under arrest. We merely wish to ask you a few questions, as I said. Showing up on your father's doorstep came as something of a surprise to us. We weren't expecting you."

"Isn't it the custom in France for children to visit their parents?" Elizabeth shot back. She felt as if Lévy was toying with her, and her eyes were drawn to the file folder.

"Indeed it is. Lamentably, however, my children don't visit me or their mother as often as we would like. I sincerely hope you treat your filial duties with more respect." Lévy tapped a blunt finger on the file folder. "As you may guess, we take a sincere interest in your father and his current activities. So long as he remains retired he is welcome to reside in France. However a question of the exact nature of his most recent activities has arisen for which we would sincerely like to talk to him."

Elizabeth tried to interrupt, but Lévy held up a hand.

"Please, Mademoiselle. Your father is in no trouble. His arrest has not been ordered, nor do we wish to interfere with his quiet enjoyment of Paris, or of all of France for that matter. So I am asking for your help. Either tell us where your father might have gone, or short of that, simply take a message to him that we'd like to speak with him. We would even agree to a telephone interview. Nothing more than that. Totally harmless. Can you find fault with us?"

"Look, I told Colonel Galan that I was just as surprised as you guys that my father is gone. I've got a few days off and I wanted to surprise him. I suppose I should have called first." Elizabeth shrugged. "But now you're getting me worried. Maybe something has happened to him. Maybe I should file a missing persons report."

A faint flicker of a smile crossed Lévy's face. "Your mother is a rich woman?"

The question caught Elizabeth by surprise. "She does okay."

Lévy flipped open the file folder, and extracted a single sheet of paper which he passed to her. "You only have a few days off in which to see your father, so your mother generously allows you the use of her Visa card. The Concorde flight alone cost nearly six thousand dollars, not to mention the ATM cash withdrawal of two thousand francs at Charles de Gaulle."

The paper with a Chase Manhattan Bank logo was a brief computer reply to a query from Air France verifying the validity of the charge.

"I assume you did not borrow the card without your mother's knowledge."

"My mother is a generous woman."

"Indeed. Would she know where your father is at the moment? Would she speak to us?"

"Probably not," Elizabeth said disconsolately. If they knew that much, they probably knew the rest. "May I telephone my embassy?"

"They won't be awake over there at this hour," Lévy said. He withdrew a plain manila envelope from the file folder, opened it, and dumped the contents, which included a U.S. passport, a Maryland driver's license, insurance card, voter registration card, and two credit cards, on the table.

Elizabeth recognized them, and her spirits sank even lower.

Lévy opened the passport, studied the photograph, then looked up at Elizabeth. "This says that your name is Elizabeth Swanson. The picture matches." He laid the passport down. "We found these where you hid them in your hotel room. Good stuff, not amateur. I'd say that the CIA supplied you with these documents. Is that so?"

"If that were the case you would know that I couldn't talk about it."

"On the other hand the papers could be first class forgeries, in which case you would be charged in France with conspiracy to conduct terrorism."

"Don't be stupid," Elizabeth flared.

Lévy was unimpressed. "It is not I who am the fool, Mademoiselle. Nor is it I who am sitting without rights in an interrogation cell. So let me ask you one last time. Do you know your father's current whereabouts?"

"I wouldn't have gone to his apartment if I did," Elizabeth said.

Lévy stared thoughtfully at her for several moments, then gathered up the papers and documents and stuffed them back into the file folder. "It is a good thing that you came into France under your real name. If you had used these we would have arrested you and deported you immediately." He got up.

"How did you know I arrived in France?" Elizabeth asked.

Lévy smiled indulgently. "Your father is a famous man. The names of his family and friends are all flagged."

"May I go now?"

"In a few minutes, Mademoiselle," Lévy said and he left.

Tom Lynch, the Chief of Paris station, came in a moment later, a sharp look of disapproval on his narrow, delicate face.

"What the hell are you doing here thirty-six hours ahead of time?" he demanded, his voice as sharply pitched as his manner.

"They're probably watching and listening to us—"

"I had them shut it off. I asked you a question. What the hell are you doing here?"

"Looking for my father. It's my job," Elizabeth answered defiantly.

"How exactly did you intend accomplishing that? Did you think that he left you a note on his door? Didn't you think that since we and the French are looking for him that his apartment would be under surveillance?"

"I didn't see anybody."

"You didn't look," Lynch shouted. "We'll have to apologize to the French government, of course, then I'll talk to Mr. Ryan and arrange to send you back to Washington."

"I don't think so," Elizabeth said.

"We'll see," Lynch shot back.

"Have you found my father yet?"

"As a matter of fact we have not," Lynch said, eyeing her. "I don't know how extensive your briefing was, but your father's life may be in danger. We simply want to get word to him, nothing more. But your little trick hasn't helped one bit. The French are going to be convinced that he's working for us again, and they'll probably try to arrest him, unless we can find him first." Lynch shook his head. "I don't even want to think what might happen."

"Sending me back won't make it any better," Elizabeth said. Her father didn't like Ryan, but he'd never mentioned Lynch.

"Do you have an idea where he is?"

"No, but I wanted to talk to two people who might know something."

"Who are they?" Lynch asked with renewed interest.

"Jacqueline Belleau, the woman he was living with."

"If she knew anything they'd have him by now."

"Is she in love with him?"

"I wouldn't know."

"Has anyone asked?"

"Ms. Belleau is a trained French intelligence officer. She wouldn't have fallen in love with your father. In any event she's not subject to an interview by us. Who's the second person?"

Elizabeth hesitated. Ryan was a jerk, but Lynch seemed to be genuinely concerned with helping her father. "I'll tell you, but I want you to keep it confidential. At least until we can talk to him. I'll need your help."

"All right," Lynch said. "That's why you were sent here. Who have we missed?"

"Otto Rencke. He's supposed to be living somewhere near Paris."

A look of amazement crossed Lynch's features. "Jesus. We never thought of him."

"He might not talk to you, but if you can find him I'll go out there."

"Damn right you will," Lynch said. "He's in Bonnières, about thirty or forty miles away."

"Can we go there now?"

"It's not going to be that easy. First of all I don't know exactly where he's living. But I can find that out. In the meantime it's going to take a couple of hours to get you out of here. The French are almost as bad as the Germans when it comes to paperwork."

"I'm warning you, Mr. Lynch, if you bring Rencke in he'll clam up. He won't talk to anybody."

Lynch's eyes narrowed. "Don't worry about it. I have my homework to do. When you get out of here, someone will drive you back to your hotel. Get a couple hours of sleep, and then come over to the embassy, and we'll do this together."

Elizabeth hoped she hadn't made a mistake by trusting Lynch, but it was too late now to do anything but go along with him. "Okay. But try to get me out of here as soon as possible."

"Hang in there, kid," Lynch said. "You did the right thing after all."

Bonnières

Three hours later Lynch stood in the doorway of the farmhouse surveying the damage that had been done to the interior. The battered remains of what had been several pieces of computer equipment lay scattered around the floor. Lynch was a computer expert himself. It was obvious to him that the room had once held a great deal of equipment. Power cables snaked throughout the house and he could see a half-dozen spots on the floor and along the walls where desks or computer consoles had stood.

"He had a visitor," Colonel Galan said, coming from the courtyard in back. He had picked up the butts of two Marlboro cigarettes. "There is no evidence that Rencke smokes, and according to McGarvey's file, this is his brand."

"The cigarette papers were crushed but not weathered. We must have just missed them."

"His daughter didn't warn them from anywhere in France," Galan said. "Which might mean that he's getting inside information from somewhere."

"We didn't know that we were coming out here until this morning. It would have taken them much longer to do this much," Lynch said.

"How do you see it?"

"McGarvey is definitely taking Yemlin's assignment, I don't think there's any doubt about it now. But he needs help, so he hired Rencke and got him out of here. By now they could be anywhere. Even out of France."

Colonel Galan laughed humorlessly. "Don't try to make me feel good, Tom. Once he leaves France he's no longer my problem."

"Might be a moot point in any case. France is where he wants to live out his retirement, if what he told Jacqueline is true. I don't think he'd do anything to make that impossible. He'd know that the CIA would help you hunt for him if he screwed up here."

"Finding this computer expert will be just as difficult as finding McGarvey, now that they're together," Galan said glumly. "What about your station in Moscow? Is there any possibility of getting to Viktor Yemlin?"

"At this point I don't think it's been passed along to Moscow. So far as Langley is concerned, we're merely helping you find McGarvey for questioning. Unless you want to take it a step farther."

"Frankly I don't know what to do," Galan said. "I'll have to take it up with my boss. But I have a gut feeling that this is not going to turn out so good for anybody. Why the *mec* didn't remain in the States, or return to Switzerland is beyond me."

Lynch had flown from Paris with Galan and a half-dozen Action Service troops aboard a Dessault helicopter. He could hear the men searching the grounds, calling to each other and joking now that they understood their quarry was long gone. The French were efficient in some matters, Lynch thought, but they tended to operate with blinders on. If France or French citizens were involved they would go to great lengths. But they tended to turn a blind eye toward anything or anyone outside of their borders.

Another thought occurred to Lynch. "Maybe we should change our tactics, Guy."

Galan looked up, interested. *"Oui?"*

"Instead of us trying to find McGarvey, why don't we arrange for him to come to us, voluntarily."

"Are you planning on using his daughter?"

Lynch nodded. "I'm thinking about letting her stay in her father's apartment. He might be keeping a watch on the place."

Galan smiled. "Jacqueline can move in with her. *Hein,* two women might be more irresistible than one."

"You told me that Jacqueline was in love with McGarvey. Isn't there a danger that she might end up helping him?"

"Jacqueline is a Frenchwoman. I will control her, and you can control his daughter."

"That might be a handful."

Again Galan laughed. "We're not schoolboys," he said. "In any event we have no other choice. But let's first give them a few days to get to know each other."

"Agreed," Lynch said. He didn't know who he disliked the most, the French collectively, or McGarvey.

Le Bourget

Elizabeth was allowed to freshen up in the bathroom under the watchful eye of a large-bosomed matron, after which she was moved to a larger, more comfortable, though plainly furnished office, where she was given a pot of tea and a plate of croissants and buns. A window looked down from the second story onto a small parade ground. When the sun came up, four soldiers marched to the flagpole in the center, raised the French tricolor, then stepped back, came to rigid attention, and crisply saluted as the national anthem blared from loudspeakers.

Twenty minutes later a helicopter came in low from the south and set down somewhere behind the building Elizabeth was in. Ten minutes after that the door opened and a slender woman dressed in a simple skirt and yellow sweater came in.

"Good morning Mademoiselle. I'm happy to see that they gave you breakfast."

Elizabeth recognized her all at once, and it showed on her face, because the woman smiled brightly.

"I'm Jacqueline Belleau, but evidently you know this." She held out her hand, and Elizabeth took it despite herself.

"I think I'm supposed to hate you," Elizabeth said.

"Whatever for?" Jacqueline asked, surprised.

"You work for the French intelligence service, and you seduced my father."

"The first part is certainly true, but as for the rest of it your father did his part. He is a formidable man."

Elizabeth knew the woman was forty, but she would never have guessed her age. She seemed self-assured, an intelligent, but amused, expression in her wide eyes.

"My father kicked you out of his apartment, then went to ground. Now you've been assigned to convince me to help you find him."

"You've gotten nearly all that correct too," Jacqueline said, her face falling a little. "I never lived with your father, although it's something I wanted. He merely told me that he was leaving and then he was gone."

Elizabeth said nothing, realizing that her remark had hurt the woman. It made her sad because she instinctively felt that her father had left because he wanted to protect Jacqueline. Keep her out of harm's way, as he was fond of explaining himself. It was one of the very few faults she could find about her father, his inability to trust the women in his life.

"If you're ready to go, I'll take you back to your hotel," Jacqueline said.

"I'm sorry."

Jacqueline's expression softened again. "That's okay, I bark when I'm cornered too."

Elizabeth had to sign a release statement downstairs when her purse was returned to her. They did not, however, return her Elizabeth Swanson passport and papers.

Rush-hour traffic was in full swing on the Autoroute du Nord as they headed back into the city. Elizabeth saw an airport that she did not recognize.

"Where are we?"

"Le Bourget," Jacqueline said. "Charles Lindbergh landed just over there when the airport was nothing more than a wide grass field with a control tower and a few buildings. But all of Paris came out to welcome him."

They drove for a few minutes in silence, Jacqueline concentrating on the traffic while Elizabeth tried to sort out her feelings. If Lynch could find out where Rencke was living, she would go out to see him. Maybe he knew something and would agree to help. It was a long shot, but for the moment there wasn't much else she could do. Or much else that she ought to do. Nobody had explained to her yet that whatever her father had been asked to do by Yemlin was wrong. If her dad were planning on killing Tarankov he'd be doing the world a favor. Certainly nobody in Washington—including the Russian diplomats—could find much fault in such an event. From what she'd read in the Russian media, Tarankov's broad-based support among the people and the military was based on a pack of lies. He told the people that Russia's problems were the fault of a western-influenced government in Moscow. Hitler had blamed the Jews, Stalin had blamed the peasants, and Tarankov was blaming the West. Of the three, Tarankov's message was the easiest to defend because in a way what he was saying had a grain of truth to it. Russia's current problems were indeed being caused by the upheaval in changing from one form of economic system to another. The Russian economy was having growing pains. If the people stuck with the reformers long enough, there was a good chance they'd come out of their depression. Russia was finally joining the rest of the major nations of the world with ongoing financial defeats and triumphs. It was called a free market economy. Everyone took their chances.

But Tarankov was convincing the rank-and-file Russians that once he was leader of the nation he could solve all their problems by going back to the old ways. The people forgot what their lives had been like before Gorbachev. They had forgotten the repressions, the gulags, the shortages. They were being dazzled by the possibility of once again becoming a superpower. It was a message that the people were taking to heart, and one that the industrial-military establishment embraced.

"Why do you want to talk to my father?" Elizabeth asked.

Jacqueline glanced over at her. "Me personally, or my government?"

"The government."

"Your father had a meeting with a Russian intelligence officer who asked him to take an assignment. We'd like to know what that's all about."

"What if it has nothing to do with France?"

Jacqueline shrugged. "Then we have no problem." She smiled wanly. "I don't think your father knows that you work for the CIA. It's going to come as a shock to him."

"I'm sure it will," Elizabeth said. "How about you? Do you want to talk to him?"

"Most certainly."

"Why?"

"I think for the same reason you do," Jacqueline said. "Your father is probably going to assassinate someone for the Russians, which will place his life in grave danger. I don't want that to happen. Or at the very least I want him to convince me that what he's going to do is worthwhile. I don't want him to throw his life away."

"What if it was worthwhile?" Elizabeth asked.

Jacqueline didn't answer at once, concentrating on her driving instead. She was having trouble keeping her emotions in check, and it showed on her face.

She turned finally and glanced at Elizabeth. "Then I would probably help him, for the same reason you came here to help him, and not merely find him for the CIA. I love him, and I'll do whatever it takes to be at his side when he needs me."

Elizabeth was touched to the bottom of her soul. "Even if it meant lying to your own government?"

Jacqueline smiled crookedly. "You've lied to protect him, and so have I."

"How do I know that I can trust you?"

Jacqueline shook her head. "I can't answer that for you Elizabeth, because I don't even know if I can trust myself to do the right thing. Right now I don't know what's right or wrong. I only know that I love your father, and everything else is secondary. I'll sell my soul for him, and if need be I'll give my life. But I don't want him to be destroyed. I want him to retire, so that I can have all of him all the time."

Elizabeth reached out and touched Jacqueline's hand on the steering wheel. "My father will never retire."

Jacqueline's eyes began to fill. "That's what I'm afraid of, my lovely man lying dead somewhere. I see it at night in my dreams and it frightens me so badly that sometimes I don't know how I can go on."

"I know what you mean," Elizabeth said. "Believe me, I know."

TWENTY-THREE

Moscow

The interim president of Russia was a deeply troubled man. He turned away from his visitor across the desk and looked out the window at Spassky Tower rising into a leaden sky as he considered his options. Whatever action they took would seriously affect the nation's future which was, at this moment in history, in more jeopardy than it had ever been. He was having a recurring dream in which he was flying over the charred, smoking remains of what had once been Moscow, a mammoth mushroom cloud roiling fifteen thousand meters above this very spot. Russia had fallen to Tarankov, who in his attempts to regain the old Soviet Union had brought on thermonuclear war. At the outskirts of the city the dead and dying lay in smoldering piles like cordwood that stretched for as far as the eye could see. The worst of the nightmare was the stench of scorched human flesh. Each morning he awoke with the horrible smell still in his nostrils, and the taste of it at the back of his throat.

"It was a mistake on my part, Mr. President," the man behind him said.

Kabatov turned back to face Yuryn, whose normally florid complexion was even more red than normal this afternoon. "There were no survivors among the crews of those six helicopters?"

"None."

"I hold you fully responsible—"

"I take the responsibility," Yuryn interrupted. "I'd hoped to stop his train with the minimum use of force, and therefore the minimum loss of life before it reached Nizhny Novgorod. An estimated one million people showed up for his speech. Had we tried to arrest him, the carnage would have been beyond belief. The nation would never have survived such an attack. Neither would this government have emerged intact. I made a decision, and I was wrong."

"Was he warned?"

"He may have been, but it would not have mattered had the attack come as a surprise, because his train is more heavily armed than we'd suspected. He has SS-N-6 missiles, and radar-guided rapid-fire cannons of some sort. I still don't have all the details."

"Next time use jet fighters with bigger missiles," Kabatov said, keeping his voice in control.

"We're working on several scenarios. But if your wish remains to take him alive so that he can be placed on trial, our options are severely restricted. Destroying the train poses no real problem. Stopping it without harming Tarankov will be difficult if not impossible."

"Nothing is impossible," Kabatov shot back. "And yes I want him taken alive. It's our only option. Anything else and we lose the nation."

"In that case, Mr. President, we have another more serious, more immediate problem," Yuryn said heavily.

"Well, what is it?"

"Viktor Yemlin has hired an assassin to kill Tarankov."

It didn't come as a complete surprise to Kabatov, still he found that he was shocked. "Is the SVR behind this?"

"No. Apparently Yemlin is working alone, but on the advice of Konstantin Sukhoruckin and Eduard Shevardnadze."

"How do you know this?"

"I didn't believe him when he said he went to Paris and Helsinki to do some shopping, so I arranged to place him in a position that he willingly told the truth." Yuryn took a thin report from his briefcase and handed it to Kabatov. "If Yemlin does remember the encounter it's not likely he'll say anything to anybody."

Kabatov opened the report and started to read, bile rising up in the back of his throat, making him almost physically ill. He looked up, unable to finish and unable to hide a look of disgust from his face. "Where is Yemlin at this moment?"

"At his office. He's done nothing outwardly to indicate he remembers what happened to him, beyond the fact that he had a pleasant evening at the Magesterium."

"We know the assassin's name, and we know that he lives in Paris. I'll instruct our people to grab him, or short of that, kill him."

"That, Mr. President, might prove to be more difficult than capturing or killing Tarankov, who after all is nothing more than a soldier. But Kirk McGarvey is a very special man who has already done our country a great deal of harm."

"I'm not familiar with the name. He's an American. What, mafia?"

"He's a former CIA officer who killed General Baranov some years ago, which subsequently threw the entire KGB into a disarray that took us years to overcome."

"We can arrest Yemlin, and force him to tell us how to find McGarvey. Or, Yemlin can call him off."

"That won't work either, Mr. President. If you read the summary on the Helsinki meeting you'll see that McGarvey has not only agreed to do the job for one million dollars—money that has apparently already been transferred to an account in the British Channel Islands—but he'll make no further contact."

"Paris is not that big a city—"

"McGarvey is already here in Moscow," Yuryn cut in impatiently. "It's even possible that he was in Nizhny Novgorod to witness the latest spectacle."

"Then he's tried and failed?"

"He probably came here to work out his plans. I think he's waiting for something, for the right moment."

"Do we have a photograph of him?"

"Da."

"Then with the help of the Militia, you will find him."

"We can try that. But if we don't succeed, and McGarvey finds out, then he'll be all the more difficult to kill. In any event he's probably here under an assumed identity, and very likely in disguise. He knows what he's doing, and his Russian is said to be nearly perfect."

"Is he working for the CIA? You said he was a former officer, but have they rehired him to do this thing?"

"I don't think so," Yuryn said. "Which does give us an advantage, if you want to take it."

"I'm listening," Kabatov said, his insides seething.

"We'll form a special task force to find and destroy this American before he gets a chance to assassinate Tarankov. The Americans want our reform movement to succeed as much as we do. So you might think about asking President Lindsay for help. Between us, the CIA, and possibly the French on whose soil McGarvey apparently now resides, we will catch him. Even a man such as McGarvey cannot outwit the combined forces of the police and intelligence services of three countries. In the meantime we'll keep this from the public to avoid any panic or possible backlash."

"We'll also maintain our efforts to capture Tarankov. Once we have him in custody, McGarvey will become a moot point."

"Agreed, Mr. President. For the moment it will be a race against us and him."

"Will you head this special commission?"

"No," Yuryn said.

"Who then?"

"When I was head of the old KGB's First Directorate a man named Yuri Bykov worked for me. When the Komityet was split apart he left Moscow."

"Is he good?"

"He's the best."

"Where is he now?" Kabatov asked.

"In the East. Krasnoyarsk, I think. I'll get word to him to come immediately."

"Will you arrest Yemlin?"

"Not yet, Mr. President. There is an outside chance that McGarvey might contact him. If that should happen we'll be ready."

"As you wish. Get Bykov here as quickly as possible. This situation must be resolved."

At 5:00 P.M. that afternoon, Kabatov placed a call to President Lindsay who was just about to receive his 9:00 A.M. CIA briefing from Roland Murphy, a fact of which he was not aware. Nor was he aware that Lindsay immediately switched the call to his speaker phone. So far as Kabatov knew he was seated alone in his office in the Kremlin, speaking to the American President who was alone in his Oval Office.

"Good morning, Mr. President," Kabatov said. "I trust your day is beginning well?" Kabatov's English was passable, so translators were not necessary.

"Good afternoon, Mr. President," Lindsay said. "My morning is busy. We'll be leaving for Moscow in a few hours. Is this why you called?"

"No, the State funeral will be conducted on schedule tomorrow, and were our meeting to be under any other circumstances I would welcome the opportunity to finally meet you."

"May I again offer my condolences, and those of the United States."

"Thank you, that is very kind." Kabatov hesitated. Lindsay was not a devious man. He seemed to have no hidden agenda as did so many American presidents before. But it was possible that McGarvey was working for the CIA after all, in which case Kabatov was about to make a fool of himself. Nonetheless there was no other choice. "Another matter has developed, Mr. President, for which I would like to ask your help."

"I'll certainly do what I can, Mr. President. But if you're speaking about the internal affair we discussed earlier, I don't know if there is much of a substantive nature that I can do for you."

"This morning I was given a report by the director of our internal intelligence service that a plot to assassinate Yevgenni Tarankov seems to be developing. The assassin may be an American citizen—as a matter of fact a former Central Intelligence Agency officer by the name of Kirk McGarvey. And, Mr. President, I stress *former* CIA officer."

"I see," President Lindsay said after a moment. "I assume that you would not have made this call if you believed this information was anything less than certain."

"That is correct. I am forming a special commission to hunt down this man and stop him. Tarankov will be arrested and brought to trial, it is the only option open to me that makes any democratic sense. I'm sure you can understand the difficulties we are facing."

"Yes, I do," Lindsay said. "How may I help?"

"It may be possible that McGarvey is already here in Moscow. On the chance that information is incorrect, or that he has returned to France, or the United States, I would like the Central Intelligence Agency and the Federal Bureau of Investigation to locate and detain him. I intend asking President Chirac for his help as well."

"That may present us with a problem," Lindsay said, and Kabatov got the distinct impression that the man was holding something back.

"Yes?"

"If Mr. McGarvey has broken no U.S. law there's actually very little that I can do. I'm sure that President Chirac will tell you the same thing."

"I'm simply asking for enough time that my police can take Tarankov into custody."

"How much time?"

"Certainly before the June elections. Less than eleven weeks."

Again Lindsay didn't respond immediately, and Kabatov got the impression that the President might have someone with him after all, an adviser.

"Mr. President, I'll do whatever is possible," Lindsay said. "I sincerely understand the problems you're faced with, and I give you my assurances that if Mr. McGarvey returns to the United States he will be detained and questioned."

"I can ask for nothing more, Mr. President," Kabatov said.

"Will you send me a report on what you have?"

"Immediately," Kabatov said.

"Then, good luck, Mr. President," Lindsay said.

"Yes, thank you, Mr. President."

TWO
APRIL

TWENTY-FOUR

Moscow

A few minutes before six Monday afternoon Leonid Chernov stepped out of an automobile in front of the Kremlin's old Senate Building, and thanked the militia driver. He'd changed his appearance over the weekend. Now his hair was short cropped and dyed gray, his eyes made deep blue by contact lenses, and he held himself in a slouch. His civilian suit fit him reasonably well, but was obviously not expensive.

His documents identified him as Yuri V. Bykov, a former chief investigator with the KGB's First Directorate Counterintelligence service. His rank had been lieutenant colonel. After twenty years of service he'd retired on a meager pension to Krasnoyarsk where he taught police science at a technical institute specializing in training private bodyguards and security service officers. The fiction would stand up to scrutiny because Tarankov's people owned the institute.

The news that Viktor Yemlin and his pro-reformers had hired an assassin to kill Tarankov sometime between now and the general elections in June, had come as a surprise only because Chernov didn't think they had the courage of their convictions. If the assassin tried and failed, they would be executed as traitors. And even if the assassin were successful, Yemlin and the others would still stand trial as traitors because Tarankov's name would soon be placed on the presidential ballot. However, the news that an independent commission was being formed to find and stop the assassin, with Chernov under the Bykov alias heading it, had been completely unexpected. What were they in Kabatov's government, he wondered, complete fools? They wanted to save Tarankov's life so that he could be arrested, tried and convicted for treason, and then executed. Why not stand back and let the assassin do their dirty work for them? The plot could be laid directly on the doorstep of the American government, and Kabatov would emerge the victor. The idiot was shooting himself in his own foot.

Chernov showed his pass to the guards at the desk inside the main entry hall, was searched, and finally directed to a bank of elevators across from a statue of Lenin lit from above by a glass and chromium steel dome. The government headquarters was busy today. In a couple of weeks the Duma would be in session, and staffs were arriving in Moscow to get ready for the legislative sessions. Russians loved politics, a fact that Chernov had not been completely aware of until he'd joined Tarankov, and of necessity became something of an expert. Riding up in the elevator he got the distinct impression that the old Senate Building was like a beehive that was being disturbed by forces outside of the legislature's control. Everyone in Kabatov's government, and in the Communist Party, were buzzing around in all directions with little or no sense of purpose. No one was at the controls. The queen bee was dead or dormant. The workers and the drones were left in a blank frenzy.

In a sense, Chernov thought, his being here was a bit of poetic irony. Who better to catch an assassin, than another assassin? In his days with the KGB's Department Viktor, he'd been among the best, because he was as brilliant as he was methodical, and his half-brother Arkady Kurshin had been his teacher. Besides being a weapons expert, he'd devoted much of his studies to human psychology. But unlike Tarankov's wife whose specialty was crowds, his was the psychology of the individual, especially the individual under stress. Arkady, before his death, had told him that being a hunter of men was much the same as being a hunter of wild animals. In order to be a success, the assassin had to understand his prey and his prey's habitat.

During the coal strikes in the eighties, Chernov had been assigned to kill three of the union's leaders. Before he'd set out for the far east, he'd immersed himself in studies of the mines and the men who worked them. He'd also studied the trade labor movement in Russia as it compared to Communism and to the trade union movement around the world. By the time he was ready he knew that above everything else these men were proud of their physical strength, and ability to endure danger. They were men for whom any sort of a challenge was irresistible.

Chernov got a job in the coal mines, where he quickly came to the attention of the union because of his outspoken criticism of what they were trying to do. The union leaders were crooks. They were skimming the union fund, and didn't care about the miners. They were only interested in politics to advance their own careers.

He didn't have to assassinate them. One by one they confronted him face to face, and in three no holds barred fights, in which hundreds of miners watched, he killed them with his bare hands. He was a hero of sorts. Afterwards his death was faked in a mine accident, and he returned to Moscow, promoted to major for a job well done. Not only had the back of the strike been broken, but Moscow was able to blame the miners' troubles on their own leadership. Chernov's action set the union movement in Siberia back by ten years.

After his brother was killed in Portugal, and the Soviet Union under Gorbachev began to fall apart, Chernov quit the KGB, and dropped out of sight. For a few years he worked as a contract killer for a number of Mafia groups, until he began hearing about Yevgenni Tarankov. Within a year he was working for the Tarantula, and six months later he was Tarankov's chief of staff, a job he was beginning to feel could only last a few months longer no matter the outcome of the assassination plot, or the election. Russia would continue to sink into chaos no matter what Tarankov did. The real fight, Chernov thought, was gaining momentum in the West.

He had to show his documents and submit to another search when he got off the elevator on the fourth floor. An aide brought him down the broad corridor and into an anteroom outside the president's office, where General Yuryn was waiting with Militia Director Captain-General Mazayev.

"Yuri Vasilevich, I'm glad you're here at last. We were just talking about you," Yuryn said. "Now we can get down to work."

"I was surprised to get your call, Comrade General," Chernov said, shaking hands. "I didn't know if you had remembered me."

"If half of what Nikolai says about you is true, you would be a man hard to forget," General Mazayev broke in.

"I'm truly flattered, sir," Chernov said, shaking hands with Mazayev. "But it has been a long time since I worked for the KGB."

"Not so long that you've forgotten your duty to your country," Mazayev said sharply. "But I'm not familiar with the Bykov name. Was your father in the military?"

"He was killed in Hungary, Comrade General. But you would not know his name because he was only a tank commander."

"Credentials enough for me," Mazayev said. "Let's not keep the president waiting." He turned on his heel and went into Kabatov's office.

Yuryn held back. "You should have been in Moscow this morning. There is something that you need to know."

"I was delayed, Comrade General. Nothing I could do about it." Chernov tried to gauge Yuryn's mood, but the FSK director's pudgy face was devoid of anything but a slight irritation. "Is it important?"

"Very. But you're going to have to watch yourself now. No matter what you learn in the next few minutes, you must maintain your Bykov identity. Do you understand?"

Chernov shrugged. "Nothing surprises me anymore, Comrade General. Not even you."

Yuryn went into the office and Chernov followed him inside. President Kabatov was seated behind his desk, General Mazayev and another man Chernov immediately recognized as Yeltsin's former chief of security, General Korzhakov, were seated across from him.

"Mr. President, this is Yuri Bykov, the investigator I told you about," Yuryn said.

Chernov crossed to the desk and shook Kabatov's hand. "It's a pleasure to meet you, Mr. President. May I wish you good luck in the June elections?"

"Thank you," Kabatov said, a little expression of pleasure crossing his features. "Do you know my chief of security, General Korzhakov?"

"No, sir," Chernov said.

The general looked at him with barely disguised contempt. But he shook hands. "Do you know why you've been summoned here, Bykov?"

"To catch an assassin who is coming to kill Yevgenni Tarankov," Chernov replied matter-of-factly. He and Yuryn sat down.

"Do you think you can do it?"

Chernov shrugged. "That depends on what we know about this assassin and his plot, who hired him, and what kind of support I'll get, Comrade General. But there can be no guarantees, though I think killing the Tarantula might be more difficult than this assassin might believe."

"Be that as it may, your job will be to catch him before he has the opportunity to try," Korzhakov said, his grave voice harsh. "As for your support, you'll have anything or anybody you need. An office has been set up for you at Lefortovo Prison. It's out of the public's eye, which for now will be one of your guiding principles."

"The Militia will not conduct an all out manhunt," General Mazayev put in. He glanced at Kabatov. "It is felt that by so openly going after this assassin, it would make it seem as if we are supporting Tarankov, when in fact the opposite is true."

"Mr. President, may I be frank?" Chernov asked, turning to Kabatov.

"Of course."

"General Tarankov is no friend of this government. In fact if what I read in the newspapers and see on television is true, he means to restore the Soviet Union to the old ways. Why not let this assassin slip through our fingers and do his best? Maybe we should help him."

Kabatov started shaking his head even before Chernov finished. "If we're to remain a nation of laws this sort of thing cannot be allow to happen."

Chernov almost laughed out loud. The man was a bigger fool than Yeltsin had been. "Tarankov is a murderer."

"For which he will be arrested, and tried in a court of law," Kabatov said vehemently, his face red. "Presidents Lindsay and Chirac have both promised me their fullest support in finding the assassin. So if you agree to direct the investigation you'll have the unprecedented cooperation of the CIA, the FBI and the SDECE."

Chernov decided that he could be surprised after all. "The assassin is a westerner?"

"He's an American living in France," Kabatov said.

"In fact he's a former CIA officer," Yuryn added a little too quickly. Kabatov and the others shot him a dirty look.

"Before we get into all of that, will you take the job, Comrade Bykov?" the president asked. "Will you find and stop the assassin?"

"*Da*," Chernov said, masking his momentary confusion. Yuryn had tried to warn him about something and now he was trying to send a signal. "Who is this American, Mr. President?"

Kabatov handed him Yuryn's report. "His name is Kirk McGarvey, a name you may be familiar with from your days in the KGB. He's done the *Rodina* a great deal of harm during his career."

It was as if a ton of bricks had fallen on Chernov's head, and it took everything within his power not to overreact, to hide his true feelings of absolute hatred. He opened the folder and began to read about Viktor Yemlin's part in the plot, his trips to Tbilisi, then Paris and finally Helsinki where he met with the American. Through the reading Chernov tried to concentrate on the content of the report in an effort to block out his other thoughts, those of loathing and bitterness and even fear. His brother had been one of the best operatives that the KGB's Executive Action Department had ever fielded. Under Baranov's direction the department had run circles around the secret intelligence services of every country in the west. Murder, kidnappings, sabotage, his brother had been the best, until McGarvey killed him in an operation gone bad in Portugal.

Coming up in his brother's footsteps, Chernov had often dreamed of revenge. But his brother had once told him that revenge was only for fools. The best operative was the man who could commit murder dispassionately, without remorse, without regret, and totally without emotion. Arkady had come up against McGarvey and lost on a number of other occasions, and Chernov had to wonder if in the end his brother hadn't violated his own principle of dispassion in going against McGarvey one last time, and it had been his undoing.

Aware that Kabatov and the others in the room were watching him, Chernov looked up. "The name is vaguely familiar. Do we have a file on him?"

"Quite an extensive file," Yuryn said. "Which will be made available to you this evening. I've also assigned you a communications assistant. If you want anyone else, you need only ask."

"Is Yemlin being watched in case McGarvey tries to contact him again?"

"Yes," Mazayev said. "Outside SVR Headquarters he can't fart without my people knowing about it."

"Why isn't the SVR represented here this morning? Aren't they in on this investigation?"

"Not for the moment," Yuryn said. "If Yemlin has help within the agency it would do us no good to share information with them. It might get back to McGarvey."

"Has anyone contacted the CIA or the French?"

"Not directly," Yuryn said. "If you haven't finished reading my report I suggest you do so."

Chernov did so, and in the next page he was struck another nearly physical blow. "McGarvey was here, in Moscow, and—" He stopped in mid-sentence. The bastard had been in the crowd at Nizhny Novgorod. The date matched, and there'd been that drunken soldier. Something about his eyes had bothered Chernov at the time. He hadn't seen a photograph of McGarvey for several years, but he remembered the man's eyes now. Penetrating, almost like cold laser beams shooting directly into a man's skull.

Gathering his wits, he closed the report. "McGarvey was here in Moscow and nobody did anything to catch him?"

"A great many Muscovites went to Nizhny Novgorod last week to see Tarankov's bloody spectacle, so it's possible that Mr. McGarvey was there. But since nothing happened, we're assuming he came here on a scouting trip, and has since left Russia—possibly back to France—where he is making his plans."

"Has McGarvey's photograph been distributed to train stations, airports, hotels, border crossings?

"Nyet," Mazayev said heavily, and a look passed between him and Korzhakov.

"What is it, Comrade Generals?" Chernov asked.

"The fact of the matter is that Tarankov has many supporters in all walks of life," Yuryn answered.

"All the more reason to make McGarvey's photograph available. You would have an army of patriots willing to help save his life."

"An odd word to use—patriot—Bykov," Kabatov said.

"They believe that they are patriots, Comrade President," Chernov replied.

"Are you one?"

"No, Mr. President," Chernov said. "But if we are to catch McGarvey, extraordinary measures will have to be taken. As you said, he has caused the Rodina a great deal of harm. It must mean he is very good at what he does."

"The best," Yuryn said.

"Then it won't be easy. Who can I trust?"

"Us in this room," Korzhakov said. "If you need something, you'll have to get it from us."

"To avoid any confusion, I think that I should work with only one of you."

"I agree," Kabatov said. "Since it was General Yuryn who suggested you, he will be your liaison to the rest of us."

"Very well. Are the files I need at Lefortovo?"

"Yes," Yuryn said.

"Who is this assistant of mine?"

"Aleksi Paporov. He's as good as they come. His English and French are flawless, he's a computer whiz and he knows how to keep his mouth shut."

"All that is good, Comrade General, but who does he report to?"

"Why, you, of course," Yuryn said.

"Who else?"

"No one."

Chernov turned to the others, his blood singing. "My methods tend to be unorthodox, comrades. But if I am allowed to do this my way, I will catch this assassin before he reaches Tarankov."

"Then I suggest you get started," Kabatov said.

"One final thing, Mr. President," Chernov said. "I would like a letter signed by you, giving me complete authority in this investigation. My methods might seem more than unusual to some people. I don't want any delays getting special authorizations."

Kabatov looked to his chief of security, who was once again staring at Chernov.

"He has a point," Korzhakov said.

"I'll have the letter sent to you at Lefortovo in the morning," Kabatov said. "Is there anything else?"

"No, Mr. President, other than catching this American."

"Then good luck," Kabatov said, rising.

Chernov shook hands with him. "Thank you, Mr. President."

Mazayev and Korzhakov also wished him luck, and shook his hand, and he left the president's office with Yuryn.

"Do you have a car here?" Yuryn asked in the corridor.

"No."

"Paporov will arrange one for you. In the meantime have you got someplace to stay?"

"I'll stay at Lefortovo for now," Chernov said.

"Good, I'll drive you over," Yuryn said and they went downstairs and climbed into the back of a Zil limousine.

The meeting had lasted less than a half-hour, and the sky was finally beginning to clear up, though the sun had set and it was dark. Yuryn's car shot out the Nikolskaya Tower gate, swept across Red Square and raced northeast toward Lefortovo Prison in Bauman suburb.

"You handled yourself very well in there," Yuryn said. "Do you really know how to catch this bastard? Or was that all talk?"

Chernov felt almost dreamy. His brother had been wrong about revenge. Arkady had to have been wrong, because at this moment nothing else seemed to matter. He would find and kill McGarvey not for Tarankov's sake, and certainly not for that fool Kabatov's sake, but for nothing more than a sweet revenge.

"I'll kill him," Chernov said softly, not caring if Yuryn heard him or not.

Traffic was heavy, but the Zil traveled in the official lane. Traffic cops waved them on, and Chernov watched, more in love with Moscow now than the first time he'd come here from the far east, because it was here that he would settle an old score, and afterward he would leave Russia forever. Right now it was as if he were seeing an old love for the last time. He was going to make the most of it.

TWENTY-FIVE

Moscow

Viktor Yemlin left the SVR Headquarters building on Moscow's ring road shortly after seven, finally ready to take action. The weekend had been horrible for him. He hadn't slept more than a few hours. He hadn't eaten much, he hadn't looked at the newspapers or watched television. Most of the time he'd sat in his favorite chair in the living room of his apartment smoking Marlboros and drinking vodka, as he watched the sun rise and set twice.

He hadn't forced himself to come to any immediate conclusions about what had happened to him because he did not have all the facts. Nor did he allow his guilt to completely consume him, although at first his shame was so overwhelming he'd been in danger of sinking into deep depression. Instead he'd gone over what he'd done at the Magesterium, what had been done to him, and the reasons behind the attack—because that's how he viewed the experience. He'd been lured to the club by Cheremukhin which in retrospect was the first troubling aspect he struggled with. The entire affair had been planned and orchestrated, possibly on Yuryn's orders. But Cheremukhin was one of the moderates who had just as much to gain by Tarankov's death as Kabatov and the rest of them. It was hard to imagine Cheremukhin working for the FSK, but if he wasn't then his appearance on the steps of the Senate at just that moment, and his insistence on taking Yemlin to his club had to have been a tremendous coincidence.

Yemlin had turned that thought over in his mind, worrying at it like a dog with a bone. Yuryn knew about his trips to Tbilisi, Paris and Helsinki, and he was suspicious. Part of that was driven by the intense inter-service rivalry between the two divisions of the old KGB. And part of it was Yuryn's surprise and discomfort in front of Kabatov when Yemlin had come up with the plan to hide the facts behind Yeltsin's death. Still there was no logical connection between Yuryn's suspicions and the setup at the Magesterium.

But the job of the FSK was internal security, which meant it not only watched the borders, the train stations and airports, but it also monitored places where high ranking Russians gathered to play. The Magesterium and all the other political clubs like it would naturally be watched. At the handful of clubs that catered to high ranking politicians, journalists and intelligence officers, security would be especially tight. As soon as Yemlin had walked in the front door whoever was controlling the FSK surveillance operation would have reported the fact, and the honey trap had been set up.

It was cunning of them to use not only the young woman, but a young man as well. They might expect that Yemlin would have little compunction about bragging about screwing a girl, but he might keep to himself the fact that he'd had a homosexual experience. No doubt the entire affair was on videotape. And from what memories he could dredge up from his foggy recollections, he'd enjoyed the experience. At least he'd gotten pleasure from the sexual act, which was a cause of his sharp feelings of guilt.

The worst part of the experience however was his inability to remember the details. He remembered Renée and the bath, and Valeri, the doll, who'd brought him champagne. He also remembered the feeling of warmth, and then of drifting, as if he were dreaming. He even remembered the rubdown, and the sex, but then it was fuzzy. He'd been thinking about Kirk McGarvey when he entered the club, and he was worried that in his drug-induced state he had spoken his thoughts out loud.

It wasn't likely that he had given anything away, or else Yuryn would have ordered his arrest. By now he'd be in the basement interrogation rooms at Dzerzhinsky Square where the entire plot would have been extracted from him. But he couldn't be sure. Perhaps he had talked, and they tried to find McGarvey but failed. Now they were waiting for him to make contact. It was something that he had to know. Because if the FSK was aware of the plot to kill Tarankov, then McGarvey would have to be stopped because he would be walking into a trap.

"Home?" his driver asked, when Yemlin climbed into the back seat of his car.

"Not tonight, Anatoli. You can drop me off at the Magesterium and then you'll be free for the remainder of the evening. But you can pick me up at home in the morning."

"Yes, sir."

Yeltsin's funeral had gone off without a hitch on Friday. Although Yemlin hadn't attended it, his people who monitored the foreign dignitaries reported that there'd been no trouble, for which he'd been heartily congratulated today at lunch by SVR director General Aykazyan. The fiction was holding. And as the general wisely pointed out, it didn't matter if no one believed it, what mattered was that the western powers were acting as if they did.

Nothing coming across his desk from North American operations gave so much as a hint that the exact manner of Yeltsin's death was being questioned. Nor did any of the product coming from the half-dozen major networks they operated in the U.S. and Canada raise questions. Yet Yemlin felt that McGarvey was right. The western powers knew what had happened, but they were biding their time to see how events unfolded over the next ten weeks before the elections. Afterward a lot of things would be different in Russia, Yemlin thought, but he was no longer so confident about his predictions for the future.

As they came into the city, he reached in his pocket and fingered the two small silver cigarette boxes that his friend Andrei Galkin in the Scientific Directorate had given him this afternoon, and he shuddered involuntarily. He had done questionable things in his long career with the KGB, things that he'd never been able to tell his wife about, things that he kept carefully hidden in a secret compartment in his mind, things that only rarely came to him in his dreams, but when they did he would awaken, his heart pounding, his bedclothes soaked in sweat. When he had finally become *rezident* in charge of the KGB's Washington station, he thought that he'd finally put all that behind him. Then when he'd been recalled to Moscow and promoted he was certain that he would finish out his long career safely seated behind a desk.

But he'd been wrong.

Twenty minutes later his driver let him off at the Magesterium, and inside at the front desk he was effusively welcomed with a guest membership.

"We know that you will be happy here, Viktor," the manager, a portly dark-haired Georgian, said confidently. "If there's anything that I can personally do to be of service, please don't hesitate to ask."

Only first names were used in the club. The manager's name tag read Josef.

"Is Renée available this evening, Josef?"

"For you Viktor, naturally." The manager picked up a telephone, spoke a few words, and then hung up, his smile widening. "One minute, Viktor. Sixty seconds, check your watch, and you'll be in heaven."

A young woman came by with a tray of champagne, and Yemlin took a bottle and two glasses. Less than a minute later Renée appeared, her face lit up in a bright smile.

"Viktor, you came back to us. Am I ever glad. You know that Vadim said you were an okay guy." She took a glass of champagne from him, and they went down the corridor.

"I haven't had such a relaxing evening for a long time, my dear. I thought I'd like to do it again."

"Just the same, Viktor? Are you a rascal then?"

Yemlin forced a grin. "You don't know the half of it."

They went back to one of the luxury suites, though it looked the same as last week, he couldn't tell if it was. Tchaikovsky's *Sleeping Beauty* came softly from hidden speakers, and the lights in the apartment were set low.

Renée went into the bathroom to check the bath water, as Yemlin got undressed. He dropped his jacket on the floor beside the bed, as if by mistake, and when he bent over to fumble for it, he slipped the heavier of the two cigarette boxes out of his pocket, unlatched the clasp and slid it out of sight under the bed. The surveillance cameras and microphones within fifteen meters would no longer work.

He laid the jacket on the bed, poured them another glass of wine and went into the bathroom where he climbed into the pleasantly hot water.

Renée disrobed, got in with him, and began scrubbing his back. "We thought you might come back this weekend," she said.

"I was too busy," Yemlin said. He sighed with pleasure. "But I'm here now. Is Valeri in the club this evening?"

She giggled and slapped him on the back. "You are wicked. Do you want me to call him over here?"

"*Da*. A rubdown would be nice."

Renée reached between his legs with a soapy hand, and give him a playful tug. "He doesn't deserve the little doll."

"What do you mean?" Yemlin asked innocently. His heart was starting to pound.

"Oh, nothing," she said sweetly. She stepped out of the tub, her black body glistening with water, and skipped into the bedroom.

As soon as she was out of sight Yemlin got out of the tub and went to the door. Her back was to him, and she was searching his clothes as she talked on the phone, the handset cradled against her shoulder. She found the second silver box in one of his pockets, opened it, then said something into the phone and hung up.

"Shall I inform Josef that my little Renée is a thief?" Yemlin said.

Startled, the girl spun around so fast she nearly dropped the box. Her eyes were wide, her nipples hard. "You almost made me drop it!"

"Did you find anything of interest?" Yemlin asked. He sipped his wine. "Are you a little spy?"

"Just curious, Viktor," she said, a mischievous look on her pixie face. "Can I have some, or don't you share?"

"It's good stuff. Maybe you can't take it."

"I'm no virgin."

"I guess you're not," Yemlin said, forcing a smile. "Be my guest. But take it easy, Renée. I don't want you passing out."

"Why not? Valeri will be here in a little while."

"Maybe I want both of you this time."

She laughed, then set the open silver box on the nightstand. Using the tiny silver spoon nestled inside the top part of the box, she scooped out a portion of the doctored cocaine, and took it up her right nostril.

Yemlin put his glass down on the dresser, and reached her as she sighed deeply, and sank slowly to the carpet. Her eyes were open and glazed, a stupid, slack-jawed expression on her pretty mouth.

"Are you okay, Renée?" Yemlin asked softly.

"Sure, Viktor. That's some good shit, you know."

"I'm going to put you in the other room for a little while. I want you to be a good girl and take a nap. Can you do that for me?"

"Sure, Viktor. Whatever you say. Then can I have some more good shit, or are you going to fuck Valeri all night?"

"You can have some more good shit, I promise," Yemlin said. He sat her up, then got her to her feet and walked her into the other room where he laid her on one of the sectional couches, propping her head on a cushion.

He was ambivalent about blacks, but he felt a tinge of sorrow for this little girl. She was going nowhere. If he'd had a daughter and she had come to this fate it would have broken his heart, and he'd had enough of that to last ten lifetimes.

Galkin had promised that the doctored cocaine taken in normal doses would not be fatal. Nevertheless Yemlin checked the girl's breathing and her pulse. Both were fast, but not alarmingly so.

Closing the door, he went back to the bathroom where he hid her costume in the cabinet beneath the vanity.

Valeri was there as Yemlin came out of the bathroom. The young man was dressed in the same skimpy white swim trunks as before. He'd brought his towels and lotions, and a bottle of champagne.

"Is Renée in the tub?" he asked.

"I sent her away. She'll be back later. Right now I want a rubdown."

A momentary look of suspicion crossed Valeri's face, but then he smiled openly. "Sure thing, Viktor," he said. "You can have a glass of champagne while I get the table set up."

"I'll have some champagne later. And this time let's use the bed, I think it'll be more comfortable."

Valeri chucked. "You're a man after my own tastes."

Yemlin closed the bathroom door, then went to the bed and lay down on his back, spreading his spindly legs. Vomit rose up in his throat gagging him, and his heart raced so rapidly that he was momentarily frightened he was going to have a heart attack.

Valeri took off his white trunks, and came over to the bed, as Yemlin reached over and took the silver box off the nightstand.

"Something new this time, Viktor?" Valeri asked.

"I think you'll like it," Yemlin said. Keeping eye contact with the younger man, he moistened two fingers with spit, dabbed them in the cocaine and spread the paste around the head of his penis. He set the box back on the nightstand and then forced a broad, wicked smile, the effort taking every ounce of his strength. "Suck my dick, you darling little pufta."

Valeri threw back his head and laughed out loud. Then he joined Yemlin on the bed, taking the older man's flaccid penis in his mouth, licking and sucking the cocaine, and smacking his lips.

"You really should have some champagne, you know," the young man said.

"Later," Yemlin replied tersely.

Valeri went back to his ministrations, and despite himself Yemlin responded.

When it was over the young man kept sucking, and Yemlin had to push him off. Valeri fell back, a glazed look in his eyes, the same stupid grin on his face that Renée had exhibited.

"S'that good?" Valeri asked, his voice slurred.

"Very good," Yemlin said, the gorge rising in his throat. "I want you to stay right there for a minute, can you do that?"

"Sure thing, Viktor. You bet."

Yemlin just made it to the toilet when he threw up. The champagne was sickly sweet and nauseating, but when he was finished he felt a little better.

He checked on Valeri who was still on the bed, and then checked Renée who was curled up on the couch and snoring softly, then he went back into the bathroom and took a hot shower. Afterward he got dressed while trying to avoid looking at Valeri, who was languidly playing with himself.

The cigarette box with the cocaine went back in his pocket, and then he sat on the edge of the bed.

Valeri reached for him, but Yemlin batted his hand away.

"Can you hear me, Valeri?" Yemlin asked.

"You bet, Viktor. You want to do it again?"

"Do you remember last week the first time I was here?"

"Sure. Georgi said you were a big wheel."

"Was the champagne drugged?"

"You bet."

"Did I talk to you, Valeri? Did I tell you things?"

Valeri laughed, and his eyes closed. Yemlin had to shake him awake.

"What did I tell you, Valeri?"

"You got big plans. You're going to kill the Tarantula." Valeri laughed. "I told them about McGarvey." His eyes fluttered.

Yemlin's heart sank. Until this moment he'd only had his guilt and his apprehensions to deal with. But now his worst fear had been confirmed by a drugged queer. The operation was over, and they had lost. He was going to have to get out of Russia immediately. Possibly to Georgia where Shevardnadze would give him asylum. Or possibly back to the United States. But McGarvey had to be called off.

"Go to sleep now, Valeri," Yemlin said.

"Am I a good boy?"

"You bet," Yemlin said. He got up and went to the other side of the bed where he retrieved the second silver box. He slipped it into his pocket, then switched the electronic device off by relatching the clasp. "I'll be back," he told the already sleeping Valeri, and then let himself out.

Lefortovo

Lefortovo Prison on Moscow's northeast side, was hidden behind a tall, yellow brick wall that surrounded the two-square-block compound. At the height of the Cold War, the maximum-security prison housed what the KGB considered its hardest cases. They were dissidents and foreign spies who had resisted the initial phases of their interrogations in the basement of the Dzerzhinsky Square KGB facility. They were sent out here to the quiet suburbs for the long haul, where psychological and scientific methods had been developed to extract every gram of useful information, without damaging the accused.

At the Lubyanka the interrogators used rubber truncheons, cold water enemas, and electrical shocks to the genitals, so that often the prisoner would tell his or her interrogators anything they wanted to know, even if they had to invent the information.

At Lefortovo it was different. Here some of the interrogators were kindly, grandfatherly men who had a great deal of sympathy for their subjects. Psychologists would listen with an understanding ear. Drugs that didn't fry your brain were employed, as was a method called "Pavlov's Rewards." It was a procedure developed in the early eighties, where electric probes were inserted into the prisoner's skull, lodging in the section of the brain that recognized and processed sexual pleasure. The same method had been used in the United States to control the behavior of laboratory mice. The interrogator could reward his subject by rotating a dial that sent varying amounts of electricity into the brain. The prisoner immediately felt the sensation of sex. If the electric current was strong enough it could induce an orgasm that could last anywhere from seconds, to indefinitely.

The prisoners soon learned that if they lied, nothing would happen to them. No beatings, no cold water enemas, no intimidation. But if they told the truth they would be rewarded with an orgasm. The more they cooperated, the longer the orgasms lasted.

In one early experiment with a Moscow prostitute, when the KGB doctors were learning to calibrate the device, they'd turned the dial to its maximum value and left it there. The woman lasted for nearly two hours before her heart finally gave out, giving rise to a lot of lewd jokes. But no one on the staff volunteered to try it out, even though the prostitute had smiled and moaned with pleasure right up to the moment of her death.

These days a section of Lefortovo was still used as a prison for hard cases, but most of the compound had been taken over by the Special Branch of the FSK. Particularly difficult and sensitive operations were planned and conducted here away from the prying eyes of the public, the Militia and especially the SVR.

Dzerzhinsky Square was often overrun by western journalists under the openness policy instituted by Gorbachev. But Lefortovo was secret from nearly everyone.

Yuryn's limousine was admitted through the main gates, and pulled up in front of the administration building that faced the assembly yard. Yuryn and Chernov went immediately upstairs to the third floor where Lefortovo's administrator, Colonel Anatoli Zuyev, was waiting for them.

"Your assistant Captain Paporov is on his way over," the hawk-nosed director said. "He can provide you with anything you need."

"I expect no interference from anyone here, Colonel—" Chernov began, but Zuyev held up a hand.

"Believe me, Colonel Bykov, I don't know what your special operation is about, and I have no desire to find out. If you want to perch on top of the flagpole at midnight, drink vodka and piss on us, be my guest. No one will even look up. But if you need something, anything, Paporov will get it for you. He is very good."

"Very well," Chernov said.

"Paporov will meet you downstairs. If there's nothing else I can do for you, I have a dinner date."

"Enjoy your dinner, Colonel."

"I will," Zuyev said brusquely.

Chernov and Yuryn went downstairs, to the darkened day room empty at this hour. Everything was institutional gray, nothing more than functional. There was no television, no pictures on the walls, no rugs on the bare tile floor, just a few steel tables and chairs.

"Kabatov will want progress reports," Yuryn said.

"Tell him whatever you want to tell him, General."

Yuryn eyed him coldly. "You and I both know the truth, so don't screw around here. You have less than ten weeks."

Chernov's left eyebrow rose. "I don't screw around, as you put it."

Yuryn nodded. "I'm having dinner at my club tonight, would you care to join me?"

"No," Chernov said.

"As you wish," Yuryn said. He turned and left.

Chernov went to the window. The prison seemed all but deserted. The outer walls were not illuminated, so far as he could tell there were no guards in the four towers and only a few windows on the one and two story yellow brick buildings were lit from within.

After Yuryn's limousine passed through the main gate, Zuyev came downstairs and passed Chernov without noticing him. Outside, his car drew up, he got in the back seat and left by the main gate, and the building fell silent.

Chernov lit a cigarette as he examined his thoughts. He had been placed in a very dangerous position, caught between the forces inside the Kremlin, and forces outside that were allied with Tarankov. Under ordinary circumstances he wondered if he would have got out while such an act was relatively uncomplicated. But these were not ordinary circumstances. McGarvey was the assassin, and whatever dangers there were here in chaotic Moscow they were worth facing for a chance at finally killing the bastard.

A dark figure came across the parade ground. Chernov stepped away from the window and stubbed out his cigarette. The figure passed through a strip of light that came through the steel gates, and Chernov caught a brief look at the man's face which was framed by long hair, and covered by a beard. Unusual for a military officer, Chernov thought, even in these times.

The man came in and walked over to where Chernov stood next to the window. "Good evening, Colonel. I'm Captain Paporov. I've been assigned to be your assistant."

"How did you know I was standing here?" Chernov asked in English.

"Your cigarette."

"That sort of a mistake could cost us our lives," Chernov said, switching to French.

"*Mais oui, mon colonel.*"

"Then we'd better not make any more mistakes."

Paporov managed a slight smile. "I think we will, Colonel. But I'll try to keep mine to a minimum."

Chernov grunted. "You're an arrogant bastard."

"Yes, sir, that I am."

"Is that why they let you get away with all that hair?"

"It's either that, or fire me. Something General Yuryn won't allow, because I'm good at what I do. And from what I was told, so are you. Otherwise I wouldn't have taken this assignment. Kirk McGarvey is a tough son of a bitch, and frankly I don't give a shit whether Tarankov lives or dies. But trying to stop a man like McGarvey might prove to be interesting."

"For the duration, then, you're mine. That means you will discuss no aspect of this operation with anyone, including General Yuryn, without telling me. Clear?"

"Yes, sir."

"From now on we have no military rank between us. Call me Yuri, and I'll call you Aleksi. It'll save time. Do you have a wife, girlfriend, parents, or anyone else who will demand your attention, or need protection when things become difficult?"

"No."

"Has anyone given you any special instructions either about this assignment or about me, personally?"

"Only that you're a demanding, cold-hearted, ruthless bastard, and that you have a habit of destroying anyone who gets in your way."

Chernov had to laugh. "Did that come from General Yuryn?"

"Personally."

"Okay. I'm a ruthless bastard, you're an arrogant bastard, and McGarvey is a tough son of a bitch who I mean to find and kill. Nothing else matters, just that one thing. Are you clear on that as well?"

"Perfectly."

They walked back to a small, one-story brick building that, Paporov said, had originally been used as the prison dispensary. Most recently it had been fitted out as a communications and operations headquarters for special FSK projects. The largest of the three rooms was equipped with several desks each with a computer terminal. A bank of sophisticated radio gear, tall grey file cabinets and map cases, a light table and a big conference desk filled the room. Another of the rooms was set up as sleeping quarters, and the third as a kitchen with a small fridge, a hot plate, a sink and several cabinets filled with food. The bathroom was at the rear. All the windows were sealed and alarmed, the glass painted black and covered with a heavy steel mesh. The front and back doors were made of thick steel with coded, eight-digit locks.

"We have ten phone lines, all of them encrypted, in addition to satellite up-and downlinks with everything we have in orbit," Paporov said. "We have communications links with the Militia, FSK and SVR as well as every command in every branch of our military. All the computer equipment is state of the art IBM which gives us good access to nearly every computer system in the world."

"I'm a computer illiterate," Chernov admitted.

"I'm not," Paporov said. "I got one of my degrees at Caltech when I worked for the KGB in California ten years ago. That's one of the reasons for this," he said, flipping his long, sand-colored hair. "Where do we start?"

"We'll need transportation."

"There's a BMW and a Mercedes parked in back. The plates are government. Do you want a driver?"

"No," Chernov said. "For now I want McGarvey's file, your file, a very good map of Moscow, above and below ground, and a complete schedule of every single event for the next ten weeks, until the general elections, in which more than a handful of people are expected to be present."

"No problem," Paporov said.

"Why aren't you writing this down?"

"I have a photographic memory."

"Very well," Chernov said. "I want you to find the best police artist in the country and get him or her here as soon as possible. Then I want you to schedule a meeting here at noon tomorrow, providing the artist shows up first, for the division chiefs of the Special Investigations units of the Militia and the FSK."

"What shall I tell them?"

"To come."

"What else?"

"That's it for now," Chernov said.

"Okay. I'll start with the files." Paporov took off his jacket, tossed it over the back of a chair and went over to the file cabinets.

Chernov walked into the kitchen where he got a bottle of beer, some sausage and a piece of dark bread, happy to be away from Tarankov and the man's insane plans for the moment.

TWENTY-SIX

Moscow

L etting himself into his apartment, Yemlin resisted the urge to go to the window and see if anyone was down in the street. So far as he could tell he wasn't being followed, but that didn't mean a thing. The FSK had a lot of good men working for it, and some of the best field officers of any secret service in the world.

They could be there, and he'd never see them.

He went into the kitchen, poured a vodka, and lighting a cigarette, went back to his chair. He turned the television to CNN, and let the words and images flow around him while he tried to work out his position.

The FSK had not arrested him because they hoped that he would lead them to McGarvey. But they couldn't be aware yet that he knew that they knew, so for the moment he would do nothing out of the ordinary. Nothing to raise their suspicions. He was an old man caught up in the allure of the

Magesterium, and the novel experience of being sexually ministered to by a young man.

The same question kept running through his mind, though, threatening to blot out his sanity. If the act were so abhorrent to him, why had his body responded? The first time he'd been drugged, but tonight he'd done it of his own free will. He'd forced himself to do the act in order to gain the one vital piece of information. Did it make him a homosexual?

He'd prided himself on being a man of experience. But faced with this situation he felt like a complete fool. Even thinking about tonight, gave him an unsettled feeling in his loins. He closed his eyes and tried to blot out the images of what he'd done.

He was going to have to get out of Russia permanently, and he was going to have to warn McGarvey off. He took the two problems as a single unit, because he felt that the solution to both would lie initially in Paris. If he could get to Paris, even if the FSK followed him, he could manage to hide himself. Once there contacting McGarvey would be easier than doing it from Moscow, even though here he had the resources of the SVR, because in Paris he would be free.

He would have to be careful about his own service, because if questions were to be raised about his behavior it might lead his own people over to the FSK, and his participation in hiring McGarvey would come out.

Despite the inter-service rivalry, General Aykazyan would not hesitate to throw him to the wolves if for no other reason than to hedge his bets against Tarankov's victory.

The FSK would probably not interfere with his movements for the time being. They might believe that he was going to Paris to meet with McGarvey. In the meantime, he was going to have to warn Sukhoruchkin. He owed his old friend at least that much.

He stubbed out his cigarette, finished his drink, then threw on a coat and left the apartment. Two blocks away he caught a taxi to the Hotel National. The driver dropped him off in front, and Yemlin stared at the Kremlin walls across Manezhnaya Ploshchad for a few moments before he went inside the ornately refurbished hotel.

It was just past 9:30 P.M. when he walked back to a bank of pay phones, and called Sukhoruchkin at home. His old friend answered on the second ring. Yemlin could hear music in the background.

"*Da.*"

"I'm at the National, how about dinner tonight, Konstantin?"

"I've already had my dinner," Sukhoruchkin said. "But I'll join you for drinks at the Moskovy."

"Fifteen minutes?"

"*Da.*"

Of the National's four restaurants, the Moskovy was the most tradition-ally Russian. Since its reopening after a four-year renovation of the hotel, it had become one of Yemlin's favorites. He and Sukhoruchkin often came here for late dinners, drinks and private conversations. They were always given good service, and if they wanted to be left alone, they were.

A woman was strumming a guitar and singing a folk song on the small stage when Yemlin walked in. The place was three-quarters full and most of the diners were paying close attention to the singer because she was very good, and the song was very old and very sad, something most Russians loved, especially these days.

"Good evening, Mr. Yemlin," the maître d' greeted him. "Will you be dining alone this evening?"

"No, Konstantin will be joining me. We would like a table away from the stage. A quiet table."

"Of course," the man said. "But you'll still be able to hear Larissa."

Konstantin Sukhoruchkin sat on the edge of the chair in his bedroom lacing his shoes as he waited for his call to Tbilisi to go through. His old friend was in trouble. He'd picked up that much from the few words they'd spoken on the telephone, and from a rumor that had been circulating around the Human Rights Commission the last few days. The rivalry between the two divisions of the old KGB was apparently coming to a head, and Yemlin was being targeted as a scapegoat for some purely internal problem. He'd heard nothing other than that, but he was astute enough to understand that something else might be happening. Something concerning McGarvey's assignment. Just the thought of anything going wrong made his blood run cold.

Shevardnadze's special number finally rolled over, rang once with a different sound, and then was answered by the man himself.

"This is Konstantin Sukhoruchkin, Mr. President. I'm telephoning from Moscow."

"What is it?"

"Has Viktor contacted you in the last two or three days?"

"No," Shevardnadze said.

"He just telephoned me to have dinner with him tonight. I have been friends with him long enough to know when he's in trouble. Big trouble."

"Have you heard anything?"

"The FSK is raising hell again. There's a rumor that Viktor might be under investigation for an internal problem."

"Nothing about the . . . project?"

"*Nyet*. But I am having these feelings."

"I know what you mean, Konstantin. I'm also having those feelings. Do you want to call it off?"

"I don't know. But I intend asking Viktor that very question," Sukhoruchkin said. "I wanted to talk to you first. To find out how you feel."

"Nothing has changed, has it?" Shevardnadze asked.

"If anything the situation gets worse every day, Mr. President. I doubt if we'll even last until the June elections."

"So the need is still there," Shevardnadze said. "Viktor may be getting cold feet. If that's it, if the project hasn't been compromised beyond salvaging, then you have to convince him to press on. Don't you agree?"

"No. Not unless I consider the alternative," Sukhoruchkin said. "I'll see what the matter is, and we'll go from there."

"It's all you can do, Konstantin. It's all any of us can do now."

Yemlin put down his glass of iced Polish vodka, opened the latch of the heavier cigarette box and laid it on the table as he spotted Sukhoruchkin coming across the room toward him. The woman was still singing, and in the past fifteen minutes no one suspicious had entered the restaurant, but this hotel was owned by the city of Moscow, which meant the restaurant was probably bugged.

His friend looked troubled, as Yemlin rose to greet him. "Has something happened, Korstya?"

"That's my question for you," Sukhoruchkin said, shaking hands. They sat down.

"I'm going to Paris to call McGarvey off," Yemlin said. "I won't be coming back." He poured a vodka for Sukhoruchkin, who glanced nervously at the door.

"I knew something was wrong."

"They know about McGarvey and it's my fault, I'm afraid."

The color drained from Sukhoruchkin's narrow face. "Is it safe to speak here?"

"Yes. But listen, you have to call Shevardnadze and tell him what's happened. There could be a backlash. They might try to assassinate him."

Sukhoruchkin was shaking his head. "I just talked to him. He told me to tell you that unless the project is beyond saving we must continue, because nothing else has changed. If Tarankov succeeds we'll lose the *Rodina.*"

Yemlin passed a hand across his eyes. "They know about McGarvey, didn't you hear me?"

"They can't know about McGarvey's actual plans, because none of us do."

"He has to be warned!"

"Why?" Sukhoruchkin demanded. "We owe this man nothing other than the money you've already paid him. If he's as good as you say he is, then he'll go ahead with it. If he succeeds we'll be in the clear."

"What if he fails?"

Sukhoruchkin raised his eyes to the ceiling. "Then nothing will matter. We'll be dead and the nation lost."

Yemlin motioned the waiter over, and ordered another carafe of vodka and another plate of blinis, and caviar.

"Would you give your life to save Russia?" Yemlin said quietly.

"If it came to that, yes, of course."

"What about your dignity, Korstya? Your pride? Your—manhood?

Would you as easily give those up for Mother Russia? Would you, for instance, give up the use of your limbs to save the nation? Would you become a quadriplegic for the sake of your countrymen? Because that's what I'm being asked to do."

Sukhoruchkin was studying his face. "My God, Viktor, what's happened? What have you done?"

Yemlin looked away for a few moments. It took courage to be a Russian. That was something they'd never understood in the West. Russia had been at war with most of her neighbors at one point or another in her history. But there'd never been a time when Russians hadn't been at war with each other. The tsars had killed peasants by the millions, as had Stalin and as Tarankov was threatening to do. Food was plentiful in the fields, but the harvests often didn't get to the population centers, so lack of food had taken uncounted millions of lives. The weather killed people. Vodka and cigarettes killed people. Even the very air and water had become deadly in many parts of the country. Nuclear fallout and poorly processed chemical wastes were killers. Infant mortality rates were up, as were abortions. More than ten percent of all Russian babies were being born with life-threatening defects. Over half of all children in school were sick. The average life span for a man in Russia was now fifty-seven years, by far the lowest of any industrialized nation. Murder was a way of doing business, and suicide rates continued to rise every year. And Tarankov would make all of that worse.

The question Yemlin asked himself was not whether he had the courage to help McGarvey succeed against all odds by whatever means he could, but whether he had the courage to continue being a Russian.

"I went to the Magesterium on Friday where I was given drugged champagne and was seduced. I told them about hiring McGarvey to kill Tarankov."

"Who does the girl work for?"

"It wasn't a girl," Yemlin said, lowering his eyes. "It was a young man. And he probably works for the FSK."

Sukhoruchkin's mouth hung open. "You were drugged, Viktor. It wasn't your fault."

Yemlin said nothing.

"But if you were drugged how do you know if you spoke McGarvey's name? Maybe you dreamed it."

"I went back tonight, to the same young man. This time I seduced him, and drugged him. He told me what I'd said."

Sukhoruchkin sat back and closed his eyes for a moment. "I see what you mean," he said softly. "But the first time wasn't your fault, and the second time you had to find out what they knew."

"If I stay, there'll have to be a third time, Korstya. The only way I can help McGarvey now, short of calling him off, will be to feed the FSK disinformation."

"We can't call him off."

Yemlin nodded.

"If it's any consolation, my old friend—and I expect that it's not—if I were in your shoes I would probably do the same thing. But you're right, it is easier to give your life for your country. Infinitely easier."

Yemlin's eyes met Sukhoruchkin's. "Do you think badly of me, Korstya?"

"On the contrary, my old friend. I think that at this moment you are the bravest man in Russia."

Paris

McGarvey watched the dawn come up over the suburb of Courbevoie, finally ready to leave. His two soft leather suitcases and laptop computer were packed, he'd bought his air ticket for Leipzig yesterday, and in addition to his Allain credit cards, he carried nearly twenty thousand francs in cash, and five thousand in British pounds. On Friday he'd arranged a letter of credit in the amount of $150,000 to be deposited in the name of Pierre Allain at the Deutches Creditbank, and had been assured that it would be in place no later than this afternoon.

Rencke, who would drive him to Charles de Gaulle, was downstairs in the kitchen, but they hadn't spoken yet this morning.

The last few days had been intense, made all the more so by the stunning revelation that Tarankov's chief of staff, Leonid Chernov, was Arkady Kurshin's half-brother. When the information had come up on Rencke's computer monitor McGarvey had been physically staggered, and he stepped back.

"What's wrong, Mac?" Rencke asked, alarmed.

"I killed his brother in Portugal a few years ago." McGarvey touched his side where he still carried the scar where the doctors had removed one of his kidneys that had been destroyed when Kurshin shot him. "I didn't know he had a brother."

Rencke looked at the picture on the monitor. "Did you ever come face-to-face with Chernov? Does he know you?"

"He has to know about me."

"Would he have recognized you in Nizhny Novgorod?"

"I don't know," McGarvey said. He was back in the tunnels beneath the ruined castle where their final confrontation had come. It was dark, and water was pouring in on them. He'd been lucky. He got out and Kurshin had been trapped. And it *was* luck, he told himself now as he had then, because Kurshin was every bit as good as he was. In some ways even better, because he'd been more ruthless, less in love with his own life, so he'd been willing to take their fight to extremes.

"Call it off, Mac," Rencke had said. "Because if he finds out that you're coming after Tarankov he won't stop until he kills you. I've read Kurshin's file. If this one is as good, he might succeed."

"We don't know that."

"There's almost nothing in the SVR's own files about him, except that he was the best. It's why he's with Tarankov. Think it out, Mac. Tarankov just isn't worth it."

"Nothing has changed."

Rencke jumped up. "Everything has changed, you silly bastard. If they get so much as a hint that you're after Tarankov you won't be able to do it. You can't fight the entire country."

"If he finds out, Otto. In the meantime I still have the advantage, because I know about him."

"You're not going to do it, are you?"

"Yes, I am."

"No."

"Bring up the probability program you worked out on Tarankov, goddammit. Nothing has changed. If he wins we could all be in trouble."

"Just probabilities, Mac. I could be wrong!"

"Have you ever been wrong?"

Rencke hung his head like schoolboy. "No," he said softly.

"Then I leave Monday morning."

"What's in Leipzig anyway?"

"An old friend," McGarvey had said.

He glanced at his watch. It was a little after 7:00 A.M. He stubbed out his cigarette, put on his jacket and went downstairs. Rencke was seated on the kitchen table, drinking from a liter bottle of milk and eating Twinkies. He looked up, his eyes round.

"Is it time?"

"Yes, it is."

"Do you want a Twinkie, Mac?"

McGarvey had to laugh. "Have you ever had your cholesterol checked?"

"Yeah, but I don't eat so many of these as I used to, and I switched to milk a few years ago."

"What'd you drink before?"

Rencke shrugged. "A half-dozen quarts of heavy cream a day. Tastes a hell of a lot better than milk, you know."

TWENTY-SEVEN

Moscow

Aleksi Paporov left the office at Lefortovo a little before nine in the morning, and returned an hour later with a distinguished looking older man in a gray fedora and western cut blue pinstriped suit, who carried an artist's portfolio.

"This is Dr. Ivan Denisov, professor of reconstructive surgery at Moscow State University and possibly the very best facial sketch artist in all of Russia," Paporov introduced him to Chernov.

"Doctor, we need your help this morning," Chernov said.

Dr. Denisov was confused. His eyes blinked rapidly behind thin wire rimmed glasses. "I don't understand, am I under arrest?"

Chernov smiled. "On the contrary, Doctor, I would simply like you to draw a face for us from a description which I'll give you. Will you do this?"

"Yes, of course," Dr. Denisov said, relief obvious on his features. "Who is this person you wish me to sketch? Is it an accident victim . . . a corpse?"

"Nothing like that. Just a man we would very much like to find," Chernov said soothingly. "But first I must inform you of something that unfortunately the law requires of me. What you see and hear this morning must remain secret. Even the fact that you were brought here must remain a secret."

"Major Lyalin told me that much already," the older man said, blinking again, and Paporov smiled.

"Well, the major is correct. Because the man whose face you'll draw for us is a mass murderer who specializes in young children. But he may be an important man with connections so we don't want to frighten him off before we have enough evidence to arrest him. Can you understand this?"

"Da," the professor said seriously. He took off his coat and Paporov hung it up for him.

He sat at one of the desks, where he took out a large sketch pad and charcoal pencils from his portfolio. He looked up expectantly.

"This is a man of about fifty, husky, a rather square face, thick hair—" Chernov begun, but the professor interrupted him.

"First things first. Is this man a Russian? A Georgian? A Ukrainian?"

"Does it matter?" Chernov asked.

"Yes, indeed. Think of the difference, for instance, between a Siberian and a Muscovite who both are possessed of a husky frame, with a rather square face and thick hair."

"He's an American."

Dr. Denisov hesitated for only a moment. "Has he lived in Russia for long?" he asked, and before Chernov could speak, he went on. "That too makes a difference. Because if he lives in Russia he will get his hair cut here. There is a distinction."

"He has lived in Paris for some years. He's come to Russia recently, but I don't think he got a haircut while he was here."

"Very well," the professor said, and he began to sketch the outlines of a head, Chernov standing above and behind him.

"His cheekbones are a little wider and higher," Chernov said.

The professor made the changes. And gradually, under instructions from Chernov, a face began to emerge from the sketch pad that fifteen minutes later was the face of the soldier Chernov had seen in Nizhny Novgorod.

"Is this him?" Dr. Denisov asked, looking up.

Chernov was mesmerized by the sketch. Especially the eyes. The professor had gotten the face exactly right. Even down to the nuances of the expression Chernov had witnessed on the soldier's face.

"Major, show the good doctor the latest photograph we have," Chernov said.

Paporov went back to the desk Chernov had used, broke the seal on McGarvey's photo file, and brought one of the 20×25 cm color glossies over to Dr. Denisov.

"This was taken three years ago," Paporov said.

"Is that the same man?" Chernov asked.

"Of course. There's absolutely no question about it. He's aged some, though not badly. And the man you described for me was obviously trying to disguise his features by not shaving, by changing the expression on his mouth, and to some extent in his eyes. But there's no doubt." Dr. Denisov looked up at Chernov. "But this is no mass murderer."

"Oh, but he is, Professor," Chernov said. "You cannot imagine the blood he's spilled, and the blood he will continue to spill if he's not stopped."

Dr. Denisov looked again at the sketch. "Then he is a very dangerous man, perhaps even more dangerous than you suspect."

"What makes you say that?" Paporov asked.

"Because the man in the photograph and in my drawing must be a master of deception. The man I'm seeing is determined, and probably hard, but he gives the appearance of a kind person. With perhaps a sense of humor."

"He's probably schizophrenic in that case, Doctor, because he is a killer."

"Then I wish you luck in catching him," Dr. Denisov said.

Chernov tore off the sketch and the next four blank pages. "Don't speak to anyone about this."

"Believe me, I won't."

While Paporov was taking the professor back to the university, Chernov compared the sketch to the dozen photographs in McGarvey's file. Whatever lingering doubts he might have had about the validity of Yuryn's report were dispelled. McGarvey had come to Russia to stalk his prey. There was no doubt that he meant to kill Tarankov. The only questions now were the where and the when. With a man such as McGarvey the assassination could come at any time and at any place, especially when it was least expected. But he wasn't a martyr, which meant he not only knew how and where he was going to kill Tarankov, but he also knew how he was going to escape afterward.

It was nearly 11:30 by the time Paporov returned. He tossed his coat aside and went to the desk where the sketch and McGarvey's photographs were laid out.

"Where did you see him?" he asked.

Chernov sat perched on the edge of one of the desks smoking a cigarette and drinking a glass of tea. He looked languidly at his aide. "What makes you think I did?"

"McGarvey's photo file was sealed. You never looked at his pictures before you described him to Dr. Denisov."

"I remembered his file from the old days. He has a face that's not easily forgotten."

"But this doesn't look like any of the photographs," Paporov said, glancing at the sketch.

"I was told that he was here in Moscow, and I thought how he must have aged, and the probability that he was here in disguise." Chernov shrugged.

Paporov gave him an odd look, then chuckled. "You're even better than I thought you were, Yuri."

Chernov forced a smile. "If you're going to run around masquerading as a major, I'd better become a general."

"That's what I thought."

Chernov glanced at his watch. "I want you to make several copies of the sketch, and one of the photographs. We'll give them to the Militia and FSK and let them hunt for the mass murderer."

"That'll get it out in public okay without tipping our hand. But where do we look besides here in Moscow?"

"Wherever Tarankov is expected to show up."

"How do we find that out?"

"Leave that to me, Major. I have a few sources of my own."

"I'll bet you do, General," Paporov said.

It was precisely noon when FSK Major Porfiri Gresko and Militia Captain Illen Petrovsky showed up at Lefortovo Prison and were directed back to the special operations office, where Chernov let them read the letter that President Kabatov had sent over this morning.

"I wondered what this was all about," Major Gresko said, impressed. He was division chief of the intelligence service's Special Investigations Unit, the same position Captain Petrovsky held in the Militia.

When Petrovsky looked up, his dark eyes narrowed. "If you ask me we ought to let the American kill him. Save us all a pain in the ass."

"You're not being asked," Chernov said coldly. "You can refuse this assignment if you wish, in which case a replacement will be found."

"Right," the Militia captain said. "How can we help?"

Paporov handed them copies of McGarvey's photograph and the sketch.

"His name is Kirk McGarvey. He's a former CIA field officer, who for a number of years has worked freelance," Chernov said. "Believe me, gentlemen, when I tell you that he is very good at what he does."

"Was he a shooter?" Gresko asked.

"One of the best."

"I think I heard of him. Something or other with General Baranov and that crowd a while back," Gresko said. "Who's hired him to kill the Tarantula? The CIA?"

"No, it's our own people," Paporov said. He gave them copies of Yuryn's report. "Needless to say this entire affair is to be considered most secret."

"You'll have no problem from me," Petrovsky said. "I'm just a cop, and I'd rather Tarankov never know my name."

Both men read the report, which with transcripts ran to about forty pages. When they were finished they sat in silence for a few moments.

"I was told that I would receive special instructions from General Yuryn when I got back from this meeting," Gresko said. "I didn't know about this operation, except that Colonel Yemlin has been under investigation for something. Those pricks out on the ring highway think they're almighty gods." He laughed and shook his head. "And here all the time they were nothing but a bunch of cocksuckers and traitors.

"From this point both your services are to conduct the surveillance operation on Yemlin and on all of his contacts. Wherever the man goes, whatever he does, I want to know about it. But he mustn't suspect anything. Nothing is to get back to the SVR. Not even a hint."

"Why not just arrest the bastard?" Gresko asked.

"Because there's a possibility that he'll make contact with McGarvey at some point," Chernov said.

"How about McGarvey?" Petrovsky said. "How far can we take this?"

"For the moment he's to be considered a mass murder suspect. Initially you'll start your investigation here in Moscow. Hotels, the railway stations, airports, restaurants."

"The Mafia?"

"If you have the solid contacts," Chernov said. "I don't want some Mafia boss finding McGarvey first, and then selling us out. He's a wealthy man. If he offered enough money to the right people we'd lose him."

"Is he still here in Moscow?" Petrovsky asked.

"I don't know, but I suspect not. He probably came here for information, and he may have gone back to France where he's making his preparations. But we'll have help. The CIA and French SDECE have agreed to find and detain McGarvey for us."

"On what charge?" the Militia cop asked. "The Americans are especially touchy on that issue. So long as McGarvey breaks no laws in his own country, or in France, there's not much they could do."

"If they find him, they'll hold him long enough for us to send someone over to interview him. Afterwards we watch him."

"But he's good, the best, you said," Gresko pointed out. "Which presents us with a number of unique problems. We don't know where he is, nor do we know his plan or his timetable. We can't use the services of our own SVR, nor apparently can we make public the real reason we're hunting for him, although I don't understand that all."

"It's political," Chernov said. "President Kabatov does not want Tarankov assassinated. He wants the man arrested and brought here for trial."

Petrovsky laughed out loud. "Not likely to happen," he said. "But we do know our timetable. It's ten weeks before the elections. Kabatov's people must either arrest Tarankov before then, or McGarvey has to kill him, or else all this becomes a moot point. Tarankov will win the election."

"Why not concentrate our efforts on arresting Tarankov?" Gresko asked.

"The military is working on it."

Gresko smirked. "Then they'd better pull their heads out of their asses, because from what I heard some good boys lost their lives outside Nizhny Novgorod."

"That's not our job," Chernov said.

"What do we do if we find him?" Petrovsky asked.

"Kill him," Chernov said.

"Then I think we should distribute his photograph to all of our border crossings. If the man is as good as you say he is, we can't leave anything to chance."

"If you have the manpower to do it, go ahead," Chernov said.

CIA Headquarters

Howard Ryan was an early riser and he habitually got to his office before 8:00 A.M. This morning a message was waiting for him in his e-mail to come to the director's office the moment he arrived. It wasn't unusual. The general often held early morning meetings before the workday began. Ryan hung up his coat and took the elevator to the seventh floor where Murphy sat behind his desk staring out the window. He was alone. His secretary wasn't due for another hour.

"Good morning, General," Ryan said, walking in.

"Close the door, Howard," Murphy said, without turning around.

Ryan did so then took a chair in front of the desk. Normally at this hour Murphy would be watching CNN and the three network news broadcasts on the bank of television monitors beside his desk. This morning the screens were blank.

"How is the McGarvey thing coming?" Murphy asked. "Any luck finding him yet?"

"No. But we're working with the French on it. Seems as if he might have been tipped off, because a lead we thought we had turned up empty. Apparently we missed him by a few hours or less."

"Would McGarvey have known that Tarankov once worked for us?"

The question was startling. "There was nothing in the files," Ryan said. "I can't think of any reason for him to have known. But with a man like McGarvey anything is possible."

"Let's hope not," Murphy said and he turned around. "We're in enough trouble as it is. And the hell of it, Howard, is that for the first time in my career I don't know what to do." He waved the comment off. "I don't mean that. I know what to do. It's just that I'm not sure what's right or wrong." He focused on Ryan. "Am I making any sense, Howard?"

"No, sir. What the hell has McGarvey done this time?"

"Apparently he's been hired by a group of Russian reformers, among them Eduard Shevardnadze, to assassinate Tarankov sometime between now and the June elections."

"Let him. If he's successful it would eliminate a potentially very large problem for us."

"It's not that simple."

It never was, Ryan thought, not at all surprised by the news. Killing

Tarankov was right down McGarvey's alley. He and that computer freak friend of his had probably already hatched some bizarre scheme to put a bullet in the Russian's brain. Whatever the plan, it would be good.

"I don't mean to suggest that we help him," Ryan said.

"We have to find him before he does it, by whatever means we can. Russian President Kabatov called President Lindsay and asked for our help. The President agreed." Murphy handed a leather-bound report to Ryan. "This came over the weekend from Kabatov's office. They've formed an independent investigatory commission to find McGarvey. A former KGB special investigations officer by the name of Bykov has been named to head it, and he sounds like a good man."

"Mr. Director, are you suggesting that we open our Moscow station to these people?"

"No," Murphy replied heavily. "We're not going to compromise any of our ongoing operations over there. But we can send someone from here, or from one of our stations outside Russia. I'll let you be the judge of that."

"Well, we can't do anything here in the States."

"The FBI has agreed to a nationwide manhunt for McGarvey. A very quiet manhunt."

"We can certainly step up our operation in France."

"The Russians have asked the French for help, and Chirac agreed."

"The son of a bitch," Ryan said under his breath.

"Do whatever it takes, Howard, but find McGarvey before it's too late and he gets himself killed, or even worse, starts a civil war over there."

SDECE Headquarters

Colonel Galan came to attention in front of General Baillot's desk, and saluted.

"Have you any progress to report in your search for McGarvey?" the general demanded brusquely.

"He and a computer expert friend of his—also a former CIA officer—have disappeared, *mon general*. It is possible that they are no longer in France."

"Our customs police have been informed?"

"*Oui*. But if he was disguised, and carried false papers, he could have gotten through."

"Yet you continue to use Mademoiselle Belleau, and McGarvey's young daughter in an effort to lure him back to his apartment. Is that not correct?"

"Yes, sir."

The general snorted in irritation. "A bad business using the child against its father."

"The Americans offered her the assignment and she agreed. She hopes to intercept her father before he takes the assignment and places himself in danger."

"He was in Moscow last week, but it is believed he has left, probably back here to France."

"Sir?" Galan muttered to cover his surprise.

"We have a report from President Kabatov who has set up a special police commission to find and stop McGarvey, who has been hired to assassinate Yevgenni Tarankov for a group of Russian moderates."

"Then it is no longer our problem, *mon general*," Galan said, relieved.

"On the contrary, Colonel Galan. President Kabatov telephoned President Chirac and personally asked for his help. Our president agreed. So it is our problem. It is your problem." General Baillot handed a leather folder across the desk to Galan. "This is the Russian report. Find Monsieur McGarvey. For now it is your only assignment, and will receive the utmost priority. Do I make myself clear?"

"*Mais oui, mon general.*"

TWENTY-EIGHT

Leipzig

McGarvey landed at Berlin's Templehof Airport a little before ten, cleared customs, and took the shuttle bus to the imposing Japanese-owned Hotel Intercontinental on Gerberstrasse in Liepzig seventy-five miles south, arriving at the front desk at 12:30 P.M.

He booked a very expensive suite for three days, paying for it with his Allain credit card. The obsequious day manager personally escorted him upstairs, and showed him around the luxurious accommodations, which included a palatial marble bathroom with gold fixtures.

"This will have to do, I suppose," McGarvey said in passable German. He tipped the man five hundred francs, and handed him another five thousand. "Change this into German currency, would you, I didn't have time at the airport."

"Yes, sir," the impressed manager said with a slight bow and he left.

McGarvey locked his laptop in the room safe then made two telephone calls. The first was to the Creditbank where he made an appointment for 2:00 P.M. with the business accounts manager Herman Dunkel. The second was to Leipzig's largest Mercedes dealer, whose number he got from the telephone book, and made an appointment with a salesman for 3:00 P.M.

The hotel day manager returned with an envelope filled with deutch-marks while McGarvey was changing into a dove-gray business suit.

"It comes to one thousand six hundred and—"

"Just lay it on the desk," McGarvey said indifferently, as he knotted his silk Hermes tie.

"If there's anything else I can do for you, Herr Allain, please inform me."

McGarvey turned and gave him a hard stare. "Not now."

"Yes, sir," the manager said, again with a slight bow and he left.

When McGarvey was finished dressing, he went downstairs to the atrium bar where he had a half-bottle of good Riesling and a Wienerschnitzel with spaetzle and dark bread. Afterward he had coffee and a cognac and signed for the bill, and by 1:40 P.M. he climbed into a taxi and ordered the driver to take him to the Creditbank's main branch on Ritterstrasse near the opera house.

The city was being renovated from the ground up after forty-five years of communist rule in which the place had deteriorated badly. Traffic was heavy, and every second car it seemed was a Mercedes or a BMW. Shop windows displayed goods from all over the world, and the stinking pall of coal smoke that had hung like a cloud over the city for so long was finally beginning to clear away.

Herr Dunkel, who'd been mildly cool on the telephone, practically fell over himself as he escorted McGarvey into his office. "Let me tell you how pleased I am to meet you, Herr Allain," he said. "Your letter of credit arrived just an hour ago."

"I'm glad to hear that," McGarvey said. "I'd like to begin conducting my business as soon as possible."

"What is your business, sir?"

"Exporting automobiles."

"To what country or countries?"

"Latvia."

"I see. And what type of automobiles would you be interested in, Herr Allain?"

"Mercedes, of course," McGarvey said. "At low volumes, at first. I think an initial order of two units might be profitable."

The bank manager opened a folder, and looked at the single piece of paper it contained. "Would this be your total capital for this venture?"

"No."

"Forgive me, Herr Allain, for belaboring this point. But two Mercedes automobiles, plus shipping and export fees, could, depending on the models of course, exceed this amount."

McGarvey got a pen and slip of notepaper from the manager, and wrote down a nine digit number. "This is an account at Barclay's on Guernsey. The code phrase is *variable*. You will not use my name, but you may verify an amount not to exceed one million pounds sterling, an addition to this letter of credit."

"May I see your passport?"

McGarvey handed it over. The manager studied it for a moment, comparing the photograph to McGarvey's face, then handed it back.

He picked up his telephone and asked his secretary to ring up Barclay's Bank. The call went through immediately, and within ninety seconds McGarvey's account was verified.

"How may this bank be of service to you?" Dunkel asked, cautious now, but extremely interested.

McGarvey had purposely brought too small a letter of credit so that the banker he dealt with would have to verify the much larger amount. It was less flashy that way. Germans instinctively mistrusted flash.

"You can act as my banker, of course. Transferring funds, establishing my credit. And I expect you may be of value in expediting the necessary licenses."

"Yes, we can do all of that," Dunkel said. "But one final question. Why did you chose Leipzig to do your business? Why not Stuttgart where the home office of Mercedes is located?"

"This is a delicate subject, Herr Dunkel, may I be frank?" McGarvey asked.

"By all means."

"Businessmen in Stuttgart, and Munich, and Frankfurt-am-Main have a reputation for being rigid, sometimes overly so. While here, in what was once the GDR, that unbending, unimaginative attitude has not yet developed."

Dunkel smiled knowingly. "Sadly it is happening here too, Herr Allain. Perhaps it's unavoidable."

"Perhaps," McGarvey said.

"Now, who do you plan on doing business with?" Dunkel asked, straightening up.

"Mercedes Rossplatz."

"Very good." Dunkel wrote a brief note of introduction on his letterhead, put it in an envelope and handed it to McGarvey. "Ask to speak with Bernard Legler. He is the president of the company, and a very honorable man. The western sickness hasn't affected him yet."

The banker had called ahead, because Bernard Legler was waiting on the main showroom floor when McGarvey showed up, and he didn't bother reading Dunkel's note. He was a very tall, rawboned man with craggy features who looked more like an ex-rodeo cowboy than a German businessman. But his broad smile seemed genuine.

"You want to buy cars and I want to sell them to you, but I don't know a lot of folks in Latvia who can afford to buy one."

"I do," McGarvey said.

"Well then, let's do some business. What do you have in mind?"

Legler spoke German as if he were translating an American western movie. It was old hat in the west, but here it was the fad.

"The sport utility four-by-four."

"How many of them?"

"Two for now. But I expect to eventually handle a dozen or more each month."

"Equipment?"

"Load them up."

"Cell phones, leather, the Bose stereo systems?"

"Everything," McGarvey said.

Legler sat back, and gave McGarvey an appraising look. "I've got one coming in this afternoon that we can ship tomorrow. It'll take me about two weeks to round up another. What kind of price did you have in mind?"

"Ten percent over invoice," McGarvey said.

"Twenty."

"Twelve," McGarvey countered.

"Eighteen, and I handle all the export licenses, prepping and shipping to Riga. We'll truck them up there."

"Fifteen, and you can handle the shipping but I'll pay for it separately."

"Throw in an extra five hundred marks per unit, and we have a deal," Legler said.

"All right. How soon can you have the paperwork ready?"

"Where are you staying?"

"The Intercontinental," McGarvey said.

"I can be there first thing in the morning."

"I'm going to drive the first car to Riga myself. So I want it equipped with an extra spare tire, a couple of cans of gasoline, and the papers I need to cross the borders. The second car should be exactly the same."

"Make it noon," Legler said. "I'll need a shipping address in Riga. We'll truck it up there."

"I'll send it to you when I get there," McGarvey said.

"On the way out, let my secretary make copies of your passport and driving license. We'll need it for the documents."

McGarvey gave the man a hard look. "This business we have together will remain confidential."

"As long as you break no German laws, that's fine with me."

"Good."

Paris

Tom Lynch met Guy de Galan at a sidewalk cafe within sight of the Arc de Triomphe on the Champs-Elysées, a few minutes before 5:00 P.M., rush-hour traffic in full swing.

"I assume that you've received your instructions from Washington," Galan said.

Lynch nodded. "Did General Baillot brief you?"

"*Oui*," Galan replied heavily. "So now what do we do? He's broken no French laws that I know of, unless he's crossed our borders under false papers."

"He's done at least that much," Lynch said. "And if he's actually accepted this assignment, he's broken our anti-terrorism laws."

"Do you think there's any doubt of it?"

Lynch shook his head. "He may still be in Moscow for all we know, in which case it's up to Bykov and their special commission."

"We have nothing on Bykov in our files," Galan said.

"Neither do we, which makes me wonder. But it's something else I can't do a damn thing about. Fact is McGarvey is too good for us to find him, unless he makes a mistake. And if that happens he's a dead man."

"My general wants us to stop him before he comes to harm."

"That's the signal I'm getting from Washington. We'd rather see him in a French or American jail, than a marble slab in Moscow." Lynch gave Galan a bleak look. "Hell of it is he might pull it off. He's done some amazing things in his career, and it doesn't look like he's slowing down."

Galan shrugged.

"Let's assume he does kill Tarankov, and comes back here," Lynch said. "What will your government do about it?"

"That depends on whether the Russians can prove he did it. But you and I both know that if ever there was a political figure who needed assassinating, it's Tarankov. If he comes to power, God help us all. McGarvey might be doing us a favor."

Lynch nodded. "That's the hell of it. But I have my orders and I intend doing everything I can to carry them out."

"As will I," Galan said. "One idea comes immediately to mind, but I don't know if I'm enough of a bastard to try it."

"Are you talking about his daughter?"

"*Oui.* And Jacqueline. McGarvey cares more about them than anything in the world if half of their conversations we've monitored are true. If they were to be placed in the middle of this investigation in such a way that McGarvey could find out, he would back off for their sakes."

"Are you thinking about sending them to Moscow to work for Bykov?"

"It's a thought. McGarvey will find out about the commission from Yemlin, there's no doubt about it. If he also finds out that Jacqueline and his daughter are there as well, it might cause him to pull out."

Lynch shook his head. "I've got to sleep on that one," he said. "In the meantime we keep looking for him."

"*Oui*. Like finding a needle in the haystack, when we don't even know which farmyard it's in."

Leipzig

McGarvey spent a pleasant evening at the hotel, which featured an excellent Japanese restaurant. After dinner, he watched CNN for an hour or so, and went to sleep early. In the morning he had a vigorous workout in the hotel's health spa, swam two hundred laps in the pool, and had a gargantuan breakfast of ham, eggs, potatoes, spinach, and very good German Brötchen.

He took a cab to the *Thomaskirche* where Bach had been the choirmaster and organist. A young woman was practicing the "Toccata and Fugue in D-Minor" for an upcoming concert. He sat at the back of the church to listen until it was time to return to the hotel, and walking to the end of the block where he caught a cab, he could still hear the music on the corner. He'd never cared much for Germans, but they had written some good music. Bach was technical, and the Toccatas appealed to him.

Legler was waiting in the lobby, and they went up to McGarvey's suite where the automobile dealer laid out the contract, bank draft, registration and export paperwork on the big coffee table.

"Would you like to see what you're buying before you sign these?" Legler asked.

"Why?" McGarvey asked matter of factly. "By the time I get to Riga I'll know if I was cheated, and there will be no further business between us."

McGarvey signed the paperwork, including the bank draft for almost DM 93.000, which was about $60,000.

Legler handed him the factory invoice which showed that he paid for the car, including transportation and prep charges. McGarvey did the rough calculation in his head, then handed the invoice back.

"Good news about the other unit. I've been guaranteed an early delivery, so I can have it to you in Riga no later than ten days from now, possibly sooner."

"That is good news," McGarvey said.

Legler gathered up the papers, leaving McGarvey's copies on the table, and stuffed his in his attaché case. "I'm curious about something, Herr Allain. You're Belgian, so what's your connection with Latvia? If you don't mind me asking."

"I do mind," McGarvey said, rising.

Legler got up, and handed McGarvey a valet parking slip. "The extra spare tire and gas cans are in the cargo area. And I put the same route map that our truck driver will use in the glove compartment."

"Thank you," McGarvey said and they shook hands.

"Have a good trip, Herr Allain. And I wish you luck in your business venture."

Downstairs at the front desk McGarvey informed them that he would be leaving in the morning, a day earlier than planned, and to have his bill ready, along with a picnic lunch.

He retrieved the gunmetal-gray Mercedes from the parking valet, and drove the heavy machine over to an automobile parts store on the north side of the city he'd looked up in the telephone book. He purchased a pair of tire irons, and an electric tire inflator that connected to the car's cigarette lighter.

By 1:30 P.M. he was on the highway to the small town of Gröbers, located in a small forest that had somehow escaped the industrial devastation of so much of the area between Leipzig and Halle. The car was massive, the knobby tires huge, but it drove like a luxury sedan, not a truck. The upholstery was leather, the stereo system magnificent and the attention to detail precise.

The day was pleasantly warm, and when he pulled up in front of an isolated house at the edge of town, he spotted a burly man stripped to the waist working in the extensive garden on the south side of the house.

The man straightened up, brushed the gray hair off his forehead as McGarvey got out of the car and came around to the front.

"*Dobry dyen, Dmitri Pavlovich,*" McGarvey said.

Former KGB General Dmitri Voronin looked as if he was seeing a ghost, but then his broad Slavic face broke out into a grin. He dropped the weeding fork he'd been using, and shambled out of the garden. "Kirk," he shouted. He grabbed McGarvey in a bear hug and kissed him. "*Yeb vas,* but it's good to see you!"

"It's good to see you too," McGarvey said. "You're looking fit." He glanced up at the house. "Where's Nadia?"

Voronin's face fell. "You could not have known, Kirk. But she died last year of cancer."

"I'm sorry, Dmitri. She was a good woman."

"We would have been married forty-five years this summer." Voronin shrugged. "But then we wouldn't have had these last years of peace without you. We often talked about you."

After Baranov had fallen, taking much of the KGB's Executive Action Service with him, the Komityet and all of the Soviet Union had gone through a period of internal turmoil largely unknown in the West. Voronin, who'd been number two in the KGB's First Directorate, had tried to make the first peace overtures to the United States, and for his effort he was branded a traitor. McGarvey was hired to pull him and his wife out of Moscow to safety, first in West Germany near Munich for months of debriefings, and when the Wall came down they'd moved here for a simpler life.

"How about a beer, Kirk?" Voronin said.

"Sure. Then I have to ask you for a favor," McGarvey said.

Voronin gave him an amused glance. "You have the look on you. You're back in the field. Are you going to tell me about it?"

"*Nyet.*"

"Good, because I no longer want the burden—" Voronin stopped short, an odd expression on his face as if something disturbing had just occurred to him. "There's a picnic table in back. I'll get the beers."

McGarvey had been here once after Voronin and his wife were settled in. Nothing seemed to have changed, it was still a pleasant spot. He sat down and lit a cigarette. His connection with General Voronin was unknown to all but a handful of people in Langley. It had somehow slipped past the traitor Rick Ames. So far as they knew no one in Russia was aware that the CIA had helped Voronin out of the country, although they might have guessed. The manhunt for him and his wife had been brief, because the Komityet was in disarray, and its officers had other, bigger problems facing them than a defecting general. So McGarvey felt reasonably safe coming here.

Voronin brought the beers out, took a cigarette from McGarvey and they sat in silence for a few minutes, listening to the light breeze in the trees, the singing birds, and the distant hum of tires on the highway half a kilometer away.

"Five years ago we were about the same size, Dmitri," McGarvey said.

Voronin chuckled. "Old age is the ultimate diet."

"I'd like to borrow one of your dress uniforms."

Voronin cradled his beer bottle in both hands, and stared out toward the woods. "There's a lot of trouble brewing in the *Rodina*. I understand this, Kirk. But you must understand that she is still Mother Russia to me. I'll do nothing to harm my country."

"Neither will I," McGarvey said. "In fact I'm trying to help save it."

"Are you working for the CIA again?"

"No."

"Assassination has almost never had the expected results," Voronin said quietly. "The situation almost always got worse."

"It might this time, too, but I don't think so."

Voronin looked at him. "There is only one man in Russia whose death would benefit the people. If he were to be killed, I might be able to return."

"If I succeed, Dmitri, there's a very good chance that you'll be able to go home finally," McGarvey said.

"What if you fail?"

"Then the situation will probably get worse," McGarvey answered without hesitation. That thought had occupied his mind since Yemlin had come to see him in Paris.

Voronin thought for a minute. "I must do this for you."

"I'm not calling in any old debts, because there aren't—"

Voronin interrupted. "I must help you help the *Rodina*, even if there's a chance things will become worse. I'm getting old, and in the end maybe you're my only real hope for going home." Voronin got heavily to his feet. "I'll get it now."

"Do you have a couple of large plastic garbage bags?"

"Yes."

When Voronin went inside, McGarvey drove the Mercedes around back. He took the extra spare tire out of the cargo area, deflated it, and by the time Voronin returned he had pried one side of the tire away from the rim.

"Ingenious," Voronin said.

McGarvey wrapped the KGB uniform blouse, trousers, shirt and tie in the plastic, forming the bundle into a long narrow tube which he stuffed inside the spare tire. He reinflated the tire with the electric pump, and put it back in the cargo area.

Next he removed the cover from the spare tire attached to a bracket on the cargo door, and took the tire down. Voronin's officer's cap went into the hub of the wheel, which he reattached to the cargo lid bracket, and replaced the cover.

The entire operation took about forty minutes, and when he was done, McGarvey was sweating lightly. Voronin brought another couple of beers, and they sat again at the picnic table.

"When do you leave?"

"In the morning," McGarvey said.

"And when will you do . . . this thing?"

"Sometime between now and the general elections."

"Less than ten weeks."

"Maybe sooner."

Voronin looked away, his eyes filling. "Do you ever miss your country, Kirk?"

"Almost all the time, Dmitri."

"When this is done, maybe we can both go home," Voronin said. He got up and without a backward glance went into the house. McGarvey finished his beer, backed the Mercedes out of the driveway and left.

TWENTY-NINE

Paris

Elizabeth McGarvey awoke at her usual hour of 6:00 A.M., got dressed in a bright pink jogging outfit and headed along the Avenue Jean Jaurès, taking the same route her father did every morning. It was only a slight hope, but she thought by being so obviously open about her moves that if her father were to be anywhere in the vicinity of his apartment he would certainly spot her.

As she ran she kept her eyes open for anything out of the ordinary. Cars, windowless vans, delivery trucks with too many antennae. A face in a window, a reflection off binocular lenses on a rooftop. But after nearly a week of the same routine, she'd come up with nothing. At times her hopes began to fade.

She and Jacqueline had taken up residence in her father's apartment, and she'd gotten to know the French woman who in some respects was like her mother. Mysterious and reserved sometimes, while at other times open and vivacious. She was very bright, very sympathetic to Elizabeth's despair, and completely in love with Kirk.

On their first full day together at the apartment, after Tom Lynch reported that he and the SDECE had apparently just missed Rencke and McGarvey at the house outside Bonnières, she and Jacqueline went through the apartment with a fine-toothed comb. The Service had already taken the place apart, finding nothing. But Elizabeth felt that the instincts of two women might turn up something the Service might have missed.

But they'd found nothing. That evening they went to an art film, had a light supper and a couple of glasses of wine afterwards and then had returned to the apartment where they'd talked until nearly dawn.

Elizabeth doubled back through the park a half-block from her father's apartment, and pulled up short in a line of trees across the street from the sidewalk cafe. A few people were seated outside, drinking coffee and reading newspapers. One man in particular looked familiar and her heart began to pound. It was her father, she was certain of it, because she wanted to be certain of it.

She moved silently from tree to tree in order to get a better look, but the man's face was blocked by the newspaper he was reading.

So far as she could determine no one was watching him. But she knew enough not to rush across the street, because if the French were following her she would tip her hand. But she had to warn him.

Moving to a position directly across the street she tried to figure out the best way of approaching the cafe. The man put his newspaper down and reached for his coffee. She got a good look at his face, and her heart sank. It wasn't her father after all. The man was far too young, his hair black, his eyebrows too thick. She leaned against the tree and lowered her head, tears coming to her eyes.

She and Jacqueline had tried everything, even placing a want ad in the personals section of *Le Figaro: Liz loves you, daddy. I'm waiting at the apartment.* So far there'd been no response.

They'd gone to a number of his old haunts, sidewalk cafes, parks, bistros, the Eiffel Tower, that he'd mentioned.

They'd even driven out to the farmhouse Otto Rencke had rented outside Bonnières. But workmen were renovating the house, and none of them had ever heard of Rencke or McGarvey.

They'd tried at a half-dozen private computer schools in Paris on the off chance that Rencke might have shown up there, again without avail.

And they'd tried the private gun clubs and the French National fencing team's practice gymnasium where McGarvey had often worked out.

She looked up. The man at the cafe had raised the newspaper in front of his face again. Elizabeth couldn't see how she'd mistaken the man for her father. It wasn't even close, except that she was a stupid kid working way out of her league. Jacqueline wouldn't have made the mistake, and she'd only known Kirk for a few months.

She headed back to the apartment disconsolately. Her father had gone to ground, and she was kidding herself thinking that she could find him when Langley's best people couldn't do the job. Come home, get married and have babies, her mother would tell her. She could almost hear the words. But it just wasn't fair.

A dark blue Citröen was parked down the block from her father's apartment but she didn't spot it until she mounted the steps to the building and one of Colonel Galan's people opened the door for her. She stepped back and looked over her shoulder.

"It's okay, Mademoiselle. Mr. Lynch is waiting upstairs for you with Colonel Galan and Jacqueline."

"Have you found my father?"

"Please, Mademoiselle, they will explain everything," the older man said gently.

Elizabeth studied his face for a hint, but she saw nothing except friendly concern.

Jacqueline, dressed in blue jeans and a sweatshirt, her feet bare, her hair a mess, sat perched on the edge of the couch in the living room, smoking a cigarette. Tom Lynch sat opposite her and Galan stood next to the window. They looked up when Elizabeth came in.

Jacqueline's face was white. Elizabeth went immediately to her.

"Have they found him? Has he been hurt?"

Jacqueline took her hand. "He's been to Moscow, but we don't know anything beyond that. He may have come back."

"Did you spot anything out there this morning?" Lynch asked. He seemed almost embarrassed.

"No," Elizabeth said. "What's going on?"

Lynch and Galan exchanged a glance.

"The Russians know that your father has been hired to assassinate Yevgenni Tarankov, and a special police commission has been formed to stop him," Galan said.

"How did they find out?" Elizabeth demanded sharply.

"Apparently Viktor Yemlin talked."

"Oh, God." Elizabeth turned to Jacqueline, who looked as frightened as she felt.

"The Russians have asked for our help," Lynch said. "And that of the French. No one wants to see your father killed. But now that they know he's coming and what he plans to do, that's exactly what will happen unless we find him first."

"How do you know that he was in Russia?"

"He was spotted in Moscow."

"But they didn't catch him," Elizabeth said triumphantly. "Because he's too good. If he's set out to kill Tarankov, then that's what he'll do, and there's nothing that we or the Russians can do about it."

"He can't fight the entire Russian police and intelligence forces," Lynch shot back.

"Then why aren't we helping my father instead of the fucking Russians?" Elizabeth screeched.

"Getting hysterical isn't going to help," Galan tried to calm her.

"Don't patronize me you son of a bitch! Your service is supposed to be one of the best intelligence agencies in the world, and all you can think to do is send his daughter and his whore to find—"

Elizabeth stopped short. She and Jacqueline still held hands. Slowly she turned and looked into the older woman's glistening eyes.

"It's all right, *ma p'tite*," Jacqueline said. "The truth isn't supposed to be bad."

"I'm so sorry," Elizabeth said softly. "It's my big mouth. Sometimes I don't know what I'm saying."

Jacqueline drew Elizabeth close and held her for a long time. "Listen, what you said was true in the beginning," she whispered. "But not now. You must believe me."

Elizabeth clung more tightly. "I'm sorry, Jacqueline," she cried. She wished her mother and father were here and together now, like the old days. Like they still were sometimes in her fantasies. "I believe you."

"Okay. All right, I'm sending you back to Washington on the first flight," Lynch said. "I'm not going to have this on my conscience."

Elizabeth pulled away from Jacqueline. "This has nothing to do with your conscience," she said, back in control of herself. She felt like a little fool. "And you're going to need every bit of help you can get. Jacqueline and I are still your best bets."

"You haven't found him."

"Neither have you," Elizabeth countered. "Who's running this Russian police commission? And what are their chances?"

"His name is Yuri Bykov, ex-KGB," Galan said. "We're told he's very good, but we don't have anything on him."

"Neither do we," Lynch said.

"As for the commission's chances, I'd say they were quite good, because they know what your father is trying to do, but your father doesn't know that his mission has been compromised," Galan said. "We thought about sending you and Jacqueline to Moscow to help out. It's possible that your father might find out and back off."

"You bastard," Jacqueline said.

Galan spread his hands. "It was just a thought. But it's up to you. I won't order you to do it. If McGarvey is going to kill Tarankov it'll happen by the June elections. Gives us nine weeks and a few days."

"At least we have a timetable," Elizabeth said. "Is there anything else we have to know this morning?"

"You don't have to do this," Lynch said, but Elizabeth cut him off with a look.

"Don't be a fool."

The Polish Border

By the time Galan and Lynch had left the apartment, McGarvey was already northeast of Berlin, the heaviest traffic behind him. The Mercedes's tank was filled with gasoline, as were the spare gas cans in the back, and the morning was bright, making driving conditions on the new autobahn from Berlin to Szczecin very good. Once the Wall had come down the first order of business for the German government was reconstructing the entire infra-structure of the old GDR. New roads, factories and apartment buildings were coming into existence at breakneck speed. McGarvey took advantage of the excellent road, pushing the Mercedes to one hundred miles per hour, the big engine barely straining.

It was less than seventy miles to the Polish border at Kolbaskowo, and although he was slowed by heavier traffic, mostly trucks, funneling into the checkpoint, he made it before 11:00 A.M.

He had to stop briefly on the German side of the border so that his export papers could be checked and stamped. Before he took such a car out of Germany the authorities had to make certain that the proper taxes had been paid. Beyond that they didn't care who he was or what else he was bringing across. Reconstructing an entire country was an expensive business.

On the Polish side, his passport and the in-transit papers for the car were briefly examined, and within a few minutes he was on his way, again pushing the car to nearly one hundred miles per hour. Although the highways in Poland were not nearly so good as those in Germany, the traffic was much lighter, so that as the afternoon wore on he made better time than he thought he would.

From Szczecin it was nearly five hundred miles along the Baltic coast to the border with a seventy-five-mile-wide strip of territory that still belonged to Russia. Sandwiched between Poland and Lithuania, the region's only ma-jor city was Kaliningrad. The Russians had held onto it because it was a major seaport.

The Intercontinental in Leipzig had made him an excellent picnic lunch of bread, sausages, cheese, potato salad, bread and several bottles of beer, plus a couple of bottles of mineral water, so he did not have to stop to eat. But he pulled into an Esso station on the outskirts of Gdansk where he filled the gas tank around five in the evening, and took a break in the wayside to relieve his cramped muscles.

It was a mistake, because by the time he got on the road again he was caught in the middle of rush-hour traffic as factory and shipyard workers clogged the highways on their way home.

He'd hoped to have reached the border with Russia at Braniewo around seven in the evening, and when traffic might still be reasonably heavy, and the customs officers too busy to check him thoroughly. Instead he arrived at the frontier a few minutes before 10:00 P.M., his the only car within sight in either direction.

On the Polish side the customs officials stamped his in-transit papers, and waved him through. On the Russian side, however, the armed FSK security officer motioned him to a parking area a few yards from the roadway. A customs officer in the dark blue uniform of a Militia cop, came out of the customs shed, and took his papers.

"Good evening," the official said indifferently, as he studied McGarvey's passport.

"Good evening," McGarvey replied in fractured Russian.

"Did you drive this automobile all the way from Brussels?"

"I bought it in Leipzig."

A second FSK security officer came out of the customs shed, a Kalashnikov slung over his shoulder. He walked over to the car, touched the hood, examined the knobby tires, and ran his fingers along the passenger side door. He stopped in back.

McGarvey glanced in the rearview mirror as the soldier studied the spare tire on the rack, and then shined a flashlight inside at the second spare tire and the gas cans.

"Why are you coming to Russia?" the customs official asked.

"I'm in transit to Riga."

"Will you be staying in Kaliningrad tonight?"

"No. I'd like to reach Latvia by morning if the roads are okay and the weather continues to cooperate."

"There is nothing wrong with Russian roads," the official said sharply. He examined the car's papers, lingering over the German export and Latvian import licenses. "Do you have a buyer for this pussy wagon in Riga?"

"I hope so."

The official laughed. "No one up there has any money these days, except for a certain class of . . . businessmen."

McGarvey shrugged but said nothing.

The customs officer gave him a hard, bleak stare, then handed back his passport. He wrote something on the Russian transit permit. "There is an additional transit fee of five hundred deutchmarks. Do you have this money with you? It says here you didn't pay it in Leipzig."

It was a bribe, of course.

"It was an oversight," McGarvey said. He counted out the money and handed it over without protest. He was being perceived as one of "those businessmen," which meant Latvian Mafia, which was giving the Russians still living in the country a horrible time. It was exactly the image he wanted to portray.

"Don't stay long in Russia," the official ordered. He stepped back, and waved the FSK security guard to raise the barricade.

An hour and a half later McGarvey was crossing the much friendlier border into Lithuania where the customs officials joked and smiled, and waved at him as he left.

Moscow

"He's disappeared and nobody can find him," Chernov told General Yuryn at breakfast in the Dzerzhinsky Square headquarters of the FSK shortly after eight in the morning. "We'll have to wait until he contacts Yemlin, or makes a mistake."

"Maybe he's given up."

"That's not likely."

"President Kabatov has to be told something."

Chernov looked at him coldly. He despised weakness of any kind, and he took Yuryn's obesity to be a sign of a lack of self control. But Tarankov needed the general, at least until after the elections. Then many things would change in Moscow.

"Sorry, General, but we've been working around the clock, and I'm getting tired."

Yuryn laughed because the remark was so obviously disingenuous. "I'll pass your complaint along to him."

"Tell him that we're working on it. McGarvey will not succeed. I guarantee it."

Paris

Elizabeth had slept poorly, and as a result she had a difficult time getting started. She didn't leave the apartment until nearly 7:00 A.M., and her heart wasn't in her jogging. She'd come to enjoy the mornings, as she was sure her father had, in part because by doing the same things he did she felt closer to him. But not this morning because she was frightened and confused. For the first time she was beginning to doubt that even a man such as her father could succeed with the deck so stacked against him.

A half-dozen blocks from the apartment, she stopped at a telephone kiosk, and using her credit card called a number in Alexandria, across the river from Washington. It was one in the morning over there, but she didn't care. She'd wake up the dead if she thought that it would help.

Her old boss Bratislav Toivich answered his home phone on the first ring as if he'd been expecting the call. "Hullo."

"Mr. B, it's Liz. I'm in Paris."

"You're up early."

"I'm jogging the same route my father takes. But we haven't found a thing. And I don't know what to do next."

"I haven't heard much here either, little *devochka*. Maybe it's time for you to come home."

"They want to send me and Jacqueline to Moscow to act as bait. But I'm afraid of what my father might do if he finds out."

"That bastard," Toivich said with much feeling. "Don't you do it, Elizabeth. Don't you let them bully you into going over there. You know the situation in Moscow. Anything can happen. You and Ms. Belleau could be swallowed up and no one would ever hear from you again."

"The Russians know what my father is planning to do, and they're waiting for him. He doesn't have a chance, Mr. B. He's walking into a trap, unless we can warn him first. But I don't know what to do anymore. We've tried just about everything."

"Have you tried reaching him through his friend, Otto Rencke?"

"He's disappeared too."

"He's a computer genius. The machines are his entire life."

"We've tried the computer schools here in Paris but no one has heard from him."

"You're young, Elizabeth. You were raised in the computer age, so think like a computer genius."

"I don't understand."

"Rencke is probably helping your father. But that wouldn't take him twenty-four hours a day. He has to amuse himself somehow in the off hours. So what would a man like that do with himself?"

THIRTY

Riga

McGarvey crossed the Daugava River that ran through the heart of the Latvian capital around eight o'clock in the morning, his eyes gritty and his stomach rumbling. The traffic-clogged streets were in terrible repair, the drivers even more reckless than in France, so he had to watch his own driving.

Using the Latvian guide book and maps he'd picked up at a truck stop this morning, he found his way to the main Telephone and Telegraph office on Brīvības Boulevard. The Mercedes attracted some attention, but nobody bothered him.

Inside, he gave one of the clerks at the counter a Paris number and she directed him to one of the booths. By the time he closed the door the number was ringing.

"Hiya," Rencke answered.

"Have you heard from my daughter?" McGarvey asked.

"She called and everything is fine," Rencke replied breathlessly. "Oh boy, Mac, it's a good thing you called because the heat's been turned up a notch. I can't get a trace on you because of my backscatter encryption program. So where are you calling from?"

"I'm in Riga. What's happening?"

"You're not calling from a hotel phone are you? Because if you are you'd better get out of there. My stuff can't protect past a hotel switchboard, and there might be bugs."

"I'm at the main telephone office. What's going on, Otto?"

"Ryan is being cagey as hell, but I picked up a reference to a special commission in Moscow that the Russians have put together to find you. It's in the SVR's system now, so there's no doubt that they know who you are and why you're coming. Ever hear the name Yuri Bykov? Ex-KGB?"

McGarvey searched his memory. "No. What'd you find out about him?"

"Not much more than Chernov. He's supposed to be one of the best cops in Russia though. But they know you're coming, Mac, so you're going to have to call it off."

"What else do they know?"

"Didn't you hear me? They know your name, and they know that you've been hired to kill Tarankov. They're waiting for you. The second they spot you, they'll kill you. But that's not all, Mac. The Russians asked for help from us and the French, and we've agreed. That stupid bastard Ryan agreed. He's sent someone here to Paris to work with the French to find you. They're going to share information with Bykov."

McGarvey weighed what he was being told. "Who'd Ryan send?"

"I don't know. But didn't you hear me? By now every cop in Europe is looking for you. Which means that if you get busted for so much as spitting on a sidewalk they'll nail your ass to the cross."

"Did they get my name from Yemlin?"

"If they did, Ryan hasn't put it on the wire. He probably sent whatever he had by courier to Tom Lynch. Which means they might suspect you've got some help."

"Maybe it's time for you to get out."

"You magnificently stupid bastard, I'm not going anywhere until you do," Rencke said, his voice pitched even higher than normal. "Do you think you can still pull it off?"

"I'm going to try."

"I'll be here."

"Watch yourself, Otto."

"You too, Mac."

McGarvey paid for the phone charge, then drove over to the Radisson International that had opened less than a year ago overlooking the river near the Vanšu bridge. He surrendered the car to an admiring valet, and checked in, booking a room for a week. Latvia was beginning to have a tourist season, but it didn't start until June, so the hotel was half-empty, and the staff was appreciative and attentive.

Upstairs, he ordered a pot of black coffee, an omelet and toast from room service. While he waited for it to come, he unpacked his bags, and took a quick shower. Afterward he sat by the window overlooking the city, and smoked.

Almost everyone he'd known from the old days at the CIA was gone. It was a safe bet that Ryan would not have come over to Paris himself, nor would the Assistant DCI, Larry Danielle. Which left no one of any importance, or at least no trained field officer. Ryan had probably sent one of his section heads with a stack of files and orders to find McGarvey or else.

McGarvey reasoned it out. The Russians knew his name, and knew that he was coming. But it was a big country, and they could not know his timetable. Nor could they know where he was planning to kill Tarankov. Since the government wanted Tarankov arrested and tried for treason and murder, it was a safe bet that no one in the Kremlin or on the special commission would send a warning to Tarankov. Although on reflection he decided that he could not be certain of that. It just seemed to make sense that there wouldn't be any lines of communications between the opposing forces.

It was possible that Ryan had sent the Russian commission the CIA's files on McGarvey. Combined with the files of the SVR, it would make a formidable record of not only his accomplishments, but of his methods of operation, his tradecraft. In the right hands that would give them a decided advantage. But Bykov was just an unknown investigator. Probably very good, but just an investigator for all that.

The only man in Russia who he had any cause to be concerned about, McGarvey decided, was Leonid Chernov. If somehow he became involved the danger would be a quantum leap greater.

On balance, then, he decided, he would go ahead with his plans made more difficult because they knew his name and face, but still not impossible.

His breakfast came, he signed for it, and the waiter left. He ate the food, drank one cup of coffee, and then went to bed for a few hours sleep. There was much to be done in the coming days, and he wanted to make a good start as soon as possible.

Paris

Elizabeth McGarvey sat on a bench in the Tuileries Gardens in sight of the obelisk in the Place de la Concorde studying the display on her laptop computer. She'd become tired of being cooped up at the apartment, so she had come down here to continue working because the day was beautiful. Jacqueline was in a cramped office at the main telephone exchange a few blocks away, sitting in front of a much larger computer that could instantly trace virtually any telephone number in Paris and its environs. She and Elizabeth were in contact via one of the two cellular telephones Elizabeth carried. The second cell phone connected her laptop to the Internet.

At the moment she was logged in under the Globalnet name of LIZMAC in a Usenet newsgroup called talk.politics.misc, in which participants posted messages in a sort of dialogue on what was wrong with politics these days.

At the top of each message was the name of the writer, the subject, the date and time the message was posted, and the location of the originating computer system. Following each message was a signature, which as often as not was the participant's nickname. And the nicknames were just as colorful as the messages.

If Otto Rencke had too much time on his hands he would almost certainly be taking part in a number of these newsgroups. His ego would make it impossible for him not to make comments, and Elizabeth hoped to be able to spot him by what he was saying, and by his nickname. It was a sure bet that he would not use his real name, nor would he use his real telephone number.

Elizabeth also hoped that if she did stumble upon a newsgroup which he posted he might recognize her own signature, and out of curiosity, if nothing else, he would have to open a dialogue with her.

His CIA file had been sent over, and combined with what she remembered her father saying about him, she thought she had a good idea what kinds of newsgroups he'd be browsing, and what kinds of messages he would be posting.

Each time she came up with a likely candidate, she passed the computer location telephone number to Jacqueline to check out. So far every possibility had turned out to be legitimate. But worldwide there were more than 60,000 Usenet newsgroups, nearly 95 million computer sites, and hundreds of anonymous remailer sites, through which messages could be retransmitted without out valid IDs.

From: Thomas LeBrun 33.1.42-74-21-31
Subject: Lindsay/Chirac trade debate
8/4/99 11.25

Who does the Monk think he's kidding? NAFTA and GATT had exactly the opposite effect he claims. Reducing trade barriers simply means a redistribution of jobs and capital. But it's never a one-way street as he suggests. Foie Gras in France, Toyotas in Japan and commercial airlines in the U.S. (bigdaddyitem7)

Elizabeth speed-dialed the telephone exchange.

"Paris exchange. Four-two, seven-four, two-one, three-one," she told Jacqueline. "He calls himself 'big daddy.' "

"Une moment," Jacqueline said.

Elizabeth continued to watch the messages continually scrolling up the screen. This went on twenty-four hours per day, seven days per week across the world. Finding Rencke would be next to impossible, but they had nothing else to go on for the moment.

"Thomas LeBrun. A street number in the twentieth arrondissement," Jacqueline said. "He's legitimate."

Elizabeth ran a hand tiredly across her eyes. "Okay, Jacqueline, I'm going to a different newsgroup. I'll try talk.politics.theory, maybe we'll have better luck."

"How about some lunch, *cherie?*"

"Let's work till noon. That gives us another half hour. I just can't stop."

"I know," Jacqueline said soothingly. "We'll find him."

"We have to."

Riga

McGarvey got up around two in the afternoon after only a few hours of sleep. He showered, shaved, and got dressed then went downstairs and had a late lunch at the hotel's coffee shop. He was still logy from lack of sleep, but by the time he'd walked two blocks from the hotel he was beginning to feel better. He caught a taxi at Krastmala Boulevard, and ordered the driver to take him out to the airport where he rented a Volkswagen Jetta for one month from Hertz. He explained that he wanted to explore the entire Baltic region, something he'd wanted to do for years. Now that they were independent from the Russians he was finally able to get his wish.

Even though only a small percentage of the population spoke Latvian, all the street signs were in that language, which sometimes caused confusion. In actuality the lingua franca was Russian, a fact that everyone despised, but that everyone lived with.

While at the airport he changed the remainder of his deutchmarks to Latvian latis, then headed back into the city. The weather continued to hold, but if anything traffic was worse than it had been this morning. Riga and its companion city Jūrmala, where the international ferries docked, were major Baltic seaports. It was one of the reasons the Soviet Union had fought so hard to keep Latvia. But the nation continued to struggle with its independence from communist rule. Still, nearly half the population was Russian, which created strong ethnic tensions. The new businessmen millionaires were Latvian Mafia, while the Russians, who were constantly being discriminated against, ran their own rackets. Just about anything went here, which was one of the reasons McGarvey had picked this place.

By four o'clock he was in the waterfront district of warehouses and dreary offices above chandeliers and other dingy shops. He found what he was looking for almost immediately, an import/export company under the obviously Latvian name of Kārlis Zālite, situated above a small machine parts warehouse. Pallets marked in English, MADE IN GERMANY, were being unloaded from a big truck.

McGarvey parked across the street, and went upstairs to a cramped, grimy office in which stacks of files and paperwork were piled on the floor, on chairs, on two small tables, and atop several large filing cabinets. A young pimply-faced man with thick, greasy hair worked at a tiny desk next to the one window, while the proprietor worked in the back from a much larger, cluttered desk. The place smelled like a combination of stale sweat, cigarette smoke and grease from the warehouse below.

"I wish to hire your firm to import Mercedes automobiles from Leipzig. Can you handle this for me?" McGarvey asked.

"*Da*, of course," Zālite, a skinny ferret-faced little man said, rising from his chair. He stuck out his dirty hand. "Mr . . . ?"

"Pierre Allain. I am Belgian," McGarvey said, shaking hands.

"Your Russian is very good."

"My father worked in Moscow and was conscripted into the army when I was a little boy. It wasn't until I was ten before my mother and I could escape."

"What of your father?"

"He was sent to Siberia to count the birches, and never came back." McGarvey lowered his eyes for a moment, his jaw tightening. "But that was many years ago. Now I wish to do some business with you."

"Do you have buyers here in Riga for your cars? Because if we can come to reasonable terms, I would certainly take one of them off your hands."

"These will be for sale in Moscow. Very cheap."

"I see," Zālite said, sitting back, and eyeing McGarvey with a sudden wariness. "Perhaps you have come to the wrong man."

"I wouldn't sell one of my cars to you, at any price," McGarvey continued. "Nor would I sell them to anyone in Latvia, or anywhere else other than Moscow. People could . . . get hurt in my cars. They will get hurt."

Zālite's eyes narrowed. "It's a dangerous game you are playing, Mr. Allain."

McGarvey sat forward so suddenly that Zālite reared back. He slammed his fist on the desk. "I'm going to stick it to the bastards for what they did to me, with or without your help!" McGarvey shook with rage. "Goddamn stinking sons of bitches!" He glanced at the young man, who watched with round eyes. "My father went there to help, and they killed him. They killed my mother too. I'm all that's left."

"How many units are coming?" Zālite asked respectfully.

"One to begin with, by truck. But there'll be many more later."

"Do you have buyers for them in Moscow?"

"Mafia," McGarvey said through clenched teeth.

"And how will you get these cars there?"

"I'll drive them, one at a time. I want to see the looks on their faces."

Zālite hesitated.

"I'll pay you one thousand deutchmarks above your usual fees," McGarvey said. "Your name will never be mentioned by me to the Russians.

I'll instruct the car dealer in Leipzig where he may ship the cars, which you'll store in a secure place until I call for them one at a time." McGarvey took a Creditbank draft in the amount of DM 1.000 out of his attache case and laid it on the man's desk. "This is for the first car, I'll have another bank draft ready for your fees."

Zālite eyed the bank draft. "You'll get yourself killed."

"That's my problem. In the meantime you'll make a profit. Do we have a deal?"

"Where can I reach you if there's a problem?"

"If there's a problem, you handle it. The first car will be here in less than ten days. Will you do it?"

Zālite looked at the bank draft again, then picked it up and put it in his desk drawer. He stood up and extended his hand. "We have a deal, Mr. Allain, if for no other reason than I too would very much like to stick it to the bastards, as you say."

McGarvey shook his hand. "I'll call when I'm ready for the first car. In the meantime I'll count on your discretion."

"Oh, you have my word on that," Zālite said earnestly.

From there McGarvey drove back to the Telephone and Telegraph office where he placed a call to Bernard Legler at Mercedes Rossplatz in Leipzig. He gave the German Zālite's address, and then rang off before Legler could ask any questions.

It was late afternoon by the time he found a parking garage a few blocks from the hotel where he dropped off the Volkswagen and went the rest of the way on foot. He stopped at the bar for a martini, then went back up to his room where he intended changing clothes and coming back down for dinner around eight. He turned on the television to CNN, lay down on the bed and fell asleep in his clothes.

THIRTY-ONE

Lefortovo

Chernov sat at his desk staring at the detailed maps of Moscow, feeling that he was missing something that was vitally important. Paporov was talking on the telephone to Captain Petrovsky at the Militia, and from the tone of his voice Chernov got the impression that there was no news. The FSK was coming up empty-handed as well. As Chernov suspected, the service did not have enough manpower to do its normal work, let alone mount a nationwide search for McGarvey. For instance McGarvey's photograph hadn't been distributed to all the border crossings yet, though Gresko promised the job would be completed within the next three or four days.

Moscow was a city of nine million people spread over nearly six hundred square kilometers, the Moscow River meandering sometimes north and south, at other times east and west through it. Defined by four ring roads, the outermost of which was fifteen kilometers from the Kremlin, the city was a maze of broad boulevards, twisting side streets and narrow, dirty back alleys down which many Muscovites feared to travel. Underground, nine separate metro lines crisscrossed the city through more than two hundred kilometers of tunnels. In addition to an extensive storm sewer system, a half-dozen underground rivers all flowed eventually into the Moscow River. In winter, subterranean Moscow was a busy place, populated by a large percentage of the city's poor and homeless.

Instinctively Chernov felt that McGarvey was no longer in the city. He had come to Moscow and to Nizhny Novgorod to stalk his prey, and to work out his plan for the kill. The fact that he'd been spotted in Red Square led Chernov to the conclusion that McGarvey had chosen the city for the assassination attempt. Putting himself in the American's shoes, Chernov decided that he would do the same thing. Because once the kill was made there was an unlimited number of places where a man could hide until the dust settled.

Paporov put down the telephone. "The Militia is getting nowhere with the Mafia. They're shitting in their pants out there on the streets."

"Did you tell them to keep trying?"

"*Da*, for what it's worth," Paporov said.

"What about Viktor Yemlin, has he made any telephone calls?"

"None of any significance from his apartment," Paporov said. "But you were right about one thing. Apparently he has some sort of an electronic device that masks video and audio surveillance equipment, because they got nothing from the Magesterium, and nothing from his dinner with Sukhoruchkin."

"He's gotten it from his own technical service, which means he knows that we're on to him," Chernov said.

"You don't think he's dragged the SVR into it, do you?"

"No," Chernov said. He figured they would have heard something if that were the case.

"Well, if he's making any important calls, they must be from public phones. I can arrange to tap every pay phone within a four block radius of his apartment."

"Do it," Chernov said.

"Still leaves us with the rest of it. I think Valeri Doyla is our best bet, but the stupid bastard gets himself cornered every time."

"Put someone in the next room. Yemlin's little electronic toy can't blind a man, or stop his ears from working."

"I'll get on it right away," Paporov said. He lit a cigarette and came over to Chernov's desk. "You think it's going to happen here, and not out in the countryside somewhere?"

"If I wanted to kill Tarankov I'd wait until he came to Moscow," Chernov said. "There'd be a better chance of escape."

"It's a safe bet that the Tarantula will be here on election day. Probably at the reviewing stand in Red Square."

Chernov looked up suddenly.

"Gives us nine weeks to catch him," Paporov said. "Because if he makes it this far, and gets mixed up in the crowds, he'll be impossible to spot. There's going to be a lot of confusion that day. Some violence too. Maybe some shooting."

"We don't have nine weeks," Chernov said, his eyes going back to the maps, specifically to Red Square.

"Not if we want to catch him before election day."

"Not election day," Chernov said. He was amazed by the simplicity of McGarvey's plan. The brilliance of the man. His audacity.

"What do you mean?" Paporov asked.

"Tarankov is going to come to Moscow on election day. Everybody knows that. Everybody is counting on it. It's the one day he could come to Moscow and be safe, because nobody would order his arrest. The people would rise up, claiming the election had been fixed."

"That's right," Paporov said. "In the confusion McGarvey could take his shot, and get away with it."

"All our efforts are being directed to that one day, that one place—Red Square. We have nine weeks, so time is still on our side."

Paporov nodded uneasily, not yet quite sure where Chernov was taking this.

"But McGarvey has another plan, because he figured out something that the rest of us have overlooked."

Sudden understanding dawned on Paporov's face. "*Yeb vas.* May Day."

"Very good, Aleksi."

"Surely Tarankov won't risk coming in to Moscow so soon."

Chernov smiled distantly. "You can count on it," he said. "And that's the day on which Mr. McGarvey will try to kill him. The day that he himself will die."

Moscow

"I think I've made a terrible mistake," Yemlin told Valeri Doyla at the Magesterium. "But I have the resources to rectify my error before it goes too far."

He and Doyla lay naked next to each other in the wide bed, soft music playing from the hidden speakers. This time he'd refused vodka and the cocaine, because, as he explained, he wanted to enjoy himself. He wanted his head to be clear. And he was not using the anti-surveillance device, because he wanted to be overheard.

"What are you talking about, Viktor? Being here like this?" Doyla asked cautiously.

Yemlin chuckled, and caressed the young man's flanks. "Heavens no. You're an old man's comfort."

"You're not so old."

"What would you say if I told you that I hired someone to kill the Tarantula? What would you think about that?"

"I don't get involved in politics," Doyla said. He giggled. "It makes my head hurt thinking about it."

"Mine too," Yemlin said. "But the bastard has to be arrested, not gunned down by some hired gun who doesn't care about the *Rodina*. I'm going to call him off. He can keep the money—it wasn't mine in the first place—and he can get out of Moscow, or wherever he is."

"Can you do this?"

"I'll figure a way," Yemlin said. He slapped Doyla's rump hard enough to leave a red mark, bile once again rising sharply in his throat. "In the meantime let's talk about something much more pleasurable, shall we?"

Riga

McGarvey rose at 8:00 A.M., after a solid twelve hours of sleep, and after he showered and shaved he got a copy of the *International Herald-Tribune* from the newsstand in the lobby, and had breakfast on the terrace overlooking the river and the old city.

In an article on the op-ed page, the writer gave a reasonably accurate, if superficial, summary of the political upheaval going on in Russia as the country headed toward the general elections. Kabatov was the front runner in every poll in which Yevgenni Tarankov's name was omitted. The general opinion across the country, however, was that although the Tarantula could easily win in any election, why bother? Any time he wanted the country it was his for the taking. The military was corrupt and would not stop him, nor would either division of the old KGB which was itself in a fierce internecine battle. The nation was in disarray, and like it or not, Tarankov was likely the one man to bring it together.

An hour later he walked down to the car park, where he retrieved the Jetta, and headed to the train station where he cruised the neighborhoods for a few blocks in a rough triangle bounded by it, the post office and telephone exchange, and the central market. After stopping to ask at several cafes and markets he finally found a black market apartment for rent not registered with the Federal Rent Control Association.

Decent housing, especially in Riga, was scarce, and between discrimination against Russians, and price-gouging which had created a lot of tensions, the government had stepped in. First choice went to registered Latvian voters, which made up only thirty percent of the population. Second choice went to well-heeled western businessmen, and the dregs went to Russians. The problem was, that the federal government levied a heavy tax on all registered apartments, so the black market thrived.

The old woman who rented McGarvey the efficiency apartment three blocks from the train station didn't even ask to see his passport once she was satisfied that he wasn't a Russian. The rent was 125 latis, or $250, a week. He paid for a month in cash, which included an old plastic radio, a small black and white television, and postage-stamp-sized private bathroom. A pay phone was located in the downstairs hall. The apartment was surprisingly clean, and looked down on Gogala Street, busy with truck traffic.

By the same process, but asking at a different set of cafes and markets, McGarvey found a secured parking stall in what once had been a warehouse near the train station, and only three blocks from the apartment, paying the rental fee of fifty latis per week a month in advance.

On the way back to the hotel he bought a heavy duty combination lock from a variety store, then parked the Jetta in the lot near the hotel, and was back for a late lunch a little before two o'clock.

He spent the remainder of the afternoon touring the old city on foot, partially to kill some time, but mostly because he'd been cooped up for so long that he needed fresh air and exercise.

There was a subtle air of sullenness among the Latvians he saw. Although the cafes and shops were filled, the streets were busy with traffic, the beer gardens humming, and every third person seemed to be speaking on a cellular phone, a sharpness of attitude was prevalent. All of Riga seemed to be pissed off. In part, McGarvey supposed, because they were finding that independence and freedom were not easy. Latvia and the other Baltic republics were still dependent on Russia for their day-to-day financial stability. The Russian economy was coming apart at the seams, yet Latvia's future remained wedded to Russia's, and nobody liked it.

Back at the hotel by six, he stopped at the front desk and told them that he would be checking out in the morning after breakfast, and would need his car out front by 8:00 A.M.

He had room service send dinner up to his room, and watched CNN with a detached interest. The real world didn't seem to exist other than as a fantasy on television. It was a strange feeling, one that always came over him at this point in a mission. It was as if he had removed himself from the human race for the duration.

In the morning he would park the Mercedes in the garage he'd rented, come back for the Volkswagen, pick up a few groceries at the market, and settle in the apartment to wait for the other Mercedes to arrive from Leipzig. He was being hunted for. It was time to lay low to see if anyone was coming after him before he made the next move.

Tarankov's Train

By 10:00 P.M., Chernov was on the M1 motorway out of Moscow heading toward Smolensk a little more than three hundred kilometers to the southwest. The BMW seven hundred series was in excellent condition, and the evening sky, though moonless, was clear and star-studded. The highway which ran nearly straight through the lake country was all but deserted, and he was able to push the car well over 130 kilometers per hour. The windows were up, and the tape deck played Mozart, so that he felt very little sensation of hurtling through the night.

He'd called a blind number in Moscow, identified himself by the code name *Standard Bearer*, and received the cryptic message Alpha-one-three-one-stop. It was a grid reference for Tarankov's train stopped on a siding fifty kilometers east of Smolensk.

"I'll arrive before midnight," Chernov said.

There'd been no answer, nor had he expected any. But his message would have gotten through to Tarankov that his chief of staff was on the way.

Since Chernov had been dispatched to Moscow, Tarankov had conducted no further raids. The first was scheduled for the day after tomorrow on the former Lithuanian trade capital on the Dnieper River, which was why the train had been moved to within fifty kilometers of the city.

The highway was totally deserted when he stopped a few kilometers west of the small city of Safonovo around 11:45 P.M. He entered Tarankov's coordinates into a handheld GPS satellite navigator, which showed that the train was another five kilometers due west.

A couple of kilometers farther, a narrow dirt road led west away from the M1, and Chernov followed it, turning off his headlights as he came over the crest of a hill. Below, nearly invisible in the dark night, the train was parked on a siding, camouflage netting completely covering it from satellite or air reconnaissance.

Chernov waited patiently for a full five minutes until he was certain that he'd spotted the six commandoes who'd established a perimeter a hundred meters out.

They would know that he was up here because he'd made no effort to mask his approach. Standard operating procedure was for him to remain here until Tarankov was informed, and someone was sent up to escort him down. The delay was only slightly irritating, but Chernov approved of the routine.

He got out of the car, and leaned against the fender when headlights flashed in the trees from the direction he'd come. He pulled out the bulky Glock-17 automatic from his shoulder holster, glanced down toward the train to make sure no one was coming up toward him, then got off the road and sprinted through the trees to the crest of the hill, keeping low so that he was not silhouetted against the starry sky.

A car, its headlights off now, bumped slowly along the dirt track. When it topped the crest, it suddenly stopped and backed down. Chernov could see that it was a dark blue Mercedes. Paporov's car from Lefortovo. The bastard had followed him.

Paporov turned the car around, then, leaving the engine running, got out, entered the woods and noiselessly hurried back to the top of the rise, passing within a few meters of where Chernov stood behind the bole of a tree.

At the top he dropped to one knee and studied the train through a pair of binoculars. Chernov, careful to make no noise himself, came up behind him.

"What are you doing here, Aleksi?"

Paporov, startled, looked up over his shoulder, his eyes wide, his face white in the starlight. "That's Tarankov's train."

"Yes it is, but what are you doing here?"

Paporov's eyes went to the gun in Chernov's hand. "You're working for him, aren't you?"

A pair of Tarankov's commandoes wearing night vision goggles appeared out of the darkness to the left.

"Who is this, Colonel Chernov?" one of them asked.

"An unfortunate mistake on my part," Chernov said, not taking his eyes off Paporov, who'd lowered his binoculars and let them hang by their strap from his neck. "I didn't see anyone on the highway. How'd you follow me?"

Paporov glanced at the commandoes. "So it's Chernov, not Bykov. Is General Yuryn in on this operation?"

"How did you follow me?"

Paporov shrugged. "I wondered about you from the start. You know too much for an ex-KGB officer living in Siberia. There's a beacon transmitter in the trunk of your car."

"We picked up the signal while you were a couple of kilometers out," one of the commandoes said.

"So now what?" Paporov asked. He was resigned. "I don't suppose it would help if I said I'd be willing to keep my mouth shut and continue helping you find McGarvey?"

"No," Chernov said. "The pity of it is that I was beginning to like you."

"What can I say to make a difference?"

"Nothing," Chernov said. He raised the pistol and shot Paporov in the head.

The captain's body flopped on its side.

"Take the car and the body back to Moscow tonight, and leave it a few blocks from Lefortovo. Take his watch, academy ring, wallet, money and anything else of value."

"Yes, sir," one of the commandoes said.

Chernov holstered his gun, and drove his car down to the train. Tarankov and Liesel were drinking champagne and watching CNN in their private car.

"We heard a shot," Tarankov said.

"It was Captain Paporov," Chernov said, helping himself to a glass of champagne. "His body will be returned to Moscow tonight, and made to look like a robbery."

"Will this cause you any trouble?" Liesel asked.

"No," Chernov replied indifferently. "You don't mean to wait until the elections, do you," he told Tarankov.

"What makes you think that?"

"Because you won't pass up the opportunity of the May Day celebration in Red Square. If you get that far, the people will be behind you and there'll be no need for the election. But McGarvey will be there as well."

"What do you suggest, Colonel?" Liesel demanded. "That we hide like rabbits because of some foreigner that you're unable to catch?"

"Send a double. The effect will be the same. And if McGarvey should succeed, it won't matter, because he won't escape, and afterward you'll miraculously rise from death like a new messiah."

Liesel was livid, but a smile spread across Tarankov's face. "That's quite good, Leonid. But are you telling me that you cannot guarantee my safety from McGarvey?"

"He was the one who killed General Baranov, and Arkady."

"Your half-brother. Yes, I know this," Tarankov said, his gaze not wavering. "It's why you were selected to stop him. It was thought that you would have the proper motivation. Instead, you seem to be admitting that he's better than you. Your thinking has been colored by . . . what, Leonid? Fear? Has your judgment slipped so badly that you allowed a FSK captain to follow you?"

"I didn't come here to play semantic games with you, Comrade," Chernov answered coldly. "I am respectful of Mr. McGarvey. In fact I am very respectful of his determination and abilities, as you should be. I came here to confirm that you plan on being in Red Square on May Day, and to warn you that if McGarvey somehow manages to slip past me, you should send a double to make your speech. You have nothing to lose and everything to gain."

Liesel's face had turned red. She jumped up, snatched a pistol from the table beside her and pointed it at Chernov with shaking hands.

Chernov didn't bother looking at her. "With all due respect, Comrade Tarantula, keep your wife away from me, and out of sight until afterwards. Just now Russians have no love for foreigners. *Any* foreigners."

Tarankov nodded but said nothing.

Chernov turned, and left the train, Liesel's enraged screeching clearly audible all the way over to where he parked his car.

THIRTY-TWO

Moscow

For ten days Chernov went about his work alone at Lefortovo, briefing General Yuryn at irregular intervals. But he was operating under a handicap now. Everyone believed that if McGarvey struck here in Moscow, it would be on election day when Tarankov was expected to make his triumphal entry into the city. If the assassination attempt came sooner, it would take place outside of Moscow. In some other city.

Kabatov and the fools he surrounded himself with hadn't put it together yet, that Tarankov had no intention of waiting for the general elections. His was to be a socialist victory. And May First was the day for the international socialist movement.

But McGarvey had figured it out. Chernov didn't know how he knew this, but he was just as certain that McGarvey would be in Red Square on May Day, as he was that Tarankov would not send a double.

With little more than a week to go, Chernov was beginning to admit to himself that McGarvey wasn't going to make a mistake. On May First he was going to be within shooting range when Tarankov took to the reviewing platform atop Lenin's tomb to speak to his people.

Even after all this time Gresko conceded that McGarvey's photograph had been distributed to less than twenty percent of Russia's border crossings, and there was even some doubt how widely the information had been spread in Moscow. At this rate it would take several more weeks to get the job done. But the FSK task force did not seem to be overly concerned, because the general elections were still more than seven weeks away.

The CIA and SDECE seemed to be having the same sort of luck as well. They'd lost McGarvey's trail somewhere in Paris, which was actually a moot point, because in Chernov's estimation they'd never had his trail in the first place. No one knew if he was still in Paris, or even in France. No one knew how he'd gotten to Moscow, or how he'd gotten back out of Russia, if in fact he'd even been here. The whole story could have been Yemlin's invention to somehow misdirect their investigation.

Nor had stationing a man at the Magesterium to eavesdrop on Yemlin's homosexual love nest produced any results other than the story Yemlin was telling his queer that he was calling McGarvey off. That story for certain was a fiction, because Yemlin's every move was being watched, now even inside the SVR. He'd never contacted McGarvey or made any effort to do so.

Paporov's body had been found about the same time Chernov had reported him missing. The autopsy took five days after which the Militia came to the conclusion that he'd been shot to death during a robbery. They refused to speculate why the Mercedes the captain had been driving had not been stolen as well.

Chernov refused another assistant, though secretly he wished Paporov were still around. It had been a stupid mistake on his part allowing the captain to follow him to the train. He'd underestimated the man, something he would have to be careful not to do with McGarvey.

Tarankov's raid on Smolensk got very little official attention inside Russia, and only a brief mention in the western media. It seemed as if the entire world was holding its breath until the June elections.

As the clock in Chernov's office slipped past midnight, he flipped his desk calendar over to the 23rd of April, eight days until May First, then got his jacket and went out. He'd been thinking about his mistress Raya Dubanova all afternoon, and he decided to spend a few hours with her tonight, because his nerves were on edge. The grinding stupidity and inefficiency of the FSK and Militia threatened to drive him crazy.

Outside, he hesitated for a moment in the darkness. The prison compound was utterly still. If the assassin were anyone other than McGarvey, he would leave now, get out of Russia, perhaps to Switzerland. There was still plenty of work for men such as him. The problem was that he would not be able to ask the Militia for much help covering Red Square until the last minute. Otherwise Kabatov would order a trap to be laid not only for McGarvey but for Tarankov too.

But he was going to have to stay, to play this little drama out to its end. For revenge, if nothing else.

At the Russian Border

By ten o'clock McGarvey left Riga behind, the morning overcast and cool, eastbound traffic fairly light. The Mercedes was running well, but he kept his speed within the posted limit of ninety kilometers per hour, which was less than sixty miles per hour.

Their main highway that ran directly from Riga to Moscow followed the railroad. It was one hundred and fifty miles to the border at Zilupe, and another 395 miles to the Russian capital, most of the distance over indifferent roads. But traffic would be light most of the way.

The second Mercedes had arrived late yesterday afternoon, and it took Zālite the rest of the day and into the evening to prepare the Russian transit and import documents.

McGarvey had picked up the car before eight this morning, and handed the Latvian a bank draft for the remainder of the import taxes and handling fees.

The car had been washed, polished and gassed, the two spare gas cans filled, and sat in the middle of the warehouse floor surrounded by a half-dozen admiring men. Zālite was practically licking his chops.

He took McGarvey aside. "It's nine hundred kilometers to Moscow, so naturally I had my mechanic check your car for defects. I'll tell you something, that Mercedes is in perfect condition. Nothing wrong. Nothing!"

"Did your man take the engine apart?" McGarvey asked.

Zālite's eyes narrowed. "*Nyet.*"

"It's a good thing, because he would have gotten a very nasty surprise. He might not have lived through it."

Zālite glanced over at the car. "But you will drive it all that way without a problem?"

McGarvey nodded. "My little secret. And since there'll already be a thousand kilometers on the car before I turn it over, no one will be able to blame me when something goes wrong."

"It's a beautiful machine," Zālite said. "Such a shame."

"Maybe when this is all over, I'll get you a good one."

"Maybe I've changed my mind about Mercedes," Zālite said sadly. "When does the next one come?"

"Depends on how this trip goes. A couple weeks."

Twenty transport trucks, empty, were lined up on the Latvian side of the border waiting to have their papers checked. Only a few trucks, all of them heavily loaded, were waiting to get into Latvia with their Russian-made products. By evening the numbers would be reversed with more loaded trucks arriving and fewer empty trucks leaving.

McGarvey had to wait nearly forty-five minutes before it was his turn. The Latvian customs official glanced briefly at his papers, stamped the exit section of his passport and waved him through. On the Russian side of the border, however, the policeman motioned him over to the parking area in front of the customs shed, where a pair of officials waited.

McGarvey handed out his passport to one of the stern-faced officers, who studied the photograph carefully, comparing it to McGarvey's face.

"What is the purpose of your visit to Russia?" the official asked in Russian.

"Business," McGarvey replied. He handed over the papers for the car. "I'm importing this car for sale in Moscow. And if I get a good price, I'll be bringing in more of them."

One of the armed Militia officers drifted over, and looked longingly at the Mercedes. It was something that he could not afford to buy with a lifetime of earnings. A certain amount of resentment showed on his face because like the customs officials, he knew that the only people in Moscow who could afford it were either corrupt politicians, the new businessmen, or the Mafia.

The customs official opened the car door. "Release the hood, then step out of the car and open the rear compartment."

McGarvey did as he was told. A third customs official came out with a long-handled mirror, which he used to inspect the undercarriage of the Mercedes, while the other two officials searched every square inch of the car, as well as McGarvey's single overnight bag and laptop computer.

As they worked, McGarvey took a picnic basket from the passenger side, and sat on the open cargo lid. The officials kept eyeing him as he opened a bottle of good Polish vodka, took a deep drink, then started on the bread, cheese, sausage and pickles.

On the way out of Riga this morning, he'd stopped at the Radisson and had them make up the gourmet picnic lunch, which also included a good Iranian caviar and blinis, some imported foie gras, smoked oysters, Norwegian salmon, and Swedish pickled herring.

The customs officers opened the gas cans stored in the cargo area and shined a flashlight inside, then bounced the spare tire several times to learn if anything might be hidden inside. Working around McGarvey, they also removed the primary spare tire from its bracket on the cargo lid, and did the same thing with it.

McGarvey finished his lunch an hour later, about the same time the customs officials were done. The one with the paperwork stamped the documents and handed them back to McGarvey.

"Take care that you violate no Russian laws," he cautioned harshly.

McGarvey nodded. "I've eaten all that I want. May I leave the rest of this here, with you and your men?" He held out the picnic basket.

The customs official hesitated for only a moment, then took the basket. The others watched the exchange.

McGarvey glanced at the paperwork, then started to raise the cargo lid, when he turned back. "You've made a mistake," he said.

"What are you talking about?" the customs officer demanded sharply.

"The import duty is supposed to be five hundred marks more than what I paid in Riga," McGarvey shrugged. "I noticed the mistake after I'd left. I thought you people might catch it." McGarvey shrugged. "But if you say it's okay—"

The officer handed the picnic basket to one of his men, took the import duty form from McGarvey and studied the document for a few moments. When he looked up he was wary. "It looks as if you're correct."

"I thought so," McGarvey said. He pulled out five hundred marks, and handed it to the official. "As I said, if my business goes well in Moscow, I'll be bringing in more of these cars. Maybe as many as a dozen or more a month, so I want to make absolutely sure that everything is as it should be. Do you understand?"

"Yes, thank you," the officer said, hardly able to believe his luck. "I'll look for you next time."

"In a week or two," McGarvey said.

Paris

Elizabeth sat hugging her knees to her chest in the window seat of her father's apartment, staring dejectedly down at the street, all but deserted at this hour of the morning. Her father was gone. It was as if the earth had swallowed him whole. For all any of them knew he could be buried in some unmarked grave somewhere. Her mother said it had been his greatest fear.

"Here it is again," Jacqueline said from across the room where she sat in front of the laptop computer. "That makes three references tonight."

"What is it?" Elizabeth asked, looking up. She was dead tired, her back ached and her eyes burned from staring at computer screens for the past couple of weeks.

Jacqueline, an expression of barely controlled excitement on her face, brushed her hair back. "He's coming on the net now." She sounded breathless. "What was that special food you told me that Rencke was fond of?"

"Twinkies," Elizabeth said. She got up and padded over to Jacqueline. "Well, take a look at this, *ma cherie.*"

From: an162885@anon.samat.po
Subject: CIA CLANDESTINE SERVICES
4/24/99 02.17

You guys don't know what the hell you're talking about. Why don't you get real or something. If the company was so bad and had a police state stranglehold etc why the hell does every swinging dick asshole want to come to the states? How many of you little darlings are shitting in your pantaloons to immigrate to Iraq, or Haiti, or some other paradise? Get real!!!!!!!!!!!!!!
(twinkieitem4)

"That's him," Elizabeth cried excitedly. "My God, you've found him!"

"Not yet, but we've made a start," Jacqueline said. "The address is an anonymous remailer in Poland, I think. But I can check on it."

"It means he could be anywhere."

"That's right, Liz. Could even be in the apartment across the hall. But I have a friend who'll know about this remailer. If it's legitimate, we'll have a shot at finding out Twinkie's real location."

She reached for the telephone, but Elizabeth grabbed her arm.

"If this gets back to Lynch or Galan, they'll screw it up."

Jacqueline grinned. "Don't worry, this is our little secret for now."

Elizabeth's eyes strayed to the hole in the wall where they'd disabled the first of the bugs they'd found. For the moment, they were secure in this apartment. She was frightened. But she was no longer tired.

Moscow

McGarvey arrived back at the Metropol Hotel around noon. He gave the car keys along with a good tip to Artur the bellman, who promised that the Mercedes would be parked in a secured spot, absolutely safe from interference. After he checked in, he used a pay phone in the lobby to call Martex Taxi Company, and left a message for Arkady Astimovich to telephone him, giving the number of the pay phone.

He bought a copy of the Paris *International Herald-Tribune* from the gift shop, then sat drinking coffee and reading the newspaper a few feet away. Astimovich called twenty minutes later.

"You're back," the cabby said excitedly.

"That's right. What's your brother-in-law's name?"

"Yakov Ostrovsky."

"I want you to set up a meeting for eleven o'clock tonight at the club. Tell him I'm bringing a proposition that he won't be able to refuse. One that will make all of us some money. Then I want you to meet me in front of the Kazan Station with your cab twenty minutes early."

"What if there's a problem, can I call you again at this number?"

"No," McGarvey said. "If you're not there I'll take this deal to somebody else."

"I'll be there," Astimovich promised.

McGarvey had a surprisingly good corned beef on rye sandwich and an American Budweiser beer at the expensive lounge in the lobby. The service was excellent but if any of the hotel staff, other than Artur, remembered him from his previous visit, they gave no sign of it.

Afterward he went up to his room, took a shower and slept lightly until 7:30 P.M., when he awoke with a start. For a brief moment he was slightly disoriented, but the sensation passed immediately. He got up and went over to the window, which looked down on the Bolshoi Theater. People were crowding into the theater, as cabs drew up, dropped off their passengers and went away. The big banner on the facade said GISELLE, which was one of the more famous ballets performed by the company.

He stood smoking by the window, until the crowds thinned out around 8:00 P.M., when the performance was scheduled to begin, then took another long shower, shaved, and got dressed in dark slacks, a turtleneck, and black leather jacket.

He switched the television to CNN, turned the volume up, and removed his gun and a spare magazine of ammunition from his laptop computer. The pistol went into a speed draw holster at the small of his back. He pocketed the silencer, and magazine.

At half-past eight he presented himself at the hotel's main dining room where he had a light buffet supper, and a bottle of reasonably good white wine. He took his time over his coffee and brandy afterwards. The restaurant was barely a third full, but preparations were being made for the after theater crowd, when the dining room would fill up.

McGarvey paid his bill, then retrieved his car from one of the bellmen, who turned out to be Artur's cousin. He tipped the man well, and was heading through heavy traffic up to the Kazan Station by 10:15 P.M.

It took nearly a half hour to get across town, and Astimovich was leaning against his cab as he watched the people emerging from the railway station. McGarvey powered down the passenger side window and pulled up next to the cabby, who turned around in surprise, the expression on his face changing from mild irritation to incredulity.

"I'll follow you to the club," McGarvey shouted out of the window.

Astimovich looked the Mercedes over with round eyes, like a kid in the candy store. "Is this the deal?"

"Do you think he'll go for it?"

"Him and every other big deal hot shot in town. I hope you've got more of them."

"A lot more," McGarvey said.

Astimovich jumped in his cab, and took off, McGarvey right behind him.

The Grand Dinamo club occupied an out-of-the-way corner of the Dinamo Soccer stadium on the way to Frunze Central Airfield. McGarvey had picked up the Russian corporal's uniform at the flea market set up on the opposite side of the sprawling sports complex. But here the front entrance was brightly lit and security was very tight with armed guards and closed circuit television cameras.

Astimovich pulled his cab off to the side, but McGarvey parked the big Mercedes under the overhang at the main entrance.

One of the guards saluted, then opened the car door. "Good evening, sir. Are you a member?"

Astimovich ran over. "Not yet. But he's here to see Yakov. We have an appointment."

A ferret-faced man came out of the club with a clipboard, as McGarvey got out of the Mercedes. "Are you Pierre Allain?" he asked. He was wearing a tiny lapel mike and an earpiece.

"Da," McGarvey said.

"You're late. Mr. Ostrovsky is a busy man—"

"Fine, I'll take my deal elsewhere, you little prick," McGarvey said, and he started to get back in the car.

"Wait a minute," Astimovich cried.

McGarvey turned back.

"You'd better tell Yakov that we're here," Astimovich told the man with the clipboard. "We're importing cars. A lot of them."

The ferret glanced indifferently at the big Mercedes. "Moscow is full of car salesmen, who if they want to make a deal, show up on time."

"Fifty thousand deutchmarks," McGarvey said.

The ferret chucked. "You've come to the wrong place. No one here buys used cars."

"It was new when I picked it up in Leipzig last week. And I can bring a dozen a month."

A corpulent man with heavy jowls came out of the club. He wore a silk shirt open at the collar, several heavy gold chains around his thick neck, a gold Rolex on his wrist, and a huge diamond ring on the little finger of his right hand. He looked amused, as if someone had just told him an off-color joke. He sauntered over.

"Yakov," Astimovich said.

"Good evening, Arkasha," the heavyset man said. He turned his intelligent eyes to McGarvey. "I'm Yakov Ostrovsky. Did I hear the price correctly? Fifty thousand deutchmarks?"

"That's right," McGarvey said.

Ostrovsky glanced inside the car, then slowly walked around it. "What's the catch, Monsieur Allain? With import duties, even if you could get this machine at wholesale, you'd have to sell it to me for ninety, perhaps a hundred thousand marks."

"I don't buy them at wholesale."

McGarvey got the car's paperwork and gave it to the Mafia boss, who handed it to the ferret.

"Do you have partners?"

"None who you'll have to deal with."

"Where would you deliver these cars?"

"Anywhere in Moscow."

"For fifty thousand marks, my cost?"

"Fifty-one thousand," McGarvey said. "I think your brother-in-law deserves a finders fee. He's already been of some assistance to me."

"The documents are legitimate," the ferret said. "But it says that you paid nearly ninety thousand including fees."

"That's about what you'd expect to pay," McGarvey said with a faint smirk.

Ostrovsky pursed his lips after a moment, then shrugged. "How would you like to be paid?"

"American hundred-dollar bills."

"Ah," Ostrovsky said, smiling broadly now. "Not so easy to counterfeit yet." He put out his hand. "I think we can do business, Monsieur Allain."

McGarvey shook hands. "I thought you might say that."

THIRTY-THREE

Riga

McGarvey decided that although his Pierre Allain work name had held up to this point he would leave Russia from St. Petersburg. The search would be concentrated for him in Moscow, and security at the three airports would be too tight for him to take the risk. He had an excited Astimovich drive him up to St. Petersburg in the morning, a distance of 350 miles, where he explained that he had further business. Astimovich was so bedazzled by his good fortune that he didn't ask any questions, though during the seven-hour drive he kept up a running commentary about what he was going to do with twelve thousand marks every month once McGarvey's business fully developed.

"Goddamn, it's good to be a businessman just like in the West," he said.

McGarvey felt a touch of sorrow for the man, because even if the deal had been legitimate he would probably have been cheated out of his finder's fee by his brother-in-law. It wasn't western business, but it *was* the new Russian business.

He was passed through passport control at St. Petersburg's Pulkovo-2 International Airport without trouble, and his Finnair flight touched down at Lidosta International's too-short main runway, the pilot standing on the brakes all the way to the end, around 10:00 P.M.

He'd repacked his gun inside his laptop, so he encountered no problem with Latvian customs either, though passengers arriving from Russia were given a closer scrutiny than those from the West. His passport and visas were in order, and he was admitted without a search of his single carryon bag.

Taking a cab downtown to the main railway station, McGarvey walked over to his apartment three blocks away, making two passes before he went in. With less than a week to May Day he was starting to get a little jumpy. So far his plan had gone according to schedule. In a few days the Russian border guards would let him cross with the Mercedes without a search, and once in Moscow he would be welcomed back by the Mafia as Pierre Allain, a well connected Belgian businessman. No one would connect him to McGarvey, the American assassin. Yet he was beginning to have a very faint premonition of disaster, and he'd been in the business too long not to heed such feelings. Long ago he trained himself to distinguish legitimate sixth-sense concerns from paranoia.

After he unpacked and took a quick shower he stood by the window looking down at the street while he had a cigarette and a bottle of beer. In another few days or so Russia would be plunged into another major turmoil, possibly even a bigger one than the 1917 revolution. This time Tarankov would die, so that he could not take the country back. However it turned out was anyone's guess. But McGarvey was already beyond the philosophical debate within himself. Now it was simply a matter of tradecraft. Of doing the job and getting away. His thoughts had become super-focused.

But something nagged at him. Some disconnected thought, some distant rationalization in a back compartment of his brain, that instinctively he thought was important.

He stubbed out his cigarette, and went downstairs to the pay phone in the back hallway. Nobody was around, and the building was quiet.

Using his Allain credit card, he telephoned Rencke in Paris. It was answered on the second ring.

"Hiya," Otto said. It sounded as if he were out of breath and anxious.

"Have you heard from my daughter?"

"Sure did, and everything's fine," Rencke responded with the proper code phrase. "You're going to have to call it off now for sure."

"Have the CIA and French picked up my trail?"

"They're using Jacqueline and somebody that Ryan sent over. I can't find out who it is, but they're serious," Rencke said. "But that's not the real problem, Mac. It's Bykov, the Russian special investigator who's looking for you. I tried to dig up some more of his background, but I kept running into a blank wall, because Yuri Bykov does not exist. There is no such man who ever worked for the KGB. But the security firm he supposedly works for in Krasnoyarsk is owned by Tarankov."

McGarvey's jaw tightened.

"I wouldn't bet my gonads on it, Mac, but I'd wager even money that Yuri Bykov is in reality Leonid Chernov. So you gotta call it off, Mac. You just gotta."

"Do they have my Allain identity?"

"I don't think so—"

"Then nothing has changed," McGarvey broke in. "They don't know who I'm posing as, they don't know when I'm coming across, nor do they know how I'm going to do it."

Tarankov's raid on Smolensk after several days of lying low, had completely convinced McGarvey that the Tarantula would be showing up in Red Square on May Day, and would not wait until the general elections. The brief mention of the raid in the *Herald-Tribune* and on CNN warned that if the reaction of the people of Smolensk was any indicator, the country would not hold together until the elections. Which meant Tarankov would make his move in Red Square on May Day, declaring himself the leader of the new Soviet Union, just as McGarvey had suspected that he would.

"You'll have to kill Chernov," Rencke said.

"If our paths cross I will."

"They will," Rencke said, after a brief strained silence.

"I need you to do one more thing for me, Otto," McGarvey said.

"What is it?" Rencke asked dejectedly.

"Do you think that the SVR knows that someone is roaming around inside their computer system?"

"No."

"Can you get a direct line to Yemlin's apartment, through an SVR secured line?"

"I think so," Rencke said with renewed interest because he was being handed another challenge.

"Call him right now, and warn him off. Tell him who Bykov is, and tell him that I'll call him one hour from now at the number I called him from Helsinki. He'll know what you're talking about."

"What if he's not there?"

"He'll have a rollover number, or he'll be carrying a secured beeper in case of emergencies. Just get the message to him, okay?"

"Mac, I'm scared big time," Rencke said. "I've got this bad feeling, you know?"

"Just hold together a little longer, Otto."

"Yeah. We're family after all. We've gotta stick together, or else there's nothing left."

Courbevoie

Rencke stared at the display on his computer screen, his shaking hands hovering over the keyboard. In the past week he'd discovered a way by which he could defeat his own backscatter encryption program to the extent that he'd gained the ability to trace a call even though both sides of the line were encrypted.

McGarvey was in the Latvian capital city of Riga, or at least within the city code 2.

He glanced at the open package of Twinkies, his last, lying on the table beside him, and tears suddenly came to his eyes. Mac was the only friend he'd ever had. Ever. The only human being who'd ever treated him fairly, who'd ever understood him, and who'd ever accepted him. Even his parents had rejected him when he was fifteen in Indianapolis. His father in a drunken rage had kicked him out of the house. His mother had pressed some money into his hand outside in the darkness, and kissed him. "You're too smart for your own good," she'd said. They were the last words she'd ever spoken to him.

The only other people who tolerated him were the geeks on the Internet. Most of them were idiots, but sometimes they provided a diversion. If they didn't always agree with his views, at least he was respected on most of the Web sites.

He flicked the Twinkies into the overflowing wastepaper basket, and with a dozen keystrokes was inside the Latvian telephone exchange system. He fed in McGarvey's telephone number, which pulled up a locator code. Within ten seconds he had an address, with a designator that the unit was a pay phone, and his heart sank. McGarvey had probably called from an anonymous booth on the street somewhere. Nevertheless, he entered the maintenance database within the Riga telephone exchange which displayed a street-by-street city map. McGarvey's number came up as a street address. A building on Gogala Street a few blocks from the train station, which the telephone company listed as a multi-unit private dwelling. An apartment building. Mac had rented an apartment in Riga.

Rencke entered the information on a tamper-proof section of a hard disk, then backed out of the program, and quickly got into the SVR's system on the Ring Road in Yasenevo on the outskirts of Moscow.

Scrolling through the personnel files, he came up with Viktor Yemlin's locator file and instituted a call to the secure line to his apartment. The telephone was answered on the first ring.

"*Da.*"

"*Is this Viktor Pavlovich?*" Rencke asked in Russian.

"Yes. Who is calling, please?" Yemlin replied. He sounded harried.

"An old friend wishes to speak with you fifty-five minutes from now at the same number he used when he telephoned from Helsinki."

"Is this a joke? How'd you get this number? Who is this?"

"Julius loves you," Rencke blurted. "Please call at once." It was the ad that Yemlin had placed in *Le Figaro* with the SVR's data number.

"*Yeb vas,*" Yemlin said, shocked. "Who is this?"

"A friend who wants to warn you that the head of the special police commission, Yuri Bykov, is in reality Leonid Chernov, Tarankov's chief of staff. Can you take this call in fifty-four minutes?"

The line was dead silent for several seconds. "*Nyet,*" Yemlin said in a strangled voice. "That phone has been bugged. They're listening with tracing equipment. He must not call that number. Do you understand me? He must not call."

The connection was broken.

Rencke stared at the screen briefly, wondering if he should reinstitute the call.

He brought back the pay phone number in McGarvey's Riga apartment, and had his computer speed dial it. After one ring a recorded announcement in Russian said the number was a simplex instrument, and the connection was broken. The phone could be used only for outgoing calls. It could not receive incoming calls.

Rencke got into the Riga telephone exchange back directory in an effort to find out if there were other telephones in the building. But there were none. Even if there had been a telephone he could have reached, he couldn't imagine what he would have said to whoever answered.

He backed out of that program, and pulled up the worldwide travel agent reservation system, and searched for flights between Paris and Riga with empty seats on any airline leaving as soon as possible.

The information came up on his screen, but he could only stare at it in frustration. What was he supposed to do? Jump on an airplane, fly to Riga and take a cab out to Mac's apartment? Then what?

He looked up at the clock. Mac would be making his call in fifty minutes, and there was nothing Rencke could do about it.

He fished the Twinkies out of the wastepaper basket and dejectedly started to eat as he moved over to a computer hooked into the Internet.

Mac wanted to be backstopped, so here he would have to remain.

Paris

"Nothing," Jacqueline said, hanging up the phone.

Elizabeth sat with a glass of white wine in front of the laptop computer, staring at the messages scrolling up the screen. It was late and she was very tired.

They'd been trying without luck for the past thirty-six hours to find out about the anonymous remailer address that Twinkie had used on the net.

"Samat doesn't exist," Jacqueline continued. "There is no such remailing service anywhere, which means it's a ghost service."

Elizabeth looked up.

"If it's Otto Rencke, then he created the address to hide his real location. But the fact is, that anonymous remailer address exists only in cyberspace. And only he knows how to access it from behind." Jacqueline threw up her hands. "The man's a genius. We'll never get close to him unless he wants us there."

"Screw the bastard," Elizabeth said. She turned back to the computer, and entered Twinkie's anonymous remailer address.

Subject: Re: CIA CLANDESTINE SERVICES
4/27/99 01.38

Twinkie, it's you who doesn't know what the hell he's talking about. Your cats probably pissed all over your pc and shorted your brain. Get real!!!!!!!
(lizmacitemone)

Several unrelated messages scrolled up her screen, until Twinkie's anonymous remailer address appeared.

From: an162885@anon.samat.po
Subject: Re: CIA CLANDESTINE SERVICES
4/27/99 01.43

I suppose you know what you're talking about from long experience, lizmac.
(twinkieitemseventeen)

"Don't lose him," Jacqueline cautioned.

"He has this number now, and if it's Rencke, and if he traces it he'll know that this computer is located in my father's apartment."

"He'll think it's a trap."

Subject: Re: CIA CLANDESTINE SERVICES
4/27/99 01.44

I grew up with my dad's stories. Twinkie handle have any significance, or is it just bullshit!!!
(lizmacitemtwo)

From: an162885@anon.samat.po
Subject: Re: CIA CLANDESTINE SERVICES
4/27/99 01.45

Do you have anything significant to add to this discussion or are you just trying to irritate us?
(twinkieitemeighteen)

Subject: Re: CIA CLANDESTINE SERVICES
4/27/99 01.46

I'm interested in the business. Care to chat?
(lizmacitemthree)

From: an162885@anon.samat.po
Subject: Re: CIA CLANDESTINE SERVICES
4/27/99 01.47

Standby and I'll download some of the highpoints.

The telephone rang, as the computer screen came alive with messages dating from last week scrolling at ten times normal speed.

"It might be him," Jacqueline said, looking at the telephone. "You answer it."

The telephone rang a second time before Elizabeth picked it up.

"Hello?"

The line was silent for a few moments, then there was a subtle shift in the sound quality of the hollowness.

"Lizmac?" a man asked. His voice sounded high pitched, and strained.

"Yes. Is this Twinkie?"

"Tell me something."

"This is an open line—"

"It's being monitored, but I've taken care of it."

Elizabeth held the phone so that Jacqueline could hear as well.

"My name is Elizabeth McGarvey. Are you Otto?"

"Do you still have the diamond necklace your father gave you in Greece?"

It was something only her father knew about.

"Actually he gave it to me when I was in school in Switzerland. But I lost it in Greece, when he found it he gave it back to me." It had happened during the operation her father had been involved with a few years ago.

"What are you doing here, Liz?" Rencke asked.

"Trying to find my father. I know that you and he are working together, and I know that Viktor Yemlin has hired him to kill Tarankov. But the Russians know about it, and they've asked the CIA and the SDECE to help out. Ryan's agreed. So my father's walking into a trap. Where is he, Otto?" It all came out in a rush.

"How do you know all this—"

"I'm working for the CIA now!" Elizabeth cut in. "Where is my father? I have to talk to him."

The line was silent.

"Otto, goddammit, don't hang up on me! Ryan's an asshole, and I don't have any intention of turning my father over to him or to the French. But

I have to try to warn him." Elizabeth was sick with fear. If she lost Rencke now she'd never get him back. "Jacqueline Belleau has agreed to help me."

The connection had not been broken, but the line remained silent.

"We've got less than seven weeks to stop him. You have to help us, Otto. You're our only hope."

"You don't have seven weeks," Otto said, his voice very strained, even higher pitched than before. "I think Mac's taking him out on May First. Four days from now."

A vise closed on Elizabeth's heart, but she immediately saw the logic in it. Tarankov wasn't going to wait for the general elections in June. He'd be in Red Square on May Day and her father would be there waiting for him.

"There's something else you don't know. The Russian police commission supposedly headed by Yuri Bykov. Well, that's not his real name. He's really Leonid Chernov, who is Tarankov's chief of staff."

"Dear God," Elizabeth said. "Is my father already in Moscow?"

"No, he's in Riga. But in a few minutes he's going to make the biggest mistake in his life when he tries to call Yemlin. Yemlin's line is bugged. When Mac calls, the Russians will know where he's calling from and Chernov will come after him."

"The Latvians will never allow it."

"Chernov might convince them somehow."

"But that'll take time," Elizabeth cried. "You can warn him first."

"There's no way to get through by phone and I've got to stay here in case he tries to call me."

"Jacqueline and I will fly up there."

"The French are watching you."

"Not now. They think we're at a dead end. They've written us off, Otto. Give me his address, we'll get there in time, I promise you."

"Put Mademoiselle Belleau on the line."

"I'm here," Jacqueline said.

"If I give you Mac's address will you turn it over to your people?"

"Only if I think that there is no other way in which to save Kirk's life."

"If you betray him, I'll kill you."

"Don't worry, Monsieur Rencke, I love him just as much as you do."

"Liz, are you there?" Rencke said, hesitating.

"Yes. Where is he?"

"He has an apartment in Riga," Rencke said. He gave her the address. "I don't know which unit he's in, but he called me from a pay phone in the building."

Elizabeth's heart sank. Her father could just as well have called from a building across the city from wherever he was holed up. But she didn't say anything. For the moment it was their only lead.

"Are you sure that you guys aren't being followed?" Otto asked.

"They want to send us to Moscow," Jacqueline said. "Until we agree to go—and they don't think we will—they're leaving us to our own devices."

"Standby," Rencke said.

Elizabeth had been holding everything in. She sat back and looked into Jacqueline's eyes. "You weren't lying to Otto . . . or to me, were you?"

"*Non, ma cherie.* In this you must believe me."

"I do," Elizabeth said. She could see how he was going to do it. Tarankov would be standing on the reviewing balcony on Lenin's Tomb in Red Square, and her father would be somewhere within a hundred yards or so with a sniper rifle. At the right moment Tarankov would fall, and her father would melt away into the crowds in a very clever disguise. She'd read his file. She knew what he was capable of.

Rencke came back. "Can you be at Orly by five this morning?"

"Orly by five?" Elizabeth said. Jacqueline nodded. "Yes."

"You're both booked on RIAIR flight 57 to Riga, first class. It wasn't cheap, but I figured that Ryan could afford it, so I put the tickets on his Mastercard."

Elizabeth laughed despite herself. "He'll hang you."

"It'd be the biggest blunder of his life," Rencke replied viciously. "By the time I got done with his computer track, he'd never again qualify for a driver's license, he wouldn't be able to afford to buy a stick of gum, and the IRS would probably want to put him away for life." He calmed down. "You guys be careful out there." He gave Elizabeth his telephone number. "Let me know what's going on, will ya?"

"We will," Elizabeth said.

"I'll keep a two-way dialogue going between us on the net. If it's being watched they'll think you guys are still in the apartment."

Elizabeth hung up and looked at Jacqueline.

"We'll go out the back way," the older woman said. "Just in case."

Lefortovo

Chernov finally got the break he'd been waiting for a few minutes before three when Major Gresko called from FSK headquarters on Dzerzhinsky Square. He was sitting in the darkness sipping a glass of white wine wondering what else he could have done when the phone rang. Every cop in Russia was looking for McGarvey, as were the forces of the CIA and SDECE. But it was as if McGarvey had simply dropped off the face of the earth. He'd gone to ground, and there was nothing they could do until he surfaced again, or made a mistake.

The FSK team assigned to watch Yemlin had learned from their source inside the SVR that he'd received an encrypted call from somewhere outside Russia an hour earlier. Fifty-five minutes after that call, a pay phone in a kiosk near the Metro station a couple of blocks from Yemlin's apartment rang. It was one of the telephones that the FSK monitored at Colonel Bykov's request. Yemlin was nowhere in the vicinity, so after two rings an FSK operator answered.

"*Da?*"

"Viktor?" a man said.

So as not to make the caller suspicious the FSK operator told a half-truth. "*Nyet.* This is Nikolai, and there's no one else around. The metro station across the street is empty."

"*Yeb vas,*" the man said, and he hung up.

"If it was McGarvey he called from a simplex instrument in Riga," Gresko said. "But I can't imagine anyone else calling a phone booth so near to Yemlin's apartment, and so soon after the call to his office."

"I agree," Chernov said.

"It's a safe bet those bastards won't cooperate with us. They'll give us the runaround if we level with them. No love lost up there, in fact if they knew the whole truth they'd probably do everything they could to help McGarvey."

Chernov thought for a moment.

"But we're not chasing an assassin. The man we're after is a mass murderer, whose specialty is little boys. Who knows, maybe it's become too hot for him here in Russia, and he may take his grim pleasures somewhere else. Like Latvia."

"That might work," Gresko said.

"Do you have an address on the trace?"

"It's an apartment building near the main railway station," Gresko said. "Could be that he's not living there. Maybe he just used the phone."

"If he called from there once, maybe he'll call from there again," Chernov said. "Get the file over to the Militia, and have Petrovsky make contact with the Riga police. Have him send a copy of McGarvey's photograph under the name Kisnelkov. In the meantime I'll arrange for an airplane to take us up there. I want to catch him just before dawn when people, even men like him, tend to be the slowest and most fuddle-headed."

THIRTY-FOUR

Riga

McGarvey awoke shortly after 5 A.M. in a cold sweat, his heart racing, his muscles bunched up. It was the same dream he often had in which he saw the light fading from the eyes of his victims. Only this time he'd been unable to focus on the face, except that whoever it was they were laughing at him. Mocking his life's work, everything he'd fought for, everything he'd stood for.

He got up and went to the window. A delivery van passed below, and at the corner a truck rumbled through the intersection. The city was coming alive with the morning.

"Get out! Get out! Get out!"

A persistent voice at the back of head gave warning like the blare of a distant fire alarm, but he wasn't at all sure it was for him. Sometimes in his dreams a part of his subconscious tried to warn his victims to get out, to get away before he came to kill them. A psychologist friend at Langley said the dreams were nothing more than his conscience.

"Proves you're just as sane as the rest of us," the company shrink said. "Only a true sociopath can kill without remorse."

He'd debated calling Rencke last night after he'd failed to reach Yemlin. But Rencke would be unable to tell him anything he didn't already know. Yemlin's position had been discovered, and by now he was either dead or under arrest.

There was an outside chance that Chernov knew about the calls to the phone booth near Yemlin's apartment, in which case McGarvey's call had not been answered by a chance passerby, but had been picked up by an FSK technical unit. It was even possible that they'd traced the call to this apartment building.

But the Latvians actively hated Russians. All Russians. So not only wouldn't they cooperate with a commission trying to stop the man who was planning to assassinate Tarankov, they'd probably throw up road blocks.

It was on this thought that McGarvey had finally gone to sleep last night. And it was this thought now that nagged at him. Someone was coming, with or without the cooperation of the Latvian authorities. If he got involved in some kind of a confrontation with Chernov, whatever the outcome, the Latvians would try to arrest them all, and someone would get hurt.

He turned away from the window and got dressed in a dark turtleneck sweater and slacks. The holstered gun went in the waistband of his trousers at the small of his back, and the silencer and spare magazine went in the pockets of his leather jacket. He left everything else, including his clothes, his shaving gear and other toiletries, and the overnight bag. If anyone came up here they might believe that he'd just stepped out and was planning on returning. It might give him a few extra hours.

Checking the street again to make sure no one had shown up, he took his laptop computer down to the Volkswagen, and drove over to the secured garage near the train station, where he switched cars for the Mercedes. Before the VW was reported missing by the rental agency, the operation would be long finished, and McGarvey would drop the keys and a note where the car could be found in a mailbox somewhere.

By 6:30 A.M., he was having breakfast on the outskirts of the city, with several hours to kill. He did not want to cross the border at Zilupe until late this afternoon, when the customs officers he'd dealt with before would be at the end of their shift, and therefore impatient to take his bribe and get home.

It was past 8:00 A.M. when the Tupolev jet transport carrying Chernov, Petrovsky, Gresko and a couple of Militia detectives was finally cleared to taxi from the holding ramp over to a customs and immigration hangar. Latvian officials had held them for over an hour and Chernov was beside himself with rage.

Riga Police Lieutenant Andrējs Ulmanis, and his dour faced sergeant Jurin Zariņš were waiting for them. Chernov forced himself to remain calm as they all shook hands, but the tension and animosity were very thick.

"We surrounded the building forty-five minutes ago, as you requested, but so far there's been no sign of the man you are looking for," Lieutenant Ulmanis said, leading them over to a police van for the ride into the city. He was a heavyset man with thinning sand-colored hair and a double chin.

"Considering the political conditions between our countries, we thank you for your help," Chernov said, carefully.

Ulmanis eyed him distastefully. "Murder is a terrible crime, and we're all police officers, jā?"

"This one is very bad. He specializes in little boys."

The Latvian policeman's jaw tightened. "I wasn't clear on his nationality. His name is Kisnelkov. Is he Russian or Ukrainian?"

"He's a Russian," Chernov said. "But he may be traveling on an American or a French passport under another name. The son of a bitch is good, he always manages to keep one step ahead of us."

"What's he doing in Latvia?"

"Trying to get away. Last week he raped and killed three young boys in Moscow. When he was finished he mutilated their bodies in ways that even you as a police officer would not believe."

"How did you find out he was here?"

"He tried to make a telephone call to a friend last night and we traced it."

"If he's here, we'll find him," Ulmanis said.

"Don't make a mistake about this one," Chernov cautioned. "Six months ago we thought we had him cornered. When it was all over, he'd killed two policemen, wounded three others and got away clean."

Ulmanis nodded.

"If you or your people come face-to-face with him, don't hesitate to shoot him like a dog," Chernov said.

"A Russian dog," Sergeant Zariņš muttered, and Ulmanis shot him a dirty look but did not reprimand him.

Twenty minutes later they pulled up at the end of the block from the apartment building. The intersections at both ends of the street had been barricaded. Police cars, blue lights flashing, completely surrounded the block. Officers in riot gear were stationed on the roof tops and in the doorways of every building within sight. Some of the cops were dispersing the crowds of curious onlookers, while other cops milled around apparently waiting for something to happen.

Chernov and the others got out of the van. He glanced at Petrovsky. "He's gone."

Lieutenant Ulmanis came over. "Not unless he was tipped off."

"Nothing against your capable police procedures, Lieutenant, but when the first of your people showed up, he would have spotted them and slipped away before the area could be secured. He's gone."

"I don't think so."

Chernov took out his pistol, checked the load, then reholstered the gun. "Well, I'm going to walk over there and search the building. Would you care to come with me?"

"I'll go with you, but we'll take a few of my people with us just in case you're wrong."

Chernov shrugged and marched down the street to the apartment building and went inside. The Latvian cops were hoping that they might get to see a Russian blown away this morning. Ambulances were standing by.

The landlady, a taciturn old woman, came out of her ground floor apartment, and Ulmanis asked her a number of questions about her tenants, and about her rent control permits, a subject on which she was vague.

Chernov walked over to the foot of the stairs and cocked an ear. The building was quiet.

"That's him," the old woman said.

Chernov turned back. Ulmanis had shown McGarvey's photograph that had been faxed down here this morning.

"What is his name?" Chernov asked.

"Pierre something," the old woman said resentfully. "He paid for a month in cash a couple of weeks ago. I didn't care what his name was."

Ulmanis came over. "I thought you said he killed some kids in Moscow last week?" he asked in a low voice.

"He must have returned here to hide out," Chernov said.

He took out his gun and went up to the top floor, taking the stairs two at a time. Ulmanis and the other Latvian cops came up behind him, their weapons drawn.

At the top Chernov flattened himself against the wall next to the apartment door and listened for a full two minutes, but there were no sounds from within.

On signal, one of Ulmanis's people kicked the door in, and they all rushed into the empty apartment.

"He's gone," Ulmanis said, unnecessarily. There was no place to hide in the tiny apartment.

The Latvian cops searched the apartment anyway.

"Maybe not for long, Lieutenant," one of the cops called from the bathroom. He appeared in the doorway. "His toothbrush and razor are still here."

One of the other cops opened the wardrobe. "His clothes are here, and a suitcase."

"There's food in the cupboards and the refrigerator," the cop in the tiny kitchen reported.

"Maybe he's coming back," Ulmanis said.

"Not with all those policemen outside," Chernov said. He took off his jacket and laid it over the back of the chair. "Place a couple of your men downstairs in the landlady's apartment, and a couple of sharpshooters in an apartment across the street. But tell them to keep out of sight. Get rid of everybody else. In the meantime I'll wait here for awhile."

"What about your people?" Ulmanis asked.

"Send them back to the airport to wait for me."

Ulmanis relayed the orders. "I'll wait here with you."

"As you wish," Chernov said. "But if he shows up he's mine."

"Believe me, Colonel Bykov, the sooner you and he are off Latvian soil the happier we'll be."

RIAIR flight 57 from Paris touched down at Riga's Lidosta International Airport at 9:00 A.M. Elizabeth and Jacqueline paid for one-time visas from passport control and had their single carryon bags checked through customs. They changed a couple of hundred francs into latis, purchased a visitors' guide and Riga street map in English from a newsstand and forty-five minutes later were in a cab heading downtown to the central railway station, which was a few blocks from the address Rencke had given them.

They traveled on their legitimate passports because at this point they thought there was no longer any need to mask their movements. Galan and Lynch were no longer interested in them. Traffic at that hour of the morning in Paris had been thin so if someone had tried to follow them out to Orly Airport Jacqueline was sure she would have spotted them. But there'd been no one behind them.

"If we run into a problem in Riga we'll be on our own," Jacqueline had cautioned. "No one except Otto knows where we are, and he won't tell anyone. At least not for twenty-four hours. Maybe longer."

"A lot can happen in that time," Elizabeth said, suddenly seeing the precariousness of their situation.

"We'll split up, so that if something goes wrong at least one of us will have a chance of getting out," Jacqueline said. "I'll leave you at the train station, and I'll walk the rest of the way over to the apartment."

Elizabeth shook her head. "He's my father, so if something should happen I'll at least have an excuse for being there that might hold up."

"It didn't work in Paris."

"It might here," Elizabeth insisted.

Jacqueline smiled wryly. "You're stubborn like your father."

"Used to drive my mother nuts."

Jacqueline's smile was set. "Is that why there was the divorce?"

"My mother was afraid of losing him so she pushed him away before the hurt got too terrible for her to bear."

Jacqueline looked out the window. "The trouble with what you say is that I understand your mother." She turned back. "Do you, *ma cherie?*"

Elizabeth shook her head after a moment. "No," she said. She'd never understood that convoluted logic. If you loved someone you did everything in your power to keep them near you.

Jacqueline squeezed her hand. "I think that you have been mad at your mother for a very long time. But there's no reason for it, you know. They both still love you."

It was Elizabeth's turn to look away.

"The divorce wasn't your fault, Elizabeth," Jacqueline said gently. "Did you think it was?"

"I probably did as a kid." Elizabeth looked at Jacqueline. "But not so much anymore." She shrugged. "It's just life. But I don't want to lose him again."

"Neither do I."

Traffic around the train station was busy. The cabby dropped them off in front, immediately picked up another fare and was gone.

They had studied the Riga map on the way in from the airport. The address Rencke had given them was less than three blocks away. They agreed that Elizabeth would walk over to the apartment building, and if everything looked clear try to find out which apartment her father had rented. If anything seemed out of place, even slightly odd, she was to immediately come back to the railroad station where Jacqueline would be waiting in the coffee shop.

"Don't fool around," Jacqueline said unnecessarily because she was nervous. "If the Russians got here before us they won't react kindly to you barging in."

"If they ran into my father, there'll be some dead people over there, and a lot of cops," Elizabeth said. "It'll be pretty obvious."

"In which case I'll blow the whistle," Jacqueline said seriously. In the past couple of weeks she'd picked up a lot of American slang from Elizabeth.

"You and I both," Elizabeth said.

She gave Jacqueline her overnight bag, then crossed the street over the tracks. The morning wanted to warm up, but a chilly breeze blew across the river, bringing with it a combination of industrial and seaport smells that were subtly different from any other city she'd ever visited.

It took her ten minutes to walk up Gogala Street to within a half a block from the apartment building her father had called from. She stopped and looked in the window of a women's sportswear shop, as she tried to calm down.

Everything seemed normal. Traffic was heavy, the shops were open and busy, and most of the tables at a sidewalk cafe at the corner were occupied. There were no police anywhere, and no one seemed to be watching the apartment building.

After a minute she crossed the street, walked the rest of the way to the apartment building and went inside. A narrow hallway ran to the rear of the building. From where she stood by the mailboxes she could see the pay phone in the back, and it gave her a little thrill that her father had used it less than twenty-four hours ago.

She didn't understand Latvian, but the word manager, in Russian, was written on a card attached to the mailbox for the ground floor apartment. She hesitated a moment, then knocked on the door.

An old woman opened it, looked Elizabeth up and down, and motioned her away. "I have no apartments here, so go away. I don't want any trouble."

The old woman was frightened.

"I don't want an apartment," Elizabeth said in Russian. "But I'm looking for someone who may have rented an apartment from you recently."

The door suddenly opened all the way, the old woman was pulled aside, and a couple of large, stern-faced men were there. Before Elizabeth could react, one of them grabbed her by the arm.

"Who is it that you're looking for?" he asked.

"I think I've made a mistake," Elizabeth said, her heart in her throat.

"Let me see your passport."

"Who the hell are you?"

"The police. Your passport, please." The cop was stern, but not unpleasant.

Elizabeth hesitated a second longer, than awkwardly dug her passport out of her purse.

The cop's eyebrows rose when he saw that it was an American passport. "Stay here, I'll take her upstairs," he told the other cop.

Elizabeth tried to pull away, but he was too strong for her. "I'm an American. I want to speak to someone at my embassy."

"You speak pretty good Russian for an American," the cop said.

"Not as good as you Latvians do," Elizabeth shot back, and she instantly regretted the remark.

His grip tightened on her arm, and he dragged her up three flights of stairs to the top floor where two men waited in a small apartment. One of them was heavyset, the other tall, and muscularly built, with short-cropped gray hair. He looked dangerous. His eyes seemed dead.

The cop handed Elizabeth's passport to the heavy man, who examined it.

"She says she's looking for someone who may have rented an apartment here not so long ago, Lieutenant," the cop said. "She claims to be an American, but I never heard an American speak such good Russian."

Ulmanis handed the passport to Chernov. "It doesn't look fake. Do you know who she is?"

Chernov studied Elizabeth's passport, a grim look of satisfaction crossing his lips. "Her name is Raya Kisnelkov. I don't know where she got this passport, but it probably came from the same source her father uses. I just didn't think she was involved with his sick games."

Ulmanis stared at her, and shook his head. "She doesn't look the type," he said. "Do you know what your father has done? Are you helping him?"

"I don't know what you're talking about," Elizabeth said in English. "I want to call my embassy."

"Her English is pretty good, too," Ulmanis said. "A lot better than mine."

Chernov stared at Elizabeth. "We'll leave now," he said. "I don't think Kisnelkov will be coming back."

Ulmanis hesitated. "Perhaps we should get someone from the American embassy up here to take a look."

"As you wish," Chernov said, unperturbed. "I would very much like to listen to your explanation how this woman got into Latvia on a fake passport." He forced a grim smile. "I trust that in the meantime you'll arrange accommodations for me and my people."

Ulmanis nodded. "I'll have the van brought around front," he said.

"Wait a minute, goddammit," Elizabeth shouted. "I'm an American!" She switched to Russian. "*Yeb vas*, you stupid bastard, don't you recognize a legitimate passport when you see one?"

Ulmanis just shook his head, and he and the cop left.

"Thank you," Chernov told Elizabeth, politely, and her blood ran cold.

From where she sat having a coffee at the sidewalk cafe on the corner, Jacqueline watched as a gray Chevrolet van pulled up in front of the apartment building. She'd been unable to simply wait at the train station, so she'd followed Elizabeth up here.

Two minutes later, a tall man, came out of the building with Elizabeth, and hustled her into the van.

Jacqueline jumped up, but before she could reach the street, the van took off and disappeared down the block. She stopped, absolutely stunned. Her worst nightmare seemed to be coming true.

THIRTY-FIVE

Riga

Jacqueline was beside herself with fear and guilt because despite her professionalism she had managed to lead Elizabeth into a trap. Although she had serious doubts, she thought that there was a possibility Liz had been arrested by the Riga Police, and not by the Russians who had traced McGarvey's call here. All the way back to the railroad station she tried to convince herself of that likelihood without success. She and Elizabeth had entered Latvia legally. There was no reason for the local authorities to detain her.

She found a pay phone in the train station's main arrivals hall and called Rencke's blind number in Courbevoie.

"They've taken her," she blurted when Rencke answered.

"Calm down. Who took her?"

"I don't know for sure. It could have been the Riga police, but I can't be certain. I hope so."

"Just a minute," Rencke said. "Okay, you're calling from the main railway station. Is anybody watching you? Anybody paying unusual attention?"

The station was busy. Jacqueline scanned the crowds, but she was picking up nothing unusual. "Not that I can see."

"Have you called your boss yet?"

"No."

"Okay, now calm down and tell me everything that happened," Otto said.

Jacqueline quickly went through the story from the moment they'd got off the plane. "Can you get into the police computer?"

"If she was arrested it wouldn't be on their machines yet, unless they asked Interpol for help. Did you get the license number of the van?"

"It was too far away to read," Jacqueline said.

"Okay, hang on for a minute, I'll see if anything is showing up."

"Mon dieu, please hurry," Jacqueline said.

"I just had another thought. Did you get a decent look at the man with Liz? Could you describe him?"

"Tall, husky. It's impossible to say more than that."

"Standby," Rencke said.

Announcements for arriving and departing trains were made first in a language that Jacqueline took to be Latvian, and then in Russian, and finally in Polish. A train had rumbled into the station while she was dialing Rencke's number, and now people began coming into the main hall from trackside. A lot of them were well dressed, and talked on cellular phones as they hurried outside to catch a taxi.

Rencke came back a couple of minutes later. "Nothing has showed up on the Riga police wire yet. But an unscheduled flight originating in Moscow landed at 6:48 this morning. It's still on the ground, but I'm betting that the man you saw with Liz was Chernov. He traced Mac's call, and somehow convinced the Latvian police to help him. I'll watch to see when it takes off back to Moscow, but it'll probably be within the next half hour. I think Liz walked into a hornet's nest, and Chernov will take her back to Moscow."

"For bait," Jacqueline said, utterly devastated. It was her fault. She should have known better.

"I'd like to disagree with you, but I can't," Rencke said, dejectedly.

"I've got to tell my boss what happened," she said. "I'll keep your name out of it. I'll say that Liz had a hunch that her father would be here, so we came to look for him, and she was taken."

"They won't believe it."

"I'll make them believe it," Jacqueline said urgently. "I don't know what else to do, but I just can't walk away from them."

"Mac must have figured it out," Rencke said distantly.

"What did you say?"

"They got Liz, but he wasn't there. It means he figured it out and he's probably on his way to Moscow now. Three days early, but he was forced into it. Which means we've still got two chances. Two options. With all that extra time it's possible he'll call me for an update. When he does I'll get him out of there."

"If you tell him that Chernov has his daughter he won't leave."

"If we can find out where she's been taken, I can convince somebody in Washington to get involved."

"How can we do that?"

"Simple, you're going to convince Galan to send you to Moscow in an official capacity. You're an SDECE field officer who has the inside scoop on Mac, and your expertise is going to be offered to the special commission which is headed by Yuri Bykov, a.k.a., Leonid Chernov."

"*Merde*," Jacqueline said softly.

"Double dip *merde*," Rencke agreed. "But right now it's our only shot."

Enroute to Moscow

Even over the roar of the jet engines spooling up Elizabeth imagined that she could hear the thump of her heart in her chest. Any doubts she might have had about who'd taken her had been dispelled the moment they'd arrived at the airport and she got a look at the Tupolev jet waiting on the apron. It carried Russian military markings, with the Russian flag painted on the tail.

Of the eight or ten others aboard, she figured four were crew, while the rest looked like cops or possibly military. All of them were surprised by her presence, but they offered no objections. The one who'd taken her was the boss, and it struck her from the moment she came aboard that he was Leonid Chernov, Tarankov's chief of staff, and the one who was posing as Yuri Bykov, chief of the police commission hunting for her father.

The aircraft had been fitted out executive-style with wide leather seats facing each other in groups of four, a pair of couches with a low table between them in the rear of the main cabin, and a complete galley and bar. She caught a glimpse of what appeared to be a conference room equipped with what looked like radio gear through an open door in the back of the plane. Forward she could see into the cockpit where the pilot and co-pilot were dressed in military uniforms.

Chernov put her in one of the seats in the forward part of the cabin, and went back to the others gathered in the conference room, and closed the door.

Elizabeth considered making a dash for the door, when one of the crewmen closed and latched it. He said something to the pilots, then came back to her.

"We'll be taking off now, so put on your seatbelt," he said pleasantly. He was young, probably not much older than Elizabeth.

"I'm an American. You have no right to take me anywhere," she said, and it sounded foolish even to her.

"If you refuse to cooperate, I've been instructed to drug you," the crewman warned. "When it wears off tomorrow you'll have a hell of a headache and cottonmouth. Sometimes it even scrambles the brain for a few days. I'm told that the effect is extremely unpleasant."

The airplane started to move, gathering speed as it trundled down the taxiway.

"I thought things had changed for the better in Russia. I guess I was wrong," Elizabeth said. She buckled her seatbelt.

The crewman sat down across from her and fastened his seatbelt. "As soon as we're airborne and out of the pattern I'll get you something to drink. It's not a very long flight to Moscow, less than two hours, but if you're hungry I can get you something to eat."

Elizabeth looked out the window, willing herself to calm down. She wasn't going to give the bastards the satisfaction of seeing the intense fear she felt. She'd walked into a trap in Paris, and she'd done the same damned thing here in Riga. The first had turned out okay, but this time she was in big trouble. When she didn't show up at the train station Jacqueline might guess what had happened, but there would be no proof. Riga had swallowed her, and there wasn't much that anybody could do to get her back.

Except, she thought, God help the bastards if and when her father found out she'd been kidnapped. The last people who'd tried that had paid with their lives.

But they'd been nothing more than a group of ex-East German Stasi thugs, not an entire government. She laid her forehead against the cool window glass as the airplane reached the end of the taxiway and turned onto the runway. Her father was only a man, and sooner or later all of his skills would be no match for an overwhelming force. When it came she would have been the one to lead him to his destruction.

The airplane took off, and as it circled the city and headed east, she searched for and found the railroad station. She touched the window with her fingers. Jacqueline would be getting worried now.

Five minutes later the countryside below was a puzzle of farmsteads, lakes and rivers, and stands of forests that stretched to the horizon for as far as she could see.

"Now, can I get you something to drink," the crewman asked. "A glass of tea, or perhaps some champagne?"

Elizabeth looked up at him.

"Champagne is permitted," he said.

She turned away without a word, and after a moment the crewman left. She heard voices at the rear of the airplane, but she didn't look up again until someone sat down across from her.

"I don't want champagne," she said.

"Neither do I," Chernov replied reasonably and Elizabeth's stomach fluttered. "You're too young to be his wife, so you're probably his daughter. The question is, what were you doing in Riga? How did you find out where your father was staying?"

His eyes were flat, lifeless. Studying his face, Elizabeth decided that he was younger than his gray hair made him look. It struck her that if he was posing as Yuri Bykov on the police commission, he would have to be in disguise. Certainly enough people had seen him at Tarankov's side and would have recognized him if he hadn't changed his appearance.

"Your father is a brilliant man. But he is dangerous. Do you know what he means to do? And do you understand why we cannot allow that to happen? Your own government does."

Chernov had something to hide, which meant he was vulnerable. But she would have to be careful what she said or did. If he suspected that she knew his true identity, she had no doubt that he would kill her.

"Your father is an assassin. But I think you know this."

"He telephoned me in Paris last night," Elizabeth said. "At my apartment. He wanted me to return to our house in Milford. He said he was flying over tomorrow."

"Did he tell you where he was calling from?"

"I traced his call."

"How?"

"With my computer. It's easy. Once I found out that he was in Riga, I got into the local phone system, and brought up the line. It's a pay phone in the building."

"That's very inventive," Chernov said. "Why did you come to Riga? What did you hope to accomplish?"

Elizabeth looked away for a moment, as if she were gathering her thoughts, as if she were making a decision, which in effect she was. Damage control, her father called what she was trying to do. If damage has been done, try to control the effects by telling half-truths to direct the inquiries elsewhere.

She looked into Chernov's eyes. "I wanted to make sure that my father was telling me the truth and was calling off the mission. Tarankov isn't worth a bullet. Nobody in Russia is. For all we give a damn, you people deserve whatever happens to you. For a thousand years you've been killing each other by the millions. Good riddance."

Chernov was impressed, she could see it on his face.

"For all *we* give a damn? Who is the we?"

"If you had done your homework, Colonel Bykov, you would know that I work for the CIA's Directorate of Intelligence. We've agreed to help you stop my father not because we think killing Tarankov is such a bad idea, but because my father's life is worth too much to risk killing such scum."

A flicker of surprise showed in his eyes, but was gone as fast as it appeared. "Then the CIA knows that you came to Riga?"

"Of course," Elizabeth said with a straight face.

Chernov thought about it a moment, then got up. "Do you think your father went back to this Milford?"

"It's in Delaware," Elizabeth said. "Yes, I do."

He nodded after a moment. "We'll see," he said, and then he went back into the conference room and closed the door, leaving Elizabeth to wonder if she'd done the right thing, or if she'd made another terrible mistake.

Riga

It was 12:10 P.M. when Jacqueline made it to the French Embassy. The young receptionist at the front desk registered no surprise when Jacqueline flashed her passport, and asked to speak with Marc Edis, assistant to the ambassador for economic affairs. In reality he was chief of SDECE operations for all the Baltics. She'd looked up his name before she and Elizabeth had left Paris. The woman put through the call, and a minute later a tall, slope-shouldered man with drooping mustaches came down the stairs, his expression frankly admiring when he spotted her.

"I'm Marc Edis," he said, extending his hand. "How may I be of service, Mademoiselle?"

Jacqueline shook hands. "I need to speak to you in private."

"May I enquire as to the nature of your business with me?"

The receptionist was paying them no attention, nevertheless Jacqueline lowered her voice. "My name is Jacqueline Belleau. I work for Colonel Guy de Galan in Paris."

The vapid smile left his face. "We'll go up to my office," he said, all business now. "Hold any calls for me, I'll be in conference," he told the receptionist.

Five minutes later Jacqueline was speaking by secured telephone to an angry Galan.

"Alexandre returned from the apartment an hour ago to report that you and Elizabeth were gone. Possibly shopping, he told me, although there was evidence that some clothing and personal articles were missing. I was getting ready to tear the city apart looking for you. But instead of that, you telephone from Latvia!"

"Elizabeth had a hunch that her father might be here. But it was just a hunch, *mon colonel.* Since we'd gotten nowhere with our other hunches I thought we would simply fly here, check it out, and immediately return to Paris if we did not find him."

"That was stupid and dangerous, Jacqueline. You should have at least warned Alexandre, in case something went wrong. As it stands we would not have had so much as a starting point to look for you."

Edis had tactfully retreated to another office, leaving her alone. She ran a hand across her eyes. She was as tired as she was stupid.

"Something *has* gone wrong," she said.

"Did you find McGarvey?" Galan asked.

"No."

"Is Elizabeth with you there at the embassy? Please tell me she is."

"She is not," Jacqueline said. "We went to the apartment that she thought her father had used on a previous assignment. Nothing looked out of the ordinary, so she went in while I waited at the end of the block. Ten minutes later an unmarked van pulled up to the curb, and a man came out of the building with Elizabeth, put her into the van and drove off."

"Maybe Riga police," Galan suggested. "Were your travel documents legitimate?"

"*Oui.* But I have a hunch they were Russian."

"Hunch? What hunch is this now?" Galan demanded.

"The man looked Russian."

"Everybody in Latvia looks Russian, Jacqueline!"

"If it had been the Riga police there would have been squad cars around. Men in uniform. But there was just the van, the driver, and the man with Elizabeth. No sirens, no lights, no radio antennas."

"I'll have to turn this over to the Americans. They can make inquiries with the Riga police. It's out of our hands now."

"Maybe the Russians tracked McGarvey here. Maybe they were waiting for him at the apartment when Elizabeth showed up."

"It's possible, but it's no longer our problem. McGarvey is out of France, if what you say is—"

"I can't abandon them," Jacqueline cut in.

"What can you do?" Galan asked. "Nothing, that's what! I want you back here on the first available flight."

"*Non.*"

"*Pourqoui pas?*"

"Because I'm convinced that McGarvey is in Moscow, and so is Elizabeth. I want you to send me there, in an official capacity."

"To do what, Jacqueline?" Galan demanded.

"To work with the Russian Police commission searching for Mac. Maybe I can find out something about Elizabeth, or her father. Maybe I can help stop this insanity."

"Where did you learn about this commission?"

"From Elizabeth. She said she was briefed before she left Washington."

Galan was silent for several long seconds.

"I think that you are not telling me everything," Galan said.

"At least let me try, *mon colonel.* I have done questionable things for France. Allow France to do something for me."

There was another long silence.

"First we'll make sure that Elizabeth wasn't arrested by the Riga police.

In the meantime you can continue to watch the apartment building. Perhaps McGarvey will return there."

"Please hurry," Jacqueline said.

"Rest assured, *ma p'tite*, I will."

Moscow

Touching down at what appeared to be an air force base, the afternoon was clear except to the north where a thick haze defined the city limits of the Russian capital. When they were on the taxiway, a pair of MiGs took off side by side with a mind-numbing roar on tails of black smoke. In the distance several helicopters seemed to be hovering over a stand of white birch. And in some of the hangars they passed, crews were working on partially disassembled fighter/interceptors.

Elizabeth had been allowed to use the bathroom, but she'd not been offered anything to eat or drink a second time. She got the feeling that they didn't care what she did. None of the crew paid any attention to her, and during the remainder of the two-hour flight Chernov had remained in the conference room with the other men.

Chernov, a smug look of satisfaction on his face, came out of the conference room with the others as the airplane stopped in front of an empty hangar. Several cars were waiting on the tarmac.

"You should have followed your orders, and not tried to interfere," one of the men said to her as he passed.

"The CIA should not have involved the man's daughter, Illen," another of the men countered angrily. "It's a bad business that will not have a happy ending for anyone."

The crewman opened the forward door as boarding stairs were pushed into place. Everyone got off the plane, climbed into all but one of the waiting cars and drove off, leaving Elizabeth alone with Chernov.

"Major Gresko is right, you should not have come to Riga, Ms. McGarvey. You've accomplished nothing. In fact you've jeopardized your father's safety."

"Will I be allowed to call my embassy?"

"That won't be possible."

"The Chief of Station here will start making noises pretty soon. President Kabatov is a reasonable—"

Chernov dismissed her with a gesture. "While it's true that you work for the CIA, you're supposed to be in Paris at this moment staking out your father's apartment with the French intelligence service in case he returns. No one knows that you came to Riga. That, you did on your own. Inventive, I'll give you that much. But stupid."

"My father is on his way to the States."

"No he's not. He's on his way here to Moscow. Probably in some clever disguise, almost certainly traveling under false papers. The last time I saw him was in Nizhny Novgorod where he was dressed as a soldier. I didn't know that he was coming then, but I know it now. And I know that he is coming here from Riga. There are only so many trains, airplanes, boat ferries and highways between here and there, and I assure you that all of them are being watched."

"Then what do you need me for?" Elizabeth asked defiantly, although she was sick at heart.

Chernov thought a moment.

"Because quite frankly, your father is very good at what he does, and I have the utmost respect for him, and maybe a little fear. He might somehow make it to Moscow. He might even be in Red Square on May Day when Tarankov makes his speech atop Lenin's Mausoleum."

"That's the day Tarankov will die."

"I think not," Chernov said. "Because you will be standing next to him on the reviewing stand. In plain sight for everyone, including your father, to see."

Elizabeth didn't know what to say.

Chernov had perched on the arm of one of the seats. He got up. "Now it's time for you to meet him. I think he'll enjoy talking to you, as I'm sure his wife Liesel will. They're very persuasive people."

THIRTY-SIX

Leipzig

At first appearances the banker Herman Dunkel and the car dealer Bernard Legler were cut of different cloth. Dunkel was an arch-conservative who habitually dressed in dark three-piece suits, and was concerned only with the bottom line. Legler, on the other hand, affected American western dress, spoke garishly, and was only concerned with hiding the bottom line from his accountant, and pocketing the money thus diverted. They had several things in common, however. Both had worked for the East German intelligence service Stasi until the Wall had come down. Both were shrewd businessmen who were profiting from Germany's reunification. And neither man trusted anybody.

They met for lunch at the Thüringer Hof, a centuries-old restaurant/tavern downtown, something they hadn't done in several weeks. They liked to get together occasionally to talk over some of the interesting cases they'd worked on in the Stasi. The darkly paneled bar was quiet and anonymous. Voices did not carry, something of interest to both men who had carefully hidden their true pasts. Legler suspected that this meeting was different, however, because of Dunkel's abrupt manner this morning on the telephone.

Their drinks came and Dunkel raised his glass. "*Prost.*"

"*Prost,*" Legler responded.

When the waitress was gone, Dunkel gave his old friend a quizzical look. "How is your business with Herr Allain proceeding? Have you received any further orders?"

"Just the two units," Legler said. "But his money is good."

"He has plenty of money, there is no doubt about that. In fact I made further inquiries into his Barclay's account—or I should say accounts." Dunkel glanced toward the door. "I have an old friend over there who has worked for the bank since the mid-eighties. In the past his information was reliable."

"It's wise to have such contacts."

Dunkel nodded sagely. "In part because of what I learned, I've asked Karl Franken to join us, I hope you don't mind."

Franken was chief investigating officer for the Federal Criminal Bureau for Saxony, also an ex-Stasi officer whose past was buried even deeper than theirs. It was rare that they had any contact with each other.

Legler held his reply for a moment, but he too glanced toward the door. "What are you worried about, Herman?"

"We have built comfortable lives for ourselves in the aftermath."

Legler acknowledged the obvious. "The future seems bright."

"I would not like to jeopardize what we have, for the sake of a minor profit."

"You're still speaking of Herr Allain," Legler said, careful to keep his voice neutral. "Admittedly the profit I made on the two units was not excessive. But if his business develops, it could turn into something worthwhile." He'd dropped his pseudo western mannerisms. "Unless of course his business is something other than he says it is."

"My thoughts precisely," Dunkel said.

A heavyset, round-faced man with curly gray hair, appeared in the doorway, spotted them seated near the rear of the bar, and came back.

"Gentlemen," he said, taking a seat.

"Good of you to join us, Karl," Dunkel said. "In point of fact we were just discussing you. We need your help with a somewhat . . . delicate matter."

The waitress came, and Franken ordered a dark beer.

"Would this have anything to do with, shall we say, past entanglements?"

"Good heavens, no," Dunkel said. "The past remains the past. All Germans are looking to the future. In that we are steadfast." Dunkel pursed his lips. "It's another matter, one possibly of an international criminal nature that Bernard and I may have been unwittingly caught up in."

"If you've gotten yourselves into trouble I don't know if I can help," Franken said quietly.

"I'm not talking about *that* kind of help, Karl. We've broken no German laws, nor do we intend doing so." Dunkel's voice was just as low as Franken's. What was being discussed here was nobody's business. "With the changing situation in the East, a businessman has to operate with care. Sometimes even forgoing an immediate profit if his business would possibly be in jeopardy."

Legler shot him a dark look, but Dunkel ignored it.

"Go on."

Dunkel explained the unexpected business deal that had fallen into their laps.

"His explanation to me why he was bringing his business to Leipzig, and not to Stuttgart, didn't ring true. Nor did his dealings with Bernard. Operating his business as he was, it would be impossible for him to make a profit. It made me wonder that either the man was a fool or he was working to another more, shall I say, mysterious purpose."

"*Es machts nichts*," Franken said, indifferently.

"But it does matter," Dunkel disagreed. "We have reputations to maintain that might run into difficulties should certain inquiries be made arising from a criminal proceeding." Dunkel looked frankly at the cop. "I'll do whatever it takes to maintain my good name. I have too much to lose otherwise. We all do."

"What can you fear from a Belgian?"

"He's not a Belgian. The passport he used was a fake. In fact the man is an American."

"How do you know?"

"His letter of credit arrived in the name of Pierre Allain, drawn on a foreign bank. When I did some checking I discovered, by accident, that Pierre Allain was apparently the name of his business, and was not in fact the name of an actual person. But the Belgian passport he showed me identified him as Allain. In fact the man's real name is Kirk McGarvey. An American, as I said."

Franken stiffened slightly, but then he shrugged and took a drink of his beer.

"Did you happen to make a copy of his passport?"

"I did," Legler said. "We needed it for the licensing and export documents."

"Fax it to my office this afternoon, would you?" Franken said. "Along with copies of all the paperwork on the cars."

"Okay."

"Is this name familiar to you, Karl?" Dunkel asked.

Franken shook his head. "*Nein*, but I'll check it out. At the very least he's broken several of our laws by using a false passport."

Dunkel hesitated a moment. "This won't affect us, will it?"

"Not to worry, Herman. You and Bernard have done nothing wrong. In fact you've done exactly the correct thing by bringing this to me."

"Then this is out of our hands now?"

Franken pushed his beer glass aside and got to his feet.

"Completely," he said to Dunkel. "But if he tries to make contact with you again, call me immediately."

"We'll certainly do that," Dunkel said.

Franken gave them an odd look, then turned and left the bar.

"*Gött im Himmel*, what the hell was that all about?" Legler demanded. "Who gives a damn what passport the man was using? I have a safe filled with them, as I imagine you do."

Dunkel smiled benignly. "Herr McGarvey's account with Barclay's bank, a secret account that can only be accessed by a number and a code word, is worth in the neighborhood of three and a half million British pounds."

Legler's eyes narrowed. "What's your point, Herman?"

"I am in possession of the account number as well as the code word," Dunkel said. "If Herr McGarvey were to find himself languishing in a German prison, he would not be in a position to challenge anyone who was to take over his financial holdings."

This time Legler smiled. "Hot damn," he said in English.

Paris

Lynch received the telephone call from Colonel Galan at his office in the U.S. Embassy at 2:15 P.M. He'd been working on his daily summary report for transmission to Langley and he was in a foul mood. McGarvey continued to elude them, and Ryan's star pupil, Elizabeth, had been of no help except for giving them Otto Rencke's name, which had resulted in a dead end. Galan sounded distant, almost resigned, as if he was at wit's end and was calling to explain why he could not go on, or even if he should have embarked on this mission in the first place.

"She's gone," he said when Lynch answered.

"Who's gone?" Lynch asked.

"Elizabeth McGarvey. And there's a good chance that the Russians have her."

"What are you talking about?" Lynch demanded angrily. If it was true he had no idea how he would explain this to Ryan, who'd taken a personal interest in the case.

"She and Jacqueline came up with the idea that McGarvey might be hiding out in an apartment he's used before in Riga. They flew up there early this morning without telling anybody and Elizabeth went in. Jacqueline was supposed to be backing her up, but before she could do anything Elizabeth came out of the apartment with a man, and they drove off together in a van."

"Was it McGarvey?"

"Jacqueline didn't get a very close look, but she didn't think it was him," Galan said. "My first thought was that the Riga police might have arrested her for some reason, but now I don't think so. I made a few inquiries up there, but one wants to say anything, beyond the fact that no young American woman was arrested anytime within the past month."

"Then it *was* McGarvey," Lynch said. "Now we're getting somewhere."

"I don't think so, and neither does Jacqueline. She was his lover long enough to recognize him even from a distance," Galan said. "In any event, the Riga police did admit that a Russian woman by the name of Raya Kisnelkov was arrested and turned over to the Russian Militia."

Lynch thought for a second.

"It's a long shot, but it could be a coincidence," he said, even though he didn't believe it himself. "At any rate how could the Russians have found out where McGarvey was hiding when we haven't been able to do it?"

"That's their back yard, Tom," Galan said. "I don't think there's any question that the Russians probably have her. And I don't think there can be any doubt what they intend using her for."

"Goddammit, we're helping the bastards. Is this how they repay us?"

"If they find out that she's working for the CIA they might ask what we were doing up there without telling about it."

"I'll call Colonel Bykov and ask him if he has her."

"Just like that?" Galan asked. "She's the daughter of a man who's gunning for Tarankov. What are you going to say when he accuses the CIA of secretly helping McGarvey? I hope you have a good answer, because if I were Bykov and you tried to tell me that you either didn't know Elizabeth was McGarvey's daughter, or that you didn't send her to Riga, I'd call you a liar."

"I see what you mean."

"What are you going to do?" Galan asked.

"I'll have to call Langley, because I don't know what the hell to do. How about you?"

"I'm sending Jacqueline to Moscow as an official liaison between the service and Colonel Bykov's commission," Galan said.

"Jesus."

"I know it sounds crazy. But maybe she can find out something before it's too late," Galan said.

"Keep me posted," Lynch said.

"*Oui*," Galan promised. "That bastard McGarvey has caused us a lot of trouble."

"He's an expert at it," Lynch agreed. "But the hell of it is that I almost hope he succeeds."

"So do I," Galan said quietly.

It took the Embassy's communications center ten minutes to find Howard Ryan at home, and establish an encrypted phone line to the DO. Lynch quickly explained what he'd just learned from Galan.

"Sending the Belleau woman to Moscow might not be the brightest move the French ever made," Ryan said.

"Sir?"

"Obviously she's under McGarvey's spell, which makes her less than worthless in this operation," Ryan said. He sounded smug.

"I'm afraid I don't completely understand, Mr. Ryan."

"Figure it out, Lynch," Ryan said irritably. "Neither we nor the French can find McGarvey. That's with all the resources of two of the best intelligence services in the West. Yet Elizabeth disappears with her father, and Mademoiselle Belleau concocts a story about how she was arrested by the Russians."

"Colonel Galan did say that the Riga police turned a woman over to the Russians—"

"A Russian woman," Ryan cut in. "The Latvians have no love for the Russians, and rightly so. I'm sure that such arrests happen all the time over there. But that's not the point, Lynch. The point is that Elizabeth is helping her father, and Jacqueline Belleau is on her way to Moscow, with her government's blessings, to work for Bykov's commission. The Russians were smart, creating that commission. But McGarvey's even smarter than they are. In one fell swoop he's recruited his daughter and managed to get one of his people inside the commission. I haven't any doubt that Jacqueline Belleau is McGarvey's little spy, and will somehow report to him every move they make."

Ryan was wrong, and Lynch was sure of it. But he also knew enough to keep his mouth shut. You might argue with some deputy directors of operations, but not with Ryan.

"It's out of your hands now," Ryan said. "I can't say that you did an outstanding job for us, but don't worry. Much better men than you have come up against McGarvey and lost. None of this will reflect badly on your record."

"Yes, sir," Lynch said, hardly believing his own ears. Not only was Ryan wrong, the man was an idiot.

Leipzig

BKA Chief Investigator Franken studied the dozen separate documents that Legler had faxed to his office, comparing the photograph in the Pierre Allain passport to that of the Kirk McGarvey photograph circulating on the Interpol wire.

"They don't exactly match, but the height, weight and date of birth are close," he told his deputy chief of special investigations.

"Passport photos never do, unless they're recent ones," Lieutenant Dieter Waltz said.

"According to the Belgians, the passport is legitimate."

"True, but they can't confirm Allain's address. Nobody by that name lives there or ever has."

"He has a proper driving license."

"Same story on the address," Waltz said. "But Allain has never been issued a voter registration card. Nor has he ever served in any unit of the Belgian military. Unusual for a man his age."

"Then you think this man is in reality Kirk McGarvey?" Franken asked.

"I think it's likely," Waltz answered carefully. "Which brings up an interesting speculation about him."

"What's that?"

"According to the Belgians, this passport was first issued fourteen years ago. Means McGarvey is a professional."

"How do you see that?" Franken asked, although he knew the answer. He liked to play devil's advocate with his people. It kept them on their toes, free from sloppy thinking.

"Why else did he maintain a false identity for so long? In all those years there's never been an inquiry about the passport. So up until now he's been a very careful man. Never made a mistake."

"Until now," Franken said quietly.

"What about his bank accounts?" Waltz asked.

"That's none of our business. For now the only law McGarvey has broken concerns his fake passport."

"Interpol wants him for something."

"Indeed," Franken said. He gathered up the papers and handed them to Waltz. "Put this on the Interpol wire."

"Shall I work up a cover report?"

Franken shook his head. "We'll leave the speculation to others. Get this out right away, and then get back to work. We've already spent too much time on this business."

"Do you want me to telephone the Latvian Federal Police?"

"I don't think it's necessary, Dieter," Franken said. "Anyone who's interested in Herr McGarvey will pick it off the wire."

Red Square

Chernov was standing on the reviewing stand above Lenin's Mausoleum when Militia Captain Petrovsky called his cellular telephone.

"Pierre Allain. He's traveling on a Belgian passport. The photos are a pretty good match."

"Where'd that come from?" Chernov asked, stepping back from the rail.

"The German Federal Police in Leipzig. But the best part is the Mercedes four-by-four automobiles. Allain is exporting them from Leipzig to Riga. Thing is the Latvian customs people show that two cars came in so far, but only in transit."

"To where?"

"Russia. It means he is coming by highway. Probably across the border near Zilupe. I sent this over to Gresko who'll alert the border crossing. We might still have a chance of stopping him."

"I want every square meter covered. What do we have up there?"

"Not much except for an air force training squadron at Velikiye Luki. That's near Toropets, about two hundred kilometers from the border. Shall I have them cover the highway?"

"Order them to send up everything they have."

"He won't get away this time, Colonel, I guarantee it," Petrovsky promised.

Tarankov's train was hidden near Klin less than fifty kilometers outside Moscow. Chernov had dropped McGarvey's daughter out there and had raced back into the city. But unless McGarvey had delayed leaving Latvia for some reason, he'd already be across the border somewhere between there and Moscow. The thought was almost too interesting to bear.

"I'm in Red Square. Have a helicopter pick me up in front of Lenin's Tomb as soon as possible. We'll follow the highway west."

"It'll be dark in a couple of hours."

"Then you'd better hurry, Captain."

Chernov broke the connection, pocketed his phone and looked out across Red Square again. In three days Russia would be Tarankov's. Before that happened McGarvey would be dead, and it would be time to get out for good. He decided that he wouldn't regret any of it.

THIRTY-SEVEN

On the Road to Moscow

About seventy-five miles east of the Latvian border, McGarvey followed a narrow dirt track off the highway down to a thick stand of birch and willows that followed a creek. Although most of the trees had not budded yet, the growth was thick enough to obscure the outline of the Mercedes from the highway and from the air. Even if someone was looking for him, which he doubted, he would be safe here until dark.

With the engine off, he stood smoking a cigarette as he listened to the burble of the gently flowing creek, and the distant hum of an occasional truck above on the highway. Through a stand of trees on the opposite side of the creek he could see a farm field rising to the crest of the hill. But there were no farm buildings or animals in sight. Nor did it seem as if the field had been worked in recent years, because it was overgrown with a brown stubble.

Crossing the border had presented no problems. When it was his turn the same customs official as before came out to examine his papers.

"No lunch this afternoon, Comrade Allain?" the official joked.

"Not this time," McGarvey said. "But I'll be back next week, and maybe I'll bring something good." He handed the official an envelope with five hundred marks in cash.

One of the border guards came out of the shack with the long-handled mirror, but the officer waved him back.

"Sometimes he takes his job too seriously," the officer said, pocketing the money. "A lot of them do."

The meaning was clear.

"Do you take a day off each week?" McGarvey asked.

"Sundays."

"I prefer to rest on Sundays myself."

"It's a good philosophy," the officer said. He stepped back and motioned for the gate to be raised.

With dusk beginning to settle in, McGarvey removed his gun from the computer, loaded it, and pocketed the spare magazines and silencer. Then he started on the extra spare tire, deflating it, popping the seal with the tire irons, and removing the plastic bags containing Voronin's KGB uniform. Next he unlatched the primary spare tire from its bracket on the cargo compartment lid, and removed the uniform cap. The cap and uniform went into a nylon zippered bag which he tossed in the back seat.

If he were to be stopped and searched before he got to Moscow he would have no explanation for the uniform. But since he would be driving at night, and planned on remaining well within the speed limit, there was no reason for him to be stopped.

He reattached the main spare tire to its bracket, then reinflated the extra spare tire using the electric pump plugged into the car's cigarette lighter.

When that was done, he tossed the pump and tire irons into the thicker brush, cleaned his hands in the creek, then lit a cigarette as he waited for the deepening dusk to turn to darkness.

A faint sound came to him on the light breeze and he cocked an ear to listen. A helicopter, he thought. Maybe more than one. He tossed the cigarette aside, and stepped away from the overhanging trees.

The sun had already set but the western sky was still dimly aglow, making it easy for him to pick out a formation of four helicopters heading cross country toward the southwest. They were Mi-24 Hind attack helicopters, their silhouettes easily distinguishable. So far as he knew the FSK did not use such aircraft, which meant there was probably a military base somewhere in the vicinity. The most likely explanation was that the formation was on a training maneuver.

McGarvey glanced up at the highway. The helicopters were heading in the general direction of the border. Such exercises were common because of the ongoing trouble between the Latvian government and Russians still living in Latvia. The maneuver could be one of intimidation.

But he doubted it. The timing was too coincidental. But if they knew or suspected that he would be coming across from Latvia, then a great deal of his preparations had somehow been blown. Possibly by Yemlin. Possibly his Allain passport had been compromised. The list wasn't endless but it was long. He'd been on too many assignments where a number of little errors and coincidences added up to a major problem for him to ever believe that he was truly safe.

When the helicopters finally disappeared in the distance, he started the Mercedes. At the crest of the hill he paused a moment to make certain there was no traffic in either direction, then headed east on the M9 toward Moscow a little over three hundred miles away, as he considered his options should the helicopters return.

In the Air West of Moscow

It was dark by the time the modified Hormone-D search and rescue helicopter finally cleared Moscow's airspace, the city of Volokolamsk directly ahead of them. Petrovsky had picked Chernov up on Red Square late because there'd been some delay in obtaining the necessary clearances from the Moscow District Military Command to overfly the city. Once they'd passed the outer ring highway the pilot found the M9 and followed it west, the throttles pushed their stops. The crew had not been told what the mission was about, but they were suitably impressed by Bykov's credentials so that when they were told to hustle they asked no questions. They hustled.

Traffic on the motorway was heavy, but Chernov expected that it would thin out to next to nothing on the other side of Volokolamsk, which was one hundred kilometers from the center of Moscow, because there were no major cities between there and the Latvian border. The problem, of course, was picking out a specific automobile in the dark, when all that was distinguishable were headlights.

Petrovsky had been speaking on the radio, and he came forward to where Chernov was braced behind the co-pilot, a concerned expression on his face.

"He crossed the border two hours ago."

"Under the Pierre Allain passport?" Chernov demanded.

"*Da.* He's driving a gunmetal-gray Mercedes sport utility vehicle, with the proper in-transit documents. There was no reason for the customs people to detain him because the warrant for McGarvey didn't show up until fifteen minutes ago."

"What about the air force up there?"

Petrovsky looked uncomfortable. "They sent up a squadron of Mi-24s, but their instructions were to remain within their training area. They're not authorized to go any farther."

"Exactly how far is that?" Chernov asked, holding his temper in check.

"Two hundred kilometers from the border."

"They spotted nothing, of course. Because he had nearly a two-hour head start," Chernov said. He turned forward and tapped the pilot on the shoulder. The man cocked his head, but did not take his eyes off the windshield.

"Sir?"

"As soon as we get to the other side of Volokolamsk, I want you to fly right up the middle of the M9, but no higher than eight or ten meters. I want to be able to identify every vehicle down there. Can you do that?"

"Yes sir," the pilot said. "What are we looking for, Colonel?"

"A gray Mercedes four-by-four."

"Will do," the pilot said.

Chernov turned back to Petrovsky. "Radio the base commander up there and tell him that I want his helicopters to start again at the border, and follow the M9 toward us, at an altitude of no more than eight or ten meters."

"You mean to catch the bastard between us?" Petrovsky said.

"That's the idea." Chernov said, although he didn't think it was going to be quite that easy.

Petrovsky started to turn away when Chernov called him back.

"When you've done that, I want every cop in Moscow to be on the lookout for that gray Mercedes. It was stolen."

"He'll never get that far, Colonel."

"Just do it," Chernov ordered sharply.

"What are they supposed to do if they spot him? My street cops wouldn't be any match for him if he's as good as you say he is."

"Tell them to report directly to you, and follow him. Nothing more."

En route to Moscow

It was nearly eight o'clock when the Mercedes pulled off the main highway near a tiny hamlet dark at this hour, followed a bumpy road up to the onion domes of an Orthodox church and parked under the shelter of a grape arbor at the entrance to a cemetery. McGarvey shut off the headlights, got the gas cans from the back and filled the tank.

He estimated that he was two hundred miles from the outskirts of Moscow, and with any luck he'd be in the city well before midnight with plenty of time to take care of one final preparation before he went to ground.

What little traffic he'd encountered were mostly trucks heading east, with an occasional passenger car, and one bus.

The only city of any size that he would have to pass through would be Volokolamsk. By then the traffic would pick up, but it was only another fifty or sixty miles into the outskirts of Moscow where he figured he might be safe unless they'd transmitted a description of his car to the police there. But he'd picked this color Mercedes because it was common in Moscow.

Finished with the gas cans, he put them back in the cargo section, and happened to glance down at the highway east of the village in time to see what at first appeared to be a truck. Its headlights were unusually bright and seemed very far off the ground.

McGarvey stepped around the back of the Mercedes to get a better look, when the lights rose up into the sky at the same moment he heard the distinct chop of a helicopter's rotors.

As the machine slowly flew over the village, a spotlight searched the main road and the side streets.

McGarvey eased back a little farther under the grape arbor. This was no coincidence. The military helicopters at the border had been conducting a search. And now this machine was coming directly down the M9, obviously searching for someone.

The helicopter's spotlight went out as it dropped down to twenty feet or so above the highway on this side of the village, and headed west.

It was possible that the military helicopters he'd seen earlier were a part of a coordinated search, and would be heading east by now. When this helicopter met them without any sign of McGarvey they would turn around and retrace the highway, greatly expanding their search pattern to include hiding places such as the trees where he'd stopped by the creek, and this grape arbor.

While he waited for the helicopter's lights to disappear into the distance he studied his road map. Three main highways entered Moscow from the west. The M9, which he was on, came from Riga. The M10 from St. Petersburg was well to his north, and the M1 from Smolensk and Minsk was about ninety miles to the south. Even the most recent Russian maps, however, showed very few of the secondary roads that connected the smaller towns and villages between the main motor routes, although he knew they were there.

The three highways funneled into Moscow, so the farther east he got before turning south, the closer he would be to the M1. If he got off the M9 now, he might get bogged down in the countryside and never reach the other highway. But if he remained on the M9 too long, the helicopter that had just passed might turn around and overtake him. One hour, he decided, as he watched the receding lights of the helicopter. Then, no matter how far he got, he would turn off the M9 and head across country to the south.

Abandoning the speed limit, McGarvey barreled down the highway at ninety to one hundred miles per hour, slowing only for small towns and villages, and the occasional truck still on the highway. Each time he saw the oncoming lights of another vehicle, he slowed down and prepared to douse his own headlights and pull off the road until he made certain that what he was seeing wasn't another helicopter.

It was a few minutes after nine when he came upon an unmarked paved road heading south. He'd been watching his rearview mirror, but so far there'd been no sign of the returning helicopter. Nonetheless he figured he'd pushed his luck far enough, and turned onto the secondary road. Within five miles he came to a collection of a half-dozen peasant houses, shuttered and dark, and on the other side of this village the road continued, but the pavement stopped.

The winter had been a harsh one, and the spring very late in coming so that the road, which at times was little more than a dirt track, was still reasonably firm. In a couple of weeks it would turn into a ribbon of deep sticky mud that even the big Mercedes might not be able to manage.

For stretches he was able to push the Mercedes to speeds in excess of sixty miles per hour, but for most of the way he had to keep below forty, and sometimes he was even slowed to a crawl as he had to detour around ruts that were five or six feet deep.

He was passing through mostly farmlands, he could tell that much but little else in the dark. Occasionally he passed through tiny villages of eight or ten crude hovels, and for twenty minutes he had a conglomeration of lights in sight, low down on the horizon to the west, which he took to be a factory, or possibly a power station.

But he never saw the helicopter again, so by 10:30 when he finally reached the M1 near the town of Gagarin with the outskirts of Moscow barely one hundred miles away, he dropped back to the posted speed limit of 90 kilometers per hour and lit his first cigarette in two and a half hours.

West of Moscow

For nearly four hours there was no sign of the gray Mercedes anywhere on the highway between the Latvian border and the outskirts of Moscow. Given the time since McGarvey had crossed the border, he could have made it to Moscow by now. So far Petrovsky had received three radioed reports of Mercedes four-by-fours in Moscow, but in each sighting the cops on the ground checked the license tags with the motor vehicle department and found them to be legitimate. In all three sightings the officers reported that the drivers were not alone, they carried passengers, something Chernov didn't think McGarvey would do.

"Where the hell did he go?" Petrovsky asked a little before midnight. "He couldn't have disappeared into thin air, unless he's hiding somewhere."

They'd touched down in a farm field just off the highway three hundred kilometers from Moscow to take on fuel from one of the air force Mi-24s, and stretch their legs.

"He might have spotted the helicopters and done just that," Chernov said, staring into the darkness. "He's not a stupid man."

"If that's true than he knows that it's all over for him. He'll probably ditch the car and try to make it to the nearest border. He might be hiding somewhere in Volokolamsk, changing his identity and waiting for the morning train."

"Do we have anyone watching the station?"

"No, but I'll see to it. We'll close that place up so tightly that even a mouse couldn't get through," Petrovsky said. "It's his only option now. He's not on the M9, which is the only route from Riga into Moscow, so he has to be in Volokolamsk."

Petrovsky went back to the helicopter to radio his instructions, leaving Chernov standing by himself in the darkness.

He shook his head, tiredly. McGarvey was smart, but he wasn't a fool. If he had seen the helicopters, and realized that they were searching for him, he would have to turn tail and run. But he had not run. Chernov was certain of it, because men like McGarvey never did.

Chernov thought about it, putting himself in McGarvey's position. His mission was to assassinate Tarankov, for which he had a plan. He would understand that things could go wrong, they always did, and he would have planned for them. McGarvey would be able to think clearly on the run. Even backed into a corner, he'd find a way. His extensive file made that quite clear.

Chernov turned and looked at the helicopters. The fueling operation was complete, and the squadron commander, who was a young man barely out of his twenties, started over to where Chernov was waiting.

Petrovsky was wrong. It came to Chernov all of a sudden. The M9 was *one* way into Moscow, but not the only highway. To the north was the M10, and to the south the M1, either of which could be reached with the right vehicle. Such as a half-track or, now before the fields and dirt road had turned to mud, a Mercedes four-by-four.

The squadron commander saluted. "Your helicopter has been refueled, Colonel. Do you want us to make another sweep back to the border, or should we concentrate our efforts toward Moscow?"

Petrovsky jumped out of the Hormone-D and came across the field in a dead run.

"Return to base, Lieutenant," Chernov said. "Thank your people for me, but your work is finished for tonight."

"Yes, sir," the squadron commander said. He saluted and went back to his helicopter.

Petrovsky came up in a rush. "The bastard's in Moscow. He must have been spooked because somehow he made it to the M1. They spotted him on the outer ring road."

"They didn't try to stop him, did they?" Chernov demanded.

"*Nyet.* They're just following him for the moment. There's enough traffic that they think they can pull it off without being spotted themselves, especially if he's tired and he thinks he's home free."

He and Chernov hurried back to their helicopter. "Inform your people that I'll have their heads if they lose him. All we need is one hour to get up there."

"The sonofabitch has made a big mistake after all," Petrovsky said triumphantly.

"Don't count on it," Chernov said.

Moscow

McGarvey parked on the outer fringes of the bustling Dinamo flea market amongst several rows of big Mercedes and BMW sedans, each with one or two bodyguards who eyed him cautiously. He shut off the engine and lights and sat in the darkness smoking a cigarette, the window down. He was very tired. His eyes were gritty, his throat was raw from too many cigarettes and his stomach was sour from lack of food. Several times he thought he might have picked up a tail. But each time he doubled back it was only a Moscow police car on ordinary patrol.

With luck they were still searching for this car somewhere along the M9, figuring that he had pulled off the highway and was hiding under cover. In the morning they would flush him out. Unless Bykov or the people with him were smarter than that. For the next two days, he thought, he would have to lay low. They knew he was coming, and by morning they would know that he had reached Moscow. It made his task even more difficult, but still not impossible.

He tossed the cigarette away, checked the load on his gun, then locked up the car and walked around to the west side of the huge parking lot where the entrepreneur Vasha was leaning up against an American HumVee and talking to a couple of surly-looking men. When he spotted McGarvey he said something to them, and they left.

"Ah, Corporal Shostokovich returns," the beefy man said. He stank of stale sweat and booze. He looked beyond McGarvey. "I just saw Arkady. Did he bring you out here tonight? He has a lot of money these days. Maybe an inheritance?"

"Something like that," McGarvey said. "Maybe you'll have an inheritance too."

The salesman got a bottle of vodka from the HumVee, cracked the seal and gave it to McGarvey, who took a big drink, then handed it back. Vasha took a deep drink, and smacked his lips.

"Do you want to purchase another uniform?"

McGarvey shook his head. "This time my needs are more specific, and perhaps even difficult to fulfill."

Vasha motioned toward his Russian army supply trucks. "I have a lot of good stuff here. Some of it pretty damned important, you know." He shrugged. "Of course if you want a MiG it would take a little longer. But I can get one."

"A Dragunov," McGarvey said quietly. "Two magazines of ammunition, ten shots each, a good telescopic sight, and a bag big enough to carry it all when the rifle is partially disassembled."

"An interesting choice," Vasha said. The 7.62mm rifle was the Soviet sniper weapon, very simple, lightweight and extremely accurate. "Would there be anything else?"

"A pair of good bolt-cutters."

"A small explosive device might be more effective, if you could tell me your exact need."

"Too noisy."

"What about the noise of the rifle? Given a few days a suitable silencer could be manufactured that would not seriously deteriorate the weapon's accuracy."

"It's not necessary."

The salesman took another drink and passed the bottle to McGarvey.

"What currency would you pay me for this . . . equipment?"

"American dollars."

Vasha thought about it for a moment. "Five thousand."

"For that amount of money I could hire a shooter who would have his own weapon and there would be no need for me to come back to you for more equipment in the weeks to come."

Vasha licked his lips. "Then this is not the *big* project?"

"Only one of many to begin with."

"How do I know that you will come back?"

"You don't," McGarvey said. "My top offer is one thousand."

"I'd need three—"

"One thousand, and I need the equipment right now."

Vasha hesitated only a moment, then grinned and nodded. "Trust is very important among businessmen," he said. He started to turn, but McGarvey grabbed his arm in an iron grip.

"It would be unfortunate if the rifle you sold me was anything less than perfect. A misfire at the wrong moment could be fatal to you."

"Trust is not only important, it is a two-way street," Vasha said, evenly. "Now if you have the money with you let's do our business."

McGarvey followed him to one of the supply trucks where the salesman produced a pair of hydraulic bolt cutters that were nearly a meter long, and a soft leather carryall with shoulder straps and lots of zippered compartments.

From a second truck he pulled an aluminum case out of a large wooden crate, and opened it on the tailgate. Nested in foam rubber cutouts was a used but apparently well-maintained, oiled and disassembled Dragunov sniper rifle, and powerful scope.

"The factory new rifles can be temperamental and often need adjustments. But this gun is nearly perfect. It's sighted in for a range of one hundred fifty to two hundred meters. If your range is outside those limits, the gun will have to be resighted."

McGarvey inspected the components as Vasha got two magazines of ammunition for the rifle, along with a gun cleaning kit and oil. "This is exactly what I wanted," McGarvey said. He counted out the money as Vasha carefully placed the rifle, magazines and cleaning supplies in the leather bag.

"Anything else?"

"No," McGarvey said, handing the salesman the money. "If all goes well,

I'll see you in a few weeks for more equipment. Maybe something quite a bit larger."

"I'll be here," Vasha said.

Slinging the heavy bag over his shoulder McGarvey walked away, taking a roundabout route back toward where he'd left the Mercedes.

A hundred yards from the car, the cabby Arkady Astimovich pulled up beside him, at the same moment he heard the sound of a helicopter coming in low and fast from the west.

"Climb in and I'll get you out of here," Astimovich said urgently.

"It's okay, I've got another Mercedes—"

"*Yeb vas*, I know," Astimovich cut in. "I saw you drive up. But the goddamn cops were right behind you. They're all over the place now."

The helicopter was getting closer.

He hated to leave the uniform, but he'd removed Voronin's name from the lining, and there was nothing in the laptop computer that would lead back to Rencke. But Chernov was damned good, even better than his brother.

He clambered into the cab, and ducked below the level of the windows as Astimovich took off in the opposite direction from the Mercedes on the heels of dozens of police cars coming out from the city, their lights flashing, their sirens blaring.

It was 1:15 A.M. when the helicopter touched down at the edge of the vast Dinamo Stadium parking lot. Chernov and Petrovsky dismounted and hurried over to the knot of policemen standing around the Mercedes four-by-four.

"Who is in charge of this operation?" Chernov asked mildly, though he was seething with rage.

A Militia lieutenant was summoned from one of the patrol cars, where he'd been busy on the radio. He saluted crisply.

"You were told to follow this car, not mount World War Three," Chernov said.

"We did follow the car, sir," he said. He gestured toward the flea market. "But the driver disappeared in there someplace, so I ordered the entire parking lot surrounded. My people are letting them out one by one after a thorough search. We'll find him."

"You think so?"

"Yes, sir," the lieutenant replied enthusiastically.

"Very well. But if you don't find him here tonight, you will be placed under arrest and tried for failure to follow orders. Is that clear?"

The lieutenant's face fell. "Yes, sir."

"I suggest that you get on with it," Chernov said, and the lieutenant scurried back to his radio car.

"Over here," Petrovsky said, from the Mercedes.

Chernov walked over. A KGB general's uniform was laid out in the backseat, along with a laptop computer.

"Well, we know how he planned on getting close," Petrovsky said. "Now that he doesn't have this, maybe he'll finally give up."

"He won't quit," Chernov said. He glanced toward the flea market. "He came here to buy a weapon, and he means to use it."

"Then maybe we're lucky, maybe he's still here."

Chernov shook his head. "He's gone. As soon as he spotted the first police car he got out. It's just as much my fault as it is that lieutenant's."

"Were you serious about arresting him?"

"Either that or just shoot him and get it over with, I really don't care which," Chernov said. "In the meantime McGarvey has made it to Moscow, and it's up to us to find him in the next forty-eight hours, whatever it takes." Chernov gave Petrovsky a hard stare. "And I do mean *whatever* it takes."

THIRTY-EIGHT

Club Grand Dinamo

McGarvey sat across the large desk from Yakov Ostrovsky, his legs crossed, smoking a cigarette and sipping French champagne, while he maintained an outward calm. Astimovich waited with Ostrovsky's bodyguards and ferret-faced accountant in an outer office, while the boss talked serious business with the Belgian who'd apparently gotten himself in some big trouble. No one else in the busy club knew what was going on, and Ostrovsky agreed to let it remain that way for the moment, although he was extremely suspicious and therefore wary, but curious. It was this curiosity that McGarvey planned on using to his advantage over the next forty-eight hours.

"I'm told that there was some excitement at the flea market this evening," the Mafia boss said. "You had to leave the car you were bringing to me."

McGarvey shrugged indifferently. "There are ten more coming by transport truck from Riga in a few days."

"If you were stopped because of one car, what makes you think that you'll be successful bringing in ten?"

"Because the next shipment won't be traceable to me. They're coming directly to you if we can make a deal. But I'll have to lay low here until they arrive."

"Then what?"

"I'll be returning to Riga to arrange for further shipments," McGarvey said. "That is if you want more cars."

"Situations change," Ostrovsky said, a calculating expression in his eyes. "Maybe we'll have to rework the conditions of our business arrangement. Maybe the risk has become too great for me. I have a serious position to maintain."

"I'm listening," McGarvey said.

"It strikes me that the Militia went to a lot of trouble to corner an ordinary smuggler tonight."

"But that's just the point, Yakov, I'm not an ordinary smuggler. In fact you've already verified that the papers for the car are valid. It's the same for the car I had to abandon tonight. The Militia was after me because I killed two of their officers outside of Volokolamsk."

"Now that's a crime those boys do take seriously," Ostrovsky said quietly. "Why did you do it?"

"I was speeding, and since I was driving such an obviously expensive automobile they suggested that I needed protection."

"Why didn't you pay it?"

"I would have been forced to pass on the extra cost to you."

Ostrovsky shrugged.

"The fact is I don't like to be pushed around," McGarvey said, allowing a hard edge into his voice. "I was tired, they were being unreasonable, and when I told them to fuck themselves they ordered me to get out of the car. So I shot them dead, dragged their bodies into the ditch, and drove the rest of the way here. Somebody must have seen something, maybe a farmer, I don't know. It was just rotten luck."

"What were you doing at the flea market?"

"I bought a couple of souvenirs for a friend in Brussels," McGarvey said. He allowed a faint smirk. "This business is a two-way street, you know."

"Let me see the gun you used," Ostrovsky said.

McGarvey hesitated a moment, then leaned forward so that he could remove the Walther from its holster at the small of his back. He ejected the magazine, locked the empty breach block in the open position and handed it across the desk.

Ostrovsky examined the gun, then sniffed the barrel. "This weapon has not been fired recently."

"I cleaned it."

The Mafia boss nodded. "You are an efficient man."

"*Da*," McGarvey said. "There's no problem importing cars to you. The only problem that exists at the moment is a place for me to stay for a few days. I would have thought that you would provide me the professional courtesy." McGarvey inclined his head.

Ostrovsky sat back, a big grin on his face. "I wouldn't have it any other way, Monsieur Allain," he said. "I will be happy to have you as a guest of the club until my cars safely arrive." His smile disappeared. "Since it's only for a few days, I'll require you to remain here, out of sight within the club." Ostrovsky smiled again. "Think of it as a well-deserved vacation."

"That's fine with me," McGarvey said, returning the smile. "But you might warn your staff that I'm a light sleeper. A *very* light sleeper."

Aboard Tarankov's Train

Elizabeth McGarvey lay fully clothed on the narrow bed in the darkness of the tiny train compartment, trying without luck to catch at least a few hours sleep. Her heart refused to slow down, and her stomach ached from fear and worry.

By now Jacqueline would have reported her missing, and word would have been passed to Tom Lynch in Paris, who would have in turn informed Ryan at Langley. But there was nothing any of them could do to help her, simply because nobody knew where she'd been taken.

She had, for all intents and purposes, dropped off the face of the earth, because even if they somehow knew she'd been taken to Russia, even the Russians had no real idea where Tarankov's train was located at any given time, nor did they seem to want to know.

In a little more than forty-eight hours, Tarankov would sweep into Moscow, mount the reviewing stand atop Lenin's tomb and tell his countrymen, and the world, that he was the new supreme leader of Russia, and would by whatever means necessary restore the old Soviet Union to all of its past glory. Sometime during the speech her father would try to kill him, but at that moment he would get the shock of his life. He would see his own daughter standing beside the madman, and there was no predicting what he would do about it. She was sick with dread.

Chernov had told her all of that on the way out to the isolated spot where the camouflaged train was parked as if he were merely telling her about the weather, or about some sports team that was campaigning for a championship. What bothered her most was his easy confidence, and the obvious competence of the rugged-looking commandoes guarding the train. Nobody had maltreated her, or had even raised their voices. She'd been politely escorted to this compartment the moment she'd arrived. They'd given her a bottle of wine, a platter of breads, cheeses, pickles, herring and even caviar. A polite soldier showed her how to use the compact shower, asking that she conserve water because their tankage was limited, and supplied her with clean battle fatigues in her size, wool slippers, and a small kit containing a hair brush and a few basic toiletries.

For the first couple of hours, expecting to be summoned by Tarankov, she refused to eat or drink anything, or take a shower and change into the clean clothes. It was an act of defiance on her part that finally seemed futile as time passed and her isolation deepened. She'd tried to open the window, but even the blackout curtains were locked in place. She'd listened at the door, but all she could make out were the sounds of machinery running softly somewhere, and the distant undertones of male voices, the words indistinct and impossible to make out.

Around 11:00 by her watch, her hunger finally overcame her stubbornness and she finished half the bottle of wine and ate most of the quite good food on the tray. Afterward she'd taken a shower, washed her bra and panties and hung them up to dry, then got dressed in the fatigues and wool slippers. Well fed and freshly bathed, she'd shut out the lights, lay down on the cot and tried to go to sleep. But as dead tired as she was her mind refused to shut down, and she replayed the events since Riga over and over.

Something brushed her lips and she woke with a start, her heart accelerating. The corridor door was ajar and in the dim light she made out the narrow, thin-lipped features of a woman standing over her.

"I mean you no harm," the woman said quietly in heavily accented English.

Elizabeth fumbled for the bedside light switch, flipped it on, then sat up.

The woman stepped back. She was slightly built with deep-set, expressive eyes, and medium-length blonde hair. She was dressed in UCLA sweats. A little color had come to her high cheeks and forehead.

"Who are you?" Elizabeth asked, her voice still thick with sleep.

"I'm Liesel Tarankov," the woman said. Her eyes lowered slightly. "You're not what we expected."

Elizabeth looked down at the front of her fatigue shirt. The top three buttons were undone, exposing her bare breasts, and her stomach did a slow roll. She clutched her shirt together. "Get out you bitch," she tried to shout, but she swallowed her words.

Liesel laughed. "I don't think that you're in any position to give orders, my dear."

"When my father shows up—"

"By then it will be too late for you," Liesel said. She reached back and closed the door.

"Are you a lesbian?"

"I haven't had that pleasure since my college days. But seeing you on that bed like Sleeping Beauty, some of the old memories came back." Liesel cocked her head to listen for something.

"I won't be so easy."

"Oh, come on, Elizabeth, you can't tell me that you didn't fool around in the dark at that school of yours in Switzerland."

Elizabeth looked around for a suitable weapon, her eyes lighting on the half-full wine bottle. She lunged for it, but Liesel was too quick for her, snatching the bottle off the tray before she could reach it.

"I believe you're going to be even more interesting than I imagined," Liesel said, and she smiled with anticipation.

Elizabeth opened her mouth to scream.

"Please go ahead and cry out for help, you might learn something about the real world," Liesel said. "Washington and New York might be dangerous places for a young woman, but you can always call nine-one-one, yes? Help is just a telephone call away." Liesel shook her head, her lips down-turned. "I'm so sorry little girl, but there is no nine-one-one for you here."

"Then I'll kill you."

"You may try, but I'm older and more experienced. And before you tell me about the wonderful hand-to-hand combat training you received at the CIA's school, it is a lie. We have checked. You have received no training."

"Maybe my father taught me," Elizabeth shot back, for want of anything else to say. Nobody was coming to her rescue. She was going to have to work this out herself. One thing was certain in her mind, however, and that was if Liesel Tarankov touched her she was going to kill the woman.

"Your father was never home long enough to teach you anything. He couldn't keep his wives, nor can he even manage to sustain a relationship with any of his whores." Liesel chuckled. "Of course what can you expect of a man whose parents spied for us?"

The woman had picked the wrong topic. Although Elizabeth was still frightened, a calmness came over her.

"You're nothing more than an ignorant slut, but then what can you expect from an East German," Elizabeth said in Russian, and she was satisfied to see a slight reaction in Liesel's eyes. "General Baranov had that story about my grandparents planted years ago, and by now everybody knows it for what it is, nothing more than a crude lie. I don't even think Colonel Bykov, or should I say Leonid Chernov, believes it."

Liesel gave her an appraising look. "Of course if you prefer, there are two hundred boys here who've been without a woman for months. They might not be so gentle."

"What's the trouble, are they tired of you already?"

Before Liesel could make a move, the door opened and Yevgenni Tarankov stuck his head in.

"Here you are," he said.

It took a moment for Elizabeth to recognize him, because he was older looking than in the photographs she'd studied, and it took a second longer for her to realize that he seemed slightly vexed and realize that she could take advantage of the moment because Liesel looked guilty.

"If you mean to use me to lure my father here, I can understand that," Elizabeth blurted.

Tarankov looked mildly at her.

"But if that includes your wife trying to rape me while I'm asleep, then your plan won't work. Because she says that she'll kill me if I resist."

Liesel laughed out loud.

Elizabeth removed her hand from her fatigue shirt to show that it was unbuttoned, and then opened it to expose her breasts. "When I awoke she was kissing me and fondling my breasts. And believe me, I think I'm in big enough trouble as it is without imagining something like that."

Tarankov's forehead creased and his wide eyes narrowed.

Liesel looked from Elizabeth to her husband. "I don't care what you believe, Zhennia, because now I don't think either one of us will let the other fuck her."

Liesel brushed past her husband and disappeared down the corridor, leaving him staring at Elizabeth.

Lefortovo

Chernov called a meeting in his office for 9:00 A.M., with Gresko and Petrovsky. It was dawn before every person and vehicle at the Dinamo Stadium flea market had been thoroughly checked out, and McGarvey had not turned up. The only news of any interest, at least to the Militia, was that twenty-seven arrests had been made for everything from illegal arms dealing to counterfeiting documents, and illegal financial transactions. Some of those who'd been picked up had been on the Militia's most wanted list for two years or more. Before last night there'd never been the initiative to clean out the flea market. But if anyone had seen McGarvey, they weren't talking.

"He was there, for maybe as long as an hour," Chernov told them. "Which gave him plenty of time to buy anything he needed. A weapon. Papers."

"But he left the KGB uniform behind, which means that part of his plan has been ruined," Petrovsky pointed out.

"Maybe it was a ruse," Gresko suggested. "To make us believe that's how he was going to get close to Tarankov."

"I don't think so," the Militia captain argued. "I agree with Colonel Bykov that he showed up at the flea market to pick up a weapon, but when he realized that he was cornered he ran."

"To where?" Gresko asked.

"Maybe back to the border. Or, maybe the bastard has help."

"It wasn't Yemlin."

"No, but there are others in Moscow who'd be willing to do it for a price. And McGarvey is a rich man. He could buy his way out of just about everything. Look at that pussy wagon he brought over. It has to be worth plenty."

Gresko threw up his hands. "Then we're back to square one. He's in

Moscow, and we've got two days to catch him. That is if Tarankov actually shows up for the May Day celebrations."

"He will," Chernov said absently, thinking of something else.

"What makes you so sure about that, Colonel?" Gresko asked.

Chernov dismissed the obvious question with a gesture. "Everybody in Moscow knows it by now. Everyone in the entire country knows it."

"Then why not concentrate our efforts on arresting him when he gets here?" Gresko said. He glanced at Petrovsky. "The military is obviously incapable of doing the job, but we could pull it off. We don't know where McGarvey is, but we do know where Tarankov will be and what he'll be doing."

"A fine idea, Major, except for two problems," Chernov said. "In the first place our job is to find and stop McGarvey. Nothing more."

"If the situation was explained to General Yuryn, I think he'd see our point."

"Maybe he'd see that we've failed so far," Chernov pointed out. "But be that as it may, the second problem is Tarankov's followers. There'll probably be a million of them in Red Square the day after tomorrow. Now, if you want to march up to the speaker's platform and clap handcuffs on the man in front of all those people, then be my guest."

"I see what you mean," Gresko said. "But I think that if the army doesn't arrest him before May Day, and McGarvey fails to kill him, then we're all lost."

"How do you mean that?" Chernov asked calmly.

"Tarankov will take over the government. I don't think anybody doubts it."

"That's politics," Chernov said. "In the meantime we have our orders, unless you want to quit."

Again Gresko glanced at Petrovsky, but then he sighed. "No, Colonel, we won't quit. But frankly McGarvey is a lot better than any of us ever expected."

"He's just a man. He makes mistakes. Already he's lost his car, and the KGB uniform."

"And he's lost money," Petrovsky said. "The documents show that he was importing the car from Leipzig via Riga. Which means he had a buyer for it here in Moscow. Find the buyer and we might find McGarvey."

"Who in Moscow can afford such a vehicle?" Chernov asked.

"A few politicians, some businessmen," Petrovsky said. "The Mafia. But they won't talk to us—"

"Wait a minute," Gresko broke in. "McGarvey was importing that car from Leipzig, right? Maybe it wasn't the first. Maybe he brought others across, to establish himself as an importer. Somebody who paid out a lot of bribes, and was well liked by the people who could hide him."

"Back to the Mafia," Chernov said. "Check vehicle registration to see who bought a similar vehicle or vehicles over the past couple of weeks. It might provide us with a lead, if your people have the balls to ask the questions of the right people. Find his buyers and we might find McGarvey. He's made at least one mistake so far, maybe he'll make another."

At the door on the way out, Petrovsky had another thought. "What did you do with his daughter?"

"We had a chat, but she's just as much in the dark as the rest of us," Chernov said matter of factly. "So I dropped her off at her embassy."

"Just as well," Petrovsky said. "We don't need to get into it with the CIA right now."

THIRTY-NINE

Club Grand Dinamo

McGarvey woke very slowly from a profoundly deep, dreamless sleep. His mouth was dry, his muscles ached, he had a tremendous headache, and as he struggled back to complete consciousness he realized that he must have been drugged. Normally he awoke instantly. It was a habit of self-preservation that every field officer who survived for long developed.

He was naked under the covers, although after he had eaten he had flopped down fully clothed on the bed to catch a few hours rest. At the time he'd thought it was possible he'd been drugged, so that they could disarm him and check the contents of the leather satchel, but there'd been little he could have done to prevent it. He needed food and rest.

The lights were on, and when he opened his eyes, Ostrovsky, who was seated astraddle a chair at the end of the bed, smiled wide with pleasure.

"Ah, you're finally awake, Mr. McGarvey. We thought you might sleep another night through."

"What time is it?" McGarvey mumbled, feigning more drowsiness than he felt. The son of a bitch knew his name already. He probably had a source within the SVR.

"Six in the evening," Ostrovsky said. "You've been sleeping for more than fifteen hours."

His ferret-faced accountant was perched on the arm of a couch across the room, and two very large men, in shirtsleeves, large caliber handguns that looked like Glock-17s in their shoulder holsters, watched alertly from where they stood on either side of the door.

The leather satchel lay open on the floor next to a table on which the bolt-cutters and the component parts of the sniper rifle were laid out.

"Christ," McGarvey said. He shoved the covers back and struggled to sit up, swinging his feet to the floor. He hunched over and held his head in his hands. "I feel like shit. What the hell did you put in my drink?"

"In your food actually, but it was just a sedative," Ostrovsky said.

McGarvey looked up, bleary-eyed. "Can I have a cigarette?"

Ostrovsky tossed him a pack of Marlboros and a gold lighter. When McGarvey had a cigarette lit he looked over at the Mafia boss as if something had just occurred to him.

"What did you call me?"

"Your name is Kirk McGarvey, and from what I was told you are certainly inventive and a very dangerous man," Ostrovsky said. He nodded toward the gun parts on the table. "You've come here to assassinate someone with that rifle. My guess is the Tarantula. Given half a chance and a little better luck, you might have succeeded. Which brings up some very interesting possibilities."

McGarvey smiled wanly in defeat.

"So you have me. Now what?"

"Now what indeed?" Ostrovsky said. "That depends in part on your co-operation, because I think you are a very valuable piece of property. The question is would you be just as valuable dead, or are we going to have to see that you remain alive? It'll be a matter of propaganda."

"I don't follow you," McGarvey said dully. He hung his head and coughed deeply as if he were having trouble catching his breath.

"Certainly the Tarantula would pay a fair sum of money if he knew that you were no longer capable of gunning for him. Contacting him, and convincing him of what and who you are, might be tricky but not impossible."

"There are methods," the accountant put in.

"The Militia and FSK are looking for you with a great deal of passion, though not for the reasons you stated," Ostrovsky said with amusement. "President Kabatov means to arrest the Tarantula and place him on trial for murder and treason. But in order to do that you mustn't be allowed to carry out your nefarious plans." Ostrovsky shook his head in amazement and glanced over at his accountant.

"It doesn't make any sense to me either, Yakov," the ferret face said, the hint of a smile at the corners of the thin mouth.

McGarvey coughed again, and had to prop himself up with his hands on his knees.

"Then there's your own government, Mr. McGarvey, which has already spent hundreds of million of dollars trying to make sure that we Russians don't slip back into our old ways. They certainly might be willing to pay a great deal of money to have you delivered alive and safe at the U.S. Embassy. It would save them from international censure if it were to come out that the CIA had plotted to assassinate a legitimate Russian presidential candidate."

McGarvey stubbed out the cigarette and looked up at Ostrovsky. "What do you want me to say?" he asked groggily.

"I'm sure that given the choice you would much rather go home. Who in Washington would be willing to make a deal?"

"Howard Ryan," McGarvey said after a moment. "He's Deputy Director of Operations for the CIA."

"What about the director himself?"

"You'll have to start with Ryan, he's the one looking for me. He'd have the most to gain."

Ostrovsky tossed a cell phone over. "Call him."

McGarvey looked at the phone and shook his head. "I need a shower first, I feel like shit."

"You can have a shower later."

"Now, goddammit. You've got me, so cut me a little slack before I puke all over your fancy carpet," McGarvey said, letting a pleading note creep into his voice. He'd been listening for sounds from elsewhere in the club, but there was nothing. Either no one was around at this hour, or this room was located in an isolated area.

"Go with him," Ostrovsky told the two bodyguards.

They came over as McGarvey started to rise. At the last moment he stumbled as if he had lost his balance, and one of the guards caught him. It was all the opening he needed. He snatched the Glock-17 out of the man's shoulder holster and shouldered the man out of the way. The other guard reached for his gun when McGarvey shot him twice in the chest, knocking him backward off his feet. The first guard caught his balance and reached for McGarvey who switched aim and shot the man in the face at point blank range.

Ostrovsky was coming out of his chair, and the accountant was starting for the door. McGarvey shot the ferret in the side of the head, sending him crashing over the low coffee table, at the same moment a panicked Ostrovsky was dragging a pistol out of his pocket.

McGarvey pointed his gun at the Mafia boss. "*Nyet!*" he shouted.

Ostrovsky ignored the warning, as he got out the pistol, which McGarvey recognized as his own Walther, and raised it.

McGarvey dispassionately shot the man twice in the chest, knocking him off his feet, where he landed in a heap in front of the couch.

At the door McGarvey listened but there were no sounds in the corridor. No one had heard the shots, and no alarm had been raised.

He went into the bathroom where he showered off the blood that had splattered on him, then found his clothes in a heap on the floor. After he got dressed, he repacked the rifle components and the bolt cutter in the leather satchel, then retrieved his own gun, spare magazine and silencer from Ostrovsky's body.

It was 6:45 when he finished, and still there were no sounds from the corridor, but by now the club would be busy with early arrivals. No one would expect trouble. In fact it was likely that no one else knew about Ostrovsky's guest.

Hefting the satchel in his left hand, McGarvey let himself out, and hurried noiselessly to the end of the corridor, which turned left through a pair of doors that led to the front of the club. Now he could hear music, and the sounds of laughter, and voices.

Without undue haste, he walked to the front of the club, through the entry foyer, past the front desk staff and doormen who paid him no attention, and outside as a valet was getting out of a BMW sedan. Several armed guards stood around, but they ignored him.

He walked around to the driver's side, nodded pleasantly to the young parking attendant, tossed his bag inside, got behind the wheel and took off before anyone realized what was happening. McGarvey watched in the rearview mirror as the valet sprinted inside, but then he was turning down the driveway and toward the highway that led back into Moscow.

Lefortovo

Jacqueline Belleau's Russian driver that the French Embassy had provided her passed through the prison gates a few minutes before 7:00 P.M., and she had to clutch her purse between her knees to keep them from knocking. As the SDECE's Paris Chief of Station Claude Navicet had told her this afternoon when the meeting with Bykov had been set up: "These people mean business, so watch yourself." Which she thought was the same as saying be careful when you stick you head into the lion's mouth. The request had been taken directly to General Yuryn, the director of the FSK. Jacqueline had listened in on the conversation, and although she spoke no Russian she detected a reluctance in his voice. Since the Russians had asked the French for help, however, he could not refuse.

A guard came out of the gatehouse, and Jacqueline powered down her window, and passed out her papers. "I have an appointment to meet with Colonel Bykov," she said in French.

Her driver opened his window and translated.

The guard took her papers back into the gatehouse, and a couple of minutes later returned with another guard. He handed Jacqueline's papers back to her, and said something in Russian.

"This man will escort us to Colonel Bykov's office," her driver translated.

The second guard climbed in the front, and they drove to the rear of the compound where they parked in front of a low yellow brick building whose barred windows had been painted black.

Chernov was alone in his office. Although he seemed impatient, he smiled pleasantly and shook her hand. "I'm Yuri Bykov," he said in French.

"I'm Jacqueline Belleau, and my service has sent me from Paris to help out." Chernov was tall, well built and in Jacqueline's opinion, handsome. But his smile was fake.

"Frankly I don't know what you can do that your government hasn't already done," Chernov said. "But I'll take any help that I can get, because we're clutching at straws. McGarvey is here in Moscow, we know that much. But this is a very big city, and we simply can't find him."

"Have you spoken with the CIA yet?"

"Not directly," Chernov said. "But I don't think they'd care to send one of their officers over here from the embassy." He smiled again. "I know we certainly wouldn't send one of our people from our embassy in Washington over to FBI headquarters if the situation were reversed."

"Well it's a good thing I came to see you tonight, because there's something that you cannot be aware of," Jacqueline said, conscious that she was taking a very large risk. But she didn't know what else to do. "Like you, we and the Americans want to see Kirk McGarvey pulled back from the brink of this madness. Nobody condones assassination, and in the past McGarvey has been a friend to France. In fact he makes his home in Paris."

"I know."

"What you don't know is that his daughter Elizabeth also works for the CIA. She was sent to work with me in Paris to find her father."

"Extraordinary," Chernov said. "I had no idea. Is she here with you?"

The bastard was lying. Jacqueline could see it in his cold eyes.

"I don't know where she is, Colonel."

"I don't understand."

"She and I traced her father to an apartment in Riga, but that's as far as we got. She disappeared into thin air, and the Riga police swear that they know nothing about it."

"What exactly do you mean, disappeared?" Chernov asked quietly.

"Just that," Jacqueline said. "We staked out his apartment that night, but when it was evident he was gone, I went over to my embassy to call for instructions. Elizabeth remained behind to continue watching the apartment. When I came back a couple hours later she was gone. The landlady knew nothing, nor, as I said, did the police. There was no sign of a struggle. She was just gone."

"What do you think happened to her?"

"She followed her father here to Moscow, I have no doubt about it. Neither does the CIA," Jacqueline said. She brushed a strand of hair off her forehead. "I hated to bring this news to you, Colonel, because I know how it will affect your investigation. But the Americans are very keen on getting Elizabeth home safe. After all she was sent over to help stop her father, at your government's request. And in the past few weeks working with the girl— she's only twenty-three—I became very fond of her. So it's become personal with me."

"Amazing," Chernov said. "In any event we can all agree that Kirk McGarvey has come here to assassinate one of our presidential candidates."

"That's still a matter of speculation, actually," Jacqueline said. "Elizabeth is traveling on her own passport. The name McGarvey is not very common, so I'm wondering if any of your people have heard anything. I assume that you're watching the border crossings, trains, planes, buses, car rental agencies, hotels, things like that."

"To my knowledge her name has not shown up on any of our surveillance reports. But if I hear anything I'll contact you at your embassy, Mademoiselle Belleau," he said. "I would ask that you let me know in turn if she shows up at her own embassy or yours."

"I'll inform the Americans, I'm sure they'll be happy to help out."

Ten minutes later Captain Petrovsky telephoned Chernov from Militia Headquarters in the old City Soviet Building.

"We may have something, Colonel."

"What is it?" said Chernov, his mind still on the French woman. Her coming here had disturbed him. It was something outside his control, something unexpected. He didn't like that.

"A Mafia boss, his money man and two of his bodyguards were gunned down about a half hour ago. The only reason we got it so fast was that one of General Mazayev's people happened to be out there and called me direct."

"Where did this happen?" Chernov demanded with his full attention now.

"That's the thing, we should have known. At the Grand Dinamo. It's inside the stadium, not two thousand meters from the flea market."

"That's it. Did anybody see anything?"

"Not the murders, but about the same time a man came out of the club, jumped into a blue BMW and took off. But it wasn't his car. The general description the valet provided more or less fits McGarvey."

"All right, put out an all-points bulletin for that car."

"I sent the bulletin before I called you. If that car is still in Moscow we'll find it."

"Don't screw it up this time, Illen," Chernov warned quietly.

"No."

Downtown Moscow

McGarvey parked near a metro station around the corner from the Bolshoi Theater at 7:20. Taking the satchel with him he found a public phone inside the station and despite the risk that the phone was being monitored for international calls, he used his Allain credit card to reach Otto Rencke. He figured that the staff at the Grand Dinamo would have been confused for the first few minutes by the theft of the car out from under their noses, and when they had gone looking for their boss, but instead found his body and those of his accountant and bodyguards, they might have panicked. It would take them time to get organized and even more time to decide what to do. The loss of a member's car was nothing in comparison to the murders. But sooner or later they would realize that the two events were connected and they would do something. They'd either call the Militia, who might put two and two together in due time, or they'd put the word out on the street, which would be a lot faster.

"Hiya," Rencke answered cautiously on the first ring.

"Have you heard from my daughter?" McGarvey asked.

"Oh boy, Mac, am I ever glad you called, because you've gotta get out of there right now. Whatever it takes, just run to the embassy and everything can be worked out."

If the line was clear and Rencke could talk, he was supposed to respond that he'd heard from Elizabeth and everything was fine. But he hadn't, and he sounded all strung out.

"I'll come for you when I can."

"Noo, Mac," Otto cried. "You don't understand. The line is clear, I'm okay, but it's Elizabeth. Something's happened. Something terrible."

A cold fist clutched at McGarvey's heart. "What's happened?"

"Elizabeth is there in Moscow. Chernov picked her up in Riga, which means Tarankov's probably got her, and is going to use her for bait."

McGarvey closed his eyes. "Christ, Christ," he said softly, as he tried to get ahold of himself. He opened his eyes. "I can't talk very long, but from the beginning, Otto, what the hell is going on?"

"Call me from the embassy, please. Just get out of there."

"Goddammit, Otto!"

"Oh shit, oh shit. The field officer Ryan sent over to look for you was Elizabeth. She's working for the CIA now. She was with the DI, but Ryan recruited her to help find you. So she came to Paris but the SDECE picked her up, and she and Jacqueline Belleau were assigned to stake out your apartment."

This wasn't believable, and yet McGarvey knew goddamned well it was true. Ryan was capable of all of it. McGarvey held the phone so tightly his knuckles turned white, but if anyone passing in the busy station noticed anything they gave no sign of it.

"Mac, are you still there?" Otto asked fearfully.

"I'm here."

"It took Elizabeth a couple of weeks, but she started surfing the net and she found me. She just put it together, Mac. I swear I was hammered right to my knees when she showed up."

"How did she find out about Riga?"

"I told her," Otto wailed. "I don't know why, but you were walking into a trap by calling Yemlin. Chernov had his phone bugged and when you made the call it was traced. I had to stay here, so Elizabeth and Jacqueline took off for Riga. They were just supposed to warn you that Chernov was on his way. But Elizabeth got caught, and Jacqueline saw it all."

"You shouldn't have told her about Riga," McGarvey said softly.

"I know that now, but there was no other way, Mac. Believe me, if I could rip my heart out I would." Otto was practically in tears. "Just go to the embassy, Mac. Please, God, just do that for me. Once I know that you're clear I'll call Murphy and he can tell the President. Between the political pressure from Washington, and Jacqueline slowing Chernov down there's a chance this'll all turn out okay. But you've got to get out of there, Mac. Right now."

"Now what are you talking about?" McGarvey demanded.

"Jacqueline convinced her people to send her to Moscow to work with the police commission—"

"Does she know who Bykov really is?"

"Yes. And so does the CIA, I think, but nobody's going to do a thing until you get out of the way. Once you're safely in the embassy Tarankov will have no reason to hold Elizabeth, and he'll let her go."

McGarvey's head was spinning. "I don't think so."

"Yes, Mac. At this stage in the revolution the man would be a fool to alienate the West over a simple kidnapping."

"He doesn't give a damn about us. In less than two days he's going to be running this country. It'll be his finger on the nuclear triggers and all the Ryans of the world won't give a damn. They'll sacrifice my daughter's life without batting an eye."

"Dammit, Mac—"

"Get out of there right now, Otto. I'll catch up with you as soon as I can."

"I'm sorry, Mac. I'm sorry—"

"It's not your fault. Just get out of there while you can."

McGarvey broke the connection, and for several minutes he was unable to do anything but sit there conscious of his beating heart, conscious of a tightness in his gut. He could see Elizabeth two Thanksgivings ago. He could feel her body, smell her scent as they hugged goodbye when she was leaving to go back to her job in New York, and his jaw tightened.

Tarankov would not harm her until after the May Day parade because he needed her until then. He was using her for bait, Otto said.

Well if you bait a hook, you should be prepared for what you catch. He picked up the phone again.

Courbevoie

Rencke caught Roland Murphy at his desk in Langley just as the CIA director was about to leave for lunch.

"General, this is Otto Rencke. I think you know who I am, because I'm helping Kirk McGarvey and you and the French are looking for us."

There was a silence on the line for several seconds.

"We don't have time to screw around, Mr. Director. If you're trying to trace this call, don't bother, because you can't do it."

"Where are you calling from?" Murphy asked, his voice measured.

"I'm in Paris. But that's not important. Kirk McGarvey has reached Moscow, but so has his daughter, Elizabeth. Your DDO, Howard Ryan, sent her over a couple of weeks ago to help the French find her father. They traced him to Riga, where Colonel Bykov, who heads the Russian police commission looking for him, picked her up. The thing is, Bykov is an alias. His real name is Leonid Chernov and he works as Tarankov's chief of staff. That means Elizabeth is probably being held prisoner by Tarankov. Do you understand what I'm telling you, General?"

"I hear what you're saying, but I don't know who the hell you think you are, or what the hell you're trying to do—"

"Mac always said you were even more stubborn than he was," Rencke cut in. "But he said you were a smart and honorable man. Watch this."

Before the call Rencke had entered the CIA's computer system. He brought up the monitor on Murphy's desk, and downloaded the Bykov-Chernov file he'd generated, along with copies of the net chat he'd had with Elizabeth, and the records of the phone trace to the Riga apartment.

"Your phone line and computer access codes are supposed to be super-secure," Rencke said. "Remind me one of these days, and if I have the time I'll show your people why they're living in a dream world and how to fix it."

There was another silence on the line, this time for nearly a minute.

"I see what you mean," Murphy said. "I'm not going to ask right now how you got this information, but it's all new to me. I had no idea that Ryan was using Elizabeth McGarvey to find her father."

"You picked him as your DDO, General," Rencke said harshly. "The man is a dangerous fool, and because of him there's a very good chance that Elizabeth will be killed unless you do something about it right now."

"Even if Tarankov has her, he won't do anything until after the elections, which gives us several weeks."

"Wrong answer," Rencke said. "Tarankov will make his move in Red Square tomorrow. And Mac will be there to try to kill him."

"My people tell me differently."

"Your people are wrong. We're not talking about political correctness here, General. This isn't what the White House *wants* to hear, this is the truth. Unless something is done immediately a lot of good people are going to get hurt, friends of mine. Not only that, Washington is going to end up with its trousers down around its ankles, as per usual. Use your friggin' head, Murphy!"

"Listen here—"

"You listen," Rencke shouted. "If you want to play games with me, I'll crash your entire system. I'll set a supervirus loose in every intelligence and Department of Defense computer in the country! That's something else your analysts tell you is impossible. But, Mr. Director, you can't believe how simple it would be to do."

"What do you want?" Murphy demanded.

"I'm not going to ask you to take my word, Mr. Director, I may be naive but I'm not stupid. Check with Ryan, and find out exactly what that bastard has been doing. In the meantime I'll download everything in my files on Tarankov and what's about to happen over there. When you've got all that, take it to President Lindsay. The Russians asked for his help, well he's in a position now to do just that."

"How?"

"Jumped up Jesus, do I have to explain everything?" Rencke said. "The Russians have to arrest Tarankov before the May Day rally in Red Square tomorrow. No matter what it takes. Because if Tarankov is sitting in a jail cell there'll be no reason to hold Elizabeth."

Murphy sighed. "I see what you mean. But I don't know if the President will go along with such a suggestion."

"Try, General," Rencke said. "At least do that much. Mac has done a lot for his country, maybe it's time that his country does something for him and his family."

Lefortovo

"We found the car," Petrovsky shouted. "It's parked on Marx Prospekt around the corner from the Bolshoi, about a hundred meters from the Ploshchad Revolyutsi metro station."

"Is there any sign of McGarvey?" Chernov demanded.

"Not yet, but we've got plenty of men down there so that if he shows up he won't have a chance."

"What about the metro station itself, you fool? Have you got any men inside?"

"*Yeb vas*, no."

"If he spots your people that's where he'll go, if he hasn't already simply walked away. I want you to shut down every metro in the city, and station men at every stop. We might still have a chance to catch him."

"I'll get on it right now," Petrovsky said.

"If your people see him, shoot him on the spot," Chernov ordered. "I'm coming down there myself right now."

Downtown Moscow

The bellman Artur wasn't expected back at the Metropol for another hour.

McGarvey hung up the telephone. He'd already been here too long. He had to put as much distance between himself and the BMW as possible, because by now the word might have gotten to the Militia. But it was hard to think straight for fear of what Elizabeth was going through at this moment. He wanted to lash out right now, strike back, but he was powerless.

A train had arrived at the metro station and a crowd of people came up the fast moving escalators and surged for the exit. McGarvey picked up the satchel and fell in behind them. Like Astimovich, Artur had connections in the city. But if he couldn't or wouldn't help with a place to stay, McGarvey would have to find an out-of-the-way workingman's hotel where he could bribe the desk clerk into not requiring identity documents. It would be risky, but he had to get off the streets as soon as possible.

The crowd slowed down and stopped. There seemed to be some sort of a bottleneck at the exit, and a commotion started. McGarvey stepped to one side in time to catch a glimpse of at least three Militia officers in riot gear, pushing their way through.

They had found the damn car.

McGarvey turned and walked back to the turnstile leading to the down escalator, the babushka in the glass booth watching him.

"Halt! Halt!" someone shouted from behind.

In three steps McGarvey was at the barrier, and he leaped over the turnstile, nearly catching the satchel handle, and tumbling down the rapidly moving escalator. But he regained his balance and took the moving stairs two at a time.

He caught up with a knot of people halfway to the bottom and bowled his way through them. He didn't think that the Militia would be desperate enough to fire in a crowded escalator or subway platform. But they wouldn't let him get away either. All the stations on this line would be covered.

At the bottom he pushed his way through the packed corridor through the arch and onto the crammed platform with its vaulted ceilings from which hung huge ornate crystal chandeliers. A train, its doors open and crowded with passengers, was not moving. The public address system was announcing that because of technical difficulties the metro was temporarily shut down, but to have patience.

The platform was a hundred yards long, and by the time he reached the far end, a buzz of excitement was growing behind him, spreading like a tidal wave. The Militia were clearing a path down the middle by shoving the people to one side or the other, and it was obvious that it would take them only a minute or so to reach the end of the platform.

With nowhere else to go, McGarvey jumped down to the track level, and raced into the black maw of the tunnel. People on the platform shouted for him to come back, and before he got twenty yards the beams of several flashlights appeared behind him.

The next stop would be two or three hundred yards away, and by now the Militia would be heading down the tunnel from that end meaning to catch him in the middle.

His suspicions were confirmed in the next minute when he spotted the pinpoints of several flashlights in the distance ahead. But at that moment he also spotted his way out, a low steel door set in a recess in the tunnel wall, and secured by an old-fashioned iron padlock.

Standing to the side to protect himself from bullet fragments, he fired three shots into the padlock, the third finally springing it.

The Militia at either end of the tunnel, thinking they were being fired upon, opened fire with automatic weapons, bullets and sparks and stone chips flying off the tunnel walls, ceiling and tracks.

McGarvey pulled the ruined padlock away and forced the heavy steel door open on rusty hinges. In what little light there was he could see narrow concrete stairs leading down into the absolute darkness. A cold breeze wafted up from below, bringing with it the damp smells of water and sewage.

He stepped through the door as something hot and very sharp slammed into his left armpit, shoving up against the open door, and nearly dropping him to his knees. But then he straightened up and raced headlong down the stairs.

Chernov shined the beam of his flashlight on the few drops of blood in the doorway off the metro tunnel. The trains were still being held, and the tunnel was busy with Militia cops searching the tracks centimeter by centimeter.

"At least one of your men got lucky," Chernov said to Petrovsky. "Why didn't anyone follow him?"

"Do you know what's down there, Colonel?"

"Yes, I do."

"With a man of his caliber I think we need reinforcements before I send any of my people into that maze. There are thousands of places where he could wait in ambush."

"He only has so many bullets."

"I'm sorry, Colonel, but I won't give that order until the Army shows up. They'll be here within a half-hour, and we'll have a good chance of flushing him out."

"In the meantime he could be anywhere."

"He won't get very far in the condition he's in," Petrovsky said. He shined his flashlight down the trail of blood droplets finally lost in the darkness. "If he keeps losing blood he'll probably pass out or become too weak to fight back." Petrovsky looked into Chernov's eyes. "The sewers aren't such a healthy place to be for a wounded man."

"Neither is Lefortovo for a healthy man," Chernov said. "Keep me informed."

"Yes, sir."

Chernov walked back out to the tunnel, and up on the street General Yuryn beckoned him over to the limousine. He climbed in back and they took off.

"Tarankov will be at the rally in Red Square tomorrow and yet with all the resources at your command you have failed to stop one man," Yuryn said coolly. "Are you going to merely stand by and let him succeed?"

"He's wandering around in the dark sewers, wounded and losing a lot of blood," Chernov said indifferently, although he was seething inside, and he was beginning to have his doubts that they'd ever had a true measure of the man.

"But I'm told he still has that shoulder bag. And we all know what that might contain."

"The Army will be here in a few minutes, and they'll make a systematic search of every hiding place down there."

"That would seem an impossible task given the time remaining."

"It might flush him out if he's not already dead."

Yuryn laughed humorlessly. "Maybe Tarankov should postpone his appearance."

"He won't do that," Chernov said. "Neither will he send a double."

"I didn't think so," Yuryn said. "So tomorrow it'll come down to you versus Mr. McGarvey. I wonder who the better man is?"

THREE
MAY

FORTY

Red Square

Chernov mounted the stairs to the reviewing stand atop Lenin's Mausoleum as the bells inside the Kremlin finished tolling midnight.

Workmen were busy putting the final touches on the platform for President Kabatov and the several dozen dignitaries who were expected to show up. Lights, banners, and a sound system were being installed here, as well as across the vast square that had been blocked off from all normal pedestrian traffic.

Soldiers and Militia officers manned the barricades and checked the papers of everyone entering or leaving, in part because McGarvey still had not been flushed out of hiding, but also because such precautions were normal for these kinds of events. This May Day parade and celebration was supposed to be the biggest in twenty years because Kabatov had made his conciliatory gesture to the Communists by assuming the party chairmanship.

But the carnival would backfire on them when Tarankov swept into Red Square at the head of his column of commandoes and announced to his people that he was returning the *Rodina* to them, the same message he'd been repeating for nearly five years. This time everybody would believe it.

Unless McGarvey killed him.

Chernov stood at the parapet and let his eyes drift across the periphery of the square, which tomorrow afternoon would be crammed with a million people. Special riot police and anti-terrorism squads would be dispersed throughout the crowd, but even Chernov had to admit to himself that spotting one man in that mob would be next to impossible.

"Let's see your identification," a gruff voice demanded.

Chernov turned to face an older man dressed in the special Militia uniform worn by guards detailed to Lenin's Mausoleum. He handed his identification book over, then glanced up at the Kremlin walls towering over the rear of the mausoleum.

"Pardon me, Colonel," the guard said, handing the booklet back. "But we can't be too careful."

"Who are you looking for?" Chernov asked.

"Anyone who doesn't belong up here," the guard said.

"Aren't you aware that we're looking for someone? Weren't you briefed before you came on duty?"

"No, sir. When we closed up downstairs I was ordered to help check everyone who came up here."

"You weren't shown a photograph?"

"No, sir,"

Chernov took McGarvey's photograph out of his jacket pocket and gave it to the guard.

"Ah, the Belgian gentleman. He was here, visiting Lenin, about three weeks ago, I think. Name is Allain, if my memory serves." The guard looked up. "What's he done?"

Chernov fought to keep his temper in check.

"There must be a thousand people visiting here every day, many of them foreigners, and yet you can recall this one?"

The guard shifted his stance. "He wasn't like most of them. He was respectful. He even brought flowers."

"Did you speak to him?"

"Just a few words," the guard responded diffidently, suspecting that he was in trouble. "But he seemed genuinely interested."

"So he came to visit the tomb, he dropped off some flowers, you and he had a little chat, and then he left. Is that correct?"

"No, sir. He wanted to come up here so that he could stand where so many . . . great men had stood."

"You brought him here?" Chernov demanded harshly.

"Yes, sir," the guard said miserably. "But he only stayed for a minute."

"What did he do while he was up here?"

The guard shrugged. "Why, the same thing you did, sir. First he looked down at the square, and then he looked back up at the Kremlin wall."

"Do you know how to use your gun?"

The guard looked down at the Makarov pistol in its holster at his side. "Yes, sir."

"The next time you see your gentleman, I want you to shoot him. Don't ask any questions. Don't stop to chat, or admire the scenery, just shoot him."

"Yes, sir."

Chernov raced back to his car, and got on the phone to the Kremlin locator to find Kabatov's chief of security, General Korzhakov, in his car heading home.

"The son of a bitch was carrying a KGB general's uniform. He's going to try for a clear shot at Tarankov from inside the Kremlin, and make his escape in the confusion."

"That's inventive," Korzhakov said. "But he's not going to last until June in the sewers."

"I want security in and around the Kremlin tightened up."

"After we get through today's nonsense I'll review our procedures with you—"

"Do it tonight, General."

The line was dead for a moment."

"Tarankov wouldn't dare show his face in Moscow now."

"Just do it."

"Where are you getting your information?" Korzhakov demanded angrily.

"It's common knowledge on the street, General. I'm not saying that Tarankov will show up, but a lot of people believe he will. Maybe McGarvey does too."

"You have a point, Bykov," Korzhakov said. "I'm turning around now. I'll be back in my office in a half hour."

Aboard Tarankov's Train

Sometime after midnight, by Elizabeth's reckoning, she finally managed to work a corner of the window's blackout shade loose so she could look outside. But it was pitch black and there was nothing to see except some woods across a narrow clearing.

In the thirty-six hours since Liesel had tried to molest her, she'd been left on her own. Except for the pleasant soldier's bringing her meals at 8:00 A.M., noon, and 8:00 P.M., nothing had happened and she was half-crazy with fear and boredom.

She sat back disappointed, then got up and pulled down the tiny sink so that she could splash some water on her face. Her eyes in the mirror were bloodshot because she'd not been able to get any sleep since the incident with Liesel. Nor had she allowed herself to get undressed so that she could take a shower. She was worried that Liesel would return and catch her in a vulnerable position.

During the day it had been easier for her, because there'd been a great deal of activity in and around the train. She'd heard machinery running, men talking and laughing, and a constant stream of footsteps past her door. Once she'd heard a woman's voice raised either in laughter or in a shout, she'd not been able to tell which. But she thought it must have been Liesel, because she didn't think there were any other women aboard.

She'd thought that perhaps they were getting ready to move out, but by the time her evening meal was delivered the activity had all but ceased, and they'd gone nowhere.

Drying her face, she went to the door to listen, but there were no sounds. She knew that she was in the last car of the train, but other than this compartment she had no idea what was in the car or who shared it with her.

She tried the knob as she had several times before, this time it turned easily in her hand, and the door opened a crack. She froze, her stomach doing a slow roll. She reached over and flipped off the lights, plunging the compartment into darkness.

Guards would be posted outside, but they'd be watching for someone to come toward the train, not get away. If she could reach the woods she thought she might have a good chance of getting several miles before she was missed. By then she didn't think they'd come after her.

Girding herself for the dash she opened the door. Tarankov was standing there, an intent look on his face. She knew why he had come, just as she knew that there was probably nothing she could do to prevent it. She was alone, and her luck had just run out.

"Were you going somewhere?" Tarankov asked. "Not such a good idea having you running around the countryside at this hour of the morning."

Elizabeth stepped back and he entered the compartment, switched on the light, and closed the door.

"What do you want?" she asked, her voice dry in her throat.

"I think you know."

"I'll fight you, and you might even have to kill me. If that happened I wouldn't be much use as bait."

"Your father wouldn't find out about that until it was too late for him," Tarankov said quietly. "They almost had him tonight in Moscow. He was wounded, and now he's trying to hide in the sewers."

"I don't believe you."

"Leonid wanted me to send an impersonator to make my speech in Red Square, in case your father got through. But I don't think that's necessary any longer." Tarankov smiled. "I don't think you'll be needed at my side on the reviewing stand either. So it makes no difference if you're damaged tonight."

"I'll tell your wife—"

"She thinks I'm a god," Tarankov cut in. "So will you after tonight."

Elizabeth lunged at him, but he easily stepped aside and backhanded her in the side of her head with so much force she was knocked across the compartment onto the narrow cot, spots and pinwheels of lights flashing in front of her eyes.

He ripped open her fatigue shirt, and pawed her breasts, the pain of the assault real but so distant she was unable to defend herself for the moment.

He tore the front of her trousers open and pulled them down around her ankles, and off, then spread her legs and opened his trousers and pulled them down, his erect penis leaping out.

"No," she cried, trying to fight him off as she regained consciousness. "Oh, God no. Please, no!"

The compartment door slammed open, and Tarankov reared back as his wife stormed in, a big semi-automatic pistol in her hand.

"I thought I'd find you here, you rotten prick," she screeched, waving the gun around.

Tarankov got to his feet, and calmly pulled his trousers up. "Well, *Schatzle*, you were right about one thing. Neither of us will get to fuck her."

"Not until after you're in the Kremlin, you mean," said Liesel, who was not mollified.

Tarankov moved away from the cot as Liesel came closer, pointing the pistol first at him, and then at Elizabeth. The woman had been drinking, and her face was flushed and she was unsteady on her feet. But she was also crazy, a maniacal glint in her eyes, spittle flying from her mouth as she ranted.

"If you and your little whore were dead, maybe the people would sing a different tune!"

"Over fucking her?" Tarankov asked mildly. "If you want her that badly, go ahead, I won't stop you—"

Liesel pointed the pistol directly at her husband's head and cocked the hammer. "First you, you cocksucker!"

Elizabeth had gathered her legs beneath her, and she sprang up suddenly, shoving Liesel aside. The gun fired, but the shot went wild. Liesel crashed against the door and Elizabeth snatched the gun from her hand, and tried to step back out of the way. But the German woman was wild with insane rage, and she charged, leaving Elizabeth no other choice except to fire.

The shot caught Liesel high in the chest between her sternum and esophagus, and she was driven backward, blood splattering the wall.

Without thinking Elizabeth spun on her heel, pointed the gun at Tarankov, who hadn't moved, and pulled the trigger. Nothing happened. The slide was back, in the locked open position.

Tarankov came forward and took the gun from her hand, just before the first of the commandoes appeared in the doorway.

"There are never more than two bullets in Liesel's gun," he told Elizabeth gently.

"There were shots, sir," one of the men said.

"An unfortunate situation here, Lieutenant," Tarankov said, staring at Elizabeth. He shook his head. "My wife tried to rape this girl, who was forced to defend herself." Tarankov looked up. "Have the body removed, please, and get someone in here to clean up the mess."

"Yes, sir."

"Make sure everybody settles down, this will be a busy day. A busy day indeed."

Subterranean Moscow

McGarvey, one hand pressed against the wound beneath his armpit, the other propping him up against the cold damp tunnel wall, held his breath for several moments to listen. It was after 2:00 A.M., and there was nothing now, other than the distant rumble of fast-moving water, probably one of the underground streams.

For a time he'd thought that he would not escape. There were too many men searching for him, seemingly coming from all directions. Several times he'd nearly stumbled into a search party, each time ducking back into a side tunnel at the last possible moment to avoid being trapped in the beams of their flashlights.

But it had been at least twenty minutes since he last heard anything. He didn't think they'd given up the search, they were probably concentrating their efforts in ever-widening circles around the Ploshchad Revolyutsi metro station. For the moment he was outside their search pattern, but it wouldn't last.

Picking up the satchel, which was becoming heavier the farther he went, he made his way along the pitch-black storm sewer tunnel toward a circle of very dim gray light about twenty-five yards away.

The news that Tarankov had Elizabeth was nearly impossible to bear, and yet the bright spark of hate it produced kept him going. She was his flesh and blood, his only child, who had been placed in harm's way because of what he was. It didn't matter that the Howard Ryans of the world gave the actual orders, it was men like himself who made those orders possible, and from a certain point of view even necessary.

If it had ever been possible for him to walk away from this, it had become totally impossible for him with Elizabeth's capture. The men responsible—*all* the men responsible—would pay.

The light on the tunnel floor came from a grate in the roof, that led two hundred feet straight up to a storm grate in the street. In a spring snow meltoff, or during a strong rainstorm, the storm sewers would become raging maelstroms as the water was channeled into the underground torrents that eventually emptied into the Moscow River. Where the tunnels sloped down they led to the rivers, and where they sloped up they led to collection points.

He cocked an ear to listen again, but still the only sound he could hear was the distant roar of rushing water.

The rally in Red Square was set for four o'clock this afternoon, which gave him something under fourteen hours to get into place undetected. But first he was going to have to take one more chance. He had to warn Jacqueline to stay in the French Embassy no matter what happened, because in the aftermath there was no telling which way the country would go, or what the crowds or the military would do.

Another fifty yards and he came to one of the maintenance openings set every quarter mile or so into the tunnel just like the one he'd used to get down here from the metro track level. The steel door at the top would be locked, but on the way down he'd spotted steel rungs set in the wall that led back up to a drainage opening in the floor of the metro tunnel.

The stairs were damp and slippery with algae so he had to watch his step. By the time he reached the top he was winded and claustrophobic, the narrow walls pressing against him in the absolute darkness.

It took him several minutes fumbling around until he found the steel rungs a half-dozen steps from the landing. He slung the satchel over his shoulder and climbed the last ten feet or so until he detected a very faint light filtering down through a grate about three feet in diameter.

Bracing himself as best he could he put his shoulder to the grate and pushed. At first nothing happened, except that he could feel a fresh gush of warm blood trickling down his side.

He tried again, this time using his powerful leg muscles to push upward with every ounce of strength he had. The grate gave way with a tremendous screech that echoed off the metro tunnel walls, then fell away with a clang.

McGarvey waited for a full minute, spots dancing in front of his face, as he tried to catch his breath while at the same time listen for the sounds of someone coming down the tunnel to investigate the racket.

But no one came, and he climbed out of the access tunnel, looked both ways down the metro line, and headed the hundred yards toward the nearest lights.

The metro wouldn't be running again until 6:00 A.M., so the only people in the stations or on the platforms would be maintenance workers, and Militia watching for him to try to make his escape.

An empty train was parked at the platform, its rear lights shining red, and its interior lights on. Ducking around the train, McGarvey looked up over the edge of the platform floor. The chandeliers had been turned low, but even so the light glinted off the tiled walls and ornately friezed arches. The long hall was empty.

Climbing up from the tracks, McGarvey crossed the platform, passed through one of the arches and found a bank of pay phones next to the restrooms near the foot of the stationary escalators. A steel accordion gate blocked the escalators for the night.

He went into the men's room where he peeled off his jacket and opened his shirt. The wound was deep, and oozed blood, but fortunately the bullet had not hit a bone or cut a major blood vessel. He pulled a wad of paper towels from the dispenser, wetted them in the sink and washed the blood away. Then he pulled another wad of paper towels from the dispenser and stuffed them under his armpit. It wouldn't stop the blood flow, but it would help.

He splashed some cold water on his face, put his jacket back on and went out to the pay phones where he dialed the French Embassy number from memory.

"*Bon soir.* You have reached the Embassy of the Republic of France," a woman's voice said. It was an answering machine, but a night duty officer would be manning the switchboard. "Our normal office hours are—"

"This is an emergency. My name is Kirk McGarvey, and I need to speak to Jacqueline Belleau immediately."

A man came on. "This line is probably being monitored."

"I know," McGarvey said.

"Stand by, *monsieur.*"

McGarvey glanced up at the station name. He'd come up at the Lubyanka, directly across from the headquarters of the FSK. The irony just now was rich.

Jacqueline came on a minute later, out of breath. "Oh, Kirk, where are you?"

"It doesn't matter," McGarvey said. "I've only got a minute before I need to leave here. I'm calling off the hit, do you understand?"

"Thank God—"

"But I know about Liz, and I'm going after her. In the meantime you have to stay inside the embassy. No matter what happens, stay there."

"I can come pick you up."

"Just stay there, Jacqueline," McGarvey said, and he hung up.

Dzerzhinsky Square

Chernov was just pulling up in front of FSK headquarters after a frustrating hour spent with General Korzhakov when Petrovsky called his cell phone. McGarvey had just now telephoned the woman at the French embassy. He was calling off the kill, and he said he knew about his daughter.

"Did you trace the call?" Chernov asked.

"He called from a pay phone in the Lubyanka metro station. So you were right, he's using the storm sewers to get around."

Chernov made a tight U-turn and shot across the broad Dzerzhinsky Square, no traffic for the moment. "I'm right across the square from the station," he shouted.

"My people are less than three minutes away."

"Do you have a map of the subway system in front of you?"

"*Da*. Right here."

"He's using the sewers, but he has to come up through a metro station. I want your people covering every station he can get to from here in case I don't intercept him."

Chernov screeched to a halt in front of the metro station, and pulled out his gun, as he ran across the sidewalk and took the stairs two at a time.

"There're four of them—" Petrovsky was saying when his signal faded and cut off.

Halfway down, Chernov heard the first sirens at the same moment he heard a gunshot from below, and he thumbed his gun's safety to the off position.

The shattered lock gave way, and McGarvey opened the accordion gate, stepped through, then stopped. He was hearing sirens, faintly in the distance, but getting closer. And another sound.

He stepped back around the corner, and held his breath. He had heard footsteps.

"McGarvey," someone called from above.

McGarvey held his silence.

"There's no way out for you."

It was Chernov, McGarvey had very little doubt. His call to Jacqueline had probably been monitored and traced here. By now the Militia would be scrambling to cover every metro station and storm sewer tunnel within a radius of a mile. Every second he remained here the tighter the net would become, and Chernov knew it.

McGarvey turned and silently headed back to the platform.

"If you turn yourself in your daughter will be turned over to her embassy. Unharmed."

"Bullshit," McGarvey said to himself, not missing a step.

"McGarvey, you have my word on it," Chernov's voice echoed down the platform. "My word as an officer and gentleman."

FORTY-ONE

CIA Headquarters

Director of Central Intelligence Roland Murphy showed up at Howard Ryan's third floor office a few minutes before 6:30 P.M., his bodyguard in tow, after first confirming that his DDO was still at his desk.

"Sorry to barge in on you like this, Howard, but the President wants to see us," he said.

Ryan looked up in surprise and pleasure. "Both of us? Right now?"

"Yes," Murphy said, masking his contempt. "We'll take my car, and I'll brief you on the way over."

Ryan put on his coat. "I don't have the day's summary ready, but I can bring my notes, and a few documents."

"That won't be necessary. All the President wants from us is the . . . truth."

Ryan's eyes narrowed in suspicion. "What do you mean, Roland?"

Since Rencke's disturbing telephone call, and the files he'd sent over, Murphy had done some checking on his own, first with Ryan's assistant, Tom Moore, who had defended his boss's action.

"The idea was merely to send her over to help the French find her father. We wanted to get a message to him, nothing more. At least that was the initial parameters we gave her."

"But it didn't happen that way."

"No, Mr. Director, unfortunately it did not. Apparently she's more like her father than we first suspected. I'm recommending that her services be terminated, once she returns."

"I see," Murphy said coolly.

Next he called Elizabeth's old boss, Bratislav Toivich in the DI's Russian Division.

"Pardon me, Mr. Director, but you wouldn't be asking me about the girl unless she was in trouble."

"What do you know about her assignment?" Murphy asked directly.

"More than I should," Toivich replied, in just as direct a manner.

"She's in Moscow, and we think Tarankov's people may have kidnapped her."

"What are we doing about it?"

"I'm taking this to the President once I have all the facts. He can take it up with Kabatov. I need to know if Ms. McGarvey contacted you at any time."

"She called from Paris worried that she and a young French woman working for the SDECE were being pressured into going to Moscow. I told her not to do it."

"Did she have any contact with a man by the name Rencke?"

"She was looking for him there in Paris, and I gave her a couple of hints," Toivich said. "Did she find him, General? Is that how you found out about this? Has Otto called you?"

"Yes, he did."

"Listen to him," Toivich said. "He's the only one I know who has the combination of brains and honesty. If Otto tells you something, you can take it to the bank."

"We'll get her back."

"See that you do, General. She's quite a young woman, and I'd hate to be in your shoes if something happens to her, and somehow her father makes it back to Washington."

Finally he telephoned SDECE Director General Jean Baillot, who confirmed that Jacqueline Belleau had been sent to Moscow in an effort to misdirect the efforts of Bykov's special police commission long enough to find out where Mademoiselle McGarvey was being held, and possibly get a message to the girl's father.

"*Pardon, Général,* but it was not a good decision to set the young woman to find her father," Baillot said quietly.

"You're right, Jean. And now it's up to me to get her back. Keep me informed night or day if you hear anything further."

"*Mais oui.* Good luck."

"The truth, Howard," Murphy said to Ryan. "About why we sent Elizabeth McGarvey to Paris to find her father."

Ryan's lower lip curled. "She's joined him in Moscow, you know. Like father like daughter."

"How do you know that?"

"It's self-evident, Roland. She met him in Riga, and together they entered Russia where she's probably going to help him kill Tarankov." Ryan shook his head in amazement. "You have to admit that the bastard is smooth. He's even enlisted the aid of his French girlfriend to spy for him on the Russian special police commission."

Murphy wondered how he could have been so blind for so long about Ryan, except that the man knew his way around the Hill. Relations between Congress and the CIA had never been better. They had half the Senate practically eating out of their hands. All of it attributable to Ryan's skills. But at what price, Murphy asked himself. At what terrible price?

"You shouldn't have used her."

"You're right, Roland," Ryan admitted. "I know that now. But at the time it was the only way I could see we had even a remote chance of finding him." Ryan spread his hands. "*Mea culpa,* Roland. *Mea culpa,* what else can I say?"

Murphy wanted to take a poke at the smug bastard, but knowing the New York lawyer, he'd probably sue.

"Well, the President is going to ask you some tough questions, and I suggest that you answer him directly, and with the truth. No artifice this time."

"What?"

"Jacqueline Belleau did not go to Moscow on her own to help McGarvey kill Tarankov, as you suggest, you sleazy bastard. The SDECE sent her to help find him. And as for Elizabeth, she was kidnapped by Tarankov's people, who are probably going to use her as a human shield if they can't use her to draw Kirk out of hiding. And as DCI it's my fault as much as it is yours. So I'm going to have to answer some tough questions as well."

Ryan's face turned ashen.

"Get your ass in gear, the President is waiting for us."

Lubyanka Metro Station

Jacqueline's Russian driver got her to Dzerzhinsky Square at 2:45 A.M. They'd encountered a great deal of military and Militia activity downtown but they weren't stopped until they reached the barricades across from the metro station.

She jumped out of the car and gave her passport to one of the Militia officers, her knees shaking so badly she was afraid she was going to trip over her own feet. What she was going to try to do could very well end up getting her and Kirk killed.

"Get word to Colonel Bykov that I'm here, and I can help him," she said in French. Her driver translated for her.

"I'm sorry, madam, but you'll have to stay here—" the guard said.

"*Merde.* If you value your stripes, just get word to him. I'm trying to save lives here!"

The cop looked nervously from her to the translator, then studied her passport. Making a decision, he walked over to a squad car, its blue lights flashing, and spoke to the Militia officer there. The officer looked at Jacqueline's passport, glanced over at her, then got on the radio. A minute later he came over, and handed back her passport.

"Do you speak English, madam?" he asked.

"Yes."

"Come with me, but your driver must remain here."

"Return to the embassy," she told her driver, then followed the Militia officer across the square and into the metro station where Chernov met her on the platform, Militia and military everywhere.

"How did you know to come here?" Chernov asked.

"We monitor your police frequencies," Jacqueline said. "Have you found him yet?"

"No, but it won't be long now. He's in the storm sewer system, but we've blocked every tunnel within a kilometer."

"How many people has he killed so far?"

"None. But he is wounded."

"He'll fight back, and believe me some of your people are going to come out of there in body bags unless you let me help out."

"I'm listening."

"Tell your people to hold their positions for the moment. I'll go down there and find him for you. When he hears my voice he'll give himself up. But you need to promise me something."

Chernov looked amused. "What is that?"

"If I find him, you'll allow him to come out unharmed."

"He'll be placed under arrest."

"I understand. But I don't want any trigger-happy cop shooting at shadows. I want to bring him out alive."

"Why?" Chernov asked.

Jacqueline looked into his flat, gray eyes. "Because I happen to be in love with the man."

"Ah, charming," Chernov said. "But then you haven't been completely honest with me."

"None of us ever are, Colonel," Jacqueline said. "How about it?"

Chernov nodded. "Very well," he said. "It'll take several minutes to get word to our people in the tunnels. It's a problem of radio communication. When we're ready I'll have you escorted below." He gave her an appraising look. "Are you afraid of the dark?"

"Not especially," Jacqueline said.

"Do you want a weapon?"

She shook her head. "We're wasting time."

The White House
Washington, D.C.

Murphy and Ryan were ushered into the Oval Office at 7:10 P.M. Besides the President, also present were his National Security Adviser Harold Secor, and the Secretaries of State, Jonathan Carter, and Defense, Paul Landry. No one looked happy.

"If what you suggested to me on the phone this afternoon is true, Roland, we don't have much time," the President said.

"Yes, sir. President Kabatov will have to be informed immediately. He's the only one who can stop this now."

"Spell it out."

"We believe that Yevgenni Tarankov will not wait until the elections to make his move," Murphy said. "It's probable that he'll attempt a military coup later today during the May Day rally in Red Square, with a very good chance of succeeding. If Kabatov has surrounded himself with enough moderates and government loyalists he still has a chance of preventing it, but only if he acts now, and only if he has all the facts."

"That's not a course of action I could recommend," Ryan broke in.

"When I want your advice, you chickenshit, I'll ask for it," said the President, his voice hard. "In the meantime keep your mouth shut."

Ryan was stunned speechless.

"Kirk McGarvey has made it to Moscow, and there's still a better than even chance that if Tarankov shows up in Red Square McGarvey will assassinate him. Or try to do it, and there's nothing we can do to stop him because now he has a personal stake. His daughter Elizabeth, who works for us, was kidnapped by Tarankov's people, and he'll do everything in his power to rescue her."

"Did you send her over there?" the President asked Ryan.

"I sent her to Paris, not Moscow, Mr. President," said Ryan, subdued.

"Go on," the President told Murphy. The others in the room glared at Ryan, who sank down in his chair.

"The former KGB officer who heads the police commission trying to find McGarvey, is in fact a man by the name of Leonid Chernov. He's actually Tarankov's chief of staff, and from what we can piece together is a former KGB assassin whose brother McGarvey killed a few years ago."

"Jesus," President Lindsay said softly. "That's quite a bombshell you're asking me to hand Kabatov."

"I'm afraid there's more, Mr. President," Murphy said. "We also learned that as a young missile service officer Tarankov worked for us."

The President and his advisers were caught completely off guard.

"His code name was Hammer, and his contact was our chief of Moscow station. It didn't last long, but what he gave us was so good that we paid him a great deal of money for it. So much money, in fact, that when he quit he was able to buy and equip the train he's been using for the past five years."

"Do we have proof?"

"Yes, sir," Murphy said. He withdrew four thick file folders from his briefcase and laid them on the President's desk. "These came to light recently, but it was my decision to sit on the information because it was so potentially damaging to us. If we were to let it become public knowledge Tarankov could accuse the United States of trying to manipulate Russian politics by inventing something which, on the surface, seems so patently ridiculous that it must be a lie."

"Why weren't we given this information earlier?" Secor asked. "It would seem to be a bad decision."

"Let's not become Monday morning quarterbacks. We've all made bad decisions," the President said. "What specifically are you suggesting I tell Kabatov?" he asked Murphy.

"Just the truth, Mr. President, something he's probably short of at the moment. After that it'll be up to him, but at least he'll know what he's actually facing."

The President glanced up at the clock. "It's three in the morning over there, they'll have to get him out of bed." He turned to Ryan. "If you'll be good enough to leave now, we have work to do."

Ryan got to his feet. "Yes, Mr. President," he said. He looked at Murphy. "I'll get back to my office and finish the daily summary."

"You and Tom Moore are relieved of duty as of this moment, Howard," Murphy said. "I've instructed security not to allow you back in. I'll have your personal items sent to you within the next day or two."

"You can't do this," Ryan said indignantly. "I'll fight you in Congress—"

"That would be the worst mistake of your life, Ryan," the President said coldly. "Everything that has taken place here this evening is top secret. Discuss the situation with anybody, and I'll have you prosecuted under the National Secrets Act."

Ryan backed up a step.

The President picked up the phone to his secretary. "Mr. Ryan is leaving, would you have a taxi pick him up?"

Ryan's color was bad.

"Not at the West Portico," the President said. "Mr. Ryan will meet the cab at the front gate."

Subterranean Moscow

McGarvey hunched in the absolute darkness of a side tunnel that sloped sharply downward as he tried to catch his breath. The sounds of running water thundered in the narrow confines of the outflow tube, and a sharply cold wind came up from below. The floor here was greasy with mud and algae, making footing treacherous. If he fell he would slide into the underground river, and be swept away and probably drowned.

It was a mistake calling Jacqueline from the metro station. But he'd thought he would have enough time to make the call, reach the street level and get away before Chernov's people closed. it. But they were closer than he thought. It was just rotten luck that Chernov himself had been nearby. He only hoped that Jacqueline had heeded his warning to remain at her embassy.

Even over the roar of the water he'd been able to pick out the noise that his pursuers made and see the beams of their flashlights on the walls. They'd been coming at him from all directions, finally driving him down here, when suddenly about five minutes ago they'd stopped for some reason.

That worried him, because he could think of a number of methods Chernov could use to literally flush him out, such as opening a series of fire hydrants to flood this section of storm sewer tunnels, or even using chlorine gas.

Slinging the leather satchel over his shoulder, he cautiously made his way back up to the main sewer tunnel, where he stopped again to listen. He was about a hundred yards from where he'd re-entered the storm sewers beneath the Lubyanka metro station, and about fifty yards from one of the main tunnel intersections where he'd been driven back by the soldiers.

If the search parties had either pulled back, or were holding their positions in the darkness, he thought it might be possible to sneak past them. Once clear he could make his way through one of the metro stations back up to the streets.

Short of that, he would either spend the rest of his life being herded aimlessly down one dark tunnel after another, or he would finally be corned.

He spotted the reflection of a flashlight beam on the wet tunnel walls at the same instant he heard Jacqueline calling his name, and he pulled back hardly believing his own senses.

"Kirk, it's me," her voice echoed down the tunnel.

What was she doing here? What could she hope to accomplish? It was beyond reason.

"Colonel Bykov has pulled back his men," Jacqueline called, much closer now. "If you come out with me you won't be harmed. They'll arrest you, but it can be worked out."

She was a trained French intelligence officer, not some giddy girl. Which meant she had a plan, and somehow she'd convinced Chernov to go along with it. There was no way they were going to let him out of here alive, no matter what she'd been promised, and she knew that.

"Kirk, thank God," she said.

McGarvey looked up half expecting to see the beam of her flashlight shining down the side tunnel, but she was at least ten yards away.

"I'm here to help you," she called. "Someone tell Colonel Bykov we're coming out as soon as he pulls his people back," she shouted loudly.

McGarvey knew exactly what she was trying to do. She meant to lead the search party away, giving him a chance of escaping. She was taking the chance that he was somewhere close, which meant she knew that all of his escape routes were blocked. But it wouldn't work, because Chernov wouldn't let either of them out of here alive.

"Mademoiselle, stay where you are," Chernov called in French.

"Don't come any closer," Jacqueline shouted.

McGarvey could hear her up in the tunnel heading toward him. She had done exactly the wrong thing but for the right reason. Instead of leading the search parties away, she had inadvertently led them to him.

"Don't move, or we will be forced to open fire," Chernov warned.

"*Merde*, you dumb bastard, he'll come out with me as soon as you pull back and nobody will get hurt!"

"McGarvey!" Chernov shouted. "Say something so that we know you're there. You have my word we will not open fire!"

Jacqueline reached the side tunnel as powerful spotlights suddenly flashed on, fixing her in their bright glare.

McGarvey reached out, grabbed the sleeve of her jacket and pulled her bodily into the tunnel at the same moment Chernov's people opened fire. Her flashlight clattered down the tunnel and disappeared below.

She struggled wildly for a few seconds until in the lights reflecting from the main tunnel she realized who it was, and the color drained from her face.

"Oh, my God—"

McGarvey clamped a hand over her mouth, until she understood that their lives depended on her silence.

The firing stopped and for several seconds nothing moved in the tunnel. But then more lights flashed on, and soldiers pounded toward them from both directions.

"I hope you can swim," McGarvey whispered urgently.

She nodded, her eyes wide.

He grabbed her hand, and together they raced down the outflow tunnel that almost immediately steepened. Jacqueline lost her footing on the slippery floor and she pulled McGarvey off balance with her. They slid in the muck, faster and faster, until suddenly the tunnel ended and they plunged ten feet down into the swiftly moving underground river.

McGarvey was pulled under water by the weight of the satchel on his back, losing his grip on Jacqueline's hand, the extremely strong current tumbling him end over end.

His knee struck the river bottom, sending a sharp pain shooting up to his hip, and he pushed upward with everything he had. His head broke the surface of the water just long enough for him to take a deep breath before he was sucked under again as the river raced down a completely submerged narrow tunnel.

He could do nothing but protect his head with his arms, as his body was tumbled end over end slamming into the tunnel walls, floor and ceiling.

Almost as quickly as he had been sucked into the underwater tunnel, he was spit out the other end, plunging another eight or ten feet into a big pool of water. His right shoulder slammed into the concrete bottom and he managed to rear up, his head once again breaking the surface long enough for him to take a breath before the waterfall from the tunnel shoved him aside.

But the water was shallow here, less than waist deep, and he struggled to his feet again, stumbling away from the outflow until his hand brushed up against a rough stone block wall.

"Jacqueline," he shouted. His voice echoed back at him. He was apparently in a large chamber. In the distance he could hear another waterfall, probably where this collection pool flowed farther down toward the Moscow River.

Jacqueline had been in front of him in the first tunnel, but it was possible that she'd never made it through the underwater tunnel. Her clothing could have snagged on a rough outcropping.

"Kirk," Jacqueline's voice came weakly from the right. "Kirk."

"I'm here," McGarvey called. "Keep talking." He started along the wall toward the sound of her voice, when he spotted a glow under the water ahead of him.

"I'm here," Jacqueline said, her voice regaining strength. "I lost you."

"Wait," McGarvey called to her. He dove into the water to the glow, and came up with Jacqueline's still-working flashlight.

"Kirk," Jacqueline screamed in panic as he surfaced.

McGarvey spotted her with the beam of the flashlight where she clung to a large iron ring hanging from a stone shelf or platform. He hurriedly slogged over to her, where she threw her arms around his neck.

"Oh, God, oh, God, I thought you were dead!" she cried. "I thought I'd never see you! I thought you were gone! I didn't know what to do! I almost didn't make it! And then you were gone, and I was alone! Oh, God, Kirk!"

He held her closely for a long time, until her cries subsided and she stopped shivering. Then he kissed her.

"I guess I was right about you in Paris," he said gently. "You *have* become a crusty old bastard from being around me."

She laughed, half-hysterically, although she was nearly back in control of herself. "Anatomically impossible, but I'll take it as a compliment."

"You can swim."

"I didn't have much of a choice."

McGarvey shined the flashlight on what he'd taken to be a stone ledge, but which was in fact a long stone platform that looked like a riverside dock or quay.

He boosted Jacqueline up, then climbed up himself with a great deal of difficulty because of the heavy satchel, his waterlogged clothing, and his weakened condition.

Jacqueline helped him pull the satchel off his back, and together they unsteadily crossed the quay to a narrow set of stone stairs leading upward but blocked by a gate of iron bars secured by an ancient padlock.

McGarvey cut the lock with three pumps of the big hydraulic bolt cutters, and pulled the gate open on rusted hinges, the squealing noise echoing harshly throughout the chamber.

"If we've come out where I think we are, our river ride was a stroke of blind luck," McGarvey said.

He started up, but Jacqueline held him back.

"Where?"

"We're either beneath the Kremlin or St. Basil's," McGarvey said. "The direction and distance are about right. If I had to bet, I'd say St. Basil's, because I think the Kremlin would be secured better than this."

"You're coming back to the embassy with me, Kirk."

"They've got Liz."

"I know. But assassinating Tarankov won't do her any good."

"It may be the only thing that will save her," McGarvey said.

"I didn't come this far for nothing," Jacqueline cried.

"Neither did I," McGarvey replied grimly. "Once we get out of here, you're going back to your own embassy and you're going to stay there this time."

"If I had followed your instructions when you called, you'd still be up there in the storm sewers with Chernov's men closing in on you."

"You're probably right. But this time you'll do as I say, because we're not going to get so lucky a second time."

"Goddamn you, Kirk," Jacqueline said in frustration.

"It's something I have to do," he said gently. "You can either accept that or not. But that's the way it is."

Jacqueline lowered her eyes after a moment.

They headed up, taking it slowly and quietly, the stone stairs switching back and forth, their path blocked by two more iron gates. McGarvey cut the padlocks free with the bolt-cutters, and through the second gate they found themselves in a series of chambers which held huge stone sarcophagi.

A stone passageway led to broad stone stairs that led in turn up to tall iron gates through which they could see the scaffolding beneath the main onion dome of St. Basil's Cathedral.

It was a few minutes before 4:30 A.M. The search for them would still be concentrated in the tunnels beneath Dzerzhinsky Square, and no one would be in the church at this hour of the morning. In fact all the buildings around Red Square would probably be closed until after the rally which was scheduled to take place in less than twelve hours.

At the top of the stairs, McGarvey reached the bolt cutter through the bars and cut the padlock free. When they were through, he replaced the padlock, and smeared some grease from the hinges around the severed metal hasp. It would fool a casual observer.

He led Jacqueline to one of the rear gardens and let her out.

"One last time, Kirk. Don't do this," she pleaded, looking up into his eyes.

"I have no other choice."

She touched his cheek with her fingertips. "Will I ever see you again, my lovely man?"

McGarvey managed a smile. "Count on it."

FORTY-TWO

Aboard Tarankov's Train

At 5:00, the morning was still pitch black and chilly as Tarankov sat on the open rear platform of his car smoking a cigarette and drinking a glass of brandy. He'd been brooding and watching the stars for the past three hours, thinking about how much he was going to miss Liesel. Her counsel as of late had become unsteady, as if the life they had led was finally beginning to unbalance her, but he missed her at his side now.

Every ten or fifteen minutes he spotted a shooting star. At first he'd made a wish on each of them. But he had stopped, because of course wishes never came true. The only truth was the reality we made for ourselves. The truth was that before the day was over he'd either be the supreme ruler of a new Soviet Union or he would be dead. At times like these he wondered if he really cared which, because throughout his life he had done questionable things. Things to which some biographer would apply his or her own truth.

He also thought about the young woman who'd infected them like a virus. She was an alien presence on the train and she was even starting to have an effect on his men. She'd not bothered to hide her nakedness as Liesel's body was removed and her compartment cleaned, and Tarankov had seen the looks on the faces of his young commandoes. It was lust, the same emotion that had affected him, and the same emotion that had resulted in Liesel's death, and very nearly his own.

But he found that he couldn't really hate the young woman who, after all, was here against her will. She'd defended herself the only way she knew how. And part of him could even admire her for her strength.

After the rally there would no longer be any need for her, he decided. He would kill her before the disease she carried infected them all beyond a cure. In a way she was every bit as dangerous to them, as her father was. They would both have to be destroyed at all costs.

Elizabeth McGarvey felt as if she had never slept in her life, or ever could. She had killed Liesel without hesitation, and had the gun contained more bullets she would have killed Tarankov as well. Afterward when the woman's body was being taken away and two of the young soldiers were cleaning up the mess she'd found that she was unable to move so much as a muscle. She'd been in shock, she supposed, but even though she was aware that she was naked, she'd done nothing to turn away or cover herself.

It was the last look in Liesel's eyes when the bullet had crashed into her chest, that troubled Elizabeth. She'd been surprised. Her rage had evaporated instantly, leaving a look on her face as if she were saying, "I'll be damned."

After that they'd left her alone, and it took a long time before she could rouse herself enough to step into the shower, turn on the water, and pick up the bar of soap. She had to carefully think out each of her movements, some of which made no sense to her, but seemed by habit to be the right thing to do. Like turning around in the shower so that she could wash her back. She could not figure out why it was necessary to do it.

When she was dressed she went back to work on the blackout screen covering her window, finally prying it completely free after a couple of hours' work, and several broken and bloody fingernails.

A soldier came out of the darkness outside and looked up at her. She stared back at him frankly, and after a minute he walked away.

The thing of it, in her mind, was that the killing wasn't finished. She was going to have to kill Tarankov before he destroyed her father. If she couldn't snatch a gun from one of the soldiers, perhaps she could take a knife from her breakfast tray. And if that was impossible, and she had to kill him with her bare hands, she would tear out his throat, or chew it open like an animal.

Thinking about what she had to do gave her a violent case of the shakes. Even though she hadn't eaten anything since eight last night, she just made it into the tiny bathroom and pulled down the sink in time to throw up.

When she finished she looked at her reflection in the mirror. She had become an animal. Tarankov and his wife had done it to her.

"Daddy," she whimpered, closing her eyes and lowering her head.

Even in the old days, when he was always gone, he'd protected her. Sometimes it was only his spirit rising within her, giving her courage. But he was always there for her.

She opened her eyes and looked up. It was her turn now to protect him.

The Kremlin

At 7:00, Chernov was called to a meeting at the President's office. His command center had been shifted to General Korzhakov's security headquarters at the rear of the Senate Building where he'd summoned the city engineer to go over the plans for the sewers and rivers beneath the city, so he only had to take an elevator upstairs.

General Yuryn, looking somewhat disheveled, was waiting for him in the anteroom.

"Any luck?" Yuryn asked.

"No, General, not yet. They probably drowned and their bodies may never be found unless they wash out into the Moscow River. I have men checking both banks as far downstream as the Krasnokholmsky Bridge but until it's completely light out, the task is nearly impossible."

"Where does that particular tunnel lead? Is it possible that they could find their way up somewhere else in the city?"

"The maps are unclear and sometimes contradictory. But that waterway may flow right beneath our feet."

Yuryn was startled.

"But no one is sure," Chernov said tiredly. He'd almost had McGarvey three times, but each time the bastard had somehow managed to wriggle free from the net. Chernov sincerely hoped that McGarvey and the French woman had not drowned, he wanted another shot at them.

"The President is waiting for us," Yuryn said.

"What does he want this time, another progress report? Well, there isn't any."

"I don't know."

They went inside where General Korzhakov was seated across the desk from an angry looking President Kabatov.

"I'm glad you're here, because I wanted to tell you this to your face. Your services are no longer needed, Colonel," Kabatov said harshly. "In fact you are under arrest as of this moment."

Chernov noticed that Korzhakov was holding a pistol in his lap, a curiously distant expression in his eyes.

"I'm also relieving you of duty, General," Kabatov told Yuryn. "You may consider yourself under house arrest until this business has been straightened out."

"What's the meaning of this?" Yuryn demanded.

"I think you and Colonel Chernov—not Bykov as we were led to believe—know very well what I mean. You recommended him to me, just as you insisted that we keep the SVR out of this affair."

"I don't know where you are receiving your information, Mr. President, but you are sadly mistaken about—"

"Enough of your lies," Kabatov thundered. "President Lindsay and I spoke at length a few hours ago. Not only about your Colonel Chernov but about the true nature of the man you so obviously support over the legitimate government. As it turns out Tarankov is not quite the Russian patriot he makes himself out to be. In point of fact he was a spy for the United States while he was an officer in the Strategic Rocket Force."

"That's not possible."

"Why isn't it possible?" Kabatov demanded. "Because you knew nothing about his past? His code name was Hammer, which is rather appropriate given the symbol on the flag he betrayed. Is still betraying!"

"Then you have already lost, Mr. President," Chernov said quietly. "Because short of completely barricading Red Square and canceling this afternoon's rally the Tarantula will come here to take over."

"If you're talking about a military coup, we're ready for him."

"I don't think you have the support in the military that you believe you do. Or else why hasn't his little train already been destroyed? He has only two hundred men with him, while you have the entire might of the Russian military."

Kabatov didn't rise to the bait, he maintained his temper. "It will be different this time."

Chernov shrugged indifferently. "Then you will still lose. No court of law in Russia will convict him."

Kabatov smiled. "You are correct, Colonel, no *Russian* court would convict him. That's why the instant he is arrested he will be flown to the World Court in The Hague where he will be tried as a war criminal."

"The American government would never admit in open court that it suborned a Soviet officer because the CIA would have to reveal its methods," Yuryn said.

"I have President Lindsay's support, and that of the governments of England, France, and Germany. I'm assured that the other major western powers will do the same. Tarankov has no chance."

"That might work," Chernov said. "Except that you're forgetting something."

"What's that?" Kabatov asked, outwardly unconcerned.

"For all your talk about rule of law, you have been reduced in this instance to trusting the loyalty of your officers and advisers. You cannot trust

General Yuryn, of course. Nor me. But you know that now. What about General Korzhakov, who was after all the chief of security for a man who despised you?"

"That needn't concern you," Kabatov replied. He reached for his telephone.

"What about Kirk McGarvey?" Chernov asked.

Kabatov's hand hesitated. "Once Tarankov is under arrest there will be no need to detain him. We'll let him go."

"That's your second mistake."

"What was my first?"

"Trusting anyone," Chernov said. He advanced closer to the desk, took out his pistol and before Kabatov could do much of anything except rear back in terror, shot the President in the forehead at nearly point blank range.

Korzhakov made no move to raise his gun.

Chernov took out his handkerchief and wiped his fingerprints off the gun. He stepped around the desk and placed the gun in the President's hand just as the door burst open and Kabatov's bodyguards pushed in, their weapons drawn.

Korzhakov had pocketed his gun. He got to his feet. "The President has shot himself, get a doctor in here now!" he ordered.

St. Basil's Cathedral

The onion domes were spotlighted from outside, which had given McGarvey all the light he needed to clean, assemble and load the Dragunov sniper rifle, and to clean and oil his Walther. With dawn finally beginning to brighten the eastern horizon he sat back against the brick wall in the arched cupola high above Red Square and allowed himself to relax.

Through the early morning hours the Square had been alive with activity in preparation for this afternoon's rally, and showed no signs of tapering off with the rising sun. In addition to the barricades, truckloads of soldiers had begun arriving an hour ago, the officers positioning their troops not only on the periphery of the square, but around Lenin's Mausoleum, and along the Kremlin's walls. More soldiers were stationed atop the walls at intervals of five or ten feet, and on the roofs of the old Senate and Supreme Soviet buildings facing the square.

It came to him that the majority of the defensive measures they were putting in place were designed to protect the Kremlin itself, possibly against an assault by Tarankov and his forces. But from his vantage point, which allowed him to see down inside the Kremlin's walls, he spotted other soldiers ringing all the buildings, and gates, and still more groups of soldiers going from building to building as if they were searching for something, or someone.

They were looking for him.

From his hiding place, McGarvey could also see the Moskvoretsky Bridge already busy with traffic. Soldiers were stationed on the bridge and on both sides of the river, and they too seemed to be searching for something.

Chernov's people would have lowered a man into the outflow tunnel down which they'd lost McGarvey and Jacqueline, until their way was blocked by the swiftly moving underground river. They would have reasoned that if anyone could survive the wild ride they might end up in the Moscow River.

There would have to be engineering diagrams of the city's storm sewer system, as well as maps of the underground rivers. Old maps because the rivers were here first and had only been gradually covered up over the years.

He looked again at the activity inside the Kremlin walls. If the old maps were inaccurate might Chernov's people believe the river was the one which ran beneath the Kremlin? Specifically the Neglinnaya River, or one of its branches that flowed under the Corner Arsenal Tower?

It would explain why no one had come here to search for him.

He lay his head back and closed his eyes for a moment, his hand pressed against the wound in his side. His shoulder and arm had stiffened up, and his mouth was so dry it was as if he'd never had a drink. But his vision was okay, and his head was still clear. He'd been in tougher spots and survived. This time would be no different, except that Liz was in danger.

He'd tried to avoid thinking about her, but sitting alone, wounded, tired, thirsty and hungry with Russian army and Militia troops earnestly searching for him, he could see her in his mind's eye, at her high school graduation, which Kathleen had tried to make a pleasant occasion, despite their bitter divorce. But in those days Liz was going through her rebellious stage in which any authority—all authority—was de facto bad. It was the only time he'd ever taken his daughter to task, and the graduation party had ended with Liz running off in tears and his ex-wife kicking him out of the house.

Good times and bad, he remembered them all, some with happiness, some with regrets.

A scraping noise somewhere directly below him on the elevated gallery which connected all the domes, woke him with a start. For a moment he thought he might have dreamed the sound, but then he heard it again. Someone was walking, trying to make as little noise as possible.

He screwed the silencer on the end of the Walther's barrel, and eased the safety catch to the off position, as he looked down through the scaffolding and tried to pick out a movement.

Whoever it was, stopped in the deeper shadows seventy-five feet below him. He could hear them breathing, almost panting, nervous, frightened.

Other than that noise, the church was utterly still. Even the technicians adjusting the sound system down in the square had finished, and traffic sounds from the bridge did not reach this far.

"Kirk?" Jacqueline's whispered voice drifted up to him.

He lowered his head and closed his eyes. "Christ," he said to himself. He switched the safety catch on.

"Kirk?" she called a little louder.

McGarvey moved away from the edge of the arch. "Here," he whispered back.

Jacqueline came into view below, her face raised up to the interior of the dome. She was carrying a blue shopping bag. When she spotted him outlined against the morning light coming through the cupola's window, she threaded her left arm through the shopping bag's handles, and climbed up the scaffolding.

When she reached the cupola, McGarvey helped her across.

"What are you doing here?" he demanded in frustration. "You were supposed to stay at your embassy. Goddammit!"

"That's what my boss told me. But there's not a chance you'll last up here all day without food and water, and without that wound bandaged up."

She opened the shopping bag, but McGarvey grabbed her arm.

"We almost died in the river this morning, and there's a good chance I won't get out alive! You have to get out of here right now."

Jacqueline nodded toward the round window. "It's crawling with soldiers and police down there. I've been hiding in the garden for the past forty-five minutes waiting to make sure it was safe to come to you. I got past them in the dark, but I'd never make it out of here without being spotted."

She pulled a small radio receiver from the shopping bag. "This scans all their police and military frequencies, and you're going to need it, because in the last few hours everything has changed. President Kabatov supposedly committed suicide this morning, which means no one is going to even try to stop Tarankov."

"It could be some kind of trick," McGarvey said.

"It came over one of the frequencies that the Kremlin security detail uses, and ever since then that channel has been silent. But military traffic is almost continuous, and just about every transmission contradicts a previous one. It's crazy out there, Kirk. They're just waiting now for someone to take over. And Tarankov is the man who'll do it."

"Unless he's stopped," McGarvey said.

Jacqueline looked into his eyes, her lips tightly compressed. She nodded.

"Like it or not, *mon cher*, you have me for the duration," she said. "Now let me bandage you up, and give you something to eat. Afterwards I'll take the first watch and you can get some rest."

FORTY-THREE

The Kremlin

It was after 3:00 P.M., and with Captain Petrovsky's help, under Chernov's direct supervision, every square meter of the Kremlin, above and below ground, had been searched with a fine-toothed comb to no avail by Kremlin security forces, the Militia and the Army.

A red dye had been dumped down the outflow tunnel beneath the Lubyanka Metro Station. It had shown up in the swiftly moving water beneath the Corner Arsenal Tower a few minutes later, but in a limited amount which an engineer suggested might mean that there was more than one branch of the river.

Three volunteer divers had been sent down the tunnel. The battered body of one of them, minus his scuba tank, his wet suit ripped to shreds, showed up under the tower eight minutes later.

That was around ten this morning. The other two divers had not shown up yet. There'd been no other volunteers.

Petrovsky came over to where Chernov leaned against the hood of his car parked in front of the Senate Building listening to reports on a hand-held radio, and debating with himself if now was the time to get out. Everything suggested that McGarvey and Jacqueline Belleau had escaped down the tunnel in a desperate attempt to save themselves, and were drowned. Their bodies might stay down there until the next series of heavy rains completely flooded the tunnels. Or they might never come out. It was a reasonable assumption to believe that McGarvey was no longer a threat to Tarankov's safety. Yet something within Chernov, some instinct, told him otherwise.

"One of my people has come up with an idea," Petrovsky said. "He thinks that we should pump a couple thousand gallons of diesel fuel down the tunnel, and set it on fire. It might work. At least it'd be better than using gasoline, which would probably blow everything from here to there off the map."

Chernov studied the Militia investigator for a moment to make sure the man wasn't joking.

"If they're still down there, they're already dead. So trying to cook them out wouldn't accomplish a thing."

"Do you think they got out?"

"I want to say no, but I'm not sure," Chernov said. "With a man like him you can never be sure."

"He has the woman with him. She might have slowed him down."

"What are the French saying about her?"

"Nothing. In fact they won't even talk to me. Word's out about President Kabatov, and it's got everybody scared shitless," Petrovsky said. He gave Chernov an appraising look. "That includes me, Colonel, because I don't know what's going on."

"That doesn't matter. You have a job to do and I suggest you get on with it."

"We're done."

"Then have your men start over again," Chernov said. "Because if McGarvey is still alive he'll be here within the hour, and we'd better be ready for him."

"What about you, Colonel?" Petrovsky said, choosing his words with care. "Your letter from President Kabatov authorizing you to do whatever it takes to catch McGarvey is no longer valid. Who are you reporting to now?"

Chernov was tired but still in control of himself. "General Yuryn."

"What about him?" Petrovsky asked. "Who is he reporting to? Who's in charge?"

"General Korzhakov," Chernov said. "For the moment."

Petrovsky nodded. "I think I'll get back to my men, now."

Chernov watched him walk away, basically a competent man who probably would not survive the next few days. There would be a lot of good and
competent men who wouldn't make it. In every revolution they were among
the first to die.

He pocketed the hand-held transceiver, checked the load in the Colt
10mm automatic he'd drawn from Kremlin security stores and took the elevator up to the presidential floor.

Security was tight. Even he had to pass through four separate body
searches, and explain who he was and why he was carrying a weapon, before
he was allowed to approach what had become General Korzhakov's temporary base of operations.

Civilians and soldiers scurried along corridors, telephones rang, computer
printers whined, and heated discussions took place in every third office. Yet
there seemed to be no order to what was going on. Half the people seemed
to be in a daze, simply standing by, waiting for something to happen. Waiting for Tarankov to show up, though nobody was saying so aloud. The other
half tried to look busy.

The president's anteroom and office were jammed with people. Korzhakov, facing the windows, was speaking to someone on the phone, while
three of his advisers hovered around, passing him notes.

General Yuryn, his uniform disheveled, looking more corpulent and dis-
gusting than ever, hurried out to Chernov.

"Have you found him?" he demanded.

"He and the French woman are probably dead, but we're still looking."

"Tarankov's train is on the move. The rally has been cancelled, but that
won't stop the crowds of course, so when he arrives the platform will be his
alone. The rest of us will wait up here."

"When's he due?"

"His ETA at Leningrad Station is 3:40, which gives him twenty minutes
to get down here if he means to make it by four."

"How about the military?"

"So far they're remaining neutral."

"Including General Vashleyev?"

Captain-General Viktor Vashleyev was commander of the Moscow Defense Forces, and a former drinking buddy of President Yeltsin and Korzhakov. But he was something of a moderate, no friend of Tarankov.

"He promises to do whatever it takes to maintain order," Yuryn said.
"Tarankov's arrest warrant is on his desk, but I don't think he'll act on it."

"Then everything is set—"

"Except for McGarvey," Yuryn cut in. "Is there any chance, even a slight
chance, that he'll get out of the sewers in time to make the assassination
attempt?"

"If it was anyone else I'd say no."

"Is there a chance that if he does somehow make it out, that you won't
be able to stop him in time?" Yuryn asked sharply.

"I don't know," Chernov said after a moment. "So far he's eluded everything we've thrown at him, even the threat that we'll use his daughter as a hostage. But he's not a fanatic, which means he knows how he's going to kill Tarankov and he has a plan for getting away."

"Tarankov will have to send a double to make his speech," said Yuryn, after first making certain that no one was listening to them.

"He won't do it."

Yuryn threw up his hands in despair. "Then it's up to you," he said. "For the next hour and a half until Tarankov is safely off the reviewing stand you must operate on the assumption that McGarvey managed to get out of the sewers and will take the shot."

Krasnaya Prensya

Viktor Yemlin had a bad three days. It was a few minutes after 3:00, and he was parked in his car down the block from an eighteen-story apartment building near the zoo, not sure if he knew what he was doing.

Ever since the untraceable but potentially disastrous call from the man who had identified himself as a friend of McGarvey's, he'd been waiting for the axe to fall. But nothing had happened, and after a couple of discreet telephone calls he was pretty sure that he was no longer being followed. His home telephone was still bugged, but the pay phones around his apartment were not.

The development was ominous, all the more so because his normal channels of communication between the FSK and the Militia had been blocked. Every cop and soldier in Moscow was looking for McGarvey, and he had no access to any information about the search except that it was going on.

Nor, despite his sensitive position in the SVR, was he able to find out anything about President Kabatov's apparent suicide this morning although he was being asked to predict Washington's likely response.

It was like working in a vacuum. Nothing was getting through.

His guest membership at the Magesterium had been cancelled, and his friend Konstantin Sukoruchkin was not answering his telephone.

One by one his contacts in Moscow were drying up. It was as if everyone he'd known was suddenly distancing themselves from him.

Earlier this afternoon he'd tried to use the SVR's secured telephone system to place a call to Shevardnadze in Tbilisi, but his access had been denied, thus completing his isolation.

Yemlin looked at his watch. If Tarankov was on schedule he would be arriving in Red Square in less than an hour. Whether or not McGarvey assassinated him, the next few hours would be extremely critical for the nation, all the more now that there was no elected leader in charge.

Yemlin looked at his watch again, then got out of the car and strode down the block to the apartment building, where he presented his credentials to the front desk security people, who were expecting him.

He was escorted upstairs where he was met in the penthouse foyer by a secretary who led him back to a corner study with panoramic views of the city.

Five minutes later, Mikhail Gorbachev, wearing a button-up sweater over an open-neck shirt, corduroy trousers and house slippers, entered the study.

"Mr. President, Russia is heading toward certain disaster and you're the only man I know who can help," Yemlin said.

St. Basil's Cathedral

By 3:40 one million people were jammed into Red Square and still more poured in from around the city. Bleachers east and west of Lenin's Mausoleum were filled with visiting dignitaries and the press. Dozens of television vans were lined up end-to-end along the Kremlin walls, their satellite dishes pointed up to the sky.

Soldiers and police manned barricades that held the people back from a broad boulevard that ran up from the river, past the Cathedral, crossed in front of the reviewing stand and opened into Okhotny Ryad at the north end of the square. It was the traditional parade route taken by the troops and their military hardware.

McGarvey had managed to get a little sleep, and afterward he'd used his pocket knife to remove the lead holding a roughly triangular piece of stained glass about twelve inches wide at its base from the round window. He crouched well back from the narrow opening through which he would shoot and studied the reviewing platform through the Dragunov's powerful scope. No one had shown up yet. No ceremonial guards, no officers, nor any of the sound technicians. Armed soldiers were still stationed on the Kremlin walls above and behind the mausoleum, but the reviewing platform was empty, the flags and banners snapping in the stiff breeze that had developed since noon.

Traditional Russian folk music thundered across the square from loudspeakers sprinkled here and there. Some people danced to it, and around the edges of the vast crowd vendors sold everything from ice cream to beer. It was a carnival atmosphere, except it was obvious that the people were waiting expectantly for something.

With Kabatov dead no one had stepped in to fill his place or else they would have come to the reviewing stand by now. The city, and the entire country was waiting for Tarankov's triumphal entrance to Red Square where he would mount the platform and tell his people that he had come to restore the Soviet Union, to give them back their dignity and their pride, to feed and clothe and house them, to give them back their jobs, their hospitals and their peace of mind.

But at what cost, almost no one seemed to be asking.

Most of the frequencies the scanner was picking up had been oddly quiet. Very little had come from the Kremlin's security detail after the search of the tunnels by divers had ended in disaster. Only the frequencies used by the Militia and army crowd control units remained busy. A dozen arrests had been made, a few fights broken up, and a number of handguns confiscated.

Jacqueline had positioned herself beneath one of the arches on the opposite side of the central dome from where she could watch the main entrance below. So far the church remained empty. McGarvey glanced over at her at the same moment something coming over the radio caught his attention.

"Azarov Brigade, say again your ETA at Leningrad Station."

"We're three minutes out," an excited voice responded. It sounded as if he were radioing from a moving vehicle.

"Pull back to point B. I repeat, pull back to point B, he's already there."

"Copy. I don't want to get into a firefight with his people up here. We won't have a chance without reinforcements."

"You'll be coming in behind him, so watch yourself," the first speaker warned. "Gamov and Sokol brigades, are you in position yet?"

"Gamov, roger."

"Sokol, roger."

"Keep your eyes open, this is a go," the first speaker said.

Apparently the government was finally doing something, but McGarvey was almost certain that they were making a very big mistake. If they meant to stop Tarankov, yet keep the civilian casualties to a minimum, the job should have been done out in the countryside by a direct attack on his train. Or else Leningrad Station could have been evacuated and as Tarankov's troops dismounted they could have been cut down. But by avoiding a firefight up there, they were taking the battle to a Red Square jammed with innocent people. No matter how many troops they had at their command, a crowd of a million people was an unstoppable force.

McGarvey carefully laid the rifle down, climbed out of the arched cupola and waved at Jacqueline until he caught her eye.

She started around the scaffolding, and he met her halfway.

"Has it started?" she asked, wide-eyed.

"His train just pulled into Leningrad Station so he could be here in fifteen or twenty minutes. But the government is going to try to ambush him."

"Good, then we can get out of here right now," said Jacqueline, relieved.

"They've missed him at the station, so they're coming down here."

Jacqueline glanced over toward the window. "It'll be a massacre with all those people waiting for him. *Merde*, are they stupid?"

"They're desperate," McGarvey said. "And they won't succeed, so I'm staying here."

Jacqueline looked into his eyes. "Then I too shall stay."

"I want you to go down to the garden entrance, the one you used to get in here, and make sure it's clear. As soon as I take my shot, we'll get out. We can lose ourselves in the crowd."

She wanted to argue with him, but after a moment she kissed him on the cheek, and then made her way down to the gallery level that provided access to the other parts of the Cathedral.

McGarvey was glad she hadn't asked him about Liz. Listening to the radio had given him an idea for a contingency plan in case everything fell apart here.

Leningrad Station

Elizabeth McGarvey was more frightened than she'd ever been in her life, yet she was still determined to somehow kill Tarankov with her bare hands, if need be because she had no weapon. They'd not fed her breakfast or lunch, so she'd not been able to steal a table knife or a fork. Nor had she found anything in her compartment that could be used as a weapon.

Two minutes ago they'd screamed to a halt a hundred yards from the big railroad station, the doors on most of the armored cars crashed open, steel ramps were extended with a tremendous din, and a dozen armored personnel carriers roared into life, forming up along the tracks next to the train.

Thousands of people up on the street waved banners and cheered, the noise they made so overwhelming that even over the roar of the APCs, Elizabeth could hear them.

The door of her compartment opened, and she spun around, ready to attack like a wild animal, but Tarankov was not with the two stern-faced commandoes.

"You will come with us now," one of them ordered.

"Fuck you," Elizabeth shouted in Russian, and she lunged at them, swinging both fists.

The commando grabbed her by the arms and sent her crashing into the compartment wall, bending her elbows behind her back so hard she thought her shoulders would be dislocated.

When she settled down they pulled her out into the corridor, where one of them pawed her crotch and grinned.

"We'll have some fun with you tonight, you little bitch," he promised.

Outside, she was hustled across the tracks and shoved into the lead APC with eight commandoes. Tarankov stood on top in the gunner's turret, and the moment the hatch slammed shut he gave the order to move out.

Elizabeth was pushed into a bucket seat near the back of the vehicle, and had to brace herself in order not to be tossed around.

It was happening as she feared it might, leaving her no chance of fighting back. But the opportunity would come, she kept telling herself. It was her only hope, her only connection with sanity.

The Kremlin

Chernov put down the telephone as one of the city engineers came rushing down the corridor into the deserted Security Center with Captain Petrovsky. The SVR helicopter he'd ordered would touch down inside the Kremlin walls on the opposite side from Red Square between the Borovitskaya and Water Drawing towers in ten minutes. The pilot, a Tarankov supporter, agreed to stand by until Chernov showed up.

"St. Basil's," Petrovsky shouted.

The engineer spread a large scale yellowed plan drawing of a part of the river and storm sewer system downtown. Over this he laid a clear plastic sheet upon which had been drawn the locations of the metro stations and tunnels, and the major buildings from Dzerzhinsky Square all the way down to the Moscow River.

"The outflow they entered drops into what is part of the Neglinnaya River System. But it branches into three tunnels so that during the spring meltoff the system won't overload and flood. It's why only a portion of the dye showed up here. A third of it went directly beneath Red Square, and the last third here." The engineer stabbed a blunt finger on St. Basil's outlined on the plastic overlay.

"Is there access from the river into the church?" Chernov asked.

"Yes, sir. Through the crypts," the engineer said. "They didn't come up here, and they didn't show up in the Moscow River. So unless their bodies are still down there, they came up inside St. Basil's."

"Within shooting distance of the reviewing stand," Petrovsky said.

"That's it," Chernov shouted, and he bolted for the door, shouting for Petrovsky to follow him.

Outside, they piled into Chernov's car and shot across the Kremlin toward the Trinity Gate, figuring they could circle around the crowds in Red Square and approach the Cathedral from Varvarka Street.

"Radio your people and have them cover every exit," Chernov ordered.

"They're gone," Petrovsky said.

Chernov glanced at him. "What do you mean, gone?"

"Just that, Colonel, and I can't say that I blame them. But we have another problem. General Vashleyev's people are going to try to arrest Tarankov."

"I heard," Chernov said. "They missed him at Leningrad Station, but if they try anything down here there's going to be a bloodbath."

"Mostly civilian," Petrovsky said dourly.

"I thought you didn't support Tarankov."

"Let's just say that I'm hedging my bets, Colonel," Petrovsky said.

St. Basil's

Tarankov's column roared into Red Square from the north, raced down the broad boulevard in front of the masses of people who were joyously screaming his name, and pulled up in a semicircle in front of Lenin's Mausoleum. The soldiers and police manning the barricades were overwhelmed by the press of people trying to get closer, aided only by the intimidating presence of the twelve heavily armed APCs now facing outward, their big diesel engines idling as if they were a pack of rabid dogs making ready to attack. The crowd surged only so far then stopped, their front ranks making an undulating line back up the square to the north.

Even the international media kept its respectful distance, though dozens of television cameras were trained on the column, and a few of the bolder photographers closed in on the lead APC from both sides hoping to catch a shot of the Tarantula.

"Target is in place, are you in position Gamov Brigade?" the radio beside McGarvey stopped at the active frequency.

"Roger, we're in place at the south end of the square."

"Sokol, any trouble at your position?

"*Nyet*, we're clear."

"Okay, Azarov Brigade, we're set down here, what's your ETA to bottle the northern route?"

"Five minutes."

McGarvey studied the lead APC through the Dragunov's telescopic sights. The top hatch of the gun turret was open but no one was manning the position as they were on the other eleven vehicles. The wind had increased in the past half hour, and whipped the exhaust from the diesel engines from McGarvey's left to right, making any attempted shot in the cross wind difficult at best.

The music suddenly stopped, and the crowd began to quiet down.

"COMRADES, MY NAME IS YEVGENNI TARANKOV, AND I HAVE COME TODAY TO OFFER MY HAND IN FRIENDSHIP AND HELP," a voice boomed from the loudspeakers.

Now the vast crowd fell totally silent, and even the soldiers at the barricades looked over their shoulders at the lead APC.

The APC's personnel hatch opened, and McGarvey switched aim, moving the sniper rifle's safety to the off position with his thumb.

Chernov and Petrovsky were stopped from entering Red Square from the east by a skirmish line of five hundred heavily armed troops backed by three T-80 tanks, with Moscow Defense Division markings on their sides, so they had to double back to Ilyinka Street that ran along the south side of the department store GUM.

Tarankov's amplified voice boomed across the otherwise silent square, as Chernov and Petrovsky left the car and hurried down the street on foot.

They had to show their IDs before they were allowed through the barricades into the square itself, which took more precious time. By now Tarankov would be climbing out of his APC, exposing himself to McGarvey's shot.

When they were through, they raced along the edge of the crowd, shoving people out of their way as they ran, Tarankov's speech continuing to roll across the vast open space.

"OUR COUNTRY IS FALLING INTO A BOTTOMLESS PIT OF DESPAIR," Tarankov said.

A figure appeared at the open hatch, paused a moment then stepped out. It was one of Tarankov's young commandoes. McGarvey held the scope's cross hairs steady on the hatch.

"OUR FORESTS ARE DYING. OUR GREAT RIVERS AND LAKES HAVE BECOME CESSPOOLS OF WASTE. THE AIR IS UNFIT TO BREATHE. THE ONLY FOOD WORTH EATING FILLS THE BELLIES OF APPARATCHIKS AND FOREIGNERS."

Seven more armed commandoes dressed in plain battle fatigues climbed out of the APC, and formed a tight knot in front of the hatch.

"OUR CHILDREN ARE DYING AND OUR WOMEN ARE CRYING, BUT NO ONE IN MOSCOW CAN HEAR THEM. NO ONE IN MOSCOW WANTS TO HEAR THEM."

McGarvey caught a glimpse of a smaller, much slighter figure emerging from the APC, and his stomach fluttered when he recognized his daughter. Directly behind her Tarankov climbed out, and taking Liz's arm immediately moved behind the protective screen of his much taller, much larger commandoes, making any shot impossible.

"OUR HEALTH CARE SYSTEM IS BANKRUPT," Tarankov said, as he and his men moved toward Lenin's Mausoleum.

"All units, sixty seconds to first air strike," the scanner radio beside McGarvey stopped at the active frequency.

A ninth commando emerged from the APC, and went immediately over to Tarankov, who was still speaking.

"OUR MILITARY HAS BECOME LEADERLESS AND USELESS."

"Azarov Brigade, what is your ETA?"

"Two minutes," an excited voice radioed.

"Sokol and Gamov will back you up if he heads your way, but you're going to have to hold him."

"HOOLIGANS AND PROFITEERS ERODE OUR LIVELIHOODS LIKE CANCER. THE MAFIA EATS BEEFSTEAKS AND CAVIAR, DRINKS SWEET CHAMPAGNE AND DRIVES CADILLACS AND—"

Tarankov's amplified voice cut off in mid-sentence.

McGarvey caught glimpses of Tarankov, and the ninth commando to come out of the APC. They seemed to be arguing. The commando pointed back at the APC, and then up to the sky to the southwest.

"Forty seconds, all units keep your heads down in case he doesn't move," the excited voice on the scanner radioed.

Liz suddenly tried to break away, but Tarankov pulled her back, slapped her face, rocking her head back, and the commandoes surrounding him closed ranks even tighter.

No shot. Even without the wind there would have been no guarantee that if he fired he might hit Elizabeth, and McGarvey was beside himself with frustration and rage.

The ninth commando said something else to Tarankov, and then the knot of commandoes headed back en masse to the lead APC.

McGarvey waited for an opening, any opening, but Tarankov ducked into the safety of the APC first, followed by Elizabeth and then his commandoes, and the hatch was shut.

"He's on the move! He's on the move! Azarov Brigade, he's coming your way right now!"

Two of the APCs moved out, leaving Tarankov's vehicle to take up the third position, the others falling in behind, and they roared off to the north, the crowds stunned into inaction, hardly able to believe what they were witnessing. Their savior was deserting them for some unknown reason.

Pocketing the scanner radio, but leaving the now useless sniper rifle behind, McGarvey climbed out of the arched cupola, and scrambled down the scaffolding to the gallery level seventy-five feet below and started for the rear of the church where Jacqueline was waiting at the garden door. He was sick at heart for his daughter, because he didn't know how he would make it in time to save her.

He reached the rear of the main onion dome, when the church doors crashed open below him.

"McGarvey," a man shouted, the same man from the storm sewers. Chernov!

McGarvey slipped back into the shadows as he took out his Walther and removed the silencer. There was no longer any need for stealth, and the silencer seriously degraded the accuracy of the gun. From where he stood he could see the arch leading to the outer vestibule.

"It's all over, McGarvey," Chernov shouted. "There's no way out for you now, but if you give yourself up you'll live to stand trial, and your daughter will be released unharmed. You have my word."

McGarvey eased a little closer to the rail so that when Chernov came out of the vestibule he would have a clear shot. At this point the Russian had to believe that McGarvey was still somewhere up inside the onion dome.

"I have him! I have him! But there's too many civilians up here!" McGarvey's radio blared.

He reached in his pocket to shut it off as a man in uniform darted out from the vestibule and fired four shots up at the gallery, two of them ricocheting off the rail inches from where McGarvey stood.

McGarvey returned fire, one of his shots catching the man in the torso, driving him backward, at the same moment Jacqueline opened fire from the rear of the church.

McGarvey sprinted the rest of the way along the gallery to one of the corner domes and rushed downstairs to the main floor.

Jacqueline was crouched just inside the corridor leading back to the garden exit thirty feet across the open floor from where McGarvey pulled up.

She spotted him and started to rise, but he held up a hand for her to stay put, and she dropped back.

The man in uniform was down, his body half in and half out of the vestibule. McGarvey didn't think it was Chernov, but the church was silent, nothing moved.

McGarvey took a few kopeck coins out of his pocket and tossed them toward the opposite side of the church, sending them clattering across the stone floor.

Two shots were fired from the vestibule.

Jacqueline returned fire, and McGarvey sprinted across to the corridor, firing over his shoulder back toward the vestibule as he ran.

Several shots ricochetted off the floor just behind him, but then he was around the corner. He grabbed Jacqueline's arm and together they raced to the garden exit at the rear of the Cathedral.

"As soon as we get outside, lose yourself in the crowds, you'll be safe," McGarvey told her urgently.

They heard Chernov's footfalls as he crossed the length of the nave behind them.

McGarvey fired the last couple of shots in the Walther's magazine down the corridor, and then he and Jacqueline emerged into the garden.

"Now go," he ordered.

"There's a van waiting for us," she said, out of breath. "It's from my embassy."

McGarvey hesitated for just a second.

"I brought a cellular phone. I called them," she explained. "They're here. They got through."

"Okay, let's do it," McGarvey said, and he followed her across the garden. He ejected the spent magazine from his gun, and put another one in, releasing the ejector slide, as the sounds of heavy weapons fire and screams came from the north end of Red Square.

FORTY-FOUR

Red Square

Something slammed into the APC with a loud clang, nearly knocking them over, propelling Elizabeth out of her bucket seat and slamming her painfully into the bulkhead next to the hatch.

They were in the middle of a fierce fire fight, the noise utterly deafening, hot shell casings falling all around her from the heavy-caliber machine guns above.

Tarankov was strapped into the command position above and behind the driver and the two weapons officers, calmly issuing orders over his headset.

Elizabeth clawed her way up to her knees so that she could see out the thick glass of the narrow port in the hatch as the lead APCs suddenly turned to the right, directly into the wall of human beings lining the Square and Okhotny Ryad.

The people tried to fall back out of the way, but it was impossible because of the confusion and press of bodies behind them.

Horrified, Elizabeth watched as the first of the people were bowled over or pushed aside, but then the lead APC gave a mighty lurch and climbed up on top of the bodies, blood and gore flying everywhere, spitting out from under the huge tracks. The second APC climbed atop the carnage directly behind the first one, plowing and smashing its way across the broad street toward Ploshchad Revolyutsi.

Elizabeth fell back, unable to do anything else but brace herself from being tossed around as the APC she was in followed the first two, climbing and bucking and heaving over the bodies. She could imagine that she was hearing the screams, hearing the bones crunch, seeing the blood oozing up through the steel plating of the floor. And still it went on.

She looked up at the same moment Tarankov glanced down at her, and she almost screamed in horror, because the look on his face and in his eyes was absolutely devoid of any human emotion. What they were doing, what he had ordered, the people they killed and whose bodies they were driving over, none of it had any effect on him. She had never seen that lack of feeling on any human being's face, not even Chernov's. And until this moment she had not even imagined that such a monster could possibly exist in the real world.

The shooting stopped and then Elizabeth *could* hear the people screaming, and she screwed her eyes shut as if she could block out the inhuman shrieks.

They lurched sharply to the right, came back onto the pavement and accelerated, but still Elizabeth could hear the screaming.

The shooting had stopped, but pandemonium had broken out as panicked people tried to get away, climbing over each other, pushing, screaming, shoving the Militia and military barricades and soldiers out of the way.

Chernov emerged from the garden gate and flattened himself against the wall at the corner. There was no sign of McGarvey or the French woman, but he knew that he was just seconds behind them, and they could not have gotten very far in this mob.

Something had gone wrong with Tarankov's triumphal entrance. He didn't think that McGarvey had taken his shot, because Tarankov's commandoes would not have fought back if their leader was dead. For some reason General Vashleyev had ordered his troops to surround Red Square and box Tarankov in. But they had not counted on Tarankov fighting back in the middle of the mob. They had made the same mistake sending helicopter gunships to stop the train outside Nizhny Novgorod.

Chernov stepped away from the wall. North or south, they could have gone either way, and once they reached the French or American embassy they would be out of his reach.

On instinct he headed north, pushing people out of his path until he came to an abandoned Militia radio car, its lights flashing. He leaped up on the hood of the car and just caught a glimpse of McGarvey, the woman and a third person as they reached Ilynka Street and disappeared around the corner.

He jumped down and yanked the driver's door open when a dozen men rushed up, pushed him aside and started rocking the squad car on its springs to tip it over.

McGarvey was getting away. It was all Chernov could think of as he fought his way up to Ilynka Street where his own car was parked. Getting across Red Square and inside the Kremlin where the SVR helicopter was waiting for him made the most sense. Once airborne he could direct the pilot to take him out of the city, and head up to St. Petersburg. From there he could catch the train to Helsinki where he could access his Swiss bank account and disappear. But McGarvey had made a fool of him, had made fools of them all. And he had killed Arkady.

Ilynka Street was jammed with people heading away from the Square as fast as they could. The T-80 tanks were gone, and the barricades had been removed or simply shoved aside.

Chernov reached his car in time to see McGarvey and the woman climb into a blue Chrysler van. He got in his car, and swung it around, gently easing his way through the crowd and then moving with it.

He was thirty yards behind the van, and he could see the top of it above the heads of the people, not moving any faster than he was, so for the moment there was little danger that he would lose them. Once they were in the clear he would speed up and run them off the road before they could reach either embassy, and kill McGarvey and the two with him.

Only then would he leave Russia, because his brother was wrong, revenge was everything.

Moscow

McGarvey looked out the back window, but if Chernov had followed them there was no sign of him. In any event he would be on foot.

"Are you okay?" he asked Jacqueline.

She nodded. "I think so, but what happened to Tarankov? Did you get a shot?"

"No, Liz was with him. I saw her." He leaned forward to the driver. "As soon as we get clear head out to the Garden Ring Road. I want you to take me up to Leningrad Station as quickly as possible."

"What?" Jacqueline screeched.

"He's got Liz—"

"The authorities will stop him! His coup didn't work!"

"I'm not willing to take that chance," McGarvey said harshly.

"*Merde*," Jacqueline said. She turned to the driver. "Take us back to the embassy, Nikolai. Right now!"

McGarvey switched to Russian. "*Yeb vas, but if you don't take me to Leningradski Station you're going to get your nine grams.*" It was a Russian euphemism for a 9mm bullet in the base of the skull.

The driver glanced at McGarvey's stern-faced reflection in the rearview mirror, hesitated a moment, but then nodded.

"You can't do this," Jacqueline cried.

"I missed him, and now he doesn't need her."

"I know how you feel, my darling. I promise I do—"

"No you don't," McGarvey cut her off savagely. "You were sent to spy on me in Paris. You've done your job, now leave."

"I love you—"

"Not now!" McGarvey shouted her down.

The van shot across the normally busy broad boulevard Staraya Ploshchad in Kitay-Gorod, the bulk of the crowds now behind them. What traffic there was all seemed to be heading away from Red Square, but Moscow suddenly seemed deserted, as if everyone had either left or was hiding behind locked doors waiting to see what was going to happen. It lent a strange war-zone feel to the city.

Liz had fought back. She had tried to get away, even in the middle of Tarankov's commandoes, even in the face of the hundreds of thousands of people and soldiers crammed into Red Square. And Tarankov had swatted her aside like he might swat an irritating insect.

McGarvey's jaw tightened, and his muscles bunched up, his face tightening in pain. He forced himself to calm down. To act rationally. To think out his options.

Five minutes later the van turned north on the Garden Ring Road just past the Ural Hotel, and traffic picked up though most of it was going in the opposite direction. In the distance they could see the twenty-six-story Hotel Leningradskaya west of Komsomolskaya Square which contained the Yaroslavl, Kazan and Leningrad Stations.

"It doesn't have to be this way, Kirk," Jacqueline said. "I want to save her life as badly as you do."

"As soon as you get back to your embassy have your people try to find out who's in charge of the government. Call my embassy and tell them that I'm not going to kill Tarankov. I'm just going to get my daughter out of there. Whoever is in charge in the Kremlin will have to understand that I want nothing more."

"You magnificent fool," Jacqueline said quietly. "You're going to get yourself killed, aren't you?"

"I can't leave her. She's all I've got. All I've ever really had."

"I know, *mon cher*. I know."

"There's a roadblock up ahead," the driver called back.

A T-80 tank and several army trucks were parked across the road a quarter-mile ahead. Barricades had been put up, and soldiers were turning cars away.

"Take a side street, I have to get closer than this," McGarvey ordered.

The driver turned at the huge Agriculture Ministry Building, but the street was barricaded just behind the Kazan Station two hundred yards from the square, across which they could see Leningrad Station. Thousands of people were milling around in the square, but it was impossible to see if Tarankov's train was still there. The driver made a left turn, then right again toward the Hotel Leningradskaya.

This time the barricades had been shoved aside by people streaming away. The street was littered with tarantula banners, and in front of the hotel something was going on in the middle of a huge crowd.

The driver was forced to stop fifty yards away.

"For God's sake don't go, Kirk," Jacqueline pleaded one last time.

"Go back to your embassy and get the word out," McGarvey said.

He jumped out of the van, and took off in a dead run.

Up on the square there was a broad path of bodies and blood, as if something had mowed its way through the crowd. Some people were helping the wounded, but for the most part everyone was trying to get away.

McGarvey entered the station, and raced across the vaulted arrivals hall filled with people who seemed to be in a daze. Trackside he pulled up short. There were three trains, none of which was Tarankov's.

But in Nizhny Novgorod he'd not pulled into the station. The train had stopped outside where the APCs could be off-loaded and make their way up to the streets.

McGarvey rushed to the end of the loading platform, jumped down to the tracks and emerged from the station in time to see the last of the APCs being loaded into the train fifty yards away.

He could see where the APCs had come down from the street, across the tracks to the west. Only a few stragglers were up there now, but the trail of blood led directly across, pointing a damning finger at what had been done.

A skirmish line of a dozen commandoes had taken up a rear guard position, but their attention was directed back the way they had come.

Keeping his eye on the rear guard, he pulled out his pistol, and staying low, raced for the right side of the armored train.

An Army truck screeched to a halt up on the road, and Tarankov's commandoes opened fire, cutting the troops down as they hit the street.

McGarvey reached the lee of the diesel-electric locomotive as its huge engines roared into life. Almost immediately it began moving backward.

Holstering his gun, he sprinted the last fifty feet to the first armored car, grabbed the access ladder and clambered to the roof.

Above Moscow

Captain Anatoli Trofimo touched off his forward looking radar as he swung his MiG-29 Fulcrum around in a tight loop at the southern edge of Moscow's inner defense ring. His wingman Captain Aleksandr Lopatin was ten meters off his port wing tip, and gave him the thumbs up sign.

Nothing was in view yet, but after the debacle up at Nizhny Novgorod nobody was taking any chances, though shooting down a few slow moving helicopters was a different proposition than shooting down a pair of high performance fighter/interceptors. Still, Tarankov was a wily old bastard, his troops were the best in all of Russia, and the defense systems aboard his son-of-a-bitch train were state-of-the-art.

The original plan was to make a surgical strike against Tarankov as he stood on the reviewing platform atop Lenin's Mausoleum. They'd been told that Lenin's body had been removed to a safe place underground, but that didn't matter as much to Trofimo as getting his shot right the first time. If they missed they'd be firing into a crowd estimated above one million people.

They'd turned inbound, armed their R85 air-to-surface missiles, and started their attack run when they were ordered to stand down less than forty seconds to target because Tarankov was on the move. Trofimo was damned glad for the reprieve. He and his wingman were ordered to keep station at the southern inner defense ring, where they had remained for the past fifteen minutes, mushing at ten thousand feet to conserve fuel.

His air controller's voice came over his comms.

"Orlov units, prime time has reached his secondary objective. You are authorized to go hot, and take out the target. Repeat, you have weapons release authorization."

"Roger, we're inbound now," Trofimo radioed. "Do you have vectors to target?"

"Roger. Relative bearing zero-four-seven, changing slowly to the north. The target is on the move and accelerating."

Aboard Tarankov's Train

Keeping low so that he wouldn't be thrown off balance as the train continued to accelerate backward through the switching yards, McGarvey leapt from car to car. The APCs had been loaded aboard the lead twelve units, leaving the rear eight for personnel. At Nizhny Novgorod Tarankov had gotten off from the rear car, which McGarvey figured was his personal quarters, and possibly the unit's operations center.

Several of the car tops contained long narrow hatches set flush into the roofs, probably concealing the missile launchers. Domes rose from the four corners of every fourth car, Phalanx Gatling gun barrels protruding from the radar-guided deadly close-in weapons systems. Other domes probably contained combat radar systems.

He'd seen the train's defensive measures in action at Nizhny Novgorod, and they'd been nothing short of awesome. It wouldn't take long for Tarankov's commandoes to realize that the government forces would be following them, and to get their act together after their hasty retreat from Red Square. That defeat had to sting, but their confusion wouldn't last.

The roof on the rear half of the last car was raised about four feet, and bristled with radar dishes and antennae. Armored viewing ports were set in the thick steel plates.

McGarvey dropped flat on the roof of the next to the last car, screwed the silencer on his gun, then swung over the edge and climbed down the ladder to the connecting platform door. The train was moving at fifty miles per hour now and still accelerating as he pulled open the door and jumped inside.

The corridor in the forward car was deserted, but peering in the window of Tarankov's car he was in time to see a commando disappear up the stairs to the upper level.

When the man was out of sight, McGarvey slipped inside, his heart pounding, the wound in his side throbbing from his exertions.

As he hesitated, a woman's voice raised in anger screamed something from the rear of the car. The words were indistinct but he recognized Elizabeth's voice, and he rushed down the corridor.

The last ten feet of the railroad car was fitted out as a comfortable sitting room, couches, easy chairs, bookcases, even a built-in entertainment center. McGarvey took all this in as Tarankov raised a fist to strike Elizabeth who was defiantly standing face-to-face with him.

Her eyes went wide as she spotted her father. "Daddy!" she cried triumphantly.

McGarvey crossed the intervening space before Tarankov could fully react, and he bodily shoved the man aside, sending him sprawling onto the couch.

Tarankov fumbled for the pistol at his hip, but McGarvey pointed his gun at the man's face and he stopped.

"Are you okay, Liz?" McGarvey asked, without taking his eyes off Tarankov.

"Now I am."

"Find the emergency stop cord or button, we need to slow down."

"There is no such mechanism aboard this train," Tarankov said calmly.

Someone rushed down the stairs from the command center. "General, I'm painting two incoming jets—" he shouted.

McGarvey turned and fired two shots, hitting the commando in the chest, driving him backwards.

Tarankov clawed his gun from its holster and he was raising it, a wicked gleam in his eyes, as McGarvey turned back and fired one shot at nearly point blank range into the Tarantula's forehead just above the bridge of his nose, killing him instantly. His body, suddenly limp, slid off the couch and landed in a heap on his side.

McGarvey checked out one of the windows. They were accelerating through an industrial section of the city, and going far too fast for them to jump.

He snatched Tarankov's gun from the dead man's hand and gave it to Elizabeth. She was badly shaken, and an angry red welt had formed on her cheek, but she had a determined look in her eyes.

"What about the jets?" she asked.

"They're going to attack, which means we have to get off. I'm going upstairs to see if I can get the engineer to slow down. In the meantime if anyone comes through the door, shoot."

McGarvey checked the corridor, then stepped over the body of the dead commando, and cautiously took the stairs two at a time. At the top he swept the cramped nerve center left to right with his gun, but the compartment was empty.

The radar screen on one of the consoles showed the two incoming jets, but he ignored it as he desperately studied the electronic panels, finally finding the handset that connected with the locomotive.

He yanked it off its cradle. "This is the command center!" he shouted in Russian. "Stop the train now! Emergency stop! Emergency stop!" Several gunshots were fired from below.

McGarvey tossed down the phone as the train gave a huge lurch, sending him sprawling, the brakes on the locomotive and all twenty armored cars locking up simultaneously.

Before he could recover, a hatch in the ceiling clanged open and a figure dropped down on top of him, smashing his head against the bulkhead, knocking the wind out of him

"McGarvey," Chernov snarled. He batted the gun out of McGarvey's hand, and smashed a roundhouse blow into McGarvey's jaw, snapping his head back again against the bulkhead, his vision momentarily dimming.

Chernov swung again, but McGarvey ducked the blow and Chernov's fist smashed into the bulkhead.

With a mighty heave, McGarvey shoved the Russian away, and scrambled to his feet.

Chernov recovered almost instantly, and he stepped back as he snatched his pistol from the shoulder holster, a look of victory in his eyes. But McGarvey was on him before he could fire, smashing his shoulder into the man's chest, sending him back against one of the electronic panels. He held Chernov's gun hand off with his left, and smashed a fist into the man's chest with every ounce of his strength. Chernov grunted in pain, and McGarvey hit him in the same spot again and again and a fourth time, until the Russian's eyes fluttered, and his body went slack.

McGarvey snatched the gun from his hand, shoved him aside and bounded drunkenly down the stairs, the train still decelerating at a terrific rate.

"It's me," he shouted as he hit the bottom. He fired four shots down the corridor and then dove into the sitting room, answering fire tearing into the bulkheads and furniture.

The moment he was clear, Elizabeth raised her gun hand up over the back of the couch and emptied Tarankov's pistol down the corridor.

McGarvey made it to where she was crouched, grabbed her arm, and together they crawled to the rear platform door.

"Ready?" he asked.

She nodded.

He popped back up and emptied Chernov's gun down the corridor at the same moment Elizabeth hauled the door open, and they scrambled outside.

Above Moscow

"Orlov leader, do you have visuals yet?" the controller said.

They had come in low directly over the top of Leningrad Station, the square still busy with people. The train was about three kilometers ahead, and was definitely coming to a stop.

Captain Trofimo dialed up two R85 air-to-ground missiles and armed them.

"We have the target in sight. We're starting our attack run now."

"We're showing no enemy weapons radars," said his controller circling high over the city in an AEW&C Ilyushin Mainstay-B.

"We're showing no response either," Trofimo responded. "Do you wish us to abort?"

"*Nyet*," the controller said. "You have final weapons release authorization."

"Roger," Trofimo said, and he glanced over at his wingman, nodded, then turned back to his look-down-shoot-down system, fired both rockets, and peeled off to the right.

At the last moment he thought he'd seen two people jumping from the rear car, while a third person was climbing up on the roof, but he wasn't sure.

By the time he made his turn and lined up with his wingman for a second attack run, it wasn't necessary. The train had literally blown itself apart at the seams, probably from ammunition and ordnance stored aboard. Every single car was burning furiously, and the locomotive was lying on its side in an embankment below an abandoned factory, flames and greasy black smoke shooting two hundred feet into the sky.

"Mission complete," Trofimo radioed. "We're returning to base now."

"Roger," his controller responded tersely.

Trackside

McGarvey and his daughter crouched in a ditch less than fifty yards from the furiously burning wreckage spread out on both sides of the railroad right of way, as the two jet fighters that had caused the destruction screamed off to the south. The heat was so intense it made their eyes water.

"Time to go home, Liz," he said.

Elizabeth looked at her father, and smiled. "I bet Mom won't believe a word I tell her."

McGarvey had to smile back. "I don't think she will. This one will be our little secret."

"And Jacqueline's too. She's in love with you, and I have a feeling she's not the type who's going to let you simply walk away."

"Maybe you're right, Liz," McGarvey said as he heard the first of the helicopters coming up from the south. Time to get out? he wondered. Maybe. But then he'd been asking himself that same question for the past few years.